Light a Candle

Chase the Devil Away

A novel

Chris Holmes

This is a book of fiction. All of the characters, organizations, and events portrayed in this novel are either products of the author's imagination or are used fictitiously.

Light a Candle

A Paranormalice Press Book
1201 Scottsdale Drive
Ormond Beach, FL 32174

www.paranormalicepress.com

Author's Note

I had always dreamed of being a writer and when I joined the Daytona Writers critique group eight years ago to pursue my dream, I discovered the journey from a first draft to a final completed novel was much longer and harder than I had thought.

The encouragement, advice and support I received from the group were key to my success in finishing this novel.

My sincere gratitude to all the members of the Daytona Writers Group and especially to leader, Veronica Helen Hart. Publisher, editor and award-winning author, Veronica's straight-forward critiques, thoughtful advice and her willingness to share her many talents to help writers improve their craft makes her the best writing mentor one could hope for. I am grateful for her guidance and lucky to call her a friend as well.

Light a Candle

Chapter 1

Nick Teravelli tugged on the sleeves of his suit jacket. They were an inch too short, but it was the only suit he owned. His mother had bought it for him three years ago for his college graduation. He wore the suit to her funeral six months later. The best and the worst days of his life were spent in this suit. Today could go either way.

Wetting a comb, he attempted to tame his long, wavy hair. He intended to have his hair cut the day before, but his father had insisted he mop the floors of the family restaurant. By the time he had finished, the barber shop had closed.

Stuffing his wallet and keys into his pockets, he hurried into the kitchen of the family's two-story apartment atop the restaurant. His father, Dominic senior, nicknamed Dom, and his younger brother, Sal, sat eating breakfast at the kitchen table. His grandmother stood on her tip-toes stirring sauce in a tall, stainless steel pot on the stove.

"Nickie, you want I make you some eggs?" she asked.

"No, thanks, Nonna." He lifted a metal pot from the stove and poured coffee into a mug. "I have to leave in a few minutes."

"Where ya goin' all dressed up, Mr. Fancy-pants?" his father asked.

Sal snickered as he slurped his orange juice.

"I told you last night, Pop, I have an interview with an agent this morning," Nick said.

"Aah, an interview. Four years of expensive college, for what? It's been three years since you graduated and you still don't have a job writing."

Nick swallowed hard and gripped the mug handle with white knuckles. "It takes time, Pop. To be a successful writer, you need a good agent."

"Agent, *smagent*. You need to give up on this writer nonsense and work in the restaurant like your brother. He's seventeen. He makes more money than you."

"I told you—" Nick started.

"Shush. Turn that up." His grandmother pointed to the television set in the living room across the hall.

Sal grabbed the remote and pushed the volume button. A photograph of a smiling, dark-haired young boy's face filled the screen. "Hey, Nonna, isn't that the kid you're making the cannoli for?" Sal asked.

She nodded her head yes. "Listen."

". . . mangled body found inside a city sanitation truck yesterday was identified as that of Robert Owens. Owens was the prime suspect in the kidnapping and murder of six-year-old Benjamin Ryan. Police went to Owens' home yesterday with an arrest warrant but found his apartment empty. Owens' employer confirmed he did not report to work yesterday. Police feared he had fled the area.

Owens, a registered sex offender, had been repeatedly questioned by police after Benjamin's disappearance and was considered a person of interest. Authorities upgraded him to a suspect yesterday morning when a warrant for his arrest was issued.

It's unknown how Owens ended up in the sanitation truck where he was crushed to death by the compactor. An investigation is underway. The gruesome discovery comes one day before a neighborhood fund raiser for little Benjamin is scheduled at Saint Michael's Catholic Church, where Benjamin's maternal grandmother is a parishioner. All monies collected will be given to the Ryan family to help pay for the young boy's burial expenses. Reporting from—"

Dom muted the volume. "Sick sonofabitch got what he deserved."

Sal and Nick grunted in agreement. Nonna made a quick sign of the cross and turned back to the stove. "The sauce is ready, Salvatore. Carry it downstairs before you go to school."

Sal drained his juice glass and stood.

Nonna wrapped thick, terry cloth towels around both handles. "Careful, it's hot."

Rising from his chair with a low groan, Dom moved his head back and forth, then rolled his shoulders. "Good thing I have a strong son to carry that. I pulled my back last night emptying the mop bucket Nick left in the kitchen." He glared at Nick as he followed Sal. "I'll get the doors."

Sal headed down the stairs to the restaurant.

His father paused in the open doorway. "So, Nick, I guess you won't be working in the kitchen today?"

"I told you I have an interview."

"Yeah, well, your brother and me could use help closing up tonight." His father shut the door behind him before Nick could reply.

"Him and that goddamned restaurant." Nick slammed his coffee mug down on the table.

"Nickie, your language!" Nonna scolded.

"Sorry, Nonna." He leaned to kiss his grandmother on the forehead. "I gotta go."

Nonna patted his cheek. "You're a good boy, Nickie. Your mama would be proud."

As he exited the door, Nick touched his fingertips to his mother's photograph hanging on the wall. He wondered whether she would have looked like Nonna had she grown older.

His mind churned during the thirty-minute walk downtown. He walked fast, the morning breeze cooled the anger burning in his face. He had never been close to his father and after his mother's death, the tension between them escalated. Nick often found himself wishing it had been his father who died instead of his mother. He missed his mom every day. She'd understand the importance of his interview today. She had always supported his passion for writing and convinced his father they should pay his college tuition.

In his senior year, his mother was diagnosed with breast cancer. In spite of the disease which ravaged her body, she promised him nothing would keep her from attending his graduation. She looked so thin in the green dress she had bought for the occasion, yet pride shone in her eyes and her smile overpowered the gauntness in her face.

After graduation, Nick mailed out dozens of query letters and manuscripts. His mother told him her dream was to live long enough to see his first book published. Nick desperately wanted to fulfill her dream. On some level, he hoped it would keep her alive.

Although he had aced all of his classes in school, he wasn't prepared for the steady stream of rejection letters he received from publishers. When his mother died, grief and depression overwhelmed him. He believed his failure contributed to her death and reluctantly gave into his father's demands to resume working in the family restaurant. His dream of becoming a writer, buried along with his mom.

Self-doubt gnawed as he neared the crowded downtown area of the city. Jamming his hands into his pockets, he quickened his pace and weaved in and out of the throng of pedestrians.

His interview was with Victor Ruby, owner of Ruby International Promotions, a prestigious agency with a proven reputation for sky-rocketing their clients to fame and fortune. He wasn't sure if talent or sheer luck had landed him as a finalist in Ruby's contest. With so much at stake, the competition would be fierce and his odds of winning, slim. If he failed his interview today, he would have to face his father's ridicule, his girlfriend, Katie's disappointment, and worse, lose the last shreds of his self-confidence as a writer.

🕯

Ruby International Promotions had its own office building, located in an upscale section of the business district. While not the tallest hi-rise in the city, its sleek steel frame and dark-tinted glass windows stood out among the older brick and mortar structures on the block. Entwined initials 'RIP' formed the logo, prominently displayed in red on the double glass doors.

His cell phone vibrated as he waited for the elevator in the lobby. *Good luck, I Luv U* displayed on the screen. Nick smiled and texted, *Luv U2.*

The smile stayed on his lips as he rode the elevator. Katie had been the only good thing that came out of working at the restaurant. He remembered every detail of the evening she came in to pick up a pizza. Nick couldn't stop staring across the counter at her. He had dated a lot of girls, but she was the most beautiful he had ever seen. Blond-haired and petite, with brilliant green eyes that lit up when she smiled. He wanted to talk to her but found himself mutely handing over the pizza box and grinning at her like a twelve-year-old boy.

As he berated himself for blowing his opportunity, he spotted her debit card lying on the counter. He ran his finger across the raised letters on the smooth plastic. *Katherine Harrington*. His father yelled when he left his post at the counter. Nick ignored him and ran down the street. He caught sight of her a block away and followed her to the local hospital.

She and her coworkers were opening the pizza box when he walked into the break room. The other nurses whispered and giggled as Nick stammered a greeting and returned her card. Asking a girl out had never been a problem for him, yet he struggled to get the words out with Katie.

After over two years together, he still smiled every time he thought of her.

Nick arrived early and opened the door to a packed waiting room. A young, red-haired receptionist instructed him to sign in and then take a seat.

Too nervous to sit still, Nick walked the perimeter of the room studying the framed photographs and posters hanging on the walls. The images showcased Victor Ruby's numerous success stories. Movie actors, television stars, musicians and authors, all united by the common theme of horror, Ruby International Promotions' specialty.

"We just hung that one." The receptionist pointed to a poster near the door. "Do you like Blood Lust?"

The poster depicted a rock band on a stage. A cloud of red mist rose from the floor around the feet of the black-clad and heavily made-up band members. A red-lined cape blew back from the shoulders of the lead singer. Along with his pale face and black-ringed eyes, he resembled a vampire.

"I know them. They're a heavy metal group," Nick said. "My brother has one of their CDs."

The receptionist smiled and returned to typing on her computer. Nick continued his slow stroll around the room. He paused at Joseph Cullen's portrait, the famous author whose books had inspired him to write horror stories. The gray-haired writer sat at an antique oak desk holding one of his best-selling novels. Nick grinned as he imagined his own photograph, looking equally as dignified, hanging on the wall next to Cullen's.

The receptionist called out a name and a young man leapt from his seat. He dropped a folder of papers in his haste. Bending, he scooped them up and crammed them haphazardly back into the folder. He sprinted through the door of Victor Ruby's office.

Nick found an empty chair in a corner next to a young woman dressed in a black gown with tattered lace trim. The ends of her short, black hair were dyed blood-red and black eyeliner contrasted against her pale skin. He settled into the chair and nodded at her. She scanned Nick from head to toe then turned away. Nick looked around the room at his competition. They eyed him back. Tension crackled in the air.

"Janis Ford?" the receptionist called. The goth-looking woman next to Nick rose and strode into Ruby's office. Nick leaned forward in his chair. His dress shoes squeezed his feet like two leather pythons.

All eyes in the room widened each time the red-headed girl approached with her clipboard in hand. She called a name and another hopeful scurried into Ruby's office. Some interviews took longer than others. For Nick, each took an eternity. He checked his cell phone for the time and found he'd missed a text from Katie. *How's it going*?

He typed, *still waiting.*

Katie had showed him the newspaper advertisement for Ruby International Promotions's search for a new horror writer. Nick shrugged it off, convinced it was yet another rejection waiting to happen. Katie prodded him daily to enter the contest. He submitted his manuscript hours before the final deadline. Weeks dragged by. He wished he had never entered. The thought of looking into Katie's hopeful eyes and telling her his work had been rejected, haunted him. When the phone rang last Friday afternoon, the news on the other end shocked him. He'd made the final cut. Victor Ruby wanted to personally interview all of the finalists before choosing a winner. Nick's mood alternated from sheer elation to gut-twisting terror for the entire week leading up to today's interview.

"Dominic Teravelli?"

Startled, Nick jumped to his feet. The waiting room had emptied. The redhead winked at him and opened the door to Ruby's office. Nick yanked on his jacket sleeves and drew in a deep breath.

Intense heat assaulted him the moment he entered. The hot, dry air proved a jarring contrast from the air-conditioned waiting room. In the center of the spacious office, Victor Ruby sat in a high-backed, red leather chair behind an enormous mahogany desk. He stood and flashed a brilliant white smile.

"Vic Ruby," he said, thrusting his hand toward Nick.

Nick shook his hand. "Dominic Teravelli. It's an honor to meet you, Mr. Ruby."

Ruby's grip was strong, and his hand felt hot. Nick forced his gaze away from Ruby's fingernails. They were long, tapered and shone with a clear, glossy polish.

"Dominic Teravelli," Ruby chuckled. "There's a great Italian name. Roman Catholic, yes?"

The question caught Nick off guard. "Um, yes sir, I was raised Catholic."

The larger-than-life reputation of Ruby International Promotions did not match the physical stature of its owner. He'd imagined Victor Ruby as a powerful giant of a man. Instead, Nick, at six foot four inches, towered over the short, wiry man standing in front of him. Yet, in spite of his slight frame, Ruby's presence dominated the room. Nick immediately felt intimidated.

Ruby sat and motioned for Nick to do the same. The guest chair, leather, black, and thickly cushioned, featured intricately carved wooden arms and legs. Nick recognized his manuscript lying on the desk. He gripped the arms of his chair as Ruby's long nails swiped at the corners of the pages. Between nervousness and the oppressive heat, sweat formed under his arms. More trickled down the center of the back. The cotton dress shirt clung to his wet body beneath the suit and tie.

Ruby glanced up from his reading. "I hope you're not uncomfortable. I'm from a hot climate, not a fan of air conditioning." His ruddy complexion confirmed time spent in the sun.

Nick forced a smile, hoping Ruby didn't see he was sweating like a pig. "No problem, Mr. Ruby."

"Mr. Ruby?" Ruby nodded. "Respect. A rare quality in young people these days." He bent his head and continued to flip through the manuscript. Except for the light scratching of Ruby's fingernails against the paper and Nick's heartbeat thumping in his eardrums, the room was silent.

Nick shifted in his seat and looked around while he waited for Ruby to finish. A green glass-shaded banker's lamp on the desk provided the brightest source of the light in the dim room. Floor length draperies covered a wall of windows behind Ruby. Ornately framed oil paintings hung under brass spotlights on deep burgundy-colored walls. One side of the room housed an entertainment center with ample seating while the other side held a computer station with multiple, wall-mounted monitors.

Nick cleared his throat. "So, what do you think of my manuscript, sir?"

Ruby looked up. His dark eyes and black hair were equally shiny. "Well-developed characters, good pace, and an interesting story line. You have talent." He stroked the black goatee on his chin, turned his head and reached into his desk drawer. Ruby's hair hung well past his shoulders, secured at the nape of his neck in a neat ponytail.

"Smoke?" Ruby offered a box of thin, black cigars.

"No, thanks."

"Yes, Dominic Teravelli, you have talent. Of course, this type of story has been done before. A vampire struggling with his conscience."

Nick slid forward in his chair. "I have others, sir. This one is the first of a trilogy. The second and third books introduce strong supporting characters, an ancient ghost, a modern-day witch and several unique plot twists—"

Ruby held up his hand, his fingers broke the swirling ribbons of cigar smoke hanging in the hot, arid air. "Yes, vampires, ghosts and witches. I get it. Giving monsters a conscience and human emotions does seem to be the popular trend." Ruby puffed on his cigar. "Not my idea of horror. But I leave most of those decisions to my publisher, Jack Conrad."

"I have other manuscripts. What type of stories are you looking for?"

Ruby grinned. "One without warm, fuzzy werewolves or sensitive vampires who sparkle in the sunlight. A monster without a moral compass, unburdened by human emotion. After all, isn't that what makes them monstrous?"

"Yes, but readers are human and there has to be an element of hope in a horror story, no matter how dark the story line. Something that makes you sympathize with the tortured soul of the monster. Or, a weakness in the monster so readers will root for the protagonist to destroy the evil," Nick said. "Good always wins over evil."

"Why?"

"Well, because . . . it just does," Nick stammered. "Otherwise the story would be pages of chaos and mayhem. The reader would have no empathy for the characters. It would be emotionless, brutal, no hope for salvation. Evil would win. That can't happen."

Ruby sat, silent and expressionless, his piercing eyes riveted on Nick. The flow of perspiration seeping through Nick's clothing increased.

Ruby's sudden burst of laughter shattered the uncomfortable pause. "That's a debate we'll save for another day." He tapped his cigar into a silver ashtray, the rim adorned with sparkling red gemstones. "There's lots of good horror writers, Dominic. It takes passion to be a true star. Ambition. And most of all, desire. Tell me, do you have desire to succeed?"

"Yes, Mr. Ruby, I do."

"How much of yourself are you willing to invest in your career?"

"Everything. One hundred percent. One hundred and ten percent."

"Hmm." Ruby tapped his nails on the polished desk. "You obviously *want* this opportunity, but will you do whatever it takes to *deserve* it?"

"Yes, sir."

Ruby stood, walked around the desk and leaned close to Nick's ear. "I choose my clients carefully, Dominic. I invest a great deal of time and money in each one. I insist they be fully devoted."

Cigar smoke clung to the fabric of Ruby's black suit, a unique odor of charred wood mixed with cloyingly sweet florals. Combined with the oven-like heat in the room, it made Nick queasy.

"I'm devoted to writing, Mr. Ruby. Becoming a published author is my dream. It would mean the world to me to have you as my agent."

Ruby patted Nick's shoulder. "We'll need to do some tweaking, but I do believe you could be my next star. Bestsellers, book signings, television appearances, and eventually movies based on your novels. Very demanding work. There will be sacrifices. Are you ready for fame and fortune?"

Sweat coated Nick's upper lip, yet his mouth felt void of any moisture. Had Ruby chosen him? His mind reeled with the impact this would have on his life.

"Oh God, am I ever ready."

Ruby snorted. "God has nothing to do with it."

Nick stared, unsure how to respond.

Ruby threw his head back and laughed, then pressed a button on his phone. "Stephanie, bring in a contract for Mr. Teravelli."

Cool air streamed through the open door when Stephanie entered carrying a packet of papers. Nick wiped his upper lip with his hand.

Folding back several sheets of paper in the stapled stack, Ruby laid the contract on the desk and placed a silver pen with a red Ruby Promotions logo on the open page.

"All it takes is your signature. Then I'll get started making you rich and famous."

Nick recalled his father always warned never to sign anything without reading it first. He picked up the pen and unfolded the contract.

"It's our standard three-year contract," Ruby said. "States that you'll agree to let Ruby International Promotions handle you, your books, publicity, et cetera. We get twenty percent. Most of our clients are millionaires by the second year. But, if you're unsure, you're welcome to take the contract home and read it over."

Nick turned the pages, scanning the small text as quickly as he could.

"Stephanie, keep Janis Ford's phone number handy. She's a decent writer. Mr. Teravelli appears hesitant. Perhaps he's not ready for such a life-changing decision."

"Yes, sir." The receptionist exited the office.

"No, wait." Nick flipped to the last page and scrawled his name on the signature line. "Here." He handed the contract to Ruby.

"Congratulations, Dominic. You've made the right decision."

"I'm ready to change my life."

Ruby hugged the contract close to his chest and stroked it with his long fingernails. "Your life will certainly change."

*

"You won!" Katie's excited squeal blasted through the cell phone speaker. "Victor Ruby signed you up himself! That's incredible!"

Nick walked in a circle inside the lobby holding his cell phone to his ear. He had called Katie the second he exited the elevator.

"I know. I'm still in shock."

"You deserve this, Nick, you're an excellent writer."

"You're the one who pushed me to enter the contest. We have to celebrate. What time do you get off work tonight?"

"Seven."

"I'll meet you at the front entrance. I love you, babe."

"Love you, too."

Nick jumped and punched the air with his fist. His excited whoop echoed through the lobby. From the corner of his eye, he saw movement. Heels rapped against the marble floor. The goth-looking woman from Ruby's waiting room walked toward him.

"You're the one he picked?" she asked.

"Yeah." Nick grinned. The stony expression on the woman's face extinguished his smile. "I know everyone up there wanted this opportunity. I'm sorry you—"

"Don't feel sorry for me. *You're* the one who's going to be sorry." Pivoting on her stacked heels, she stormed out the front doors.

At a quarter past seven, Katie still hadn't exited the hospital. Nick paced back and forth on the concrete landing outside the entrance. He checked his cell phone for a message. Katie kept her phone turned off at work, though she sneaked text messages to him.

Entering the sliding glass doors, he immediately spotted Katie coming down the main hallway. Her pale blond hair shone under the fluorescent lights. A handsome young man in blue scrubs walked next to her, chatting and smiling. Nick's stomach tightened. Straightening to his full height, he strode toward the pair.

"Nick!" Katie ran the last few feet and threw her arms around his neck. "Congratulations! I'm so thrilled for you."

Hugging her tightly, he stared over her head at the man in scrubs.

Katie stepped back. "Oh, Nick, this is Jon Gerber. Jon, this is Nick Teravelli."

Jon stepped forward and held out his hand. "Nice to meet you."

Nick squeezed Jon's hand hard. Jon's discomfort showed in his strained smile.

"Sorry I'm late," Katie said. "This is Jon's first day. I was showing him around."

Jon nodded to Nick. "Hope I didn't keep her too late. Katie's been so patient teaching me the ropes." He grinned at Katie as he turned to leave. "See you tomorrow."

"You have that look," Katie said as they sat at the sidewalk cafe table.

"What look?"

Katie sighed. "Your jealous look." She reached across the small round table and squeezed Nick's hand. "This is a celebration, right? I'm not the least bit interested in Jon. I love you."

Her touch melted his anger. "I'm sorry, I can't help—"

The waitress placed their drinks on the table.

"Let's forget it, okay." Katie raised her wine glass and smiled. "To my soon-to-be outrageously famous, best-selling author boyfriend."

Nick clinked his glass against hers. "How about your soon-to-be outrageously famous and rich, best-selling author *husband*?"

"You know I want that more than anything."

Nick leaned close and kissed her. "I promise you, my first royalty check is going for a diamond ring."

With the day's surreal events replaying in his mind, Nick sauntered from Katie's apartment to his family's restaurant. His grin reflected in the darkened plate glass window of the closed restaurant.

Upstairs, he found his grandmother asleep in her chair in the living room, her baby-blue Rosary beads wrapped around one hand. His father's steady snoring vibrated through the ceiling from his bedroom on the third floor while sounds of electronic carnage emanated from Sal's room, next to his father's, where he spent most evenings playing video games.

Nick stood in the hallway outside his bedroom. He wished his mom was still alive. He pictured her smile, the tiny crinkles at the corners of her brown eyes turning upwards when he told her his incredible news.

"Who's there?" Nonna called from the living room.

"Me, Nonna." He walked into the room and offered his hand to help his grandmother up from her chair.

"It's late, Nickie. Where you been so late?"

"Celebrating with Katie. Good news, Nonna. I have an agent. A famous agent who's going to publish my books."

"Good, Nickie, good. You happy? You make money? Maybe now you marry that nice Irish Catholic girl, eh?"

Nick smiled. His grandmother adored Katie. His whole family appreciated how she had helped care for his mother during the last months of her life. Nonna even relented in her stubborn belief that her grandsons should only marry Italian girls.

"Oh, Nickie, you help me bring the cannoli to the church tomorrow morning? It's the fund raiser for little Benjamin, God bless his soul. It's Saturday. Your father needs Sal in the restaurant."

"Sure, I'll help you, Nonna."

"Okay, good. Get some sleep, Nickie."

"Night, Nonna."

Nick stretched out on his bed with his hands behind his head grinning up at the ceiling. His cellphone vibrated on the night stand. Thinking it must be Katie, he reached for his phone and saw an unfamiliar number.

"Hello?"

"Mr. Teravelli? Hi, this is Stephanie from Mr. Ruby's office."

"Yes?" Nick's stomach knotted, fearing the late-night call meant Ruby had changed his mind.

"I'm calling to tell you to report to the Ruby building tomorrow morning at ten o'clock for your photo shoot. You know, publicity photos and a bio picture for your book jacket. We'll have Wardrobe and stylists on site."

"A photo shoot?" Nick exhaled a breath of relief. "Uh, sure. I'll be there. Ten o'clock?"

"Yes, ten sharp. Oh, and don't shave."

"Don't shave?"

Stephanie giggled. "We don't want any cuts from a nervous hand. Like I said, there's a style team on site. They'll take care of everything. Be sure to be here on time."

Chapter 2

Saturday mornings offered Nick an opportunity to enjoy some quiet time in the usually noisy Teravelli household. His father and brother were downstairs in the restaurant preparing for the eleven o'clock opening. His grandmother indulged in an extra hour of sleep, so she would be rested to help greet the dinner guests that evening.

Too excited to sleep, Nick woke early, showered, dressed and made coffee. He sat at the kitchen table typing a new horror story on his laptop. The words flowed so quickly, his fingers had trouble keeping up. It had been months since he had felt the urge to write. He watched the computer's clock so he would have plenty of time to walk downtown for the ten o'clock photo shoot.

"Nickie! Shave your face. You can't go to church looking like a bum."

"Church?" Nick peered over the lid of his laptop at his grandmother's scowling face. "Oh, right. I forgot. The cannoli." He closed his laptop and glanced at the wall clock. Eight-forty-five. Even with the detour, he still had time. The church was only two blocks away, although in the opposite direction of Ruby's office. "You ready to go now, Nonna?"

"Almost. I put on my hat."

Nick waited by the door, eyeing the clock. Fifteen minutes later, his grandmother emerged dressed in a rose-colored suit with matching hat and gloves.

"You no shave?" she scolded.

"I can't stay at the church. I have an appointment."

"This appointment, it's for your new job?" she asked.

"Yes, so we need to get going, okay?"

"I'm ready. I wait on you."

Nick steadied the stack of pizza boxes filled with pastries under his chin as he made the trek to the church with his grandmother. Although she walked at a brisk pace, Nick slowed his long strides to allow her to keep up with him. She stopped often to greet people along the way, especially children. A matriarch of the neighborhood since she and his grandfather had opened the restaurant fifty years ago, she knew most of the residents by their first names and doled out hard candies and shiny quarters to the kids.

A group of older women converged on the pair as they arrived at the church. Most were the grandmothers of Nick's old high school classmates. The women stayed friends after their grandchildren graduated. They organized community events like today's memorial fund raiser for Benjamin Ryan. Nick's grandmother assumed the role of chairwoman for the group. She held frequent meetings at their restaurant and ruled over the committee the same as she did her family.

Maria Gonzalez, a short plump woman in her seventies, led Nick to a row of long tables laden with baked goods and glass donation jars. Business owners and residents manned tables around the perimeter and offered merchandise and crafts for sale. They donated their profits to the charitable cause.

"Mrs. G, I have to go," Nick said.

"Let me get you some of my cookies," Maria said. "Remember when you and my Raymond, were little boys? You two would come home from school and eat all the cookies I kept in the big yellow jar by the stove."

Nick smiled. "I remember. But, no cookies today, thanks. I have an appointment and I need to leave now."

Maria Gonzalez was his best friend, Ray's, grandmother. Ray joined the army four years ago and had only been home twice on short leaves between tours in Iraq and Afghanistan. Maria worried about Ray constantly. In his absence, she doted on Nick whenever she saw him.

"Oh, Nick, how could I forget to tell you. Ray is coming home."

"That's great news, when?"

"One week or two weeks. It's confusing. Depends on what base he goes to and what flights they have. I think I have his letter in my bag." She plunked her over-sized purse on the table and dug through the contents.

"Tell Nonna the date. She'll let me know."

"I have it right here. Where is it?" She pulled a coin pouch, a prayer book and rosary beads from her bag. The unusual-looking beads had multi-colored, semi-precious stones strung on a delicate silver chain. "My Mama's beads," she murmured as she kissed them. "I'll find the letter. Give me a minute."

"Mrs. G, I really have to go." He gave her a quick hug.

She reached up and pinched his cheek. "Nick, you need a shave, honey."

After pecking his grandmother on the cheek, Nick jogged down the street. He checked the time on his cell phone. Nine-forty. He ran the twenty-three blocks to Ruby's office.

At three minutes after ten he burst into the waiting room.

"Sorry I'm late," he panted. "Had to help . . . my grandmother. Fund raiser . . . for that poor murdered kid."

Stephanie rushed around her desk with her finger pressed to her lips. "Shh! I told him you arrived ten minutes ago and were in the restroom." She pushed Nick toward the closed bathroom door. The light and exhaust fan were on inside.

"Mr. Ruby is an absolute fanatic about punctuality," she whispered. "Tell him you felt sick. Nerves or whatever."

"Thanks," Nick mouthed as she eased the door shut.

Nick inspected his sweaty face and dark beard stubble in the mirror. He splashed cold water on his head and smoothed his hair back with his wet hands. Smudges of cannoli cream and perspiration stained his black dress shirt. He scrubbed at the stains with a wet paper towel, but his efforts only made the white streaks more prominent.

The whir of the fan motor muffled the voices outside the bathroom door. Loud raps shook the door. "Mr. Teravelli," Ruby called. "Are you all right?"

Quickly tucking in his shirt, Nick opened the door to a visibly irritated Victor Ruby.

"Mr. Ruby, I apologize. I felt sick. Nerves, I guess. I'm better now."

"I will not tolerate lateness." He glanced at his receptionist. "But Stephanie tells me you arrived early. I suppose a nervous stomach is understandable."

Stephanie stood behind Ruby holding a clipboard. "If you're ready, we can go downstairs to the photo studio," she said.

Ruby patted Nick on the back. "Relax, son. Enjoy the photo shoot."

"Thanks for covering for me, Stephanie," Nick said once the elevator doors closed.

"Don't mention it," she replied, staring down at her clipboard. She looked up. "Seriously, don't *ever* mention it. You'll get me fired, or worse."

The elevator stopped on the second floor and Stephanie led the way down the hall. Men and women in business attire hurried past in both directions.

"The photo studio is this way. The make-up and dressing rooms are attached. And a shower, if you want to freshen up." She eyed his shirt.

Nick read the signs on the doors as they walked. "Ruby owns this entire building?"

"Yes. It's a huge operation. Legal is on the first floor. The third and fourth floors are Creative Services. Fifth floor is Publishing and Editorial. IT and Marketing take up the sixth and seventh floors. Mr. Ruby's office suite is on the eighth floor, as you know. The recording studio's in the basement. It's an awesome set-up, sound-proofed with state-of-the-art equipment. I love to watch the musicians record. Oh, and Mr. Ruby's private residence is on the ninth. Takes up the entire floor."

"I've never realized all that's involved to promote people," Nick said. "Are the books printed here, too?"

"No, only cover designs, editing and pagination are done here. Mr. Ruby owns a separate printing company."

"We're done." The tall blond hair stylist nodded to the shorter blond woman holding a make-up brush. The make-up artist whisked a touch of powder across Nick's forehead. Then the stylist swiveled the chair around to face the wall mirror. She leaned over Nick's shoulder displaying a deep cleavage line above her tight, pink tank top.

"Don't you love it?"

"Um, my hair looks the same, except . . . messier."

The stylist rolled her eyes. "This is Gino Marco's newest look. Very hot."

Nick looked at her blankly. "Gino Marco?"

She sighed. "The famous hair designer, you must have heard of him?"

Nick studied his reflection. "Don't you think a shave and trimming my hair might be better?"

The stylist ran her hands through his hair. Her breasts pressed against the back of Nick's neck. "It's the look Mr. Ruby ordered for you."

"Ordered for me?"

The make-up artist hopped onto his lap and cupped her hand under his chin. "Why do you want to shave? Stubble is so-o-o sexy."

The short, terry cloth robe they had given him after his shower made him feel both ridiculous and vulnerable to the woman squirming in his lap.

Stephanie appeared in the doorway. "Mr. Teravelli needs to go to wardrobe now. We're running late."

He politely nudged the girl from his lap and stood.

"Hey, Stephanie," Nick whispered as he followed her to the adjoining wardrobe room. "Can I have a minute with an electric razor and a comb so I can neaten myself up?"

"Why? This is the look Mr. Ruby wants for you, Nick."

"What's with this *look* thing you all keep talking about?"

"It's part of what a promoter does. Creating an image for the client. Mr. Ruby is very specific about the image he wants for each of his clients." Stephanie grinned. "I think it suits you."

Nick shook his head.

The dressing room had four mirrored walls with a bench and a chrome clothing rack in the center. Leather boots stood in a neat row beneath the bench.

Nick surveyed the leather jackets and blue jeans. "Where's the shirts?"

"No shirts. It's what Mr. Ruby ordered." Stephanie fanned through the clothing on the rack. "How about these?" She held up a pair of faded blue jeans with holes in the knees.

"Seriously?" Nick's pulse beat in his temples. "The Barbie twins in there did nothing but give me a lap dance for the past hour, now you want me to wear jeans with holes in them and a leather jacket with no shirt?"

Stephanie bit her bottom lip. "What did you want to wear?"

"A suit and tie or a dress shirt and slacks. Something dignified, like Joseph Cullen's photo upstairs." Nick ran his hands through his unkempt hair and paced the room.

"Joseph Cullen is like a hundred years old. You're young and . . . cute." Stephanie's cheeks flushed bright pink beneath her freckles.

"Why don't I get you a drink to help you relax." She slipped out the door before Nick could answer.

Taking advantage of the privacy, he pulled on the jeans she had draped over the bench. Balling up the black robe, he tossed it across the room.

When the door opened, Victor Ruby entered carrying two glasses. "Stephanie tells me you have a problem with my wardrobe choice?"

"My problem is this." He pointed to himself. "I wanted to look like a serious author, Mr. Ruby. But between the wild hair, no shave and these torn-up jeans, I look like a homeless guy."

"Homeless? Hardly. Those torn-up jeans cost over four hundred dollars." Ruby thrust a cold glass into Nick's hand. "Sit. Relax. Drink."

Ruby settled on the bench and sipped his drink. Nick remained standing.

"How old are you, son?"

"Twenty-five."

Ruby shook his head. "I employ a team of highly-paid, marketing professionals. Our research indicates your main appeal will be with the fifteen to forty-year-old female market. Do you think they want to see a young, virile man in a stuffy suit and tie? No, they do not." Ruby took a piece of paper from his suit pocket and waved it in front of Nick's face.

Nick's eyes focused on the fluttering paper, a check made out to him in the amount of ten thousand dollars.

"What's this for?" he asked.

"Your first advance. Our research maps potential book and merchandise sales. We have blind orders coming in simply because you're the newest Ruby Promotions talent. Next week is the press conference formally announcing you as the winner of our talent contest. When your book hits the stores, so will the hard sales. Which translates to more money for me—and you."

"Wow, that's fantastic," Nick said. "But, don't you think a writer should look—"

Ruby stood. "Mr. Teravelli, you have a decision to make. You either put on the clothing I had hand-picked for you, or I tear up this check and you can go back to slinging pizza in your family's dive." He jabbed a tapered fingernail into Nick's chest. "We have a contract. And

I assure you, if you walk out that door any chance you have of publishing a book in this city walks with you. I'll make certain of it."

Although nearly a foot taller than the angry man in front of him, Nick stepped back. The temperature in the dressing room rocketed to a blistering heat.

"What's it going to be?" Ruby demanded.

Nick muttered, "I'll wear the clothes."

The heat dissipated as Ruby smiled. "Nick, I realize this is all new to you, but you need to trust I know best in these matters. I've been changing people's lives for a very long time. My job is to make you rich and famous. Your job is to do what I tell you to do. Understood?"

"Yes, sir."

Ruby slapped the check into Nick's hand and walked out the door. "Stephanie! Get this photo shoot done."

"It's a different look from what you're used to, Nick." Katie reached up and tousled his hair as they strolled hand in hand from the hospital to her apartment.

"Yeah, except it's not me. And not who I want to be either. I wonder about Ruby. The guy's pushy and very strange."

"Lots of famous people are eccentric. Focus on the positive, you're getting your book published. That's your dream. And your own photo shoot is so cool. Plus, they let you keep the clothes." She fingered the butter-soft leather. "This jacket looks expensive."

"Probably is. Ruby said these jeans cost four-hundred bucks. They took my clothes. I got out of the shower and they were gone. His secretary said she'd have them cleaned for me." He smirked. "My shirt was covered with cannoli cream and sweat from running over twenty blocks to make the appointment on time."

"I think you look sexy." Katie traced her fingers through the hair on his chest down to where it tapered into a thin line above the waistband of his jeans.

"Sexy, huh?" Nick grabbed her around her waist and lifted her up until her face was even with his. He kissed her and then pressed his lips into the curve of her neck.

Katie shivered and wrapped her arms around his neck. "Tara should be leaving for her shift any minute." She lightly bit Nick's earlobe. "We'll have the place all to ourselves."

Chapter 3

Sunlight filtering through the window blinds formed horizontal ribbons of light on the walls of Katie's small bedroom. Nick slid his hand under the covers and ran it down Katie's naked body. She stirred and snuggled against him.

"Hey," he whispered, "I've gotta go home and get ready for a meeting with Ruby this morning."

"Okay," Katie murmured into his chest.

"You have another hour before your alarm goes off, sleepy head. See you tonight." He kissed her forehead, then tucked the sheet around her. Pulling on his jeans, he searched the dim room, then remembered he didn't have a shirt. He backed out of the bedroom, easing the door closed and bumped into Katie's roommate, Tara, as she exited from the bathroom.

"Sorry." Nick skirted around her, pulling on his jacket.

"That's your new look? Bad Boy Nickie?" Tara looked him up and down. "Or did you leave your shirt in someone's bed?"

Nick ignored the comment. He disliked Tara and wasn't in the mood to get into an argument. He shut the front door on Tara's shrill laughter.

※

"You work on a Sunday?" His grandmother shook her head. "What about church, Nickie?"

"Sorry, Nonna, the agency keeps odd hours. This meeting is important."

"You always walk to church with me on Sunday. Since you were little boy. I don't understand this new job." His grandmother threw her arms in the air. "Salvatore! Get dressed. You walk to church with me."

"But Nonna, I'm resting," Sal called from the living room. "I gotta work in the restaurant later."

"You come to church!" His grandmother stood over him with her arms crossed. "Rest later."

Sal pushed himself up from the couch. He punched Nick in the arm as he walked past. "Thanks a lot."

Nick grinned. "Church is good for you, little brother."

※

The door of Ruby's office muffled the words shouted behind it, but the volume and tone of the two voices inside indicated a heated argument.

Nick sat on the corner of Stephanie's desk. "Who's he got in there?"

She shook her head, keeping her eyes focused on her computer screen.

"C'mon, you can tell me." Nick opened the lid of the white bakery box he held. "Try one. It's a thank you gift for not telling Ruby I was late yesterday." He waved the box near Stephanie's nose. "My grandmother's cannoli are practically world famous."

Stephanie raised her eyes from her computer and smiled. "They smell amazing." She reached into the box. "I've never had a cannoli." As she bit into the pastry, the sweet cream filling squeezed out the opposite end of the crunchy tube into her hand.

Nick laughed when she licked her fingers. "Messy, but good, huh?"

"Delicious." She giggled and licked her fingers again. Watching her, Nick realized beneath the heavy make-up, was a girl of maybe eighteen. He wanted to ask how old she was, but instead asked, "How long have you worked for Ruby?"

"About four months," she said.

"You like working here?"

"Uh huh. I get to meet actors and rock stars. And the pay is more than I'd ever dreamed of making back home."

"Where's home?"

"Oklahoma."

"Do you have family here?"

"Nope. Just me. Packed up one day and got on a bus heading east."

"That took guts." Nick stepped into the rest room and grabbed some paper towels. "Here."

"Thanks." She wiped her hands on the towels. "I auditioned to be a singer when I first got here. That's how I met Mr. Ruby. He said I sounded too country for him to represent me." She shrugged. "He offered me this job instead."

"So you're a singer? Pretty cool."

Stephanie dabbed around her glossy, red lips with the corner of a paper towel. "Not a good enough one, I guess." She pointed to Ruby's door and lowered her voice. "Ian Slaughter's in there."

"Who's Ian Slaughter?"

Stephanie rolled her eyes. "Seriously? The lead singer of Blood Lust." She pointed to the poster of the band hanging on the wall.

"Oh yeah, right. The metal band."

"Like, only the biggest heavy metal band in the world. How old are you anyway, Nick?"

"Twenty-five. That's not old. What are you, fifteen?"

Stephanie straightened her shoulders. "Twenty-one."

"Really? You look a lot younger."

Stephanie's eyelids flitted downward, and her lips pulled tight.

"But you needed to be twenty-one to work here, right?" he asked.

"I have to get back to work." She stared at her monitor.

"Hey, it's all right. I won't say anything."

Another volley of shouting exploded in Ruby's office.

A man's voice bellowed, "Fuck you and your contract! I don't need you!"

Stephanie and Nick looked at each other. He cleared his throat. "Should I leave and come back later?"

"Oh, no," Stephanie said, "Ruby would be furious if you missed your appointment."

They both jumped when Ruby's door swung open, crashed into a large ceramic planter and toppled it.

A tall man with sandy-colored hair stormed past. He slammed the outer office door.

Stephanie hurried around her L-shaped desk to close the door to Ruby's office while Nick righted the potted plant. She barely made it back to her chair when the door opened.

A smiling Victor Ruby strode out with his hand extended. "Nick, good morning."

"Good morning, Mr. Ruby." He shook Ruby's hand.

"What's this?" Ruby motioned to the box of cannoli on the desk.

Stephanie jumped to her feet. "I'm sorry, sir, I'll put them away."

"Don't be silly." Ruby glared at her. "You'll insult Mr. Teravelli."

"Did I do something wrong?" Nick instinctively stepped between Stephanie and Ruby.

Ruby laughed. "Of course not. Stephanie knows I don't allow food in the office. But it's Sunday and who could resist your grandmother's famous cannoli?" He reached into the box and took one.

"How did you know my grandmother made them?" Nick asked. "And you also knew we have a family restaurant."

Ruby didn't reply. Instead he made loud sucking noises as he slurped the filling from the pastry tube. He nodded his head toward his office. "Come in. We have a lot to discuss." He waited for Nick to enter, then shut the door.

"Exciting time for you, hey Nick?" Ruby crunched the pastry shell between his teeth.

"Yes, sir, it is."

"You survived the photo shoot, I see." Ruby led Nick to a round conference table. Two posters lay side by side on the table. One, a full-length enlargement of Nick from yesterday's photo shoot. The wild hair and dark stubble accentuated his brooding expression. The second poster included the two bikini-clad models who were brought in to pose with Nick. The tall blond had her arm draped around his right shoulder while the raven-haired girl crouched, cat-like on his left, her arm encircling his leg. Purple colored mist swirled around the trio's feet and gave a surreal effect to the image.

"Posters?" Nick asked. "Who'd want a poster of an author?"

"Merchandising," Ruby said. "That's where the money is. You underestimate your appeal with females, your target market. These are only proofs, the printed ones are on order. But I have a bigger surprise for you." He placed a hardcover book on the table.

A single word *Thirst* shone in metallic silver letters on the glossy black jacket. Elongated descenders on the title text twisted into sharp points. Red ink, mimicking blood, dripped from the points. Below the title, Nick Tera was printed in red block letters.

"My book's printed already?"

"A press proof. I had the publisher start work on it as soon as you signed your contract."

Nick chewed on his lower lip. "The title's changed and my name–"

"Genius, isn't it? Terror-Tera. Perfect for a horror author." Ruby smiled.

"But, Mr. Ruby, sir, that's not my name."

"It's your name now. Do I need to remind you of our discussion in the dressing room yesterday?"

Nick felt the air temperature rising along with his frustration.

Ruby continued, "Nick Teravelli sounds like a pizzeria owner, or worse, a priest."

Nick's jaw muscles tensed. He couldn't believe Ruby changed his name without asking, but feared if he argued, he'd blow his book deal of a lifetime and the ten-thousand-dollar advance.

"We had to move fast. I told the publisher to have his staff writers make a few changes to your story." He took a cigar from his pocket as he studied Nick's face. "Your vampire character is, let's say, a bit less repentant. He revels in the dark side now. A much more enjoyable read."

The words exploded from Nick's mouth, "You had my story rewritten?"

The reflection of the flame from his silver lighter danced in Ruby's dark eyes. "Problem, Mr. Tera?"

Nick rubbed his face, his skin slick with sweat. Drawing a deep breath, he forced himself to speak in a measured tone. "I understand manuscripts are edited. I expected that. But I hoped to do the revisions myself, to keep the integrity of my story."

Ruby waved his hand sending a trail of cigar smoke above his head. "Normally, yes, you would work directly with my editors. But we needed to push this one through to meet the deadline."

"Deadline?"

"Another surprise." Ruby handed Nick a folded black card. Inside, an invitation to the annual Ruby International Promotions VIP Ball dated for the coming Saturday night.

"It's a very swanky party, Mr. Tera. My top clients, celebrities, and every elite society snob in the city will be there. More importantly, there will be a live press conference. You'll be introduced to your future fans and unveil your new book." Ruby tapped the book cover with his shiny fingernails.

Nick's mind reeled over his rewritten story and name change. Posters, parties and press conferences were not things he had anticipated when he signed on with Ruby.

"I'll have Stephanie make arrangements to get you the appropriate clothing for the party. Something to match the image we're building for you. In six short days your book will be on the shelves of every bookstore in the city." Ruby's eyes narrowed. "You have nothing to say?"

Nick felt like he'd been punched in the stomach. Yesterday's argument over clothing for the photo shoot was miniscule compared to today's shock. He struggled to maintain self-control and not let his anger show. His prolonged silence appeared to bore Ruby, who busied himself rolling the two posters together into a neat paper coil.

"Here you go, Nick. Your first book and posters." Ruby slapped the posters into Nick's hand. "Enjoy. Just don't show either in public before the press conference."

Nick turned to leave. He craved cool air and distance from Ruby.

"One more piece of business. You said you had two other books in your trilogy? I'll need those manuscripts ASAP. There's time for you to do the edits on those. What other story ideas do you have?"

"I started a new novel. It's going slow, but I'll—."

"Ah, the dreaded writer's block." Ruby took a business card from the holder on his desk. "There's a quote on the back of my card. Latin or some ancient language. I'm embarrassed to say I've forgotten which. Loosely translated it means, open your mind to inspiration. Call me superstitious, but I give one to all my authors." Ruby tucked it between the pages of Nick's novel. "Are you familiar with Joseph Cullen, Nick?"

"The king of horror? Of course, I've read all of his books."

"And *my* client, I might add." Ruby grinned, exposing perfectly white teeth. "You know, ol' Joe tells me he reads the quote aloud every time he sits down to write. Seems to have worked quite well for him, don't you think?"

"Yes. I suppose it has."

"I can see you're still digesting everything, Nick. It's a lot happening in a short time. Go on, take off. I'll have Stephanie call you to set up a time to shop for clothing for the VIP party." Ruby opened his door. "Focus on writing your new book. I'm betting you'll outsell Cullen one day."

Nick mumbled good-bye to Stephanie and left the office. He punched the down button on the elevator and stared at the book in his hand while he waited for the doors to open. Stephanie called out as he stepped inside the elevator.

"Nick, hold the door please!" Her tall heels clacked down the hallway. She hurried into the elevator carrying a bulky shoulder bag, the box of cannoli and a black shopping bag.

"Here." She held out the black bag emblazoned with a red RIP logo.

"What's this?"

"Your clothes from yesterday. They've been dry cleaned."

"That was fast." Nick snorted. "Does he own a damn dry cleaners, too?"

"What's wrong? You looked upset when you came out of Mr. Ruby's office."

Nick shook his head. "Most guys would be thrilled to be posing with hot models, having posters made—not to mention the fat pay check." Nick dropped the book into the shopping bag and slid the rolled-up posters in beside it. "I want to be published, but this all feels like a circus side show." He gave Stephanie a wry smile. "Sorry, I don't expect you to understand."

Stephanie touched his arm. "I dreamed of being a country singer. Yet, here I am, a secretary. I'm doing it for the money. I understand more than you think." The girlish smattering of freckles across her nose contrasted her world-weary tone.

Nick sighed. "So, where're you going?"

"Mr. Ruby said I could leave for the day." Stephanie's face brightened. "Guess I'll grab some lunch. Maybe, do some shopping."

"It's Sunday. Most of the stores are closed. But it's a nice sunny day. Go hang out with your friends. Have some fun."

"I've spent every day at this office since I moved here. Including weekends. I don't have any friends. Unless salesclerks count. I've become a shopaholic." She stared at her feet and asked in a meek voice, "Want to have lunch with me?"

Nick started to say no, but, with Katie at work and sulking over his revised book his only plan for the afternoon, he reconsidered.

"Sure." He smiled. "Hey, have you ever had a City Dawg hot dog?"

"No." Her giggle sounded like a sixteen-year-old girl's.

"You're in for a treat."

They settled on a bench in a small park across the street from the hot dog stand. Nick laughed at Stephanie's dainty attempt to bite into the over-sized hot dog piled with toppings. She put the cardboard container down next to her on the bench and wiped her mouth with a handful of napkins.

"Can I see?" She pointed to Nick's book in the bag at their feet.

Nick shrugged. "Sure."

She picked up the book. "The cover's awesome."

They both turned at the rapid clicking sound behind them. It came from the 35mm camera a woman aimed at them.

Nick stood as Stephanie rushed toward the woman.

"You can't print those, Janis! The book isn't even in stores yet. Mr. Ruby will be furious!"

The woman lowered the camera, revealing deep-set, dark eyes. Though she replied to Stephanie, she looked at Nick. "It's a public park. I can photograph whoever, or whatever, I want."

"If I tell Mr. Ruby, you'll lose your press pass to the VIP party."

Stephanie's statement made an impact. Janis pursed her lips. "Fine. I won't print the pictures–yet." She glared at Nick, then stalked away.

"Who was that?" Nick asked. "She looked familiar."

"Janis Ford, a reporter for *The Entertainer*." Stephanie walked back to the bench and slipped the book into the bag.

"I've heard that name before."

"She was a finalist in the talent contest. She came to the interview all Gothed-out. I guess she thought if she looked freaky enough, Mr. Ruby would pick her."

"Oh yeah, the Goth girl, now I remember. Why's a reporter trying to get a book deal?"

Stephanie shrugged. "She said she wanted to change careers. Ruby said she's a talented writer. Maybe that's why he gave her the press pass for the VIP party. A consolation prize."

"She gives me the evil eye every time she sees me," Nick said.

"Probably jealous. And a sore loser." Stephanie nibbled at her hot dog. "I don't like her, she's pushy. And the tabloid she works for is a real rag. I'm surprised Ruby gave her a pass. Reporters are only allowed to ask questions that he pre-approves. Janis doesn't like to follow rules."

After lunch, Stephanie and Nick said goodbye and then walked off in opposite directions. He texted Katie while he waited for the green light at a crosswalk. *"CU@6."* A few moments later his cell buzzed. Katie's text replied it would be eight o'clock, or later, when she finished work.

Nick shoved the phone into his pocket. Katie worked long hours at the hospital, especially since she started training to move to the Radiology Department. He was anxious to talk to her about the revisions in his book. She'd understand. The two had spent many late nights discussing the characters and story line. Katie was almost as invested in the original story as he was.

He checked the time as he neared the family restaurant. Twelve thirty, leaving him too many hours to wait before he could talk to Katie. His grandmother's church group sat around the large table near the front window. Not in the mood to socialize, he ducked past the restaurant's window and ran upstairs to his room.

Flipping open his laptop, he sat at his desk to work on the story he had started that morning. After several minutes of staring at the blinking cursor, he closed the computer and paced the room. Too agitated to write, he stripped off his clothes and changed into a tee shirt and sweatpants. He packed clean clothes, his book and the posters into his gym bag. As he jogged down the street to the neighborhood gym, he envisioned a punching bag with Victor Ruby's face on it.

A few treadmills and stationary bicycles with peeling paint comprised the only modern additions made in years to Eddie's Gym. A regulation-size boxing ring took up half of the old, high-ceilinged building. The other half housed free weights, benches, slant boards, pull-up bars and boxing bags. A row of dented green metal lockers lined the back of the big room; hidden behind them, a dressing room with white-tiled shower stalls.

Nick waved to the gym's owner, Eddie, who sat in a raised corner office. His windowed perch allowed him to survey the entire gym. The old man's docile appearance belied a gritty and tenacious personality. He had trained champion boxers for over five decades, including Nick's paternal grandfather, Joe *The Hammer* Teravelli. Framed photographs of famous fighters, including his grandfather's, cluttered the gym's walls.

Eddie's Gym had been a staple in Nick's life since childhood. His father brought him and his brother, Sal, here as young boys, hoping one or both, would continue their grandfather's boxing legacy. Nick's preference for weightlifting over boxing maddened his father. His workouts intensified in his teens, when he concluded larger muscles attracted more girls.

Nick warmed up by punching one of the heavy bags. When he tired, he moved on to free weights, then a pull-up bar and finally over to a weight bench. He slid weight plates onto a bar and spun the end nuts tight. Positioning himself on the bench under the bar, he closed his eyes and gripped the bar.

"Need a spotter?" a male voice asked.

Nick opened his eyes to a familiar, though upside down, grinning face.

"Ray! When did you get back?" Nick slid out from under the bar, jumped up and hugged his best friend.

"Nick, man, it's good to see you." Ray thumped Nick's back as they embraced.

"You on leave?" Nick asked.

"Nope. I'm done. I'm a civilian now," Ray said. "Discharged last week."

"That's great. It's been a long time."

"Four years," Ray said.

"I saw your grandma at a church benefit yesterday. She said you were coming home, but she couldn't remember the date. I'd thought she'd have it memorized."

"Yeah, she's getting a little forgetful, but it doesn't slow her down. She's still running around doing her charity work at the shelter and the church."

"Her and Nonna talk about you all the time. I hear you're a hero. Medals and all."

"I'm no hero." Ray shrugged. "I only did what anybody would do in that situation."

"So, you gonna grow your hair out?" Nick rubbed Ray's crew cut.

"Working on it." Ray laughed and lightly jabbed Nick in the chest.

"You here to work out?" Nick asked.

"Did that this morning. Eddie told me he has a new kid he's training. A welterweight. There's a three round practice match today I wanted to watch."

Nick smiled. "Watch, or bet on?"

"Maybe both, we'll see."

"Let me do a few sets on the bench. I'll meet you over there."

A small crowd gathered around the ring. Nick wiped his face with a towel and walked over to stand next to Ray. "Is that the guy?" He nodded to a man in one corner being fitted with a mouth guard.

"No, he's the sparring partner." Ray pointed toward the locker room. "There's the guy Eddie's excited about."

A young man with a towel draped over his head jogged toward the ring. Old Eddie shuffled along a few feet behind him.

"Holy crap!" Nick said.

"What?" Ray asked.

"That's Sal. My freaking little brother."

Sal's eyes widened when Nick entered the locker room after the match. "Don't tell Nonna."

Nick hugged his brother. "That was an impressive fight, Sal. You've got talent."

"Thanks, Nick." A slow grin spread across Sal's face. "You really think so?"

"Hell, yeah. Eddie's picky about who he trains. He had that proud papa smile on his face when he watched you in the ring. I've never seen you here. How long have you been training?"

"A while. Pop lets me sneak out of the restaurant to come train. Evenings, mostly," Sal said. "But Nonna, geez Nick, she'd pitch a fit if she found out. You know how she feels about boxing."

"Don't worry. I'm not gonna rat you out to Nonna."

Nick unzipped his bag and pulled out a towel. He walked into a shower stall.

"Hey," Sal called. "Is this your book, Nick? You changed your name?"

"Put it back in the bag."

"Why? This is a big deal. My big brother has his own book."

"Look, Sal, do me a favor, don't mention it to Pop or Nonna, okay?"

Ray congratulated Sal on his win as the two brothers emerged from the locker room. "Good fight. I can't believe you're Nick's little brother. You were, what, twelve or thirteen when I left for Iraq?"

Sal shrugged. "I grew up."

Ray waved a small stack of bills in the air. "I'm buying the beer with the money I won off your brother. Is Mulligan's still open?"

"Yeah. Looks the same, too," Nick said. "Let's go celebrate your homecoming and my brother's win."

"Cool," Sal said, following the two to the door.

Nick shoved his brother in the chest. "Just 'cause you can kick ass in the ring, doesn't make you legal to drink. And, if I catch you in a bar, I will tell Nonna."

Ray and Nick each carried two bottles of cold beer from the bar to a high-top table near the jukebox. "You're right," Ray said, "The place look's the same."

"Except the two-for-ones on Sundays is new."

"I'm not complaining." Ray clinked his bottle against Nick's. "So, you seeing anybody, Nick?"

"Yeah, I am. More than seeing."

"Seriously?" Ray asked.

"Uh, huh. Her name's Katie. She's a nurse at Saint Mary's. We've been together over two years now." Nick scowled when Ray broke into a huge grin. "What?"

"What? I've seen all kinds of shit in that God-forsaken sand pit overseas, but I never thought I'd see Nick Teravelli in a serious relationship."

"Like my brother, I've grown up."

"What's Katie like?"

"Beautiful, inside and out. Smart. Sweet. Most incredible woman I've ever known. She was at my mom's funeral. The nurse. You remember?"

Ray's eye's widened. "Oh, yeah. I remember her. She's gorgeous. So, what happened to horny dog Nick that I went to school with?"

Nick took a sip of beer. "We were teenagers then. When I met Katie, I wanted to be better, for her."

"Damn, and here I am depending on you to hook me up."

"What about Carla? I thought you two were serious."

Ray grunted. "For a while. It crashed and burned on my second tour in Afghanistan. She married a friggin' accountant and moved to Jersey."

"That sucks. Sorry."

"Just as well. So, does Katie have a sister? Roommate? Hot mother?"

Nick laughed. "She's got a roommate. A real piece of work. I wouldn't wish her on my worst enemy."

"Well, I'm happy for you, Nick. What else is going on with you?"

"I recently got an agent. Getting my book published."

"Damn, you're full of surprises. That's awesome."

"Yeah, it is, except the agent's a little weird. Tell me about all the medals your grandmother keeps bragging that you got."

"I got a few. Mainly I'm grateful I got out with all my body parts and my sanity. Some guys weren't so lucky. Let's leave it at that."

"So, what are your plans now that you're back?"

Ray laughed. "You mean besides getting my buddy to hook me up with one of his hot ex-girlfriends?"

"Yeah, besides that."

"My old man wants me to take over the body shop. I'm thinking, I'd like that. I've always loved restoring old cars. It's in my blood. I'd be third generation."

"You fixed up the old wrecks we ran around in."

Ray laughed. "Then we'd wreck 'em again."

A waitress placed four beer bottles on the table. She pointed to the bar. "Compliments of those gentlemen." The group of men waved and called out. "Ray, welcome home!"

Nick sat on the hospital steps waiting for Katie. She finally walked through the doors after eight-thirty.

Katie wrinkled her nose when he kissed her. "You've been drinking."

"Only a few beers." He hoped she wouldn't ask how many, he had lost count. "Ray Gonzalez is back from the army. We were catching up. Some neighborhood guys kept buying rounds." Katie didn't like it when he drank too much. After hearing her talk about her alcoholic father, he understood she had her reasons.

"You don't have to walk me home. You look . . . tired."

"Of course, I have to walk you home. I'm fine, just a little buzzed." He slowed his speech so his words wouldn't slur together. "You're the one who looks exhausted."

"Exams are in two days. I'm trying to get in all the Radiology training I can after my regular shift. And I still have a lot of reading to do tonight." She held up the pile of medical books she carried.

"Here, give me those." Nick packed her books into his gym bag and hoisted it onto his shoulder. He put his free arm around her and kissed the top of her head.

Katie slipped her arm around his waist. "At least you're a sweet drunk." She leaned her head against his chest. "Do you realize you've walked me home every night since our first date?"

"Damn, over two years of walking you home. Maybe I'll get lucky tonight, huh?" He laughed when Katie punched his arm.

Nick waited in the living room while Katie changed her clothes. She returned wearing one of his tee shirts, the hem hanging below her knees.

"I'm so beat." She yawned and cuddled next to him on the sofa. "I need to read two chapters tonight."

"I know you're tired, but I wanted to show you something."

"What?"

He dug his novel out of his gym bag and handed it to her.

"Oh my God, your book's printed! But wait, the title's wrong. It should be *Thirst of the Soul.* And your name's wrong, *Nick Tera?* What's going on?"

Nick told her about his meeting that morning with Ruby.

"He had other writers edit your story? I thought the author made the changes?"

"Yeah, me too."

"What did they change?"

"Honestly, I don't even know, I haven't had the heart to read through it all yet."

"I'll read it." She flipped open the book. Ruby's business card fell face down into her lap. "What's this?' She pointed to the odd writing on the back of the card.

"Ruby's card." Nick pushed it back into the book. "It's a Latin quote. He said it inspires his authors and cures writer's block. Supposedly Joseph Cullen swears by it. I'll have to try it, especially if Ruby expects me to spit out books as fast as Cullen."

Katie squeezed his hand. "This sucks, Nick. Your story was perfect. I can't believe they changed it. And without telling you until after it was printed." She turned to page one.

"Not tonight, babe." Nick took the book from her hands. "You have to study."

"My tests will be over in two days. Can I keep it and read through it for you? I'll make notes. Maybe whatever changes they made can be modified somehow in the rest of the trilogy."

"I hate to put that on you, you have work and exams."

"I want to read it." Katie put the novel on top of the pile of medical books Nick unpacked from his bag.

"Thank you. I know I should read it, but I just don't have the heart to see the changes yet." He picked up the stack. "Where do you want these?"

Katie gave a sheepish smile. "I usually study in bed."

"Sounds like a fun night."

Katie followed him into her room and curled up on the bed next to the textbooks.

"Be right back." He went into the bathroom to relieve his beer-soaked bladder and brush his teeth. Returning to the bedroom, he found Katie sound asleep with an open medical book lying across her stomach. He thought about waking her, but decided she needed the rest. Piling the books onto the floor, he turned off the light and climbed into bed beside her. Between his workout at the gym, and the beer fest that followed, he passed out within minutes.

Chapter 4

He awoke the next morning to an empty bed. He found Katie sleeping at the kitchen table, her head resting on a notebook. Open textbooks lay scattered across the table. She jumped when he gently massaged her shoulders.

"When did you get up?" He picked up the empty coffee pot.

"Around two." She stretched her arms above her head. "Oh, it's almost seven. I have to get ready for work."

"Go ahead, I'll make us coffee."

He set up the Mr. Coffee pot and pushed the button. Katie had plugged his cell phone into the charger he kept at her apartment. He checked it for messages. Finding none, he left the phone to continue charging. While he waited for her to shower, he flipped through the morning news channels on the television. When he heard her hair dryer turn on, he knew she was done in the bathroom. He showered and dressed before she had finished doing her hair and make-up.

"It's not fair," she grumbled, watching him tie his sneakers. "Guys are ready in ten minutes. It takes girls an hour."

"Coffee's ready." He smiled and left her to finish dressing. When she emerged in her nursing uniform, Nick set a mug of hot coffee on the table for her.

"Thanks." She stood, organizing her books and sipping coffee.

"Want me to make you some breakfast?"

"No, thanks, I'm not hungry."

"At least sit for a few minutes. Relax."

Katie looked at him with watery, pink-rimmed eyes. He thought she might burst into tears. Wrapping his arms around her, he whispered, "One more day, then your exams will be over."

She snuggled against him. "I'm sorry. I'm a mess this morning. I'm so stressed over the Radiology tests."

"You're fine," he said. "C'mon, I'll walk you to work." Katie grabbed her bag and Nick scooped up her books.

"It's like you're walking a damn kid to school with all these books," she said. "What have you got planned today?"

"Ruby's secretary is supposed to call and let me know the schedule for the week. And, oh yeah, I'm supposed to write more books." He purposely left out the news about the upcoming VIP party. He planned to surprise Katie once her tests were over.

"I know you're upset about your novel," Katie said. "I'll try to read some of it tonight."

"Focus on your exams. There's nothing I can do about the book now, it's already printed."

They had reached the driveway of the hospital when Nick stopped. "Damn it!"

"What?" Katie asked.

Nick shook his head. "I left my cell phone and gym bag at your place."

"Oh." Katie said. "If you weren't so busy baby-sitting me this morning."

"No big deal. I have my key. I'll run back." He kissed her goodbye. "Try to relax."

Nick cursed his forgetfulness as he ran back to Katie's apartment. He hoped he could get in and out, without running into her roommate, Tara. Her work schedule at the hospital varied so much it was impossible to know when she'd be at the apartment. His encounters with Tara were always uncomfortable to say the least. She blatantly flirted with Nick whenever Katie wasn't around.

"Crap." Nick spotted Tara's red Mazda parked in front of the apartment. He put his key back into his pocket and rang the doorbell.

"Well hello, Nick!" Tara smiled, opening the door wide. "I was just getting ready for bed. Want to join me?" She stood in the doorway in a short, leopard print nightgown. The thin material clung to her bulbous breasts and well-padded hips.

"I came by to grab my stuff. Be out in a second." Nick squeezed around her to enter the apartment.

"Who's Stephanie?" Tara's high-pitched, nasally voice made Nick's head ache. "She's called you three times in the past fifteen minutes. Must be important." Tara held up Nick's phone.

"Give me that, Tara." Nick reached for his phone.

She spun around and held the phone away from his grasp. "Come and get it."

"Stop playing games." Nick walked toward her. "Give me my phone."

"Oh, come on Nickie, don't get mad," Tara cooed. "I won't tell Kate about Stephanie, especially if you're nice to me." She tilted her head sideways and twirled a long blond hair extension on the right side of her head. It was the newest addition to her ever-changing, multicolored hairdo.

"Go ahead and tell Katie," Nick snapped. "I've got nothing to hide." He pried the cell phone from Tara's hand.

"Ow!" Her eyes squeezed into black-lined slits. "I could tell Kate you barged in here and attacked me."

"You wish." Nick retrieved his bag from the living room floor and turned to leave.

Tara's stocky body blocked the front door. "You think you're too good for me, don't you? You wouldn't know what to do with a woman like me!"

"You're right. I wouldn't." With Tara's weight leaning against it, Nick tugged the door until the opening was large enough for him to slide through. She yelled out an obscenity as he walked down the path.

Tara's behavior angered him. He kept her suggestive comments to himself so as not to upset Katie. He had tried everything he knew to discourage Tara's advances, but she continued to taunt him. Tara tested his rule of never hitting a woman.

Once he had put distance between himself and Tara, he pressed the call back button on Stephanie's last call.

"Hi Nick, I've been trying to call you."

"My phone was on the charger. I didn't hear it."

"Mr. Ruby wants you to get clothes for the VIP party. Can you meet me downtown at eleven? The store is called Male Storm Clothiers. That's M-A-L-E."

"Of course, it is." Nick chuckled. "Where's it at?"

"Two blocks north of the hot dog stand we went to, left-hand side."

"All right, I'll meet you there at eleven."

Nick had errands he wanted to do before meeting Stephanie. He stopped at home to drop off his bag, change his shirt and retrieve the ten-thousand-dollar check he'd tucked away in his dresser drawer. As he walked toward the front door, his grandmother called after him.

"Nickie, there you are. I didn't hear you get up."

Smiling, he leaned down to kiss her. His grandmother knew he had been gone all night and she knew exactly where he had been. Though she would never allow Katie to stay overnight in Nick's room, she had reluctantly adopted a don't ask, don't tell attitude about the reverse situation. She would never be as forgiving if he were a granddaughter. Being a male in his family had its advantages.

"You look happy today," she said.

"I am happy, Nonna."

"You want something to eat?"

"No thanks, I'm on my way to an appointment."

"This new work, it make you happy?"

"Yes." He surprised himself with how easily he answered. "It does make me happy."

Walking downtown, he thought about his grandmother's comment. He did feel happy, in spite of knowing his story and name had been changed. Lots of authors wrote under pen names and had their manuscripts edited. He focused on the fact his first novel would soon be in print. And with Victor Ruby as his agent, he was on the path to success. Although Ruby marketing him like a new toy at Christmas made him uncomfortable, he accepted it as a trade-off for getting his book published.

Seeing his bank account balance also made him feel good. He was finally earning a living on his own, away from the family restaurant. But it was his next errand that made him feel the happiest. Leaving the bank, he headed to the jewelry store to buy Katie an engagement ring.

He had taken Katie ring shopping on a whim several months ago. At the time, he had no idea what diamond rings cost. The excursion proved both educational and humiliating for Nick. He soon realized he couldn't afford the smallest diamond in the store. Katie told him she didn't need a ring, then took his hand and led him out of the store. Though they never spoke of rings again, Nick vowed someday he would buy Katie a ring worthy of his feelings for her.

Scanning the jewelry store window, he immediately focused on a ring in the center display. He pointed it out to the clerk inside the store. The man told him it was an eighteen-carat gold ring with pavé diamonds in a halo bezel setting. Katie had admired a similar ring. The diamonds in this ring were significantly larger and more brilliant than the one she had tried on. The only positive that came from his ring shopping excursion with Katie, was he'd learned her ring size.

The clerk slipped the freshly polished, size-six ring into a black velvet box and commented it was the fastest sale he had ever made.

The final cost came to just over forty-three hundred dollars. Nick slid the box into his front jeans pocket and left the store grinning.

He arrived early at the Male Storm clothing store. Looking in the windows, he saw mostly black leather and denim items. Small placards on the mannequins boasted designer names, but no prices.

His cell rang at eleven o'clock. A breathless Stephanie informed him she was running late. Nick walked a few doors down and bought a coffee to go. He sipped it while he waited in front of the store.

"Sorry I'm late," Stephanie said.

"No problem."

"Well, there was a *huge* problem at the office. Chris and Ruby got into it. Again."

"Who's Chris?" Nick asked.

"Oh, sorry. Ian Slaughter from Blood Lust. His real name's Chris Turner."

"Ruby changed his name, too?"

"Yeah, he does that a lot." Stephanie made quote marks in the air with her fingers. "It's all about the *image* with Ruby."

"Why were they fighting this time?"

"Same thing. Chris wants to break his contract." Stephanie looked up and down the street, then lowered her voice. "His wife is threatening to divorce him because he's away so much."

"Chris looked pretty lethal in that poster hanging in the office. Ruby better watch out."

"All the stuff on stage with the knives and fake blood is theatrics. All Ruby's idea. Chris is a sweetheart. And a great musician, classically trained on guitar. He's written some beautiful ballads."

"Yet Ruby puts him in a heavy metal band. Go figure," Nick said.

"He has a little girl, Brittany. She's three. He misses her and wants to go home to the west coast. Ruby has him booked non-stop for concerts across the U.S. and Europe. They both know without Chris as lead singer, Blood Lust would be Blood Bust."

Nick touched the velvet box inside his pocket. "Chris's wife and daughter have to come first. You think Ruby will let him out of the contract?"

Stephanie frowned. "Not easily."

Having choices when it came to his attire for the VIP party pleasantly surprised Nick. Ruby's only stipulation was he wear black leather; either pants or a jacket. Nick opted for the jacket.

"None of this stuff looks formal, Steph."

"The VIP isn't traditionally formal, it's more like a masquerade party. It's the horror industry. Think outrageous, sexy," she said. "Even the society snobs let loose at this party."

"This is more comfortable than a suit and tie." Nick stood in front of the full-length mirror and admired the sleek, black leather jacket styled like a suit jacket, a white silk shirt and black jeans. The open neck and oblong pewter buttons gave the shirt an edgy look. A tailor tugged on the hem of the jeans and inserted pins. "And it's not too outrageous, considering I've been told my taste in clothes is 'fuddy-duddy'"

Stephanie's face reddened. "I only meant you're too young for an old-guy suit and tie. She draped a long, black silk scarf with thin red pinstripes around his neck. "There, that's better."

"A scarf? Isn't that kind of girly?"

"No. A lot of French and Italian designers feature scarves in their men's collections." She tucked the scarf under the back of his shirt collar. "I never noticed the scar on your neck before. How did you get it?"

He laughed. "I used to make up cool stories to tell the kids at school. But truth is, when I was about two years old, I grabbed an open soup can off the kitchen counter. Cut my neck on the metal lid."

"Ouch," Stephanie said.

"I don't remember it. My mom told me about it. She cut her hand a lot worse trying to take the can away from me. It left a big scar on her palm."

The tailor stood up. "All set, sir. We'll have everything ready in two days."

Stephanie looked at Nick. "If you're satisfied with the clothes, I think we're done."

"I'm good. How much is all this stuff?"

"Don't worry." She flashed a platinum credit card. "There's major perks to working for Ruby."

"Seriously? He's paying for all of this?"

"Yup, all part of creating the perfect image for his client."

"The cost comes out of my future royalties, right?"

"Trust me, Ruby's got the money figured out. He's convinced you're going to make him a lot of money or he wouldn't be so generous."

"I hope so. I could get used to a lot of money," Nick said.

"I *am* used to it." She waved the credit card. "Now, I get to shop for my dress for the party."

"Nice. So, where do young women find dresses for the VIP party?"

"My favorite place is across the street. Damned Divas." She giggled when Nick rolled his eyes. "It's a funny name, but they specialize in one-of-a-kind dresses. Perfect for the VIP. You wanna come with me?"

"That's okay, I'll pass. Enjoy your shopping."

When Nick met Katie outside the hospital that evening, she looked exhausted. He carried her books and listened to her describe her day as they walked to her apartment.

". . .and on top of that, I only had forty minutes of Radiology training, 'cause two girls were out sick on my floor." Katie sighed. "Sorry, I've been whining for blocks. How was your day?"

"Pretty uneventful." He cupped the ring box inside his pocket.

When they reached the door of Katie's apartment, Nick saw lights on inside.

"Is Tara off tonight?" he asked.

"She pulled the graveyard shift. She leaves for work at ten-thirty. Aren't you staying?"

"Not tonight." Nick put her books on the kitchen table. "You're beat. Get some sleep so you're fresh for your exams." He hugged her. "You're going to ace those tests tomorrow."

Katie's body relaxed against his. "I hope so." She wrapped her arms around his neck.

He kissed her. After several minutes, he pulled away. "If I don't leave now, you won't get any sleep tonight."

Nick stayed up late working on his new novel. He labored over each sentence. No matter how many times he rewrote the paragraphs, the words sounded awkward when he read them back. He finally shut down his laptop after midnight and stretched out on his bed, too tired to undress.

A ringing sound roused him from a deep sleep. Disoriented, it took him several seconds to realize it was his cell phone. He finally located it in the back pocket of his jeans. With his eyes closed, he answered, "Yeah?"

"Nick, oh thank God! I've been calling you." Katie's tone sliced through the thick fog in his mind and made the hair bristle on the back of his neck.

"What's wrong?" He bolted upright in bed.

"Someone's here."

"What? You mean a break-in? Did you call 911?" He held the phone to his ear with one hand while he pulled on his sneakers with the other. "Are you all right? Where are you?"

"No, not a break in." Her breaths sounded sharp and rapid. "There's—I can't explain it. I'm scared. Can you—"

"On my way." He pulled on his jacket and patted the pockets to check for his keys and wallet.

"Nick!"

"Yeah, babe?"

"Please, don't hang up. Stay on the phone."

"Okay. I'll be there in ten minutes, or less." He started out of his room, then turned back to grab his grandfather's old M1911 automatic pistol he kept in the top of his closet. He checked the magazine, then jammed it into the back of his waistband.

He ran down the stairs, jumping over the last three steps. "I'm out the door now."

"I know it sounds crazy. Something's here. I can't . . . describe it."

"I'm at the end of the block by the florist." He sprinted around the corner. The wet pavement shone under the streetlights after last night's rain. A strong, cool breeze whipped his jacket behind him as he ran. Although he couldn't make sense of Katie's words, the fear in her voice spurred him to run faster. Maybe he shouldn't have brought the gun. If he found anyone hurting Katie, he'd end up in prison for murder. He wondered if he should break their connection and call the police. Before he could suggest it, Katie gasped into the phone.

"A–are you there?" Panic choked her voice.

"I'm at Fountain Park. Just a few more blocks."

"Please, hurry."

With one hand clamping the phone to his ear, he ran full-out for the last five blocks, his breath huffing into the speaker.

"At your complex . . . now," he panted. "Coming up . . . the path." His outstretched hand slammed into the front door, stopping his forward momentum. He banged on the door. "Katie!"

The door opened two inches. Katie stared up at him with glassy eyes. The opening narrowed while she fumbled with the chain lock. He pushed the door open and Katie grabbed onto him.

"You all right? What's going on?" He scanned the small apartment. The living room and kitchen lights were on. A dim line of light showed under Katie's closed bedroom door. The bathroom and Tara's bedroom doors were shut. Katie's breathless jumble of words disintegrated into unintelligible sobs.

Nick closed the front door and locked it. "It's okay." He led Katie to the couch in the living room. Her fingers clutched the material of his tee shirt as he eased her onto the couch.

"My room," she said between sobs.

"Stay here." He pulled out the gun. Twisting the knob, he shoved her bedroom door open until it hit the inside wall. Her bedside lamp illuminated the room. Books, papers and her laptop lay strewn across the rumpled bed. He looked inside the closet, under the bed and checked the locked window. Shaking his head, he walked back into the hallway.

Katie stood petrified at the edge of the living room and pointed toward Tara's room. Nick heard the scratching sounds on the other side of Tara's door. He motioned for Katie to stay back. Adrenaline pumped through his body. Grabbing the doorknob, he turned it, and then kicked open the door. He moved the gun from side to side as he scanned the darkened room. He felt for a switch with one hand and flipped on the light. Furniture, clothes, shoes, toiletries and stuffed animals cramped the small room. Flowered curtains billowed inward through an open window. Aiming the gun, he swung the door closed expecting to find the intruder. Nothing. The scratching sound started up again.

The poster of himself and the two models hung on the back of Tara's door. The bottom corners had come loose and rolled. Gusts of wind moved the corners of the slick paper against the door.

"Shit," he mumbled. Ripping the poster down, he crumpled it and threw it on the floor. He slammed the window closed and locked it.

"Nick?" Katie called from outside the door.

Katie cowered in the corner of the hallway. He reached out and hugged her. "Nobody's here. Your stupid roommate left her window open. The wind was blowing a poster on her door."

Nick dropped a tea bag into a mug of boiling water while he listened to Katie recount her evening. It had taken him ten minutes to calm her down enough to talk coherently. She sat at the kitchen table fingering the tiny gold cross hanging from the chain around her neck as she rocked back and forth in the chair.

"I was in my room, studying. For hours," she said. "My brain needed a break from all the medical books, so I started reading your book. Victor Ruby's business card fell out with that odd phrase on the back. I know some Latin from nursing school, but the spelling didn't look right. I sounded out the words and they didn't sound Latin either. I opened my laptop to Google the phrase."

She nodded when Nick set the hot tea in front of her.

"All of a sudden my room got so hot. The air became thick. And a smell, like something burning. I could barely breathe. I thought the apartment was on fire." She closed her eyes. "I ran out here to check the kitchen. Out of the corner of my eye . . . I saw it."

"Saw what?"

"A black shadow. Shaped like a man. He was behind me. But when I turned around, he disappeared. I kept seeing him, but only glimpses. Everywhere I turned he was there . . . then gone. He was taunting me." She rubbed her forehead. "I ran into my room to grab my cell and I felt his breath on the back of my neck. It felt evil. Then hands grabbed my neck. They kept tightening. I tried to pull them off, but there was nothing there." She covered her neck with both hands. "It was choking me. I thought I was going to die. Then, it just let go. I ran out and slammed my door closed. That's when I called you. I should've run outside, but I was so scared, I couldn't think straight."

Nick didn't know how to respond. Hearing Katie say she had been spooked by a shadow baffled him. She excelled at nursing partly due to her ability to stay calm in an emergency. He had never seen her behave like this. Something had obviously terrified her.

"You've been stressed over your exams and you haven't slept a full night in weeks. Then you start reading a horror story. Maybe you dozed off and dreamed—"

"No! It wasn't a dream." Katie stood and leaned across the table. "Something was here. I saw it. Smelled it. Felt it. It tried to kill me."

"Okay, okay calm down. Do you see, or feel, anything now?"

She shook her head. "No."

"Well, that's good."

"You don't believe me, do you?" Katie paced the small kitchen. "You're humoring me, like a child who had a nightmare."

Nick massaged her shoulders. "I do believe you saw something, but what, I don't know."

Katie crossed her arms and stared at him.

"It's late. Why don't you try to get some sleep? You have exams tomorrow."

Her chin dropped and her bottom lip quivered. "You're gonna stay, right?"

He smiled and touched her cheek. "Of course."

Lying on his side in bed with Katie's back tucked against him, Nick stroked her hair until her body stopped trembling and her breathing slowed to even breaths. Her words played in his mind, but still didn't make sense. She must have had a bad dream. He fell asleep holding her. The alarm clock woke them both a few hours later.

Chapter 5

Nick scrambled eggs while Katie showered.

"Oh look, a hottie who cooks." Tara's voice dripped with sarcasm. She closed the front door and flung her key ring on the table. "I like mine boiled *hard*."

Nick glared over his shoulder. "Don't start, Tara."

"Somebody's testy." Her laughter reminded him of a bleating goat.

"You left your bedroom window wide open. This is a first-floor apartment. Katie's here alone all night." Nick jammed the lever down on the toaster.

"You were in my bedroom?" Tara sidled up next to Nick, "If I had known, I would have called in sick last night."

"You don't even care. You're an inconsiderate bitch—"

"Be nice, Nickie." She patted Nick's cheek.

He grabbed her wrist. "What wrong with you? Katie's supposed to be your best friend. Stop coming on to me. How many times do I have to tell you, I'm not interested?" He released her wrist and stared down at her. "And what were you doing with my poster hanging on your door?"

Tara's eyes widened in mock innocence. "I found it in the living room. That's our common area."

"Inside my zipped-up gym bag is not your common area."

"Everything okay?" Katie padded barefoot into the kitchen in her robe with a towel wrapped around her wet hair.

"Everything's fine," Nick said. "Breakfast's ready."

"I'm going to bed." Tara yawned loudly and walked toward her room. She held up her middle finger to Nick behind Katie's back.

Nick set the two plates of eggs on the table with more force than he intended. He turned to retrieve the toast.

Katie lowered her voice. "I know you don't like Tara, but what did she say to make you so angry?"

"It's what she didn't say. She never apologized about the window. She's an inconsiderate bitch and I told her that."

"She usually does close her window. I guess she forgot."

"Forget about Tara. You have your exams to think about. Relax. Eat some breakfast." He buttered a slice of toast and placed it on her plate. "Are you feeling better this morning?"

"Yeah." She paused and looked down. "Look, Nick, I can't explain it and I know how crazy it must sound, but there was someone—or something—here last night."

Before he could respond, she looked up at him and shook her head. "Forget it. I don't want to talk about it now."

After walking Katie to the hospital, Nick stopped by his home to change clothes and then went to the gym. The image of Katie's terrified face stayed in his mind as he went through his workout. The only logical explanation was she had a nightmare, or a panic attack brought on by stress and lack of sleep. He decided it best to wait and talk to her about it after her exams were over.

He returned home, opened his laptop and read over his first chapter with fresh eyes. After smoothing out the paragraphs which had stumped him the night before, he continued typing. He completed the second chapter as his cell phone vibrated on the desk. Seeing a message from Katie surprised him. She said cell phones weren't allowed in the exam room. She texted she was on a break. A row of smiley faces preceded the next line telling him she would be finished with the tests by five o'clock and she had the next two days off.

Nick immediately started planning for tomorrow evening. He wanted to propose to Katie in the same restaurant he had taken her to on their first date. The *Cafe´ Bella Luna* offered the perfect atmosphere; candlelight, soft music and intimate seating. He found the phone number online and made the reservation.

His cell rang as he ended the call to the restaurant.

"Hello, Nick," Victor Ruby said.

"Good morning, Mr. Ruby."

"I need you to come to the office. In one hour."

"Yes sir," Nick closed his laptop. "I'll be there."

Nick changed his clothes and walked at a brisk pace to get to the office within the hour. In the waiting room, he found the reception desk vacant and Ruby's office door wide open.

"Come in, Nick." Ruby stood in the doorway. "Stephanie's out running errands."

The air conditioning streaming through the open door made the interior office temperature bearable.

"How did you get here today?" Ruby asked, settling into his chair.

"I walked."

"It's a long walk, yes?"

"About thirty minutes, I—"

"Let me get to the point, Nick." Ruby tossed a key ring on the desk in front of Nick. "There's an older model Ford in the parking lot. Space number eight. It's yours to use."

"A car? Mr. Ruby, I can't accept—"

"Do you have a valid driver's license?"

"Yes, sir."

"Then you can accept." Ruby held his hand up to silence Nick's objections. "As my newest client, I can't have you walking clear across town to your debut at the VIP. I'm working on scheduling book signings and media appearances for you. You'll need reliable transportation."

"Thank you, sir. I appreciate it. I planned to buy a car—"

"There's an apartment key on the ring, also," Ruby interrupted. "I own the building. It's six blocks west of here. I use it for out-of-town clients and a few employees. Stephanie lives there."

"Mr. Ruby, the car is more than enough. I couldn't possibly accept an apartment."

"I insist. Writers need a quiet place to work. I expect many bestsellers from you in the future."

"Let me pay you rent at least."

"You couldn't afford it." Ruby laughed and then leaned forward. "Soon you'll be able to afford to live anywhere you like. Until then, enjoy." He pressed the keys into Nick's palm. "I have some routine maintenance and cleaning scheduled, but you can move in Saturday morning."

"I don't know what to say, Mr. Ruby. I want to repay you for all of this."

"No need to say anything, Nick. Settle in. Finish your next book." Ruby led Nick to the door. "You'll repay me soon enough."

Nick left the office in a daze. He nearly walked into Stephanie as he exited the elevator in the lobby.

"Nick? I didn't know you had an appointment today," she said.

"Me neither. Ruby called and told me to come down."

"What for?"

Nick held up the keys. "He gave me a car and an apartment to use. He said it's in your building."

"Awesome! You'll love it there. I told you there were major perks to working here." She pointed to an exit at the rear of the lobby. "The parking lot's out back. He has several cars he loans to clients. Which one did he give you?"

"A Ford in space number eight. Maybe an older Taurus or something?"

"You'll flip when you see it. C'mon." Stephanie pulled Nick by the hand toward the back door.

The parking lot had only one row with numbered spaces. Nick's mouth fell open as they walked up to space number eight.

"Holy sh–"

"Told you."

Nick stared at the classic, fully restored 1966 Mustang convertible. He walked around the car admiring the Raven Black paint that shone from every angle. The interior, upholstered in red leather with chrome trim, looked brand new. The signature pony emblem centered on the slotted chrome front grill, gleamed in the sunlight.

"I've always wanted a '66." He popped the hood to check out the engine and was awed by its spotless condition. "It's the high performance 289 with the four-barrel carb," he said.

A snippet of Johnny Cash's *Ring of Fire* played from Stephanie's cell phone. "Yes, Mr. Ruby. On my way." She wrinkled her nose. "I have to get back to work." She hesitated a second, then gave Nick a hug. "I'm so happy for you. I can't wait until we're neighbors."

Nick gaped at the car for several more minutes before he unlocked the driver's door and slid inside. He moved the seat back to accommodate his long legs and breathed in the earthy leather scent. Running his hands across the steering wheel and dash, he caught his smile reflected in the rear-view mirror as he realized he could drive Katie to the restaurant tomorrow night instead of taking a cab.

Katie exited the hospital with a small group of coworkers a few minutes past five. They congratulated each other on completing the exams. Jon Gerber stood next to Katie. He hovered too close for Nick's liking. Gerber looked more like a surfer than a nurse with his sun-streaked hair, deep tan, and athletic build. Nick's jaw tightened involuntarily when Katie hugged Gerber. She waved to her friends and then ran over to greet Nick. He picked her up and spun her around, glancing over her head at Gerber, who watched them from the group.

"You look happy tonight," he said to Katie.

"I'm so relieved exams are over," she said. "We have to wait a couple of weeks to get our scores, but I think I did okay."

"I had no doubt you would," he said. "As hard as you've trained and studied, I'll bet you get the highest scores in your class."

"As long as I pass, I'll be thrilled. Working in Radiology would mean higher pay and better hours." She stood on her toes and kissed Nick on the lips. "Let's go home and celebrate." She tugged on his hand, but he didn't move.

"I can't walk you home tonight," he said.

"How come?" Her expression changed from disappointment to concern. "Is something wrong?"

Nick couldn't keep himself from grinning any longer. "No, something's right. C'mon, I'll show you." He took Katie's hand and led her around the corner of the hospital building into the parking lot. He stopped in front of the Mustang. "I'm going to drive you home tonight."

"It's beautiful. You bought a car today?"

"I wish. It's a loaner from Ruby. Get in." He opened the passenger door for Katie and then ran around to the driver's side. He turned the key in the ignition and the deep, throaty engine rumbled to life.

"Love it," he said. "Doesn't she sound sexy?"

"I don't know about sexy, but gas-guzzling, yes."

"She's worth every drop."

"She?" Katie laughed. "I'm jealous."

"Let's go for ride. I'll tell you about my meeting with Ruby."

Nick had pulled the car into a lookout near the river.

The sky turned from orange, to crimson and then to a deep purple as the sun dipped below the horizon. Nick and Katie watched as the colors of the sunset rippled across the surface of the river. As night fell, the water turned to a glossy black mirror reflecting the myriad of sparkling lights from the city.

"It's so pretty here." Katie leaned her head against Nick's shoulder.

"Yeah, it's pretty cool to be able to drive down to the river on a whim and watch the sunset."

"Yes, it is. A car and an apartment. That's very generous of Mr. Ruby. He must have a lot of confidence in you and your book sales."

"I hope so." He squeezed her hand. "Hey, do you mind if I plan your day off tomorrow?"

"What did you have in mind?"

"First, I want to take you dress shopping."

"Shopping? You hate shopping." She frowned and then cocked her head. "A dress for what?"

"Ruby's annual VIP party is this Saturday night. It's a big event in the horror industry. A lot of Ruby's clients will be there, actors, musicians and authors. And a press conference where they'll announce I won his talent contest and introduce my first novel."

"Nick, that's so exciting!" Her eyes sparkled. "Oh no, wait, this Saturday? I have to work."

"I was hoping you could swap a day with one of your—"

"Julie," Katie interrupted him. "She owes me a favor. I'll work Thursday for her and she can cover Saturday for me." Katie grabbed her cell phone and called Julie to confirm the arrangement. She ended the call and grinned. "All set."

"One more thing, I want to take you out to dinner tomorrow night," Nick said. "To celebrate your exams being over."

Katie touched his cheek. "You're so sweet to me. But you don't have to spend your money—"

Nick touched his finger to her lips. "I want to."

Katie wriggled in the bucket seat to move closer to Nick. He leaned across the center console to kiss her. The gear shift lever jabbed into his ribs.

"Ow! This car's sexy, but not built for romance," Nick said.

"There's always . . ." Katie glanced at the narrow back seat, then at Nick's six foot plus frame and burst out laughing. "Let's go to my apartment."

Chapter 6

The following morning, they drove downtown with the top down, enjoying the warm, sunny morning. Katie's windblown hair streamed behind her in long, shiny ribbons. Nick couldn't stop glancing over at her and smiling. He slowed and parked the Mustang in a space in front of an upscale boutique.

"I thought we were going to the mall. *Damned Divas*? What is this place?" Katie asked.

"Ruby's secretary recommended it."

The sign on the barred front door instructed to ring the bell for entrance. A tall, bony woman dressed in a red leather corset and a tattered, lime-green skirt opened the door. Her cheekbones dominated her gaunt face. She studied them with icy eyes. "May I help you?"

"My girlfriend needs a dress for the Ruby International Promotions VIP party."

The woman's pencil-drawn brows raised. "Come in. Please, be seated." She sauntered off into a back room. Layers of shredded material on her skirt ruffled in the air as she walked.

Nick and Katie grinned at each other. "I guess we sit," Nick said.

The tall, narrow display windows outside belied the spacious interior. Glossy black walls with back-lit cubby holes showcased displays of clothing and shoes. Groupings of bright-colored upholstered chairs dotted the plush, snow-white carpeting.

"This place looks pricey, Nick. And if the dresses here are anything like hers—"

"Don't worry about price. This is my treat." Nick leaned close to Katie's ear. "She looks like an old dominatrix who fell into a chipper-shredder."

Katie stifled her laughter as the sales woman returned rolling a small chrome rack with a colorful selection of evening gowns. She held up each dress and recited its list of designer features in a monotone voice.

"This one's cute." Katie stood and admired a black cocktail dress. "May I try it on?"

"Certainly, follow me."

Katie waved to Nick and then followed the woman to the dressing room.

"It looks nice," Nick commented when she returned. While the simple dress flattered Katie's figure, the plunging neckline and back held Nick's attention "How does it stay on?" he asked.

The saleswoman pursed her thin lips but kept silent.

"It feels more secure than it looks," Katie said. She walked to an alcove with mirrors on three walls and studied the dress.

"This one would better suit you." The woman removed a dress from the rack and held it up. The pale golden material shone under the florescent lights.

"I thought a black dress would be the safest choice for a formal party," Katie said.

"The VIP is definitely not about safe choices," the woman said. "You'll stand out in this. Your coloring and body type are a perfect match for this gown."

Nick shrugged. "Try it on."

Several minutes later, Katie and the dour-faced saleswoman walked back into the show room.

Nick stood. "Wow!"

The dress fit Katie's slender body like a shimmering glove. Beneath the sheer outer layer, matching pearlescent fabric provided coverage and accentuated Katie's tiny waist and full breasts. The deep V-back ended at her waist in a cascade of sparkling fabric. The long asymmetrical skirt had a daring slit to the upper thigh on one side.

The saleswoman's grim red lips twitched at the corners. "I told you."

Katie pulled Nick by the hand over to the mirrors. "The dress is gorgeous, but she said it cost nine-hundred dollars," she whispered. "Then she brought me these heels to try with it. They're one-hundred and seventy!" Katie lifted her long hair to simulate an up-sweep and slowly twirled around in front of the mirrors.

"You look fantastic. We're getting it." Nick said. "Of course, I'll have to bring my gun and a couple of Dobermans to keep the guys away from you."

"No, Nick, it's too expensive. I can find a nice black dress for eighty dollars at the mall. Maybe less, if there's a sale. I already have black heels—"

"Nope. This dress looks incredible on you. Face it babe, the ol' dominatrix is right."

Although he knew Katie loved the dress, she couldn't get past the price of the extravagant purchase. As they drove away from the boutique, she still protested.

"Nick, over a thousand dollars for one outfit. I feel terrible you spent so much."

"You can't back out, they're doing alterations. I'll pick it up for you tomorrow. I have to get my clothes across the street."

"Let's pass on going out to dinner tonight," Katie said.

"Why? I made reservations."

"To save money. We can make dinner at home."

"We?" Nick grinned. "You plan on making your special pasta soup?"

"You're never going to let me forget, are you?"

"I know I won't." He enjoyed teasing Katie about her first and only attempt to cook him dinner. After boiling spaghetti in a covered pot for over two hours, she was horrified when she discovered the glutinous mass inside the pot.

"You're a fantastic chef," she said. "You cook. I'll wash dishes."

"Nice try, but I'm not cooking tonight. We're going out."

Despite her earlier objections, Katie's face lit up when they pulled up outside the Cafè Bella Luna.

"Oh, Nick, I love this place!"

Nick couldn't remember the last time he felt as elated as he did escorting Katie into the cafe. He couldn't afford to take her here before receiving Ruby's check. They followed the maitre d' to a secluded alcove in the rear of the dining room. He seated them in a booth next to an arch-shaped window overlooking the river. The Venetian plaster walls reflected the warm amber light from candles flickering in the wrought iron and glass wall sconces. More candles glowed in the center of the table. A ceramic planter filled with ivy sat on the windowsill, its delicate green tendrils trailed down the wall and curled onto the table.

Nick picked at the selection of tapas-style dishes he and Katie shared. An unexpected bout of nerves dulled his appetite. Until this moment, the possibility Katie might reject his marriage proposal hadn't occurred to him. If she turned him down, he couldn't imagine how the rest of the evening would play out—much less, the rest of his life.

He ran through a mental check list of reasons why he believed she would accept. They could talk to each other about anything or be equally as comfortable together in total silence. While Katie voiced her disapproval if he drank too much or acted jealous, they had never had a serious argument.

Beyond the long list of practical reasons, Nick knew in his heart he and Katie belonged together. He put all of his feelings into a proposal he had written months ago. He had read it and edited it over and over, as if it were a page from one of his novels. He kept the folded sheet of paper inside his wallet.

"Nick?"

"Sorry, what?"

"I said you're not eating much. Aren't you hungry?" Katie asked.

"Not really. But everything's delicious."

When they finished eating, Katie excused herself to go to the ladies' room. As the waiter cleared their plates, Nick asked him to wait five minutes after Katie returned and then bring a bottle of champagne to the table. He clutched the velvet ring box in his hand.

"Excuse me." Nick motioned to the same waiter again. "Make it ten minutes, okay?"

The waiter smiled and nodded.

He gulped the remaining wine in his glass, then picked up Katie's untouched glass and drained it.

Nick drew a deep breath as Katie settled into the booth. She gazed out the window and remarked about the beautiful skyline. He moved from his seat and knelt on one knee beside her. Katie stopped talking in mid-sentence. He took her left hand in his.

She clasped her right hand over her mouth. Her eyes widened more each second she waited for Nick to speak.

His mouth felt dry and his stomach hollow. The proposal he had memorized and rehearsed so eloquently in his mind completely eluded him.

"Katie, I, I've loved you from the minute I first saw you. Even more now . . . and I, I . . . will you marry me?" With damp hands, he flipped open the velvet box. Katie gasped as he slid the ring onto her finger. She gaped at the diamonds glinting in the candlelight and then stared at Nick with wet eyes. Katie leaned over, wrapped her arms around him, and pressed her face into his neck. He stayed on one knee holding her.

His words came out in a hoarse whisper. "Um, does this mean you will?"

Katie sat up and stroked his face.

Nick's heart beat hard and fast in his throat as he waited for her response.

"Yes." She nodded and smiled. "Yes, of course I will."

He slid into the booth next to her and kissed her. They glanced up when they heard a smattering of applause. Diners smiled from the surrounding booths, some waved, and others held up their glasses. The waiter placed an ice bucket with a bottle of champagne and two fluted glasses on the table. The pop of the cork brought more applause.

"Congratulations," the waiter said. He poured the champagne and then left them alone.

"Nick, I had no idea you were going to propose. This ring is stunning." Katie dabbed at her eyes with a corner of the linen napkin. "When I saw you kneeling there, my heart started beating so fast."

"Not as fast as mine," he said. "I was afraid you we're going to say no."

"Never." Katie kissed his cheek. "I was so choked up, I couldn't talk."

Nick smiled. "Me neither. I had memorized a romantic speech but," he paused and blew out a long breath, "my mind went blank."

"You'll have to tell me your speech sometime."

"Or, you can read it." Nick pulled the paper from his wallet. "I wrote my proposal six months ago."

Katie carefully unfolded the paper and read. Fresh tears rolled from her eyes. "Oh my God. This is the most beautiful. . .." She kissed him. "May I keep it?"

"Only if you pretend I actually said it."

"Are you sure you want to do this tonight?" Nick parked the Mustang a few doors down from his family's restaurant. "I thought we'd go back to your place and, you know, celebrate."

"Don't you think we should tell your family?" Katie asked.

"Of course. I just hadn't planned on doing it tonight," he said.

"It'll be fun to share the news with them," Katie said. "I always wanted a family like yours."

Nick grinned. "Be careful what you wish for, it's about to come true."

"I know they get on your nerves sometimes, but they're so loving compared to my parents, especially my father. I love being around your family, it helps me forget—"

"I know."

"It was six years yesterday."

"Since your parents died?" Nick clamped his hand on his forehead. "Oh, I'm so sorry. I can't believe I proposed to you so near the date of their deaths."

Katie took his hand. "No, that date was yesterday. Six years ago today, I was all alone and feeling sorry for myself. I'm not sure if I was grieving for them or crying for the parents I wished I had."

"I can't imagine what that must have been like for you."

"When the cops came to the door to tell me about the car accident, they asked how old I was. I said nineteen. Legally, I was an adult. The officer handed me a card for a grief counselor and left. It's like remembering a bad dream. I wasn't surprised my father was drunk. He was always drunk. And angry. My mom shouldn't have let him drive. But she never stood up to him. She was always so afraid." Katie sighed. "I used to get as angry at her as I did at my father."

"But you sold the house and put yourself though college. Became a nurse. Landed a good job here in the city. That's amazing for a nineteen-year-old."

"My neighbors helped me. He was a lawyer. She was a retired baker. They were so sweet to me. Even before the accident, I sometimes wished they could be my parents."

"I'm sorry, Katie. I didn't know the date they died."

"Don't be sorry. Six years ago today, I was alone and lost. Now, I have you."

"You have a family, too. After all you did for my mom, my family adores you, Katie." Nick squeezed her hand and sighed. "Let's get this over with."

"It'll only take a few minutes," Katie said. "We'll have the rest of the night to ourselves."

"Uh, huh."

They strolled the half block to the front door of Rosa's Ristorante. Nick held the door open for Katie. His grandmother sat at a large table near the window surrounded by the ladies from her church group. Near closing time, a lone customer stood at the back counter as Nick's father, Dom, piled take-out boxes into his outstretched arms. Nick waited and held the door for him to exit.

Nonna rose to greet them. "Come sit," she said dragging two chairs from a smaller table over to the large table. Like a circle of dominoes, the ladies inched their chairs over one by one to make room. "You come for supper?"

"No, thank you, we've already eaten." Nick smiled and grasped Katie's hand. "Nonna, we have wonderful news to share."

Nonna and her friends turned their expectant faces toward the couple.

"I asked Katie to marry me tonight." Nick held Katie's hand up to show Nonna the ring. "The wonderful part is, she said yes."

The women jumped up from their chairs and swarmed around the couple, kissing and hugging each in turn. Nonna hugged Katie and kissed both her cheeks repeatedly. Nick's father edged his way through the crowd.

"Let me kiss my future daughter-in-law." He cupped his hands around Katie's face and kissed her on the forehead. Taking both her hands, he stepped back to look at her. His brown eyes shone with tears. "I already think of you as my daughter." He thrust a beefy hand toward Nick. "You did good, son." He shook Nick's hand, then pulled him into a tight hug.

Sal called from the pass-through in the kitchen. "What's going on?"

His father motioned to him. "Your brother's gonna marry Katie!"

Sal untied his apron and tossed it on a chair as he sprinted over. "Awesome, Nick." He slapped Nick on the back. "Hey, I get to kiss Katie." He stood with his lips puckered and eyes closed. Katie tactfully avoided his mouth and kissed him on the cheek. Sal's face flushed bright pink, sparking laughter from the ladies.

Nonna clapped her hands above her head to quiet everyone. "When is the wedding?"

Nick and Katie looked at each other. "We haven't set a date yet," Katie said.

Nonna made a tsking sound. "It's spring now. You have the wedding in the summer, yes? Or maybe fall? Fall is nice for a wedding."

"Nonna, we don't know yet," Nick said.

"I call Father Santore. I need a date to reserve the church."

Mrs. Gonzalez patted Katie's cheek. "My daughter-in-law's family owns a bridal boutique. We can all go shopping to find your dress! You'll be a beautiful bride."

A tall, thin woman with bluish-grey hair tapped Katie on the shoulder. "My neighbor has a hair salon. She does my hair. I can make appointments for you and the bridal party. How many bridesmaids will you have?"

Another woman's voice called out. "My grandson works for a printer. He can print your invitations. I'll need your guest list."

"What flowers you like?" Nonna asked Katie. "I talk to Loretta tomorrow."

"Who's Loretta?" Katie asked.

"The florist, on the corner. You like roses, yes? Everybody likes roses."

Nick sat sprawled in a chair with his hands folded behind his neck grinning up at Katie. "I warned you."

"What you mean you warn her? *Agitatore*! Troublemaker!" She waved her hand dismissing his laughter.

"I haven't even thought about a dress, or flowers, or anything yet," Katie told the chattering women. "I've only been engaged twenty minutes."

"That's okay. Loretta will know what's nice for a fall wedding. Nickie, I call your cousin Sophia tomorrow. Her daughter's five, she make a beautiful flower girl. But first we need to redecorate the restaurant."

"Redecorate?" Dom asked.

"Yes, yes," Nonna bustled around the dining room pointing as she talked. "Fresh paint, maybe new upholstery for the booths and chairs, and linens for the tables."

Sal snickered as he watched his father's mouth fall open.

"Salvatore, you paint on Mondays when the restaurant's closed," Nonna said.

"Me? This place is huge, Nonna," Sal said. "Why not hire a painter?"

"You a big, strong boy. You paint. We buy the paint next Monday. Then you start."

"What does Nick getting married have to do with me painting the restaurant?" Sal asked.

Nonna smacked the back of his head. "How can we have the reception here unless you paint and make it nice?"

Nick smirked at his brother.

Nonna poked Nick in the chest. "Nickie you taller, you do the ceilings. Oh, and I make that cream cake you like for your wedding cake. Katie, you like that cake? Or, maybe you like the chocolate one? Eh, I make both."

A plump, white-haired woman leaning on a cane joined in. "Rosa, my niece, Angela, had a cannoli tree at her reception. It looked so grand. With your delicious cannoli, it would be fabulous!"

"Cannoli tree? Why you put cannoli on a tree?"

"No, no," the woman said. "They piled them all up and made it look like a pyramid." She made a triangular shape with her hands.

"I can do this. You two want this cannoli tree?" Nonna asked, repeating the shape with her hands.

Katie stood with her mouth open looking from Nonna to Nick.

"Nonna," Nick stood and put his arm around his grandmother's shoulders. "I love you, but you need to slow down. Katie and I need time to set a date."

"Slow down? What, I wait for you? *Dio aiutami*! God help me! I want to hold my grandchildren before I'm dead!"

"Told you." Nick chuckled as they drove toward Katie's apartment.

"Yes, but they meant well. Nonna looked so happy. Your dad, too."

Nick grunted.

"I saw him hug you. He loves you, Nick. Your dad isn't comfortable showing his feelings. I saw how hard it was for him to handle his emotions when your mom was sick."

"I guess," Nick sighed. He would gladly give up a hug from his father if it would bring back his mother. She would have been thrilled over his engagement to Katie.

"You got quiet all of a sudden, are you okay?" Katie asked.

Nick blinked his eyes. "Excellent." He squeezed her knee and laughed when she squealed.

Chapter 7

When Nick drove Katie to work the following morning, she expressed her concern again about the price of the dress.

"Don't worry about the money," he told her as he kissed her goodbye. He understood why she worried. The last six years had been difficult for her after the loss of her parents, emotionally and financially. Their life insurance payment and the money from the sale of their house were the only money she had. Katie used a large portion to pay for the college where she earned her nursing degree. When she graduated, Saint Mary's hospital offered her a well-paying job. Still, she chose an apartment within walking distance of the hospital to save the expense of a car. She found another nurse, Tara, to split the rent. Nick knew Katie lived frugally and banked most of her earnings. Money, or rather the lack of money, had been the main reason Nick delayed asking Katie to marry him. But now, with Ruby as his agent, Nick felt confident he could provide financial security for them both.

Nick carefully placed Katie's wrapped dress and shoes into the back seat of the Mustang. The same saleswoman from yesterday convinced him to buy an evening bag to match the shoes. The woman's first genuine smile came with the approval of the purchase on his debit card.

Nick's clothes for the VIP party were laid out in a garment bag on the back seat. He put the top up on the car to protect their clothing. His cell rang as he pulled out into traffic to head home.

"Nickie, I need a ride. Can you take me to pick up a few things at Maria's house? And then over to the Shelter?" Nonna asked.

"Sure, Nonna. When?"

"I be ready in an hour," she replied.

Nick had planned to drive home and work on his book, and then bring Katie her dress when he picked her up from work. He knew if his grandmother required a car to transport a few things, the load would probably take up the entire back seat, as well as the trunk. Nonna, and Ray's grandmother, Maria, regularly donated clothing and other items they collected to a neighborhood domestic abuse shelter. Nick didn't want to damage Katie's expensive outfit, so he made a quick right turn and headed to her apartment. He hoped to sneak in and put the dress in Katie's room while Tara slept.

Nick parked in front of the building, not far from Tara's Mazda. Tara and another woman stood talking outside the front door of Katie's apartment.

He waited in the car for the woman to leave. Although the delay annoyed him, knowing he would have to deal with an awake Tara annoyed him more. He considered bringing the dress in while Tara was occupied but feared she might make an embarrassing scene.

Ten minutes later, the woman finally turned and walked down the path. As she approached the sidewalk, Nick recognized her. Janis Ford, the reporter who had photographed him and Stephanie in the park last week. She crossed the street and got into a white Camry. Nick ducked down in his seat as she drove past. In the rear-view mirror, he watched as her car turned left at the end of the block and disappeared from view.

Gathering up the boxes, he carried the shoes and bag under one arm, and held the dress in his other hand so it wouldn't touch the ground. He rang the doorbell with his elbow. Tara talking to a reporter worried him. Although he had only a few brief encounters with Janis Ford, she had been openly hostile each time. Seeing both women together gave him a bad feeling.

Tara peered through the narrow door opening secured with a chain. "Nick, what are you doing here?"

"Dropping off some things for Katie," he said.

"Can't it wait till she's home?"

Although relieved not to hear Tara's usual crude come-ons, Nick wondered why she seemed reluctant to let him inside. "C'mon, Tara. I don't want to drop this stuff. It'll only take me a minute to put it in Katie's room."

"Oh, all right. Hang on."

He heard Tara's footsteps run across the linoleum kitchen floor. A few moments later, she returned, unlatched the chain, and then stood in the kitchen flipping through a magazine while Nick hurried into Katie's bedroom. He hung the dress in her closet and placed the boxes on her bed. Tara glanced up as he closed Katie's door, then quickly looked down at the magazine. The magazine cover was upside down.

"What did Janis Ford want?" he asked.

"Who?"

Nick sighed. "Janis Ford. The reporter from *The Entertainer*. You were outside talking to her for ten minutes or more. What was she doing here?"

Tara dropped the magazine on the table. "I don't know what you're talking about. And if you don't mind, I'd like to get some sleep. I've been working all night." She stomped to the front door and held it open.

"Tara, I saw you talking to her. Tell me what she wanted."

"Oh, her." Tara twirled one of her long, black hair extensions around her finger. "Just some woman selling make-up." She snorted. "Took me forever to get rid of her." She averted her eyes from Nick's piercing gaze.

"You're lying. I know who she is. Now tell me what she wanted."

"Why were you watching the apartment? Are you spying on me?" Tara backed up against the kitchen table. She reached behind her back and slid her purse closer. "Leave, or I'll—I'll call the cops."

"Oh, please Tara, cut the drama crap." Nick walked to the side of the table and spotted a white card sticking out from the side pocket of her bag. He snatched the business card before Tara could react.

"So, the Avon lady's name is Janis Ford. And her business card has *The Entertainer's* logo on it, isn't that strange?" Nick held the card above his head while Tara swatted the air below attempting to grab it. "And look, she wrote her cell number on the back. Why does Janis want you to call her, Tara? Is she asking questions about me? Or Katie?"

"Give it back! You can't just take stuff out of my purse!"

"It's no different than you taking the poster out of my gym bag. Isn't the kitchen part of your common area, too?" Nick pocketed the card and walked out the front door.

Tara followed him part way down the path screaming at him. "You bastard! Don't you ever come here again when I'm alone! I swear I'll call the police!"

A middle-aged couple walking in the courtyard stopped and stared. Nick hurried to his car and drove away.

Nick carried the last box from his car into the lobby of the Domestic Abuse Shelter. He surveyed the pile of cardboard boxes and plastic bags, amazed it had all fit into the Mustang.

Nonna stood talking to the shelter's director. "The clothes are washed and packed by size. And toys for the kids." Nonna pointed to the neatly labeled boxes. "Sheets, blankets and towels in those bags. Maria's cookies are in the white plastic bin."

"This is wonderful, Rosa. Thank you, and Maria, so much," The woman took Nonna's hand. "You two are our biggest and most consistent donors. It's all so appreciated. The children look forward to Maria's cookies every week."

Nick helped his grandmother into his car. "Do you need to go anywhere else, Nonna?"

She shook her head. "No. I go home. Thank you, Nickie. I feel better now. The kids have clothes and shoes."

Nick smiled at his grandmother and started the car. His cell phone rang. He saw Stephanie's name on the screen.

"Hi, Nick. Listen, I have the prepared questions for the press conference and an outline for your biography. I meant to give them to you the other day when we went shopping, but I forgot. Mr. Ruby wants them completed tomorrow morning. Can you come by the office or should I email them to you?"

Nick glanced over at his grandmother. She sat stiff-backed in the car seat, looking straight ahead, her knuckles white from gripping the rosary beads she clutched in her lap. Riding in cars made her nervous. On the drive to the Gonzalez's house and the shelter he had purposely stayed on the less trafficked side streets. The busy downtown avenues near the Ruby building would terrify her. "Email them to me, okay Steph?"

Stephanie verified his email address. "I'm sending you two files. One is an outline for you to use to write your bio. The information will be released to the media. The other is a list of five questions Mr. Ruby chose for you to answer at the press conference Saturday night. It might be narrowed to three, for time constraints. He wants you to write out your answers and then review them with him tomorrow morning at nine o'clock. I'm so sorry, you should have had more time to work on this. I screwed up. Please, don't tell Mr. Ruby."

"Don't worry, I'll knock it out this evening. Sounds easy enough."

"Damn, this is harder than I thought." Nick sat at Katie's kitchen table typing on his laptop.

"They didn't give you much time." Katie poured coffee for Nick. A tea bag steeped in her cup.

Katie insisted Nick stay at her place and offered to help him with his project. Although she refused to talk about the shadowy figure that had terrorized her the other night, Nick sensed she feared being alone at night. He brought his laptop and a change of clothes with him when he picked her up from work.

"Okay, bio's done. What do you think?" He turned the screen toward Katie.

She read the page. "It sounds good. I see a typo. I'll fix it."

"Now, the dreaded press questions." Nick sighed.

"Dreaded?"

"Yes, I dread standing on a stage answering questions from reporters," Nick said. "One of them is Janis Ford, the goth-looking woman I told you about. For some reason, she doesn't like me. I told you she made a nasty comment the day Ruby picked me."

"She's probably jealous."

"And she was bitchy the other day in the park when she took pictures of me and Steph."

"Took pictures of you and Steph? What are you talking about?"

"Last Sunday. Steph and I grabbed a hot dog at a City Dawg cart."

"I didn't know you were that close with Ruby's secretary."

"I wouldn't say close. She has no friends here. I told you she's from the mid-west, right?"

Katie chewed on her bottom lip and dunked the tea bag up and down in her cup. "Do you think she's looking for a friend, or something more?"

"Oh, c'mon, babe. Steph's a kid. I don't even think she's twenty-one like she says." Nick put his hand over Katie's. "It was a hot dog on a park bench. She was lonely and I felt sorry for her. Then Janis Ford showed up and started snapping pictures."

Seeing Katie's adverse reaction to his lunch with Stephanie, he decided not to mention Janis Ford speaking to Tara today. He wanted to ask Katie to talk to Tara about Janis. But, knowing Tara's spiteful nature, she'd use it as an opportunity to cause trouble between him and Katie. He had tried calling Janis to find out why she was at Katie's apartment. He left messages on her office phone and her cell, but she never returned his calls.

"You told me Stephanie went shopping with you, but I didn't know you had lunch with her. It's just . . . don't you notice how girls are always looking at you?" Katie looked down. "Especially now with the designer clothes and the sexy, single image Ruby's pushing. It's not that I don't want you to be successful, you know I do. I guess I wasn't prepared for all this."

Nick laughed. "Now you know how I feel. Guys stare at you all the time."

"I'm not interested in any other guys."

"And I'm not interested in any other girls." Nick lifted Katie's hand and pressed it against his lips. "That's why I asked *you* to marry me."

Her pout broadened into a smile. "I never thought of myself as the jealous type. Guess I am."

"I kinda like you being the jealous one for a change," he teased. "Besides, you'll meet Steph tomorrow night. You'll see what I mean. She's a naive young girl, all starry-eyed about meeting rock stars and shopping for designer clothes. I think of her like a kid sister."

"Okay." Katie scrolled to the page of press questions. "I know you have to get this done tonight. I'll read the questions and you can practice answering and . . . oh, for— seriously?"

"What?"

"Question one. Are you single and what turns you on the most about a woman?"

"You're kidding?"

Katie pushed the laptop across the table. "No, look."

"Must be Ruby's idea." Nick looked over at Katie chewing on her lip again. He scanned down the page. "Here we go, question two, who or what inspired you to write horror stories?" Nick typed as he spoke out loud. "I'd say Joseph Cullen. I started reading his books when I was twelve. Read every one he's written. He revolutionized the horror genre. Unique story lines, intricate plot twists, and in-depth characters. I don't like his newer books, though. Too much senseless violence and gore. Same plot over and over. Cullen's gotten lazy in his old age."

Katie sat with her arms crossed staring into her cup. "Aren't you supposed to answer all of the questions, and then Ruby picks out which three the press will ask?"

Nick sighed. "Okay, fine. Question one." He typed for about a minute and then turned the screen toward Katie.

Katie read his answer.

No, I am not single. I'm engaged to a beautiful, intelligent, woman with an incredibly hot body. What would turn me on the most is if she would help me answer these stupid press questions so we could make love instead of sitting here at her kitchen table talking about silly crap that's never going to happen.

Katie giggled. "Smart ass."

Chapter 8

How did your meeting go with Ruby? Was he satisfied with your answers?" Katie asked.

Nick sat in the Mustang in the Ruby Promotions parking lot talking to Katie on his cellphone. "Yeah, he was fine with all of it. I'm surprised. The guy's usually a real control freak. I think he's preoccupied with the last-minute details for his VIP party tonight.

"I'm glad the meeting went well for you. I know you were worried."

"So, how about I pick you up and we'll go check out my new apartment?"

"This morning?"

"Yeah, it's available for me to move in today. Why, did you have something planned?"

"Tara scheduled a spa day for me at the salon she worked at before she became a nurse. A very expensive salon. She's getting me in for free. I'd hate to turn her down after the trouble she went to."

"What's a spa day?"

"Massage, facial, manicure, pedicure, the works. Plus, Tara's going to do my hair."

Nick pictured Tara's multi-colored, choppy hair. He wouldn't put it past her to purposely ruin Katie's long, beautiful hair. "Babe, do you think that's a good idea? Tara's hair looks like something chewed on it—"

"Oh, stop. She's a talented stylist. She showed me a picture in a magazine of this sophisticated up-sweep. It will look great with the new dress."

"This is going to take all day?" Nick asked.

"Well, yes, I wanted to look nice for you tonight."

Nick pushed back his disappointment. "Okay. Enjoy your spa day. I'll pick you up at seven."

"You plan on moving today? How will you have time to move and get ready for the party tonight?"

Nick laughed. "Cause all I have to do is take a shower and get dressed, like any other day."

"Must be nice being a guy. Can I see the apartment after the party?"

"Plan on it. Pack an overnight bag, okay?"

"I will. Love you."

Nick put the phone on the passenger seat and pulled out of the parking lot. It was a short drive from Ruby's office to the high-rise apartment building.

The building's lobby had white marble floors, linen wallpaper, and live trees housed inside massive ceramic urns. He rode the elevator to the fourth floor. The doors silently parted revealing thick taupe-colored carpeting and walnut wainscoting. Elegant brass wall sconces illuminated the corridor.

Turning the key in the lock, he swung open the door. "You've got to be kidding me."

He walked across the polished, hardwood floor and stood in the center of the open-plan suite. To his right was a kitchen and small dining area. Gleaming stainless-steel appliances coupled with rich cherry wood cabinetry gave the room a warm yet modern look. He ran his fingers over the glassy surface of the black granite counter tops and imagined cooking a gourmet meal for two on the high-end gas range. The cabinets and drawers were well-stocked with dishes, glasses and flatware.

Across from the kitchen, the room expanded into an L-shaped living area. A dark walnut desk stood in front of a picture window overlooking a park below. Richly grained brown leather chairs and a matching sectional sofa created a cozy seating area in front of a gas fireplace. A huge flat screen television hung above the sleek stone mantle.

"So, what do you think?"

Nick turned to see Stephanie standing in the doorway grinning at him. She wore skinny blue jeans, a tee shirt and tennis shoes. Without make-up and her long red hair pulled up into a ponytail, she looked more like a twelve-year-old peddling Girl Scout cookies than a receptionist for a prestigious international agency.

"It's fantastic. I can't believe Ruby's letting me live here. He must be losing a fortune in rent."

"Are you moving in today?" Stephanie's ponytail bounced as she walked toward Nick. "I can help. Well, for a couple of hours, then I have to get ready for the party."

Nick laughed. "It's only ten-thirty. The party's not till eight tonight."

"I have appointments to get my nails, hair and make-up done."

"Yeah, I get it." Nick smiled. He walked down a hallway, directly in line with the front door to another door.

"Must be the bedroom." Nick turned the knob.

"Uh, huh, this apartment has the same layout as mine." Stephanie tagged along beside him. "Bathroom's over here." She pointed to an open door to the right of the bedroom. Floor to ceiling earth tone-colored tiles surrounded a glass-enclosed shower that took up the entire width of the room.

"Nice." Nick looked over Stephanie's head. "You're shorter today."

She giggled. "I'm wearing flats. And I'm not short, you're just really tall."

Nick entered the bedroom. His shoes sank into the steel-grey colored carpet. "That's a big bed."

The platform bed formed the centerpiece of the room, piled high with decorative pillows and dressed in silver and burgundy satiny fabrics. The right wall of the room had two floor-to-ceiling windows and double French doors that opened onto a small balcony. The left wall featured an enormous walk-in closet, with built-in dressers and shelving units.

"My bedroom doesn't have that." Stephanie pointed upward.

"What the hell?" Nick looked up at the huge ceiling mirror above the bed. He laughed. "Did Scarface used to live here?"

Stephanie fiddled with a panel on the upholstered headboard. The overhead mirror dimmed, then lit up with different colored lights as she pressed the various buttons. "Interesting." Her pale cheeks flushed red. She walked over and looked out the doors to the balcony.

"The mirror's a little over the top for my taste." He strolled back into the main living area.

Stephanie followed. "Do you have a moving van outside? I'll help you bring your stuff upstairs."

"No, I stopped by to see what I'd need. But this place has everything, like a luxury hotel. I'll run home and grab my laptop and clothes. Should fit in the Mustang."

"That's it?" She rolled her eyes. "I'd need a semi just to hold my clothes and shoes."

"I have some specialty kitchen stuff, too. I like to cook. And I'll need to do some grocery shopping and buy a coffee maker. Can't write without coffee."

"Well, if I don't see you later, I'll see you tonight. Don't forget, the party officially starts at eight, but Mr. Ruby wants his clients there at seven-thirty. The press isn't allowed in until later."

"I'm not looking forward to the press conference. Or Janis Ford. Hey, Steph, do you know why Janis was snooping around my girlfriend's apartment yesterday?"

"Girlfriend?" Stephanie's smile faded. "No, I don't. You never mentioned you had a—" Her cell phone interrupted her. *The Ring Of Fire* ring tone played. "Hello? Yes, sir. I told the caterer. I'll call and confirm now." She slipped the phone back into her pocket. "Gotta go. Mr. Ruby needs me to make some calls. See you tonight."

Nick returned an hour later with his things packed inside the Mustang. He would have returned sooner, except he had to tell Nonna he was moving out. He knew she wouldn't be happy, which is why he had waited to tell her. He put a box of cannoli and a foil container of ziti she insisted he take with him into the refrigerator. Despite his reassurances he would visit often, she worried he wouldn't eat enough.

A gift-wrapped box sat outside his apartment door when he returned with his second load from the car. A small card taped on top read, *Welcome to the neighborhood! Luv, Steph.*

He tore off the wrapping and found an elaborate coffee machine inside. He set it on the kitchen counter along with its packet of attachments. The thick manual that came with it boasted the machine brewed espresso and latte as well as regular coffee.

By early afternoon, Nick had all of his personal belongings moved in. He hung his cooking pans and utensils on the copper pot rack in the kitchen and placed the case of professional chef knives his grandfather had given him on the counter.

His clothes looked lost inside the cavernous bedroom closet. The 'Ruby-approved' wardrobe hung on one side and his regular clothes on the other.

The massive desk in the living room dwarfed his laptop and inkjet printer. He sank into the high-backed leather chair and gazed out the window at the picturesque view. He grinned, putting his hands behind his head he thought, so this is how it feels to be a successful author.

He decided to go grocery shopping so he would have food and drinks in the house for when Katie stayed overnight. He hoped to convince her to move in permanently. The thought of never having to deal with Tara again made him smile as he wheeled the cart up and down the aisles of the supermarket.

As he paid for his groceries, he realized his bank account had dwindled substantially since he deposited the ten-thousand-dollar check. Ruby indicated at this morning's meeting a larger check would be forthcoming soon. He hoped Ruby wasn't being overly optimistic about his future book sales.

After putting away the groceries, Nick checked the clock on the kitchen wall. Only three-fifty. He thought about calling Katie, but she never pampered herself and he didn't want to interrupt her spa day. He smiled thinking about her saying she wanted to look nice for him tonight, he couldn't imagine her ever not looking beautiful.

He grabbed a bottle of beer from the refrigerator and sipped it while he wandered around the apartment, taking in the luxurious surroundings. The beer helped settle the butterflies building in his stomach. He tossed the empty bottle in the trash can and opened a second. The party worried him. On one hand, he felt excited knowing his book would be debuted tonight and in stores by Monday. Yet, the thought of giving a synopsis of his novel in front of an audience made his stomach quake. Reporters asking him questions made it even worse. He set his cellphone alarm for five-thirty, removed his shoes and stretched out on the bed. His feet didn't hang over the edge of this mattress, like they did in his bed at home. Looking up at the ceiling, he laughed out loud and wondered what Katie's reaction would be to the immense, shiny voyeur looming above the bed. He felt certain she wouldn't like it.

The smell of buttered popcorn wafted outside when Tara opened the door. She looked him over from head to toe. Nick braced for an onslaught of crude innuendos.

"You look hot, Nick. Katie's almost ready." She turned back to the kitchen table, tore open a bag of microwave popcorn and emptied it into a bowl.

Katie's bedroom door opened. Nick gaped as she walked toward him.

"Do I look all right?"

"All right? You look amazing." He walked around her taking in every inch. The dress, the shoes, and her glowing face and eyes. "I like your hair like that."

"Isn't it cool? Tara styled it." Katie jerked her head toward Tara and raised her eyebrows.

"Very nice job, Tara," Nick said.

"Thank you." Tara beamed at him as she munched popcorn. She turned to Katie. "You're wearing your cross?"

Katie touched the delicate gold chain and tiny cross that hung around her neck. "I always wear it. It's the only jewelry my mom had left. She had to pawn everything else."

Tara shook her head. "It doesn't go with the dress. I have some necklaces if you want to borrow one."

Nick saw the frown on Katie's face. "It's fine, babe. It's gold, like the dress."

Tara shrugged. "Whatever." She carried the popcorn over to the couch and sat. "Have fun."

"Tara's in a pleasant mood for once." Nick held the car door open for Katie.

"She's not a bad person, Nick. All of the services at the spa were free because she performed them. It would have cost me a fortune otherwise. She's happy she has the next two days off. She can stay up late and watch the VIP party. I didn't realize how big a deal this event is. Tara said it's televised on three cable entertainment channels. She's recording it for us."

"Televised?" Nick pulled away from the curb. "That helps my nerves."

The valet opened Katie's door and helped her out while Nick walked around to hand him the keys. Onlookers gathered in designated sections cordoned off with velvet ropes. Huge monitors hung facing the street audience. Video crews bustled around stringing cables and setting up equipment. Camera flashes went off like a wave of silent fireworks as the two walked the red carpet into the lobby of the Grande Plaza Hotel.

Nick handed his invitation to a young man in a tuxedo who led them to a bank of elevators reserved for party guests. A uniformed man inside the elevator greeted them and pressed the button for the rooftop.

Katie stepped from the elevator onto the rooftop expanse. "It's breathtaking!"

Three sides of the open venue contained round dining tables and chairs. Metallic silver cloths with black lace overlays and tall vases of black orchids adorned each tabletop. Shimmering scarlet and silver curtains covered a stage in front of the railing near the edge of the roof. Beyond the steel and Plexiglas railing, lights from the city sparked to life as twilight darkened into night. Overhead, white lights entwined in a fine mesh stretched across the roof. The midnight blue sky camouflaged the dark mesh, creating the illusion of thousands of low-hanging stars. The twinkling lights reflected from a glossy black, dance floor in front of the stage which looked like a dark pond of rippling water.

"Not many people here yet," Nick said. "Want to get a drink?"

"You don't need to be drunk when they call you up on stage," Katie chided.

Nick laughed. "Yes, I do."

"Relax, you're going to do great tonight." Katie kissed his cheek. "I'm so happy for you, Nick. And you look so handsome. The silk scarf is a sexy touch."

"Steph picked it out. I would have never thought of wearing a scarf indoors."

"Hmm. Steph has good taste. Is she here yet?"

"I don't see her. But, look, there's Joseph Cullen! I recognize him from the pictures on his book jackets." Nick nodded toward a slim, gray-haired man dressed in a black tuxedo. He stood alone by the railing, sipping a drink and smoking a cigarette.

"He's the author that inspired you?"

"Yup, that's him. I'd give anything to be like him. A best-selling author and a multi-millionaire." Nick grinned and grabbed Katie's hand. "C'mon, let's go meet him."

Cullen leaned against the railing staring out at the skyline.

"Excuse me, Mr. Cullen?" Nick called a third time. The author finally turned his head.

"It's an honor to meet you, sir. I'm Nick Teravelli. This is Katie Harrington."

Cullen's gaze flitted past Nick's outstretched hand and settled on Katie. "Hello, beautiful swan." He flicked his cigarette butt over the railing and reached for Katie's hand. Closing his eyes, he brought her hand to his mouth. Cullen slowly moved his lips across the back of Katie's hand as if he were in a trance. Nick cleared his throat. Cullen pressed his mouth against Katie's hand and lingered there.

Katie jerked her hand away and moved closer to Nick.

Cullen studied them with glazed eyes while he took a long drink from his glass. He wavered on his feet and grasped the railing with his free hand to steady himself.

Nick wasn't sure if it was alcohol or age affecting the famous writer's behavior. His patience thinned when Cullen's leer settled on Katie's cleavage.

He attempted to distract Cullen with conversation. "I was recently signed by Ruby International Promotions. I have my first book coming out next week. *Thirst,* a vampire novel. It's the first in a trilogy." As he talked, Nick eased his arm around Katie's waist and turned to face the railing. The subtle movement blocked Cullen's view of Katie. "One of my all-time favorites is your *Veiled Secrets* trilogy."

Cullen leaned sideward and peered around Nick. "Are you a writer, Katie?"

"No, Mr. Cullen, I'm a nurse."

Draining his glass, Cullen glanced up at Nick and commented, "So, you're the new meat."

"Excuse me?"

"Victor always likes to have the young ones in place before the old ones rot and die."

"Mr. Cullen, you're still writing bestsellers. I can only hope to achieve half the success—"

"Katie." Cullen interrupted Nick. He scuttled along the railing for a better vantage point. "My next novel is set in a hospital. Your knowledge of the field would be invaluable. Perhaps you would come by my apartment for an interview?"

"My work schedule is so hectic, I'm afraid I . . . couldn't." Katie's tone sounded polite but strained.

"I'd love to talk to you sometime about writing horror. I've been a fan of your books for years," Nick said. "Mr. Cullen? Stop staring at my—"

"We have to go now," Katie blurted. Nick felt her fingers dig into his side. "Nice to meet you."

"Do give us a call." Cullen fumbled inside his jacket pocket and pulled out a white card. He pressed the card into Katie's palm, then turned and staggered off toward the nearest bar.

"What a rude asshole," Nick said. "Staring at you like that."

"I knew you were getting upset," Katie said. "That's why I told him we had to go. And, I have to find a rest room." Katie's eyes flashed with anger.

"Are you okay?" Nick asked.

"The disgusting pig licked my hand."

"He what?"

"I pulled my hand away because I could feel his tongue and his slobber . . . ugh."

"Are you sure? He's pretty hammered and he is older, you think maybe he just drooled?"

"You couldn't see it, but I could feel it." Katie laughed despite her annoyance. "And, no, he wasn't drooling for God's sake, he's not *that* old. He's a drunken old lech. Every time he looked at me, I got the chills."

"I'm not letting him get away with this." Nick spun around.

Katie grabbed his arm. "Where are you going?"

"To find Cullen. I don't care who he is, or how drunk he is, there's no excuse for licking your hand."

"Nick, please." Katie tugged on his hand. "Let it go. He's not worth it. A scene will only make you look bad on your big night."

Nick took Cullen's card from Katie and slid it into his wallet. "All right, but I will pay the old bastard a visit when he's sober. So much for my inspirational author." He sighed. "I'm sorry, babe."

"It's not your fault. I wanted to slap him, but I didn't want to make a scene either. Let me go wash my hand." She shivered. "I feel like I need a shower."

"I saw rest rooms next to the elevators. I'll wait here."

Despite Katie's plea, Nick walked the perimeter of the rooftop searching the growing crowd for Cullen. Not finding him, he ordered a beer to quell both his anger and his nerves. The first icy glass went down quick. He ordered a second.

A steady stream of guests poured from the elevators and filled the rooftop. Nick sipped his third beer, as he waited for Katie and watched outrageously dressed guests pass by. The women's outfits ranged from elaborate ball gowns covered in sequins and feathers to skimpy leather bikini tops and skin-tight shorts. Many of the men sported tuxes, while others wore eighteenth century period suits and Dracula-inspired red satin-lined black capes.

Nick spotted Katie winding her way through the crowd toward him. He smiled and waved. She glowed like an angel. Her blond hair and the shimmering pale gold dress stood out in the sea of predominately dark clothing. Stephanie walked by her side. The two talked as they approached.

"Hey, Steph." Nick raised his glass in greeting. "I see you met Katie."

"Yes, Katie's a lifesaver! I had a wardrobe malfunction. She helped me fix my dress in the lady's room." Stephanie wore a floor-length strapless gown in a silky black material with thin red pinstripes. The low-cut dress clung to her thin frame. Two side slits exposed her pale legs from mid-thigh down to her red high heels. Her eyelids drooped at the corners from the weight of false lashes caked with silver glitter.

Katie smiled at Stephanie. "Glad I could help."

"I'd better check in with Mr. Ruby. I feel like I've been stuck in the bathroom forever. I'll catch up with you guys later. Thanks again, Katie." As Stephanie hurried away, Nick noticed her dress exposed her milky-white back down to her waist.

"Is it me, or does Steph look like a little kid playing dress-up?" Nick asked.

Katie sighed. "She's trying to look glamorous and older."

"What was her wardrobe malfunction?" Nick grinned.

"I promised her I wouldn't tell anyone."

"Not even me? I won't say anything."

"Let's just say thanks to the roll of magic boob tape Tara lent me, and lots of toilet paper, all is well now." Katie smiled.

"Magic boob tape and toilet paper?"

"Never mind." Katie laughed. "You're right about Stephanie. She's naive, but very sweet."

"Told you."

"Yes, you did, but I'm right, too. She has a huge crush on you, Nick. Her eyes lit up every time she talked about you. Not to mention her shocked expression when she saw my engagement ring. And did you notice her dress matches your scarf? I doubt it's a coincidence."

"No, I didn't. I had a hard time getting past all the make-up. But now she's met you and she knows we're engaged. She's got to know I'm not interested in her romantically."

"Be careful what you say to her. She could easily get the wrong idea."

"I will." Nick touched Katie's cheek. "Have I told you how beautiful you look tonight?"

"Thank you." Katie looked around. "Compared to these women I feel plain, even in this dress. They all look like super models. Some of them are practically naked."

"I didn't notice." Nick ran his hand down her bare back.

"Hmm, half-naked women everywhere and you didn't notice." Katie rolled her eyes.

They both looked up when they heard their names. Across the room, Stephanie sat at one of the numerous mini bars waving her hand above her head and calling for them to join her.

"Oh, God. Look at that creepy-looking character with Stephanie," Katie whispered to Nick as they made their way through the crowd. A tall, spiky-haired man stood talking to Stephanie. His white face, black-ringed eyes and deep red lips gave him an evil, vampirish look.

"He's that guy from the metal band, Blood Lust," Nick said.

"I hope that's fake blood dripping from the corners of his mouth. If the normal-looking old guy in a tux licked my hand, I can only imagine what this freak might try." Katie tightened her grip on Nick's hand.

"If he does, I'd have no problem punching him. He's more my size and age."

"Hey guys! I wanted you to meet Chris Turner, aka Ian Slaughter, lead singer of Blood Lust," Stephanie said. "Chris this is Nick Teravelli, aka Nick Tera. He's a writer and our talent contest winner. His first horror novel will be released tomorrow. And, this is Katie, Nick's fiancée."

Nick accepted Chris's handshake.

"Congratulations, mate. I'll be sure to pick up a copy of your new book," Chris said.

Katie hesitated when the rocker offered her his hand. He gently shook it and said, "Lovely to meet you, Katie."

"Your accent sounds Australian, is it?" Katie asked.

"Yes, ma'am. Born and raised in the ol' Down Under. Of course, I've been in the states for about fifteen years now." Chris' teal-colored eyes twinkled when he smiled. "By the way, I recognized the expression of horror on your face when you looked at me." Chris winked at Nick.

"I'm sorry, I didn't mean to stare. It's stage make-up, um, right?" Katie stammered.

Chris' laughter cut her off. "No, I meant I saw the same look of horror in the mirror when I was getting ready for this little soiree. Glad I did theatre in college. It helps with my stage act. Trust me, dressing like a vampire is not my idea."

"Let me guess, it's Victor Ruby's?" Nick asked.

"Yes, but not entirely as he wanted. If I let the little bast—," Chris nodded at Katie, then Stephanie. "Pardon me, ladies. If Ruby had his way, I'd have permanent two-inch fangs cemented to my ivories and glowing red contact lenses glued to my corneas."

Nick laughed. "Guess I got off easy. I'm forbidden to get a haircut or a close shave."

"Which suits you," Stephanie chimed in. She sat on a bar stool between the two men with her eyes open as wide as her heavy eye make-up would allow. She swiveled back and forth as each spoke.

"My roommate loves Blood Lust," Katie said. "I've heard some of your CDs."

"It's heavy metal, not everyone's taste. I prefer softer rock myself," Chris said.

"Chris writes beautiful ballads." Stephanie beamed up at him. "He has a phenomenal voice."

"Thank you, Love." Chris tousled Stephanie's hair. "Unfortunately, I can't convince Ruby to let his record company release any. Doesn't fit my image, he says."

"He can be pretty stubborn about the image thing," Nick said.

"Yes, but don't let him bully you when it comes to your principles, mate," Chris said. He leaned closer to Nick. "Tell him to shove his infernal contract where the sun doesn't shine. I did. Tonight is likely to be my last gig with Blood Lust."

"Chris, don't say that! Ruby will renegotiate your contract," Stephanie said. "He's got to, the band would be nothing without you. Everyone knows that."

Chris sighed. "I'm not holding my breath. Besides, I'm sick of reading the twisted lies in the tabloids. Ridiculous headlines like *Ian Slaughter Has Meth Lab Backstage* or *Ian Slaughter Performs Blood and Sex Rituals With Unsuspecting Virgins*." He laughed. "Like there's any virgins floating about this God-forsaken city. Oh, what was the latest one, Love?" Chris looked at Stephanie.

"*Ian Slaughter Sucks The Blood Out Of A Kitten On Stage.*" Stephanie shook her head.

"I don't need my daughter hearing that rubbish. At least she's too young right now to understand. Now my wife, let's just say that kind of publicity is not conducive to a happy marriage."

A female bartender in a glittery red bikini top interrupted to ask if anyone wanted a drink.

"Another ginger ale, please." Chris handed her his empty glass.

The bartender winked at him. "Can't I get you something stronger?"

Chris shook his head. "No, thanks, alcohol wreaks havoc on my vocal cords."

"I'll take a draught," Nick said.

"Nothing, thank you," Katie said. "Nick, go easy, you just had a beer."

"I'm fine." Katie would be appalled if she knew how many beers he'd downed tonight. Yet, despite not eating the entire day, the alcohol didn't calm his jittery nerves.

"A Bloody Nightmare, please." Stephanie grinned when Katie, Chris and Nick looked at her. "What?" She giggled. "It's a drink created especially for the VIP party."

Katie turned to Chris. "So, you have a daughter?"

"Brittany, my pride and joy. She turns four today. Which reminds me." Chris took out his cell phone and held it up to show off his daughter's photograph. "It's party time on the west coast. Pardon me, will you?" He walked a few feet away and made a call.

As the bartender placed their drinks on the bar, the three turned to listen to Chris softly singing Happy Birthday to Brittany.

"He does have a nice voice," Katie commented.

When Chris returned to the bar, Stephanie raised her glass. It was a tall glass with alternating layers of red and blackish colored liquids, adorned with a red plastic pitchfork sticking out of the top. "To Ian Slaughter and Blood Lust. May they make music together, forever!"

As Nick and Chris reached over to touch their glasses against Stephanie's, an unusually tall woman sporting black feather wings on her back pushed between them and leaned against the bar. Her left wingtip hit Stephanie's glass, nearly knocking the drink from her hand.

"Hey!" Stephanie said.

The woman ignored Stephanie and slammed her fist on the bar. She yelled at the startled bartender, "Tequila, straight up!" Standing several inches taller than Nick, her toned, sculpted body looked like bronzed marble in a bikini top and thong bottom. Taut, narrow triangles of black leather strained to contain her breasts. Her shiny, black hair was pulled tightly into a ponytail secured on the top of her head. It hung in a straight line down her back, between her feathered wings.

Grabbing her drink, she spun around, brushing both Stephanie and Chris with her massive wings.

She smirked at Chris, then strutted off into the crowd.

"Who was that?" Katie and Nick asked at the same time.

"Talon," Stephanie said, glaring at the woman's back.

"Talon?" Nick asked. "Like a bird's claw?"

"She's more like a big, nasty toenail," Stephanie muttered.

"Is she an actress?" Katie asked.

"I'm not sure what she's supposed to be," Stephanie said. "I saw her for the first time yesterday at Ruby's office. She was rude then, too. Walked right by my desk and into Mr. Ruby's office without even knocking. A minute later he calls me on the intercom and says he doesn't want to be disturbed." Stephanie's cheeks blushed redder beneath her make-up. "I heard the door lock. Then there were all these . . . noises. You know, like they were doing it in his office. Gross."

"I'm six four and she made me feel short." Nick laughed. "Ruby must have been standing on his desk."

Chris laughed. Katie rolled her eyes. "Nick!"

"Obviously you haven't met Victor Ruby, Katie," Chris said. "He's a short little bugger."

"When she finally came out of his office, she blew right by me and out the door. Then Ruby comes out and tells me to put her name on tonight's guest list." Stephanie wrinkled her nose and stuck out her tongue.

"Did you see her tattoo?" Nick asked. He referred to a colorful snake on her left leg. The tip of its tail began at her ankle and wound around her long, shapely leg up to her hip. The top portion of the serpent encircled her abdomen and ended with the snake's head pointing downward below her navel. Her tiny thong hid the tip of the snake's tongue.

"That was a tattoo? I thought it was body paint," Katie said.

"Must have taken days to do all that ink." Chris grunted. "And hurt like hell, too."

Katie sighed. "She has a perfect body. I guess you'd have to if you walk around basically naked."

"I can't imagine her and Mr. Ruby—" Stephanie began.

"Shush, Love. Speak of the devil." Chris nodded toward the crowd. Ruby strode through the throng of guests. Despite his short stature, he exuded an aura of power and the crowd parted in waves to let him pass. He curled one finger at Stephanie as he approached. Jumping down from the stool, she hurried to meet him. Ruby glowered at her and spoke in a tone too low for the three at the bar to hear. Stephanie stared at the ground in silence. He left her standing alone and strolled to the bar.

"Nick, Ian! Are you enjoying the gala?" he asked.

"Quite a spectacle, as usual, Victor," Chris answered.

"Yes, sir, everything's amazing," Nick added.

"Mr. Slaughter, show time approaches. Get your band together and check the set up on stage."

Chris shook Nick's hand and squeezed Katie's. "Fun talking to you both." He patted Stephanie on the head as he walked past.

"And, who is this lovely young lady?" Ruby cocked his head and smiled at Katie.

"Katie Harrington, sir. My fiancée," Nick said.

Ruby's thin black eyebrows arched. "Fiancée? Well, well, Katie, it's my pleasure."

He extended his hand and bowed his head slightly.

Katie's eyes widened when he brought her hand to his lips. He kissed and released it.

"Very nice to meet you, Mr. Ruby," Katie said. "Your party is spectacular."

"I'm pleased you're enjoying yourself. Though, I do hate to be the bearer of bad news." Ruby flashed his white, toothy smile. "I need Nick to accompany Stephanie for a few minutes to familiarize himself with tonight's program. My apologies Katie, I neglected to tell Nick there would be work tonight."

Nick looked at Katie. "Will you be okay waiting here?"

"If Katie will allow me, I'd be honored to keep her company while she's waiting." Ruby held out his arm. Katie looked at Nick, and then back to Ruby. "Yes, thank you, Mr. Ruby." She slipped her arm into his.

"Call me Victor."

Ruby motioned to the bartender. "Two Champagnes."

"I'm not much of a drinker," Katie said.

"Just a sip, I insist." He handed her a glass. "We must toast to your engagement and to Nick's debut tonight." He clinked his glass against Katie's as he escorted her into the crowd. "Let me introduce you to some of my guests."

Nick followed Stephanie across the rooftop. He scanned the crowd as he walked and caught sight of Ruby gesturing and smiling as he led Katie around on his arm.

Stephanie opened a door near the elevators. Inside, a small storage room housed surplus folded tables and stacks of chairs. She plopped into a chair at an opened table and put her drink down next to a clipboard and pen.

"Tonight's program is pretty straight forward," she said. "Excuse me." Turning her back, she pulled a length of toilet tissue tucked inside the neckline of her dress and dabbed at her eyes.

"Something wrong?" Nick asked.

"Glitter in my eye." She turned away again. Nick saw her narrow back trembling. He put his hand on Stephanie's shoulder.

"Did Ruby give you a hard time about something back there?"

Stephanie looked at him with tears running down her cheeks. "I screwed up. Again. He said if I don't do better, he'll fire me."

"Why, what happened?"

"I lost track of the time. I'm supposed to be working. He said I should have gone over the program with you five minutes ago."

"He threatened to fire you over five minutes?"

Stephanie nodded and blew her nose. "Staying on schedule is important to him. I need this job and the apartment. I don't know what I'd do if he fired me."

"Don't cry," Nick rubbed her shoulder. "You do a great job, Steph. Like all the arrangements you made for this incredible party. Ruby's not an easy man to work for. Don't let him upset you. I'll make sure I tell him how well you handled everything you did for me."

Stephanie jumped up and flung her arms around Nick's neck. Her sudden embrace surprised him. He instinctively hugged her and then remembered Katie's warning about giving Steph the wrong impression. Letting his arms drop, he lightly patted her bare back.

Stephanie released her hold and returned to her chair. "I'm sorry, I—" She looked down and rolled the pen on the table. "Needed a hug. Thank you, for the sweet things you said."

"No big deal."

She took a deep breath and picked up the clipboard. "Mr. Ruby will host tonight. He'll introduce his top stars, Joseph Cullen, the television and movie actors, Chris and the band. You're last. There's a small corridor behind the stage where everyone will wait until their name is announced. That's your cue to go on stage. Mr. Ruby will talk to you about your book. You'll give your synopsis. Then he'll open the floor to questions from the press. They'll take turns asking everyone the prepared questions. That's it." Stephanie grinned.

"That's it, huh?" Nick paced around the room running his hands through his hair. "I wish I could relax. I've lost count of the beers I've had, yet I barely feel a buzz."

"Here," Stephanie held up her glass. "You can have this, if you want. I only took a sip. It's a lot stronger than I thought."

Nick hesitated, then took the glass. "Why not. Thanks." He chugged it down and then laughed. "I need a Bloody Nightmare to get me through tonight."

"Do you see Katie?" Nick searched the crowd when he and Stephanie returned to the party.

Stephanie craned her neck to look past the tall, red devil horns on one of the male guests' heads. "No, but here comes Mr. Ruby."

"Nick, bad news I'm afraid," Ruby said. "Katie suddenly became ill. She had to leave."

"Ill? But she was fine a little while ago. What happened?"

Ruby shrugged. "She said she felt sick and excused herself. I had one of my waitresses check on her in the rest room. She reported back that Katie wished to go home. She said she felt terrible about leaving on your big night, but she needed to go."

"Go home, how? I drove her here. I have to find her—"

"Calm down, son," Ruby said. "I had my driver take her home. He has instructions to escort her to her front door. And, I had the same waitress accompany her in the car, to make her feel more comfortable."

"Thank you, but why didn't you come get me?" Nick reached into his pocket for his cell phone. "I need to call and make sure she's all right." He patted his jeans and jacket pockets. "My phone's gone. I must have dropped it. Is there a phone I can use?"

"No time, Nick. The program starts in five minutes. Call Katie after the press conference. Stephanie, take Nick to the waiting area backstage." Ruby motioned for them to hurry.

Stephanie took Nick's hand and they wove their way through the crowd toward the stage. "Maybe you dropped your cell in the storage room, or by the bar," she said. "I'll look. Or, you can use mine later. It's in my purse, locked in a room downstairs we're using as a temporary office."

They saw Ruby directing reporters and a video crew to a cordoned off area in front of the stage. Nick recognized Janis Ford among the group.

Stephanie stopped at the entrance to a narrow corridor hidden behind the stage where a line of people waited and chatted in hushed tones. Nick checked his pockets again, hoping somehow he had missed his phone the first time he'd searched.

"Relax." Stephanie squeezed his hand. "The press conference will be over before you know it."

"You'll look for my cell?"

"I'll go and look now."

"Thanks, Steph." Nick ran his hands through his hair and took a deep breath. He worried about Katie. She probably called his cell and wondered why he didn't answer. A blast of guitar chords and drumbeats rang out followed by a burst of applause. Everyone in the back-stage corridor fell silent as Victor Ruby's amplified voice boomed across the rooftop.

"Welcome to the Ruby International Promotions third annual VIP gala! As you know, this is the event where we celebrate the horror industry, in film, video, music and print. I'm proud to represent an extremely talented group of movie and television actors, musicians and authors this year."

Ruby waited for the applause to subside. "Let me first introduce the infamous Ian Slaughter and Blood Lust!" On Ruby's cue, the band played a short instrumental and drew loud cheers from the audience.

"I have an announcement I've held especially for tonight. Not even Mr. Slaughter is aware of the news." Ruby paused, letting anticipation build. "As of yesterday, the band's second album, *Blood Sacrifice*, has sold over one million copies, making it their first platinum record!"

The thin back wall of the stage vibrated with the audience's thunderous ovation and the band's celebratory drum solo. Chris Turner's smooth voice congratulated his fellow band members and thanked their loyal fans for the honor.

When the hand clapping and cheering died down, Ruby resumed his announcements. "And the distinguished gentleman sitting on the stool to my right is, of course, the king of horror, best-selling author, Joseph Cullen."

Nick snorted. The audience probably presumed they put a chair on stage in deference to Cullen's age, but he knew it was because Cullen was too drunk to stand upright. Ruby informed the crowd that Cullen's newest novel would be released this fall. He asked Cullen what the book was about. Nick couldn't understand the author's slurred reply. Ruby's voice took over, describing the book as another terrifying tale from the horrific mind of Joseph Cullen. "A terrifying story set in a hospital, *The 13th Ward*, will be the forty-ninth bestselling novel of Mr. Cullen's long and illustrious career!"

If the book would be on the shelves by fall, Nick knew Cullen's invitation to interview Katie had been a cheap ploy to get her to his apartment. Any admiration he once felt for the author turned to disgust and renewed his desire to call Cullen out for his appalling behavior toward Katie.

Ruby introduced eight teen-aged actors who sprinted up the steps onto the stage in pairs to a warm reception from the crowd. They were the stars of two new hit television series, one featuring werewolves, the other vampires. Their departure from the backstage waiting area placed Nick third in line. His stomach knotted tighter and he wished Katie were in the audience.

Ruby introduced two more actors, a young man and woman, as the stars of a new horror movie, *Night Birds*, to be released next spring. After expounding upon their acting skills and on-screen chemistry, Ruby told the crowd some scenes in the movie were so graphic, the

Motion Picture Association couldn't agree on a rating for the film. The audience responded with approving shrieks.

"Lastly tonight, I have a special announcement. This is the first year Ruby International Promotions has held a talent contest. I focused on upcoming, unpublished writers in the horror genre," Ruby said. "I wanted someone fresh with an edgy writing style and youthful appeal."

Nick climbed the three steps leading to the stage. His legs felt rubbery as he waited behind the curtain. Closing his eyes, he prayed he would remember his book synopsis and the answers to the press questions he had memorized.

Ruby continued his speech. "The response to my contest proved incredible! So many talented authors came forward, making it difficult to choose only one. The final decision fell to me . . . of course." Ruby's unabashed tone sent a ripple of laughter through the crowd. "I am proud to introduce the winner, my personal choice, Mr. Nick Tera!"

Nick parted the black curtain. A spotlight temporarily blinded him as he walked onto the stage. Chris Turner stood a foot away holding his guitar. As Nick passed by, he slapped him on the back. "Smile, mate. You'll do fine."

Nick stopped at the only opening left on the crowded stage. The audience applauded. He clasped his trembling hands behind his back and tried to muster a natural-looking smile.

"Nick Tera's debut novel, *Thirst*, will be in bookstores tomorrow. Nick, this is the first novel of a trilogy you've written, is it not?" Ruby asked. "Tell us about your story."

Nick swallowed to moisten his throat and leaned toward the microphone stand. "Thank you, Mr. Ruby. Yes, the trilogy begins in 1813 with the first volume, entitled *Thirst*, where I introduce the protagonist, Julian Rentworth, and his fiancé, Caroline. Although deeply in love, and engaged to be married, a series of dark events upset their plans. Julian is seduced by Diana, a beautiful, but evil vampire. In a fit of jealous rage, she turns Julian into a vampire, ending any hope for his marriage to Caroline.

"The three books chronicle over two hundred years of Julian's immortal life and the constant conflict between the vengeful woman who made him a monster and his search for his reincarnated lost love, Caroline. Julian's thirst is a metaphor for his hunger for human blood as well as the spark of humanity inside him which longs for a soul. He is forced to make a critical choice, and then he must face the dire consequences of his choice."

Applause erupted from the crowd, surprising Nick. He let out a long breath, relieved he had delivered his synopsis smoothly.

"Excellent, Nick. I predict all three books will be bestsellers!" Ruby proclaimed above the clapping. "Nick has other merchandise available in stores and online." Ruby waved his arms indicating two huge monitors on either side of the stage displaying the poster of Nick and the two models. He chuckled. "Ladies, I'm sure you'll want a poster or perhaps a tee shirt."

Female voices screamed 'Nick' from the darkened sea of bobbing heads in front of Nick.

"Thank you all for coming tonight," Ruby said. "I'll turn the floor over to our media guests. After the press conference, Blood Lust will entertain us. Drink, eat, dance, and enjoy the night!"

A female reporter shouted, "Nick! How did you feel when you heard you won the Ruby Promotions contest?"

"On top of the world," Nick answered. "Being a published author is my dream. Having Victor Ruby represent me is . . . well, it's making my dream come true."

"Ian! Ian!" A male reporter waved his hand. "Is it true you're leaving Blood Lust to pursue a solo career?"

Chris stood stunned for a moment, then struck a deafeningly chord on his guitar and leapt to the front of the stage. "My mates and I have just gone bloody platinum! Leaving the band? Are you insane?" Boisterous laughter rose from the crowd.

Reporters took turns questioning the young television stars about each of the show's story lines and rumors of real-life love affairs between the cast members. The youthful exuberance reflected in their answers sparked spontaneous rounds of clapping from the party guests.

Another string of questions focused on the movie actors and the band. Nick's tension eased. The abundance of alcohol and the knowledge the press conference neared an end filled him with relief. The effects of the alcohol kicked in. He hoped the reporters were finished questioning him.

"Nick Tera!" A male voice called to him. "Who or what inspired you to write horror stories?"

After meeting Joseph Cullen, Nick edited his rehearsed reply. "Mostly the classic gothic horror writers, Stoker, Lovecraft, and a few of Joseph Cullen's earlier works."

"Hey, Nick!" The female voice shouting out his name sounded louder and closer than the other reporters. He squinted into the bright lights. Janis Ford's silhouette stood right below him.

"There are rumors about your personal *thirst*, as in the long list of women you've seduced. Are these lurid affairs truth or fiction?"

The audience reacted with whistles and hoots. It wasn't one of the rehearsed questions.

"That isn't true," Nick said. His voice didn't carry. The microphone wasn't working. He saw movement from the corner of his eye and the crowd broke into wild cheers. The two models from the poster, Rachel and Ebony, walked up on either side of Nick and grabbed his arms. Rachel, the taller blond, yanked his scarf jerking his head down close to hers. She planted her lips on his mouth. Her clip-on microphone recorded her loud moans to the delighted screams of the onlookers. Ebony unbuttoned Nick's shirt and ran her hands across his chest. She yelled, "We know all about Nick's *thirst*, don't we, Rachel?"

Nick tried to push Rachel away. She wound his scarf around both her hands and pulled it tighter. Aware of the cameras aimed at the stage, he fought to keep both his balance and composure. Ebony clutched at his open shirt and laced her legs around his. She shimmied up and down, egged on by lewd comments from the crowd. Shocked, humiliated, and unsteady from alcohol, Nick attempted to extricate himself from the pair without physically hurting the women.

"Give the man some air, ladies!" Chris' voice blared over the microphone. A guitar played. "Start the song. Now!" Chris yelled. A driving drumbeat muffled the crowd's rowdy jeers. The spotlights shifted from Nick and the models to the band. Rachel released her death grip on his scarf. The women each latched on to one of Nick's arms and escorted him off the stage as Blood Lust played their first number.

Nick shrugged off the models as they exited the back-stage curtain. He shouted over the music, "What the hell was that all about? Who told you two to come on stage?"

Ebony's lips formed a pout. "What's the matter, sweetie, don't you like us?"

Rachel ran her long blood-red fingernails through his hair. "Victor hired us. To help you sell posters."

"Screw the posters!" He pushed past the two women and hurried along the narrow backstage corridor.

When he emerged from behind the stage, he blinked to refocus to the darkness around him. The rooftop lights had been dimmed to accentuate the bright stage. Between the poor lighting and the drinks he had consumed, he had difficulty navigating through the swaying throng of guests. Dancing bodies blocked him in every direction. Peering over the heads in front of him, he searched for Stephanie or Ruby. He didn't see either. Women screamed his name. Several tried to kiss him, and others tugged at his clothing. Bursts of light popped in the darkness. Reporters called to him, then blinded him with camera flashes when he turned his head.

The energy in the room accelerated. The guests were inebriated, loud and aggressive. They screamed over the music, bumped against each other and spilled their drinks. Costumed women danced suggestively, pressing their bodies against him and the other guests.

Rachel and Ebony emerged from the unruly mob surrounding him. "We'll help you, sweetie," Ebony said. She threw her arms around Nick's neck and hoisted herself up, wrapping her legs around his hips. When he yelled for her to get down, he felt her tongue push hard into his open mouth. A bitter tasting pill lodged in the back of his throat. Nick staggered in a circle as he tried to pry her arms from his neck. The bright camera flashes and the constant, deafening drumbeat made him dizzy. He fell backwards and landed in a chair. Rachel sat close to him holding a glass to his lips. Ebony straddled his lap and danced to the loud music. She poured a shot glass of fiery liquid into his open mouth when he attempted to speak. Tequila washed the bitter residue down his throat.

The heavy metal music stopped. A mellow drum rhythm with rich guitar riffs started. Nick heard Chris's voice ring out. "Here's something different. A medley of new ballads I've written."

Chris sang the lyrics to the love songs in his deep, smooth voice. Couples paired off on the dance floor. Others gravitated back to their tables, sat and swayed in their chairs in time to the music. The slow, hypnotic melodies blended from song to song. Nick felt dazed but welcomed the calm after the previous chaos. He stopped resisting the two models who hung on him and fed him drinks. The liquor they poured into his mouth masked the bitter taste lingering in his throat.

Nick focused on Chris's soothing voice. He felt light-headed. His body relaxed and his mind drifted. He wanted to leave to check on Katie and escape the chaotic party, but he couldn't maintain the thought long enough to make himself stand up. His eyelids involuntarily drooped shut and he kissed the soft lips pushing against his. *Katie?* He embraced her and opened his eyes to see Ebony's dark eyes staring into his. She licked her lips and kissed him again.

Applause thundered as Chris ended his last ballad with a soft flourish of guitar strings. The mood in the room suddenly changed. The guests stopped clapping. They shouted and pointed at the stage. Nick forced himself to look up. A mythical-looking creature with huge black wings strode to the front of the stage. The tall, winged woman shoved Chris with both hands. He lost his balance, fell and crashed into the drum set behind him. Women screamed. Cymbals clanged as he pulled himself upright.

"Enough of your pathetic bawling! Let's make some real music and take this party back!" Talon shouted to the raucous crowd. Chris stormed off the stage. The band hesitated, playing random drumbeats and awkward guitar twangs.

"Play the damn song!" Talon's screech ricocheted across the rooftop like the scream of an eagle flying over a canyon. The drummer pounded out a loud beat and the rest of the band joined in. She loomed over the audience waving the microphone stand above her head and shrieked out lyrics to their heavy metal accompaniment. Her voice didn't soothe like Chris's had, it assaulted Nick's eardrums.

Although her mouth still moved, the volume faded. Farther and farther away, until it became a muted, tinny sound. The enormous snake wound around Talon's leg mesmerized Nick. Its iridescent scales rippled and changed colors under the lights. The snake's movements fascinated him. Its eyes flashed yellow and its long, forked tongue flicked against Talon's taut lower belly. It wriggled, slithered and undulated, yet never loosened its tight grip on her flesh as she strutted back and forth across the stage.

Chapter 9

Nick awoke to the sound of a doorbell and the reflection of three naked bodies entwined on a bed in the mirror above him. Disoriented, he stared up at himself and the two models sleeping next to him. He rubbed his eyes and struggled to push himself into a sitting position on the slippery satin sheets. Rachel's head rolled off his chest. Ebony's bare leg slid off his hip as she rolled onto her stomach. She moaned and stretched a limp arm toward him.

The doorbell rang again. It took all of his strength to swing his legs over Ebony's prone body and stand up. His head pounded and his tongue stuck to the roof of his dry mouth. A bitter taste mixed with sour alcohol coated the back of his throat. Nausea and dizziness swept over him when he bent to rummage through the tangle of clothing strewn across the floor. He grabbed the nightstand with both hands to steady himself. Empty glasses and beer bottles rolled off the table and fell on the carpet with soft *thunks*. The tabletop felt gritty. He lifted his hands. Traces of white powder clung to his palms. The doorbell rang again, a rapid succession of rings this time.

"Shit, what if it's Katie." His mind reeled and his heart raced as he made his way to the bedroom door. He shut it behind him. Holding the hallway walls for support, he staggered to the front door.

"Who is it?" He pressed his aching forehead against the cool, metal door.

"It's me, Stephanie."

"Steph? Whaddya want?"

"Can I come in?"

"No. Um, not now. Later?"

"Nick, it's important. Mr. Ruby wants to meet with you at nine o'clock sharp."

"Shit." Nick fumbled with the double locks until the knob turned and the door opened.

Stephanie gasped. "You're naked!"

"Sorry." He stumbled toward the living room. Stephanie stomped past him, grabbed a chenille throw from the sofa and flung it at him. He caught a corner of the material and clumsily wrapped it around his waist before collapsing into a chair. He covered his face with his hands and rubbed his temples.

"What the hell happened last night?" he mumbled through his hands. "Katie got sick and left, right? Then the press conference. Those two models. I can't remember after that."

"Well, apparently you partied all night," Stephanie said. "And yes, Katie left sick about an hour after you got there. You need to get cleaned up and dressed now."

"Let me rest a few minutes. My head's killing me."

"Absolutely not. Get up and take a shower. I'll make coffee."

She tugged on his arm and nagged at him until he managed to stand on wobbly legs.

"C'mon." She slung his arm around her shoulders, slid her arm around his waist and led him to the bathroom. He leaned against the door jamb with his eyes closed while she turned on the water in the shower.

"Get in," she said. "The hot water will help sober you up."

The throw slipped to the floor as he stepped into the shower.

"Oh God, you have lipstick on your. . .." She rolled her eyes and walked out, slamming the door.

Twenty-five minutes later, Nick emerged from the steamy bathroom. Although his head still throbbed, the long shower refreshed his body. The smell of coffee filled the apartment. He paused outside the opened bedroom door and peeked inside. The bed had been stripped. The naked women were gone, along with the mess of clothing, drink glasses and drug paraphernalia. A clean shirt and a pair of jeans were laid out on the bed.

He dressed and then found Stephanie sitting at the kitchen counter. She handed him a mug of black coffee and four aspirins. "We have to leave in fifteen minutes to get to the office on time."

Nick tossed the aspirins into his mouth and swallowed a long drink of coffee.

"I'm sorry about before. I wasn't thinking straight."

"Forget it." She sipped her coffee.

"Those models, were they really in my bed this morning? Please, tell me I was hallucinating."

"You weren't hallucinating. I sent them home."

"Oh God, I can't believe I . . ." Nick buried his face in his hands. "What the hell have I done? Man, I really screwed up." He looked for his cell phone. It wasn't on its charger. "I have to call Katie. Have you seen my cell?"

"You lost it at the party last night, remember? I looked everywhere but couldn't find it."

"Damn it." Nick walked back to the bedroom and dumped the contents of his clothes hamper onto the floor. His head felt like it would explode when he bent over to search through the dirty laundry. The sickening sweet scent of Rachel's perfume permeating the sheets nauseated him.

Stephanie stood in the doorway. "Let me do that. You look like you're gonna puke any second and I'm not cleaning *that* up." She picked through the laundry on the floor. "It's not here. You can use mine." She held out her metallic pink iPhone.

Nick took the phone. He had to think before pressing each number. The phone went straight to a mailbox. "Katie, it's me. Hope you're feeling better. I have a meeting with Ruby this morning, but I'll come see you as soon as I'm done. Love you."

"Thanks." Nick handed Stephanie her phone. "What does Ruby want? It's freaking Sunday and I feel like crap."

"He loves working on Sundays. Says it's a day when everyone else rests, but not him. He said to make sure you were there at nine but didn't say why."

Nick drove behind Stephanie's Volkswagen beetle. Dark sunglasses shielded his eyes from the sun glinting off the neon yellow paint. At three minutes before nine, Stephanie unlocked the office door and flicked on the lights.

"Sit down, you look awful," she said. "Mr. Ruby's not in yet."

"Can I use your desk phone to call Katie again?"

She sighed and pushed the phone across the desk.

Nick put the receiver to his ear as Ruby entered the office. He hung up the phone.

"Hello, my dear." Ruby nodded to Stephanie. "Nick, you're looking a bit under the weather this morning. Come in."

Nick followed Ruby into his office and sank into the guest chair. The smothering heat in Ruby's office magnified the steady pounding in his head.

Ruby didn't waste time. "You should have consulted with me first before bringing a date to the VIP party."

"Katie's not a date, Mr. Ruby. She's my fiancée," Nick said.

"I'm marketing you as an available bachelor, Nick." Ruby tapped his fingernails on the desk. "Lose the fiancée."

"Lose Katie? You can't be serious?"

"I am. Though, after your infamous debut last night, the situation may resolve itself."

"What do you mean?"

Ruby pointed a remote toward the enormous flat screen television mounted on the wall. He flipped through the channels and settled on an entertainment news show. "It's been playing all morning."

The screen displayed the entrance to the Grande Plaza Hotel. A female reporter described the gala event. The camera panned across the long line of guests entering the hotel for the VIP party. The scene switched to video clips of the party in progress with a voice-over detailing the celebrities present.

". . . featured an all-star line-up including best-selling horror author Joseph Cullen, heavy metal rock star Ian Slaughter and his band Blood Lust, film actors Bethany Grant, Lee Woods, and the cast of two hit cable TV series, Full Moon Coming and Dark Reflections. A newcomer on the music scene, Talon, turned heads in her leather bikini and black feathered wings. The six-foot-six singer caused quite a spectacle when she shoved Ian Slaughter off the stage and led the band for the rest of the evening. Ruby International Promotions will not confirm if it was a rehearsed publicity stunt or something more serious. On the heels of their first platinum record, rumors have been circulating that Ian Slaughter is quitting the band to pursue a solo career. Neither Talon nor Slaughter have answered our calls to comment.

"During the press conference portion last evening, new horror author Nick Tera, was introduced as Ruby Promotion's talent search winner. Mr. Tera is said to have a quite a reputation with the ladies. As you can see from our clips, he did not disappoint."

"And there you are, Mr. Tera." Ruby chuckled and pointed at the screen.

Nick watched Rachel and Ebony kissing him and opening his shirt on stage. The two models hung on Nick in every video clip. The segment ended with a dimly lit shot of the three entering Nick's apartment building. The final shaky footage depicted Nick shoving a camera man who attempted to follow the three into the lobby of the building.

The reporter closed with, "Nick Tera's outrageous behavior, made musician Ian Slaughter look like a choir boy tonight. It's unusual for a writer to outdo the antics of a rock star, but Nick Tera's debut is causing quite a buzz in the entertainment world this morning."

"No! That's on television?" Nick stood. A sour bile taste inched up his throat from his queasy stomach.

"Yes. And in newspapers and on the internet." Ruby grinned showing his unnaturally white teeth.

"You think it's funny?"

"I think it's a gift. We couldn't get this much publicity if I'd taken out a full-page ad in the Sunday *Times*."

"I look like a drunken jerk. How's this going to sell my book?"

"Ah, Nick, so naive. Book orders are pouring in as we speak. As are requests for you to appear for book signings and talk shows. The reporter hit on something I hadn't considered. A writer acting more outrageously than a rock star. Mr. Slaughter has lost his edge. It appears you're my new poster boy for bad behavior."

Nick eased himself into the chair. Leaning forward, he pressed his palms against his temples. "Mr. Ruby, I don't understand what you want from me. I'm grateful you agreed to publish my book. But this image you've created, it's not me. I wanted to be a writer. The only publicity I want is for my books. Putting those models on the stage with me last night was embarrassing. And, if you're asking me to choose between Katie and the book deal—"

"Ah, yes Katie," Ruby interrupted. "Beautiful girl, I understand your attraction. I enjoyed talking with her last night. She's very bright. It's unfortunate, the poor girl fell ill."

"I should have taken her home."

"The show was about to start, and she didn't want to interfere with your debut. Besides I told you, my driver took her home."

"Yes. I appreciate that."

Ruby patted Nick on the shoulder. "How about a compromise, Nick? You'll appear solo at all promotional events. Keep your engagement private for now."

Nick looked at him with bloodshot eyes. "If Katie sees the video of those two models going into my apartment, I will be solo."

Ruby pressed his intercom button. "Stephanie, send one dozen red roses to Ms. Katie Harrington at," he glanced at Nick, "her address?"

"737 Piermont. Apartment 7."

"737 Piermont. Apartment 7. And send a box of those chocolate covered strawberries. The ones we had at the VIP party. She remarked how much she enjoyed one last night. Put Nick's name on the card." Ruby cut off the intercom. "There, feel better?"

"Thanks, but I doubt flowers and fruit will make up for the two women in my bed this morning."

"Then lie to her." Ruby waved his hand. "Tell her it was a publicity stunt. Blame it on me. Keeping up the bachelor image." He laughed. "After all, the video is at the entrance to the building, not inside your bedroom. Celebrities leak controversial videos and photos all the time. It's the oldest trick in the book to gain instant publicity."

"I hate the thought of lying to Katie."

Ruby rolled his eyes. "Fine. Tell her the truth. While she was home wretchedly sick, you got shit-faced drunk and after your very public foreplay, you banged two gorgeous models all night. Does the truth cleanse your Catholic guilt?"

"No. It has nothing to do with religion. I don't want to hurt her." Nick sighed. "I've never lied or cheated on Katie."

"Such dramatics over one night of sex." Ruby lit a cigar. The cloying odor of the smoke mingled with the suffocating heat. "You like to screw women. So what? A juicier story will come along. The media will get bored with your sexual antics. Who knows, tomorrow a Hollywood starlet could overdose or a rock star might fling himself out a window. Embrace the publicity. It doesn't last forever."

"Katie's the woman I want to marry, have a family with. I'm not interested in other women. If I hadn't gotten so drunk—"

"Enough." Ruby tapped his cigar against the edge of his ashtray. He walked to his computer station and pressed a key on the keyboard. Six large monitors lit up on the wall.

"Ha! I so love the Internet," Ruby said. "Hits on your website have quadrupled since last night. The digital age. Makes it so easy to reach thousands of souls, possibly millions."

"I have a website?" Nick joined Ruby in front of the bank of monitors.

"Of course, and a Facebook fan page, and Twitter account. All necessary for marketing."

Nick squinted at the bright screens. "Who's doing the tweets and the posts on the website?"

"Not your worry. Part of my publicity staff are devoted solely to social media." Ruby pointed to another screen. "Look. Book orders. And posters and tee shirts. Fantastic! The electronic version of your book will be released shortly and will open up another market. I'll cut a check for you tomorrow. From the looks of these numbers, quite a large check. That should assuage your guilty conscious."

Nick's temples throbbed. Sweat coated his body from the oppressive heat in Ruby's office. Simply standing upright made him feel like he might vomit.

Ruby took him by the arm and led him to his office door. "You have a busy week ahead. I'll have Stephanie call you tomorrow with your itinerary. We'll need to get the manuscripts for the rest of your trilogy over to the publisher. Finish your next book. You've got a long way to go to catch up to ol' Joe Cullen."

Ruby stooped to pick up a long, bluish-black feather from the carpet. "Go to your apartment and rest, Nick. I need you fresh for next week."

"I'll be fine after I get some sleep. I apologize for getting so drunk last night."

"No need to apologize. I'm a huge fan of self-indulgence." He stroked the feather against his carefully groomed beard. "I couldn't be more pleased with your debut."

Nick left the building upset over Ruby's dismissive attitude toward his engagement and confused about his gleeful reaction to the bad publicity. He should have balked against keeping his engagement secret, but his hangover left him little energy to debate Ruby.

His started up the Mustang and drove to Katie's apartment. As he passed the hospital, he remembered Katie was scheduled to work today. She turned her phone off when she was at work. He hoped that was the reason he reached her voice mail earlier and not Katie refusing his calls after seeing his televised fiasco.

He made a U-turn and parked in the side lot of the hospital. The nurse sitting at the desk recognized him and told him Katie had called in sick.

Katie never called off work. Worried, he sped down the four short blocks from the hospital to her apartment. Seeing an open parking space, he hit the brakes hard. Something slid on the floor of the car and bumped against his foot. He picked up his cell phone. The battery was dead.

The sunny morning turned cloudy and cool. Thunder rumbled in the distance as he walked up the path. Katie's front door stood wide open and bags of groceries lined the stoop.

His head hurt as he bent to scoop up the plastic bags and carry them inside. Tara stood with her back to the door talking to Katie.

". . . sorry, sweetie, I know you love him, but let's face it, he's a no-good whore dog."

Katie sat at the kitchen table, dressed in pink leggings and one of Nick's tee shirts. Her hair was tied back in a ponytail emphasizing her pale, drawn face. She looked up when Nick entered. Tara continued her monologue as she unpacked groceries. "You know what they say, the bigger the rock they give you, the more women they have on the—" She turned to see what Katie was staring at behind her. Her eyes widened. "Nick! I didn't hear you come in."

"You were too busy bad-mouthing me." He plunked the bags on the table and looked at Katie's red, puffy eyes. She pushed herself up from the chair and hurried to her bedroom. Nick followed a few steps behind. She closed the door, leaving him standing in the hallway.

"Katie?" He knocked softly on the door. "Can I talk to you, please?"

Nick glanced over at Tara. She stood in the kitchen with her arms crossed, watching him.

"Mind your own business."

"It is my business," she said. "Katie's my best friend."

"Since when." Nick knocked again. When Katie didn't reply, he turned the knob and the door opened. He slid inside and closed it. Katie lay on her bed, her back facing him.

"Go away." Her voice quivered.

He walked around the bed and knelt on the floor to face her. Tears ran from her eyes. She rolled over, putting her back to him again.

"Babe," he said stroking her hair. "How are you feeling?"

Katie inched away from his touch. "How do you think I feel?" she murmured into her pillow.

"I'm so sorry." He eased himself onto the bed next to her and put his arm around her waist.

Katie shrugged off his arm and moved to the far side of the bed. "What exactly are you sorry for?"

Nick sighed. "Everything. I'm sorry you got sick and couldn't be there last night. And that I wasn't there to take you home. Sorry I drank too much and—"

Katie turned and glared at him. "Sorry you slept with those two—" Soft sobs cut off her words.

"No," Nick moved toward her.

"You're not sorry?"

The betrayed look in Katie's eyes wrenched at his heart. "I meant no, I didn't sleep with them." In a split second, he decided to lie to spare her more hurt. He feared the truth would end their relationship.

"It's all over the TV and the Internet. Tara showed me your tweets and posts on your website."

"Of course, she did," Nick mumbled. "Katie, Ruby set up everything. It was a stupid publicity stunt. Those aren't my tweets, or posts. He pays a staff to run the social media."

"The video of the party shows you kissing those women and more. And then all three of you going into your apartment building." Katie drew her knees close to her chest. "You proposed to me only three days ago. How could you do this?"

Nick pulled her shaking body close to him. "I didn't sleep with them." A hollow feeling filled his stomach and throat. He felt thankful he didn't have to look into her eyes as he lied. "I was drunk. And nervous, so I kept drinking. I didn't feel anything from the alcohol until after the press conference. It hit me all at once. I was passing out when they were hanging on me at the party. I wanted to leave and come see you. I couldn't think straight. Ruby told me this morning it was all planned. He's marketing me as an available bachelor. He hired the models to pose for photos outside the apartment building. I was too damn drunk to stop it." He put his arm around her. "And, for that, I am the most sorry."

Katie pulled away from him and hugged her pillow. A folded piece of paper poked out from beneath the pillow. He recognized his typed marriage proposal.

"I called you so many times. You never called me back," she whispered.

"I lost my cell. When Steph and I came back to the party, Ruby told me you were sick and left. I wanted to call you, but my phone was gone. The show was starting, and I had to get backstage. I asked Steph to look for my cell." Nick rubbed Katie's back. "After the press conference, I went home and passed out. I called you this morning, from Steph's phone. I left a message."

"I didn't get any message," Katie said.

"Babe, I swear I called you. I'm used to pushing one programmed button. Maybe I dialed wrong." Nick sighed and rolled onto his back to ease the incessant pounding headache. "I found my phone in my car when I pulled up here. The battery's dead."

"I watched the press conference on TV. The question about all the women you've seduced– why didn't you deny it? Then those models came out. You never told me they were at the photo shoot with you. Tara showed me the poster with the three of you," Katie said.

"Janis Ford asked that question. It wasn't one of the approved questions. You saw the press questions. Janis hates me. I said it wasn't true, but the microphone wasn't working. As for the models," Nick blew out a long breath, "I never mentioned them being at the photo shoot because it was stupid. I didn't know Ruby planned on printing a poster. I thought I'd never see them again."

Katie lay silent, curled up away from him. He closed his eyes. The cool, quiet room and the rhythmic drumming of rain falling outside soothed this head. "Katie, I was on a stage. I tried to push them away. What could I do, punch a woman on live TV? Not that it matters, I came across looking like an ass—"

Katie jumped up and rushed out of the room. The bathroom door slammed. Pain jolted through his temples as he sat up and followed her. He heard her coughing and retching behind the closed door. The sounds made his own queasy stomach lurch. He walked into the kitchen to wait.

Tara sat in the living room watching the recorded VIP party. The Sunday newspaper and *The Entertainer* were on the kitchen table, both opened to stories and pictures of the VIP party.

"Tara," Nick said. "Would you please stop playing that?" He folded the newspapers. Tara muted the television and strolled into the kitchen. She opened the refrigerator and took out a shiny, gold box. "These are delicious, want one?" She offered a box of chocolate-dipped strawberries.

"No. Did the roses come?" he asked.

"Yes! They're gorgeous. Katie didn't want them. I hated to throw them away, so I put them in my room. Wanna see?"

"No. Would you check on Katie? It sounded like she was throwing up."

"Duh. She's been vomiting all night. Not sure if it's a stomach bug or food poisoning. I bought Gatorade and ginger ale, so she won't dehydrate, and some saltine crackers."

"Thanks."

"It sounded really lame, by the way." Tara made a loud slurping sound as she bit into a strawberry and sucked the juice.

"What sounded lame?"

"Oh, c'mon, Nick," Tara laughed. The high-pitched sound sent shock waves of pain through his head. She deepened her voice to mimic him, "I lost my phone. The microphone stopped working." She laughed some more. "You're a writer, couldn't you come up with something better? What's next, I tripped and my penis accidentally fell into a super model? Oh, I mean you tripped twice and—"

"Shut up. You were listening outside Katie's door?" Nick took a step toward Tara. "You have no right making up lies about me. Katie's sick and you're making things worse. Some damned best friend you are. Did you tell her about all the times you came on to me when she wasn't around? If I'm such a dog, then why didn't I take you up on your offers?"

"Dogs don't poop where they eat. If I didn't live with Katie, you'd be all over this." She pointed to herself and wiggled her hips.

"Oh please, don't flatter yourself."

"Please stop yelling." Katie stood in the open bathroom doorway with her palms on her temples. Her red-rimmed eyes stood out against her paper white face. She turned, and holding onto the wall, walked into her bedroom.

Nick hurried after her. She sat on the edge of the bed and tried to sip a glass of water. Her hands shook so, she couldn't bring the glass to her mouth.

"Here." Nick held the glass to her lips. Katie nodded when she had drunk enough and then slumped backwards onto the bed. He swung her legs up onto the bed and slid a pillow under her head. "What can I do to help?"

"Just go." Tears dripped from the corners of her closed eyelids. "I can't talk now. I feel awful."

"Can I get you more water or something?"

"Excuse me." Tara brushed by Nick carrying a small tray. She placed it on the nightstand. "Here's some ginger ale and crackers. And a cold rag." Tara wrung out the washcloth in a small bowl of ice water and draped it over Katie's forehead.

Nick stood watching Katie after Tara left the room. His frustration and guilt grew by the minute. He wanted nothing more than to lie down next to her and fall asleep holding her. He saw his book under the tray on her bedside table. Yellow post-it notes stuck out from between the pages. Sliding it out, he saw Katie's neat handwriting detailed the changes from his original story on each note.

"I read it. Go ahead. Take it." Katie pulled the sheet up to her chin.

Nick leaned and kissed her on the cheek. "Get some rest. Call me if you need anything."

Katie didn't reply.

"Call me later, please?"

Katie lay silent with her eyes closed. Nick whispered in her ear. "I love you."

He quietly closed the door. Tara sat at the kitchen table staring at her laptop. He saw his website's home page displayed on her screen.

"Tara, keep an eye on Katie and don't upset her."

"What do you think I've been doing? I am a nurse, you know. I'm the one who's been taking care of her all night while you were out taking care of yourself." Tara giggled and pointed at the screen. "One click, and I joined your new Fan Club." She laughed again. "And you posted that you gave Rachel a nine score in bed, but, gave Ebony an eleven because she used to be a gymnast."

"I'm standing right here. It's obviously not me posting that bullshit." He grabbed some of the empty plastic grocery bags from the table and wrapped his book to protect it from the rain. He crumpled up the newspapers on the table and stuffed them into the bag.

"Hey!" Tara yelled. "I bought those as souvenirs for Katie."

Nick restrained himself from yelling so as not to disturb Katie. He held up his middle finger as he opened the door. He stepped off the front stoop into the rain. Tara leaned out the open door and called after him. "Is that an invitation?"

Halfway to his car, a loud clap of thunder signaled a torrential downpour. Drenched to the skin and too exhausted to run, Nick trudged to the curb with his book clutched against his chest. His jeans made a squishing sound when he sank into the leather car seat.

The hurt in Katie's eyes wouldn't leave his mind. The guilt of cheating on her and then lying about it burned an acidy hole in his empty stomach. If Katie found out the truth, she would leave him. A wave of nausea swept over him. He pulled into an empty parking lot and opened the driver's door to vomit, but only dry-heaved. The wrenching motion in his gut tore a new blinding pain in his head.

Nick peeled off his wet clothes, hung them in the bathroom and then showered. He pulled on a pair of his old sweatpants. A small comfort from before Victor Ruby ruled his wardrobe.

After plugging his cell phone into the charger, he studied the maze of buttons and digital displays on the coffee maker Stephanie had given him. A one-inch thick instruction manual sat on the counter next to it. He didn't have the patience to look up how to brew a simple cup of coffee. Instead, he poured the cold, leftover coffee Stephanie had made that morning into a mug and heated it in the microwave. He shook out four aspirin from the bottle she had left and carried the warm mug to the couch.

Sitting on the overstuffed leather sectional, he took a drink of coffee and swallowed the aspirin. As the pills washed down his throat, it triggered a memory. Ebony had used her tongue to push a pill into his mouth. She drugged him. That's why he couldn't remember most of last night. He almost called Katie but thought of Tara's words. He hated to agree with her, but his explanations did sound like lame excuses. Any conversation about the VIP party would involve telling Katie more lies. He stretched out and rested his aching head on the cushioned sofa arm.

It was late afternoon when Nick woke. To his relief, the headache was gone and hunger pangs replaced the sour churning in his stomach. Although the rain had stopped, a dense grey blanket of clouds covered the late spring sky.

After checking his cell phone for any missed calls from Katie, he went around the apartment and opened the windows. The French doors in the bedroom opened inward. Gusts of wind cleansed the last clinging traces of Rachel's perfume from the air.

He found clean sheets in the linen closet along with a flyer detailing the building's laundry services. After making up the bed in fresh, cotton sheets, he stuffed the soiled satin ones and his clothes into a canvas laundry bag. He set the bag in the hallway outside his apartment door with the filled-out form.

After purging the apartment of all remnants of his indiscretion, he cooked bacon and eggs and ate at the counter as he thumbed through his novel. He had read the words on his computer screen countless times, yet this was the first time he read them in a hard-cover book. Katie's post-it notes demonstrated how she had pored over each line and added more weight to his guilt.

He checked his cell phone, though he knew it hadn't rung. It had finally charged enough to retrieve last night's messages. There were seven from Katie. She had called him from the rest room when she first felt ill. The series of calls continued throughout the night into early morning. Her voice sounded increasingly shaky with each message. In her last, after one in the morning, she broke into sobs. Nick pushed the delete button and then texted Katie, *Don't want 2 wake U. Call me. We have to talk. Luv U.*

An eighth message from his brother, Sal, had come in later this morning. Nick pressed the call back button.

Sal answered on the first ring. "Hey Nick, Nonna wants to talk to you." He lowered his voice. "She's super-pissed."

Nick waited while Sal handed the phone to his grandmother.

"What's the matter with you? *Disgrazia!*" she shouted. She alternated between Italian and English when she was upset. She said her friends told her he was on television. She turned on the set and saw for herself. "We raised you better than that! You embarrass the family and yourself! *Disgrazia!* You disrespect Katie! The girl you want to marry! What kind of people you work for?"

Nick listened to her tirade in silence. During her brief pauses, he mumbled, "Yes, ma'am," and, "I'm sorry."

"I say an entire rosary for you this morning, Nickie," Nonna said. "You apologize to Katie. Stop acting like a *prostituto maschio! Disgrazia. Cane in calor!* You hear me?"

"Yes, Nonna. I already apologized to Katie and I'm sorry I embarrassed you. I drank too much. I promise, it won't happen again." His grandmother wouldn't understand Ruby's manufactured publicity. It was simpler to blame his behavior on alcohol.

"You go to confession, Nickie. Ask God's forgiveness. Talk to Father Santore."

"Yes, Nonna."

After a few seconds of silence, Sal came back on the phone. He whispered, "Hey, Nick, did you really do it with those models? Two at the same time?"

Nick ended the call and slammed his cell on the counter. He paced the apartment. In one night, he had screwed up his relationships with Katie and his family. Ruby's publicity stunt and his own drunkenness cost him dearly. He had to repair the damage.

Picking up his book, he walked to his desk and turned on his laptop. Referring to Katie's notes, he focused on mending the story line in his second and third books. The revisions Ruby ordered changed key scenes which resulted in the protagonist, Julian, becoming a blood-thirsty murderer. Nick's original story portrayed a sympathetic Julian who reluctantly abandoned his love, Caroline, in order to protect her from evil Diana a jealous vampiress. Ruby's version allied Julian with Diana, and had Julian kill Caroline in a blood-filled vicious attack scene.

With the book now printed, there was nothing he could do to salvage his first story. Instead, Nick typed for hours revising the second book to bring his main character back to redemption. He stopped long enough to skim a few pages of the coffee maker manual and brewed a fresh pot of coffee.

At midnight, he sat in front of his computer screen, sipped coffee and read over his work. He liked it better than his original. In the third volume, Julian reunites with his reincarnated love, Caroline. After a climactic battle with Diana, Julian kills the evil vampires. He added a twist at the end; to save Caroline from becoming a vampire, Julian must destroy himself. It would be a bitter-sweet ending, with the hero regaining his soul but sacrificing his life to save the life of the woman he loves. He started typing the new ending when his cell phone beeped. He ran to the kitchen to check his phone.

Katie texted *good nite*. The simple message made him smile. While he would have preferred she had called, her text was a positive sign. He texted back, *Good nite, I Luv U.*

Feeling wide awake after his long nap and a pot of coffee, he returned to his computer and continued to write. Bringing his story closer to the original version made him feel in control of at least one aspect of his life. The real test would be convincing Ruby not to change it again.

The sound of the doorbell startled him after one in the morning. He wondered if the laundry service worked this late. He opened the door to find a thin, barefoot girl with two long, red pony tails. It took him a second to recognize Stephanie without her usual make-up, designer clothes and high heels. She looked prepubescent in a baby blue tank top and pink shorts.

"Steph, is everything okay?"

"Chris is dead." She stared up at him with wet, blank eyes. Her arms hung limp at her sides. She clutched a brown envelope in one hand.

"Chris Turner? What happened?"

Stephanie opened her mouth, but only ragged gasps came out.

Nick put his arm around her shoulders. "Come inside." He led her to the couch, and she collapsed onto it, sobbing.

Nick knelt on the floor in front of her and squeezed her hands. "Steph, calm down. Tell me what happened."

She buried her face against his bare chest. The gesture made him uncomfortable and he excused himself and left the room. He had no tissues, so he grabbed a roll of toilet paper from the bathroom and a T-shirt from his closet. Setting the tissue roll on the sofa arm, he hurried into the kitchen to get a glass of water. He pulled his T-shirt on as he walked.

Stephanie sat, wiping her eyes when he returned with the water. As soon as he sat down, she cuddled next to him.

"What happened?" Nick said.

"It's on the news. They said he jumped out the window of his hotel room."

The hair on the back of his neck prickled. Ruby's words about a rock star throwing himself out of a window replayed in his mind.

Nick picked up the television remote and scanned through the channels. It didn't take long to find a news station with Chris's picture displayed above a red breaking-news banner. He leaned forward and listened to the reporter.

". . . hotel staff told police a loud party raged on for hours tonight in the rock star's room. Shortly after eleven o'clock, police responded to noise complaints and ordered the guests to leave the premises. A young woman at the party told reporters that Slaughter was high on drugs and alcohol. Chris Turner, whose stage name is Ian Slaughter, has been rumored to use crack cocaine and methamphetamine.

Allegedly, he bragged to several party guests he could fly. Witnesses claim the thirty-two-year-old singer climbed atop the balcony railing outside his window. Details are murky and police have declined to comment about this open investigation. Speculation is, he either fell, was pushed, or he jumped fifteen stories to the parking lot below. Ian Slaughter was pronounced dead at the scene. This story is still breaking. Stay tuned for updates."

Stephanie covered her face with both hands and cried harder.

"Sorry." Nick muted the set and stared at the silent images of Ian Slaughter and the Blood Lust band flicker and fade across the screen. Finally, a photo without the stage makeup revealed a smiling young man with a tan complexion, strong jaw line and brilliant teal blue eyes. Aware of Stephanie's muffled sobs, Nick turned off the television. She burrowed against him. He sat back and put his arm around her. Although he had only talked to Chris for a few minutes, he liked him and found it difficult to believe he was a drug addict, especially after he refused any alcohol before taking the stage last night.

Stephanie's sobs gradually subsided. She sat up and dabbed at her eyes with the tissue.

"What's in the envelope, Steph?" The sealed envelope had Stephanie's name and address on it.

"My demo CD. It came in the mail today. I can't open it now. Chris helped me record it. We sneaked into the recording studio a few weeks ago in Ruby's building. Chris said I was a talented singer and wanted me to quit Ruby Promotions."

Stephanie unrolled more paper and blew her nose. "It's mostly country songs, but he and I did a couple of ballads together, too." She picked up the glass of water. "Do you have any alcohol?"

"I have beer and wine in the fridge."

"Could I have some wine, please?"

Nick's first instinct was to tell her she was too young, but he had grown up drinking wine with dinner since he was a child. Under the circumstances, he didn't think a glass of wine would do any harm and it might calm her. "Sure." He walked into the kitchen. Stephanie followed and sat on a tall stool at the counter while he poured two glasses of red wine.

"Mmm." Stephanie drained her glass in two long gulps, then picked up the bottle and poured herself another. "I drank about a half a bottle I had upstairs, but I don't feel drunk yet."

"Take it easy. Getting drunk won't help. Trust me, I know."

"I want to numb out. I can't believe Chris is gone. I just talked to him at the party last night." She poured more wine into her empty glass. Nick took the bottle from her hands in mid-pour. "That's enough, Steph. You're a lightweight." He put the nearly empty bottle back into the refrigerator.

"I don't believe Chris killed himself," Stephanie blurted. Her eyes filled with tears. "He was going home tomorrow to see his daughter and to work things out with his wife."

"I didn't really know him, but he didn't seem like a drug addict, either."

"He wasn't! That's all Ruby's doing. His stupid stereotype image for rock stars. Drugs, sex and wild parties. Chris is . . . was . . . so sweet, kind. He was my friend." Stephanie buried her face in her hands. "Now I have no friends."

Nick rubbed her back. "I know what it's like to lose someone you love," he whispered. "It takes time, but it will get easier."

Stephanie grabbed Nick's glass on the counter and gulped it down. She swayed when she stood. "Ruby had Chris killed."

"What?"

She leaned against the counter for balance. "He hated Chris. Chris hated him. All they did was fight over that stupid contract."

"A dispute over a business contract is a long way from murder, Steph."

"Victor Ruby's evil." Stephanie clamped her hand over her mouth and looked around the room.

"Ruby's strange. The fingernails. Keeping his office like a damn oven. His unorthodox ways of promoting people. The guy definitely lacks morals, but murder?"

"I've seen and heard stuff." Stephanie stared wide-eyed at Nick.

"Steph, you're upset. Hearing about Chris is a shock. And you've had too much wine. You want to lie down awhile? Or, do you want me to walk you upstairs to your apartment?"

Stephanie took a few faltering steps toward Nick. Her knees buckled. Nick grabbed her under her arms before she fell. She clutched his shirt. "I'm afraid to be alone. Can I stay here tonight?" She managed to stand by holding on to him. "Please? I'll sleep on the couch."

"I'll take the couch. You sleep in the bed. C'mon, you need to lie down before you fall down."

"I don't mean to be any trouble."

"You're no trouble. Besides, I owe you one after yesterday morning."

Nick carried her the last few steps to the bedroom. As he leaned over to lay her on the bed, Stephanie threw her arms around his neck and pulled him off balance. He landed on top of her in the bed, straddling her shoulders with his hands and her legs with his knees.

"I love you." She pushed her lips against his.

"Whoa, Steph, stop." Nick extricated himself from her arms and eased himself off the bed.

She tugged on his hand. "You can make love to me, if you want to."

"You've had too much wine." Nick gently pulled his hand away. "Try to get some sleep, okay? If you need anything, I'll be in the living room."

Stephanie sat up. "You don't want me." Her narrow shoulders shook as she cried. "Katie's so beautiful. I'm ugly, skinny."

Nick sighed. "Don't say that. You're not ugly."

"Yes I am. I used to think Chris loved me, but he loved his wife. And you have a gorgeous fiancée. Nobody wants me. I try so hard to look grown-up and pretty, but everyone sees me as a stupid, ugly kid."

"That's not true, Steph. You're a very pretty, smart girl. You'll find a guy. One who's not married or engaged. You need to meet people your age."

"I thought if Chris got divorced, he'd marry me. We could raise little Brittany together. Then he told me he thought of me like a second daughter. You don't want to make love to me. I'm the one who should kill myself!" Stephanie bolted across the bed.

The French doors leading to the balcony stood wide open. Nick dove onto the bed, grabbed Stephanie's ankles and dragged her back onto the bed.

"Jesus, Steph! What are you doing?" Nick knelt over her, pinning her arms and legs.

"Let me go! I don't want to live anymore. I hate you! I hate my life!"

"If I have to freaking tie you to this bed, I'm not letting you jump off a damn balcony. Now, please, Steph, calm down."

She kicked Nick. He rolled to one side to protect his crotch from her flailing feet. She squirmed one arm free and punched him until he managed to grab her arm and stop her. He held her down until she stopped fighting, twisted onto her side and sobbed. He sat next to her until she passed out.

Nick closed the balcony doors and then took a wire hanger from the closet. Straightening it, he wound it around both handles to secure the doors. He left the bedroom door ajar so he could hear if Stephanie attempted to open the doors.

Exhausted, he sat on the couch and stared at the television screen. He kept it muted and listened for Stephanie, fearing she would wake and try to kill herself.

Chapter 10

The sound of the front door closing woke him. He jumped up, ran to the door and opened it. Stephanie climbed the staircase to the upper floor.

"Steph, you okay?" he called.

She glanced over her shoulder. "Yeah. Thanks for letting me stay."

"Wait." Nick sprinted up the stairs. "Are you sure you're all right?" He lifted her chin with his hand and looked into her eyes. "You're not going to hurt yourself, are you?"

"No." She shrugged his hand away and stared at her feet. "Sorry for all the stupid stuff I said. I made a real ass of myself."

"Forget it." Nick hugged her. "I'd say me answering the door buck naked takes the being-an-ass grand prize." He touched the bruises on her arms. "I'm sorry, Steph. I didn't mean to hurt you."

She gave a weak smile. "They don't hurt. It was my fault. I'm going to call Mr. Ruby and ask for a personal day today. I need some time alone."

Returning to his apartment, he saw Stephanie had started a pot of coffee brewing for him. He checked his cell phone but found no messages. It was seven o'clock. Katie would be getting ready for work, if she felt well enough to go in today. After their tense exchange yesterday, he felt apprehensive calling her. She answered on the third ring.

"Are you feeling better?" he asked.

"Yes, I'm getting ready for work."

"Can I see you tonight?"

"I'm working a double. I won't get out till midnight."

"I can come by on your dinner break."

After long pause Katie answered, "Okay."

"What time?"

"About eight," she said.

"I'll see you at eight. I love you."

A steady stream of people walked in and out of the front doors of the hospital, but Katie wasn't one of them. Nick sat waiting on the top step outside the main entrance. The digital time display on his cell read eight twenty-two. He worried she changed her mind about meeting him. A soft "Hey" startled him. He stood and stared at Katie across the two feet of space between them. Two days ago, he would have scooped her up in his arms, but tonight, tension paralyzed him.

"How long is your break?" he asked.

"It's too busy for me to take dinner. This is only a five-minute break," she said.

He reached for her hands and held them. "Babe, we really need to talk."

She stared past him, over his shoulder. Her eyes shone with tears. "I know," she murmured.

"We can't talk in five minutes. Call me when you're done work. I'll drive you home."

She slipped her hands from his grasp and tucked them inside her uniform pockets.

"It'll be after midnight," she said. "I need to sleep. I have the early shift tomorrow."

"I'll still drive you home. We can talk tomorrow."

"I have a ride."

"Who?"

A flicker of annoyance crossed Katie's face. "Jennifer. She drives by my place on her way home."

"I'd rather drive you and make sure you get into your apartment safe." He brushed away a wisp of her hair that had blown over her eyes in the cool breeze.

"It's silly for you to come all the way back here." Katie took a step back. "I'll be fine." She glanced at her watch. "I have to go."

Nick put his hands on her shoulders. "Katie, promise you'll find time to talk. Please."

She looked up at him with wet eyes and nodded.

"I'll pick you up after work tomorrow. We can go to my place," he said. "I'll make dinner, okay?"

"Okay," she whispered. She turned and ran back into the building.

Hot tears stung Nick's eyelids. He stomped down the steps and stopped at the edge of the parking lot. Pacing in a circle, he considered running after Katie. Instead, he slammed his fist down on the top of a metal newspaper rack.

"Everything all right, big fella?" A security guard pointed a flashlight in Nick's face.

"Yeah, sorry," he mumbled to the old man. He walked to his car.

After driving aimlessly for blocks, Nick found himself at his family's restaurant. Although past closing time, the lights were on inside. He parked on the side street. A galvanized-metal mop bucket propped open the back kitchen door. Inside, his brother, Sal, stood peering through one of the porthole windows in the double swinging doors which led into the dining room. Sal jumped as the back door screeched on its hinges.

"Nick! Geez, you scared the shit outta me," Sal said. "Did Pop call you?"

"No, why?"

Sal motioned toward the dining room. "Tonight's the big meeting."

"What big meeting?"

"Nonna and Eddie."

"What're you talking about?"

Sal snorted and wiped his eyes with his palms. "Nonna found out about me boxing."

"Ah, shit. So, what's the meeting about?"

"Nonna insisted on talking to Eddie, face to face. They're all out there now." Sal peeked through the round window again.

"Pop will stick up for you, Sal. So will Eddie."

"You know Nonna. If she decides she doesn't want me boxing . . ." Sal walked over to the big stainless-steel cooler and leaned his back against it. "Shit, it's not fair. I don't care what Nonna thinks. I love boxing. I'm good at it. I'll be eighteen in a few months. She can't stop me then." He crossed his arms and jerked his head at Nick. "Right?"

"Once you're an adult, you can do whatever you want."

Sal threw his hands in the air. "What's she got against boxing anyway?"

"She probably doesn't want her youngest grandson to get hurt."

"I'm not a damn baby."

"I know."

The kitchen door swung open. "Sal, come out here, son," their father said. "Oh, hey Nick. Didn't know you were here. You can come out, too."

Nick held the door. Sal walked ahead to the table where his grandmother and Eddie sat opposite each other.

"Sit, Salvatore," Nonna said.

Sal slumped into a chair and glared at her over his crossed arms.

"Me and Mr. Eddie reach an agreement," she said. "You can keep training, as long as you get good grades and graduate high school next spring."

Sal straightened up in the chair. He looked from Nonna to Eddie. "Really? I can box?"

His father patted his shoulders. "Yes, but you have to do good in school, like your nonna said. And help in the restaurant. And once you turn eighteen, we want to be included in any decisions. You know, like what fights you take, and money you get. Understood?"

"Yeah, Pop. Sure." Sal jumped up and hugged his father. He ran around the table and shook Eddie's hand.

"You should thank your grandmother," Eddie said in a voice that sounded like tires on a gravel road.

Sal crouched down next to his grandmother. "Thank you, Nonna."

She cupped his face in both hands. "I forget sometimes, you not a little boy anymore. You promise me, you be careful, Salvatore. I don't want you to get hurt. And remember, you can talk to your father, or me, about this boxing, or anything."

"Yes, Nonna." Sal stood, his face beamed with happiness.

Nick gripped his brother in a bear hug. "Glad it worked out."

Eddie rose to leave, tipping his grey fedora toward Nonna before planting it on top of his white-haired head. "My pleasure to meet you, Miz Rosa." A younger man sitting near the front window stood to help Eddie. Eddie pushed the man's arm away. "I can walk by myself, Danny. You drive the car."

Nick's father locked the front door after the two exited. "It's late. Help me finish cleaning up in the kitchen, Sal," he said.

Nonna nodded at Nick and patted the chair next to her.

Nick sat down. "You made Sal very happy, Nonna."

"I want to say no. *Stupido* sport. Hitting each other, for what? Money? *Machismo*? But, if I say no, he do it anyway. He be angry. It only push him away. *Testardo ragazzo*, stubborn boys, both of you." She shook her head. "Why you look so sad tonight, Nickie?"

"It's Katie, Nonna," he said. "She's still angry at me."

"Ah," she said, nodding her head. "You say you apologized? From your heart?" She placed her hands over her heart.

"Yes, I did." Although he didn't intend to, Nick found himself pouring out the details of the last two days to his grandmother. He told her how Ruby manipulated the press conference to gain more sensational publicity. He stopped short of telling her about sleeping with the models. Instead, he talked about how much he regretted drinking too much and how he loved and missed Katie. His grandmother sat in silence and listened until he had talked himself out.

"You bring Katie here for dinner tomorrow," Nonna said.

"I wanted to make dinner for her at my new apartment. It's quiet. We can talk," Nick said.

"What you gonna cook?"

"I hadn't really thought about it."

"Come in the kitchen," she said getting up from her chair. "We got some nice veal today." She took Nick's hand. "Salvatore, get a box for your brother. Nickie, you take this fresh basil and some of the good Romano." She packed meat, cheese and herbs into the box. "You make her a nice dinner, Nickie. She loves you. You love her. Everything will work out. You see."

Chapter 11

The sky had barely begun to lighten in the east when Nick climbed out of bed. He had spent most of the night lying awake thinking about seeing Katie tonight. Every time he looked up at the ceiling, he saw the image of himself with Rachel and Ebony. He hated that mirror.

He showered, dressed and made coffee. At seven o'clock, he called Katie and tried his best to sound upbeat. "Hey babe, I'll pick you up after work, okay?"

"Okay," Katie answered.

"I have your overnight bag in my trunk. From Saturday night."

"Oh, right, I forgot," she said.

"I'll see you at five?" The long pauses and cool tone of Katie's voice unnerved Nick. He wished he could see her now, he couldn't read her expressions through a phone. He also wanted the awkward phone call to end.

"Yes," she said.

"Love you." There was no reply. "Katie?" The call ended. He put the phone down on the counter, then picked it up and called Stephanie.

"Hey Steph. Are you still at home?"

"Yes, why?"

"Do you have a vacuum cleaner I can borrow?"

Nick steered the small vacuum around the bedroom carpet. He wiped down the nightstands and put the freshly laundered sheets on the bed. When he finished in the bedroom, he moved on to the bathroom. By mid-morning, the entire apartment was spotless. He poured lukewarm coffee into a mug and called Stephanie at work.

"I had no idea they made purple vacuum cleaners, but it did the job. Thanks," he said.

Stephanie giggled into the phone. "I bought it because it was purple."

"Hey, I have another favor to ask. Can you ask Ruby if I can meet with him today?"

Her tone turned somber. "He's dealing with the aftermath of Chris' death. I'll ask and call you back."

While he waited for Stephanie's call, he mixed up a flat bread dough. He used one of his grandfather's fine-edged chef knives to mince the fresh herbs his grandmother had given him and folded them into the dough. He covered the bowl with a towel and set it on top of the stove to rise.

Stephanie called a few minutes later. "Mr. Ruby said he can fit you in at two-thirty this afternoon."

"Perfect. Thanks, Steph."

"Is everything all right?"

"Yes, I need to talk to him about my manuscripts. Thanks, again."

Stephanie greeted Nick, but she wasn't her usual bubbly self. She sat slump-shouldered in front of her computer with red, puffy eyes. Ruby's office door opened at two-thirty sharp. He stood in the doorway holding his cell phone to his ear and motioned for Nick to come inside as he talked.

"We all have problems, Mike," Ruby said. "I have a platinum rock band scheduled for a world tour with no lead singer." Ruby paused and rolled his eyes as he listened. "Yeah, yeah. What do you expect me to do about it? Scrape the bastard off the ground, put him in a envelope and mail him to his wife? Tell her the body will be shipped after the damn autopsy." Ruby put his cell down on the desk.

"What can I do for you, Nick?" Ruby settled into his chair and lit a cigar.

"I have several things, Mr. Ruby," Nick said.

"Well, spit it out. Slaughter's suicide is taking up my whole damn day. Especially since my sensitive secretary took a personal day yesterday. Her absence delayed several projects."

"It was a suicide?"

"Who knows? The press is leaning that way. All this media speculation is making a bigger splash than Slaughter made when he hit the pavement." Ruby threw back his head and laughed.

Nick shifted in his chair and cleared his throat. "I have my manuscripts ready to submit for the second and third books of the trilogy."

"Excellent. I'll call Jack, my publisher. You can drop them off to him downstairs."

"I want to make the edits. And I don't want my story changed like it was in the first book."

Ruby puffed on his cigar and studied him with narrowed eyes. "Your overnight fame has gone straight to your balls, hey, Nick?"

"No sir. I just feel strongly about my story."

"Whatever. Work it out with Jack." Ruby got up, walked to his computer and studied the monitors. "Anything else?"

"There won't be any more events like the VIP party, will there?"

"Why, you horny, Nick?" Ruby grinned. "I'll give you Rachel and Ebony's phone numbers."

"That's not what I meant. You said from now on it would be interviews and book signings, right?"

"Yes. In fact, I've scheduled two book signings for the end of this week. I wanted you to do them sooner, but I didn't want Slaughter's messy exit to overshadow your events."

"I don't want any more public humiliation."

"Humiliation? Look at this." Ruby tapped on a monitor with his fingernail. "Half a million books sold. I've had to reorder the posters and T-shirts. All sold out."

"Half a million books?"

Ruby returned to his desk and took a check from his drawer. "Here you are, Nick, as promised."

"Holy shit." Nick stared at the check in his hands made out for over six hundred-thousand dollars. "Is this for real?"

"Your royalties. Do the math. Anything else on your mind, Nick?"

"Um, yes." Nick slipped the check into his shirt pocket. "I'd like your permission to remove a mirror in the apartment. I'll do the work myself. I have experience with patching and painting."

"I pay you to write," Ruby said. "I pay a maintenance company to service the building." Ruby cocked his head and asked, "Where is this mirror? Can't you simply take it off the wall?"

"In the bedroom. And, no I can't, it's attached."

Ruby scrawled a note on a pad. "The maintenance staff aren't the brightest bulbs. I'll need to tell them which wall exactly in the bedroom?"

"It's not on a wall, it's on the ceiling."

"Huh? The former tenant must have installed it." Ruby smirked. "A ceiling mirror in your bedroom and you want it taken down?"

"Yes, sir."

"An odd request for a virile, young man." Ruby leaned across his desk. His upper lip curled into a sneer. "What's the problem, Nick? Is your fiancée shy?"

Nick ignored the taunt. "There's one more thing I'd like to ask you."

"Make it quick. I have a meeting at three concerning Slaughter. That prick is becoming as annoying dead as he was alive."

"I'd like to buy the Mustang from you, if you'll consider selling it."

Nick tasted his pesto sauce and added a pinch more salt and some fresh lemon zest. He put the bowl into the refrigerator. Hesitating at the open door, he took a beer from the shelf and made a mental note to brush his teeth before picking up Katie. As he walked around the apartment sipping the beer, he straightened a picture on the wall and rearranged the items on his desk for the third time. He hadn't felt this nervous since his first date with Katie. His cell phone rang. Seeing Katie's name displayed, he answered on the first ring.

"I wanted to let you know you don't have to pick me up at the hospital," Katie said.

"Why?" Had Katie decided to dump him? Nick took a breath to steady his nerves. "Should I pick you up at your apartment instead?"

"No. I have an errand to run with Tara. She'll drop me off at your place on her way in to work."

"So, I'll see you . . . when?"

"About seven."

Nick sat at the kitchen counter. Katie's voice sounded strained. He wondered what the errand with Tara could be. Katie never kept secrets from him. Tara's involvement gave him a bad feeling. He finished his beer and grabbed another from the refrigerator.

At seven twenty-six, Nick stood by the living room window looking down at the street below. He gripped his cell phone, debating whether or not to call Katie when a light blue sedan pulled up in front of the entrance. The driver and passenger doors opened at the same time. Katie stepped out from the passenger side. A man ran around from the driver's side and opened the trunk. He handed a large box to Katie and kissed her on the cheek. As the man turned to get back into the car, Nick recognized him. Jon Gerber, the male nurse. Nick's jaw tightened. Katie lied about Tara giving her a ride. He feared Gerber was taking advantage of the rift in their relationship. He walked to the front door taking deep breaths to calm his temper. When the elevator bell sounded, he opened the door. Katie hurried down the hall carrying a large, gift-wrapped box.

"Let me take that for you," he said holding his arms out.

"I've got it." She slipped past him and headed for the kitchen counter. "Oh, shoot," she said.

"What's wrong?"

Katie pointed to the new coffee maker. "I brought a housewarming gift, but you already have one. A nicer one. Mine's just a Mr. Coffee pot, like the one I have."

"Your's makes the best coffee, plus it's a no-brainer in the morning. This one's too complicated. Steph gave it to me, that's the only reason I set it up."

"Oh," Katie said. "I'll take it back and get something else."

"Are you kidding me? It stays." Nick ripped open the box and set the coffee maker on the counter in front of the other one. "I love it. Thank you." He leaned to kiss Katie.

She abruptly turned her head. "Your apartment is very nice." She strolled into the living room.

"I like it." Nick followed her as she wandered around the room. Each time he stood close to her, she moved away to admire something. Feeling frustrated, he walked back into the kitchen. "Do you want something to drink? I have the tea you like," he called out.

Katie stood near the kitchen. "Do you have wine?"

Nick bit his tongue and nodded. Katie rarely drank alcohol, but her request suited the strange way she acted tonight. He poured two glasses and handed one to her.

"Thank you."

Nick watched her take a tiny sip and then put the glass down. Her eyes darted around the kitchen, looking at everything but him. She wrung her hands and twisted the diamond engagement ring on her finger.

"You look fantastic, is that a new outfit?" He admired her tight black jeans and the black lace bra which peeked above the neckline of her pink tank top.

"Yes." She removed her leather blazer, walked into the living room and draped it over a chair. He noticed her matching pink high heels. It was not her usual style of clothing.

"You're all dressed up and I look like a slob." He motioned to his sweat pants and tee shirt.

"You look fine. Besides, you've been cooking." She picked up a knife he had left lying on the cutting board and positioned it over a plump, ripe tomato. "I'll help," she said. "How do you want this cut?"

"Careful." Nick reached and held her hand. "This is one of my grandpa's chef knives. Really sharp." He wrapped his arms around her. She slipped sideways to escape his hold. Her bottom brushed against him as she moved past. He eased himself down onto a stool to hide his arousal. Katie picked up her glass and raised it to her mouth but didn't drink. Her whole body trembled, and she gripped the wine glass with both hands to steady it.

"What's wrong, babe?" he asked.

"Oh, God, I can't do this." She put the glass down on the counter and ran toward the front door.

Nick ran after her and put his hand on the door above her head so she couldn't pull it open.

"Can't do what?" he said. "Katie, please, talk to me."

Tears misted her eyes. Her breath came out in short gasps between her words. "I can't pretend to have polite conversation when I know you asked me here to break our engagement."

"What? No! Why would you think that?" He took her hand. "Please, let's sit down." He led her to the couch and sat next to her.

Katie perched on the edge of the seat. "Tara said you told her you were breaking our engagement as soon as I got over the stomach bug."

"What? Katie, that's a lie, I never said—"

"That's why I put off seeing you. She said you posted on your website you were looking for girlfriends."

"Freaking Tara. I should have known." Nick let out a long sigh. "Katie, the last thing I want is to break our engagement. I didn't even know the website existed until Tara told me about it. And I have no control over it, Ruby's staff runs it." He buried his face in her hair and breathed in the familiar, sweet scent. "The only thing I want is for us to be us again. I'd do the last three days over if I could. I know you're angry and I don't blame you."

"I *was* angry, Nick. I felt so sick last weekend, I could barely think." She touched his hand. "I shouldn't have let Tara get me upset. But I felt so hurt and her constant chattering about those models and all the women propositioning you on your website . . . it got to me." Katie smiled for the first time that evening. "Nick, I believe you didn't sleep with those models. I remembered what Chris told us at the party.

The awful lies about him in the press. Ruby's doing the same thing to you. Poor Chris. I heard about his death on the news. Do you think all the media pressure drove him to kill himself?"

"I don't know." He didn't want to think about poor Chris right now. Nick pressed his face deeper into Katie's hair and pulled her closer. *She believes me.* Relief and then shame flooded over him. He wondered if his guilt would ever go away. "If you believe me, then why would you think I wanted to break our engagement?"

"Because everything's changed."

"Nothing's changed."

"Yes, it has. You proposed to me before the VIP party—before you got a taste of fame and beautiful women falling all over you. Ruby insists on promoting you as an eligible bachelor. What if he drops you because you're engaged? You'd lose your book deal because of me. I was afraid you regretted proposing to me. I don't fit into your new life—"

He stopped her words by pressing his lips against hers. He wrapped his arms around and pulled her close. The need to lose himself in Katie's embrace overwhelmed him.

"Nick? If you're not breaking up with me, then what did you want to talk about tonight? You sounded so urgent."

He grabbed a throw pillow and covered his lap to hide his arousal. "I've missed you. Talking to you. Being with you. Making love to you. You're more important to me than a book deal or Ruby's crazy publicity stunts. None of it matters if I can't be with you. I want you in my life, every day, like it was before all this."

"I missed you, too," she said. "Three days is the longest we've ever been apart."

He picked up his wallet from the coffee table and took out a slip of paper. "Here."

"What's this?"

"My bank deposit slip."

"Sixty-thousand, three-hundred and eight. Wow! Is this from your book sales?"

"Look again," he said.

"Oh my God! Six-hundred and thirty-eight thousand dollars? Is that right?"

"Yeah, pretty wild, huh? My book's sold half a million copies. Plus the stupid posters and shirts."

"Nick, this is amazing. What are you going to do with it?"

"You tell me. You're the sensible one when it comes to money." He grinned. "But I do have one purchase I want to make."

"What's that?"

"Ruby's agreed to sell me the Mustang. Thirty thousand. Ray checked out the car. It's a good deal."

"You love that car. Now it'll be yours."

"That's my point, Katie. The VIP party, posters, that damn website, I hate all of it. I don't want to be dependent on Ruby for everything in my life. The car is only the first step. The second is I want you to move in with me. I'll pay Ruby rent. If you don't like this apartment, we'll find another place. Whatever you want to do."

"Oh." She fanned her flushed face with her hands.

"Are you all right?"

"Yes, it's just . . . I expected tonight to be awful. I'm so relieved. And happy."

He grinned. "Maybe you should go into the bedroom and lie down." He nuzzled his face against her neck.

She smiled and kissed him. "You can put that pillow down now."

Katie walked into the kitchen barefoot wearing one of Nick's tee shirts. She watched him roll out the flat bread dough and place it on a baking sheet.

"Nick, that ceiling mirror has got to go."

"Already talked to Ruby about it. His maintenance guys are taking it down this week."

"Good."

"Here, this is for you." Nick pointed to a legal pad and pen on the kitchen counter.

"What for?"

"I asked you to move in. You always make a list of the pros and cons before you make a decision."

Katie stretched her arms above her head and then hugged herself. "Unlimited access to your comfy tee shirts is a definite pro. But, how will your family feel about us living together? They're planning a big wedding. Nonna is so religious. We'd be living in sin, according to her."

"I'll be a very happy sinner," Nick said. "We're adults. And besides, they don't need to know."

"It wouldn't be right to lie to them."

"Not lie. Just not mention it."

"Tara will have to find a new roommate to cover half the rent."

"Don't expect me to feel bad for her after all the trouble she caused."

"How will I get to work? My apartment is close to the hospital so I can walk."

"I'll drive you."

"What if you have a meeting or something? I want to be able to get to work on my own."

"Then I'll buy you a car. It's not a big deal for me to drive you, though."

"I guess. But the Mustang's old. Is it reliable? What if there's a snowstorm?"

"It's fully restored with brand new parts. The car's old school, I can maintain it myself. And if it ever needs major work, my best friend, Ray, owns a classic car shop. Plus, there's a bus stop out front and a cab stand." Nick dried his hands and picked up the pen. He wrote on the pad and then turned it back toward Katie.

She read the items he wrote out loud. "What ifs . . . tsunami, earthquake, zombie invasion." She smacked his arm with the pad. "Very funny."

"Just wanted to make sure you covered all the cons."

"Fine." She wrote on the list.

He read her addition to the con list over her shoulder. "What? No appreciation for expensive lingerie?"

"The underwear on your bedroom floor cost me sixty dollars. You didn't even look at it."

"Sure I did. It was, um . . . pretty."

"You took my bra off before we made it to the bed. Then you pulled my thong off. With your teeth."

He grinned at her. "I'm not apologizing."

Katie laughed and shook her head. "I should have known better. It was Tara's idea to go to the mall tonight. After spending all that money, here I am, naked under one of your old T-shirts."

"You went clothes shopping with Tara?" Nick focused on cutting a tomato into thin slices.

"Yes." She sighed. "I let Tara brow beat me into stepping up my game, as she put it, to keep you interested. She said I needed to dress sexier, like the models at the VIP party. Stop wearing my frumpy nursing uniform."

"You couldn't look frumpy if you tried." Nick put the knife down and squeezed her hand. "Katie, please stop listening to Tara. She's a liar and wrong about everything."

"I usually don't listen. She is a drama queen. Guess I was feeling insecure."

"So, Tara drove you here?" He tried to sound nonchalant.

"No. She planned to, but we stayed too long at the mall. She barely had enough time to get to work. I rode back to the hospital with her. I was going to call you, but Jon offered me a ride. He lives near here."

"Did you ever think he might want to give you more than a ride?"

"Don't worry about Jon. He's a nice guy, but not my type. I think he has a girlfriend."

Nick breathed a sigh of relief as he slid the pan into the oven. He had jumped to conclusions about Gerber. "Hey, I want you to read something." He went to his desk and came back with a stack of papers. "I talked with Ruby's publisher today. I can't fix the first book, but I modified some chapters of the other two volumes to get my original story back, or close, at least. Your meticulous notes helped me a lot. Thank you."

Katie's face lit up. "Can I read it now?"

"If you want. Dinner's not for another thirty minutes."

He turned on the gas fireplace while Katie snuggled into a pile of pillows on the living room floor to read.

"I put your drink on the coffee table," Nick said.

Katie wrinkled her nose. "Oh, the wine—"

"I know you don't like wine. I made you a cup of tea." He slapped her bottom as he walked past on the way to the kitchen. "That's for listening to Tara."

"Nick, how could you do this?"

He dropped the hot pan on the cutting board and looked up. Katie stood at the counter with his manuscript pages in her hand.

"Do what?"

"Kill Julian."

"I had to. He sacrificed his life to save Caroline."

"Well, I absolutely hate it. Your new ending sucks."

Nick grunted and then smiled. "Don't sugar coat how you feel about it, babe."

"I can't help it. Julian and Caroline have to end up together."

"It doesn't work anymore since Ruby changed the first book. There's suspension of disbelief in any horror novel. There are also vampire rules, I can't change them. Remember the old vampire he met in the second volume who explained everything to him? In order to save a victim from becoming a vampire, you must kill the vampire who bit them. Diana tricked Julian into biting the reincarnated Caroline. Now he has to die in order to save her life. Period."

"Forget the vampire rules. The story is about their romance. After all they've been through, for over two centuries, readers will feel cheated with this ending."

"Julian is over two hundred years old, Katie. When he kills Diana, he becomes mortal and rapidly ages. Having an ancient dust-bag hook up with a twenty-year old woman, *that* would be real horror."

"You have to figure out another way then. I want Julian and Caroline to be together. Period. Killing himself, even to save her life, is not romantic."

"To give your life for someone else is the ultimate expression of love. Hell, it's biblical."

Katie shook her head. "For someone who's so sweet and passionate, how can you possibly think that's a romantic ending?"

Nick shook his head. "Dinner's ready."

"So, what do you think about moving in with me?"

"Let's see, you made love to me, cooked a gourmet dinner and now you're giving me a back rub in front of the fireplace." She closed her eyes and sighed. "You're making it difficult for me to say no."

"Say yes."

"I have to finish my list. Then wait twenty-four hours before making my decision. My list has rules. I can't change them."

"You're making me suffer for killing Julian, aren't you?"

"Maybe." She smiled. "I'll have to add gaining weight to the con side of the list." She picked up a piece of the herbed flat bread and dipped it into the pesto. "Dinner was incredible, Nick. If you hadn't decided to become a writer, you could have easily been a five-star chef."

"I enjoyed cooking at the restaurant. Unfortunately, no one has built a kitchen big enough for me and my father to be in at the same time." He picked up the legal pad. "You have nothing written on the pro side of your list."

Katie sat up and put her arms around his neck. She brushed her lips against his ear and whispered, "I will."

Nick lay with his head propped on his elbow watching Katie sleep next to him in bed. He rolled on his back and smiled up at their reflection in the ceiling mirror. If she didn't have to work in the morning, they would have stayed up all night talking about their future plans. Too excited to sleep, he quietly slipped out of bed so as not to wake her.

He walked to his desk and sat down at his computer. His new novel had stalled after three chapters. Writing under the pressure of a deadline was new to him, and he didn't want to sacrifice quality to meet the deadline. He opened his computer file of story ideas, hoping one might spark a plot strong enough to carry a full-length novel. Several of his ideas involved vampires, but since his trilogy featured vampires, he wanted something different. He scanned the short blurbs he had written about vengeful ghosts, pacts with the devil and a modern-day witches coven. Another file held dozens of short horror stories he had written. Joseph Cullen had published several short story collections. Nick decided he'd email Ruby's publisher, Jack, about doing his own book of short stories. It would buy him time to work on a new novel. He liked working directly with the publisher, rather than with Ruby. Jack was knowledgeable, welcomed Nick's ideas and was eager to work with him.

He pulled a small stack of business cards from his wallet and found the publisher's card wedged between Joseph Cullen's and Victor Ruby's. After sending Jack the email, he started to slide the cards back into his wallet.

The phrase on the back of Victor Ruby's card caught his eye. He worried he might have writer's block. The phrase worked for that asshole Cullen and if Ruby expected Nick to outsell him, he figured he'd give it a try. Unsure how to pronounce the words, he sounded each one out loud. *"Peta Babkama Luruba Dalkhu Anaku."* He laughed to himself as he sat with his fingers poised over the keyboard waiting for instant inspiration to strike. After a minute or two, he felt silly and went back to searching through his idea files.

The apartment grew warm. Although certain he had turned it off before they went to bed, Nick got up and checked the fireplace. The glass front felt cool and no flames burned inside the hearth. Yet, the temperature in the room continued to climb. He opened the living room window. The cool night air offered no relief from the rising heat. Perspiration soaked through Nick's tee shirt and sweat rolled in rivulets from his scalp, down his forehead, and into his eyes. He checked the thermostat on the wall. The digital display read seventy-two, but the air felt more like one hundred and seventy-two degrees.

An odor of sulfur mixed with charred wood filled his nostrils. Maybe there's a gas leak or electrical fire. He hurried to the bedroom to check on Katie. Hesitating in the bedroom doorway, he wondered if he should wake her, but then decided to let her sleep. He looked around the kitchen and examined the gas range. All of the knobs were in the off position and the foul odor wasn't coming from the oven.

From the corner of eye, he saw movement in the living room. In spite of the oppressive heat, a chill ran down his back as he hurried to investigate. He found nothing unusual or out of place.

Returning to the kitchen, he grabbed a dish towel, wet it with cold water and pressed it against his sweaty face. His body burned with a feverish heat. The last thing he needed was to get sick, he had too much to do. The cold towel helped. As he lowered the towel to run it under the water again, a smoky, black mass hanging in the air inches from his face startled him. His mind reeled to make sense of it.

The swirling black mist slowly formed into a face, suspended bodiless in the air, with dark cavernous eye sockets and a gaping hole for a mouth. Two tiny red points appeared in the blackened voids where eyes should be. They burned brighter and grew larger. His initial confusion turned to terror. His heartbeat raced, yet his arms hung like lead pipes at his sides and his legs stood frozen. His mind screamed for him to run, but his body refused to react. The suffocating stench of sulfur made him gasp for air. He stared, open-mouthed and paralyzed, as the undulating face loomed closer and expanded. Long black tendrils stretched down into the shape of a body beneath the gruesome head. Shadowy arms lunged out and hot fingers clutched his throat. Nick willed his stiffened arms to move. He clawed at the air around his neck, but his fingers passed through the vaporous claws that strangled him. His vision narrowed to a long tunnel focused on two burning red circles at the end. A wriggling sensation like thousands of fiery worms burrowing beneath his skin revolted him. Blackness engulfed him.

When he opened his eyes, he found himself sitting at a desk in front of a laptop computer. A red haze colored the room. He squinted at the blurry text on the computer screen but couldn't focus his eyes to read it. He stood on unsteady feet. His body felt uncoordinated and his legs lurched in a stiff, awkward motion when he walked. The apartment and its furnishings were unfamiliar. He slowly dragged his feet across the floor and scrutinized everything in the room. A leather jacket lay draped over an easy chair across from the kitchen. He picked it up with rigid fingers, raised it to his face and breathed in a floral scent from the jacket's lining.

An open case of knives on the kitchen counter drew his attention. The bright ceiling light reflected in the shiny, steel blades. Mesmerized, he ran his fingertips over each one, admiring how they gleamed and shone. He selected a fillet knife and pulled it from its strap. The sight of the finely-honed edge and long, slender blade sent a shiver of excitement through his body. The handle felt good in his hand. His coordination returned. He turned and walked toward the partially open door at the end of the hall. The same sweet scent from the jacket, only stronger, enticed him to enter the darkened room.

He stood at the foot of the bed and watched the woman sleep. Long blond hair partially covered her face. The sheet clung to her body. Her deep, slow breathing teased him, alternately pulling the material taut across her breasts when she inhaled, and then loosened when she exhaled. Women always teased him, mocked him. They were inherently cruel creatures. He despised them.

He flexed his fingers to adjust his grip on the knife handle. It felt like a familiar old friend. He focused on the woman in the bed. This one wouldn't tease him anymore. The anticipation of the razor-sharp blade slicing into her flesh aroused him. He planned each thrust, each slice, and thought about her blood soaking into the white sheets. Each stick of the blade had to be done slowly, carefully, or else his pleasure would end too soon. She'd beg him to stop, promise to do anything he wanted. But he knew it was a trick, lies to distract him from his work. Soon she would lie helpless and bloody, like the others.

He relished the thought of releasing the coppery scent of her blood. Letting it envelop him like a lover's perfume. He licked his lips in anticipation of the warm, salty drops splattering across his face. The final slash would be to her throat. He'd savor the gurgling sound as air mixed with the blood. He would gaze into her eyes, her pupils wide with terror, and watch until they turned glassy, and then finally, dull. Dead.

He drew a deep breath, smiled and raised the knife.

The woman stirred and opened her eyes. "Nick?" She shielded her eyes with one hand against the light from the open door behind him.

Nick's body shook. His limbs jerked with the sudden spasms. Gasping, he forced his fingers to release their vice-like grip on the knife handle. It dropped from his hand and banged against the wooden sideboard of the bed.

"What are you doing?" Katie pushed herself up into a sitting position.

Doubled over with convulsions, he pressed his arms tightly across his stomach. He coughed, wretched and defied the voice which screamed inside his head to pick up the knife and stab Katie. He kicked the knife away from his reach. It slid soundlessly across the carpet and disappeared into the dark void under the bed.

"Are you sick?" Katie swung her legs over the side of the bed. "What's wrong?"

"N-nothing," he stammered. "Go back to sleep." He turned and grabbed the door knob. Twisting the lock on the inside knob, he pulled the bedroom door shut, locking Katie in and himself out. He staggered into the bathroom and locked the door. Hunched over the sink, he vomited.

"Nick? Are you all right?" Katie wiggled the bathroom door knob.

He rinsed away the vomit and then splashed cold water on his face.

"Open the door. Let me help you."

"I'm . . . all right. J-Just sick." He leaned on the counter with shaking arms and stared at his reflection in the mirror. His face wet and void of color except for an odd glint of red in his eyes. His clothing, drenched with sweat, stuck to his trembling body.

"Sweetie, let me in." She gently knocked on the door. "I'm a nurse, remember? I've seen sick people before."

He unlocked the door and opened it a crack. "I need some time. I threw up."

Katie pushed the door open and put her hand on his forehead. "You're pretty warm," she said, "but it looks like your fever broke. You're soaked in sweat."

His muscles tensed as she touched him, and a burning sensation crawled through his veins. The red haze returned, clouding his vision and his thoughts turned dark. Grab the bitch by the hair, drag her to the bed, get the knife. . .. The bloody images flashing in his mind first thrilled and then revolted him. He fought the murderous urges. Bile rose in the back of his throat. He turned and heaved into the sink basin.

Katie wet a wash cloth and pressed it against his forehead. She cradled his head between the cool cloth and her other hand clasped on the back of his neck. "You need to get out of these wet clothes."

The softness in her voice and the scent of her perfume fanned a dark fire inside him. He had to make Katie leave before his last thread of self-control snapped.

"I-I'm going to take a shower. Go back to bed. Leave me alone."

He saw her hurt expression as she turned to leave. "I'll get you some clean clothes."

Nick twisted the door lock after she exited. He struggled to peel off his wet clothes and stepped into the shower. He turned the cold water on full force. The jolting spray calmed the intense burning in his body and he leaned his back against the cool tile wall and let the water flow over him. He slowly slid down the shower wall and sat. He buried his face in his hands to muffle his sobs as the icy water flooded over him.

Shivering, he reached over and turned off the faucet. He rubbed himself dry with a towel and inched open the door. A clean pair of sweat pants and a tee shirt hung on the outside door knob. The bedroom door stood wide open. Katie lay sleeping in the bed. He locked the bedroom knob and shut the door. He didn't trust himself to be near Katie.

He dressed and found a blanket in the linen closet. Wrapping it around himself, he shuffled to the living room. It was after four in the morning. He had been in the shower for three hours. Cold and exhausted, he huddled on the couch and tried to make sense of what happened.

Katie would be waking soon to get ready for work. She expected him to drive her to the hospital. The thought of being alone with her in the car made him shudder more than the chills that wracked his body.

He pulled the blanket tighter. What had come over him and what if it happened again? He drew his knees up under the blanket and squeezed his eyes shut. Tears leaked down his face.

He wanted to kill Katie.

Chapter 12

Nick opened his eyes. A tiny gold cross dangled inches above his face. His gaze followed the delicate chain up to Katie's neck. She leaned over him dressed in her nursing uniform.

"I didn't mean to wake you. I was checking your temperature," she said. "Your fever's gone."

"What time is it?" he asked.

"A few minutes before seven."

He struggled to sit up. "I have to drive you to work."

Katie gently pushed on his shoulders. "No, you need to stay here and rest. I called a cab. It'll be here in a few minutes."

"I'm sorry," he closed his eyes and sank back into the couch. "I'm so sorry."

"There's nothing to be sorry about. You're sick. I wish I could stay and take care of you, but I couldn't find anyone to cover for me on such short notice."

"No. You go to work. I'll be fine. I just need to rest."

"I fell asleep waiting for you to get out of the shower last night." She smoothed her hand through his hair and smiled. "I thought you'd drowned in there. I tried to check on you, but the door was locked."

"Sorry," he mumbled.

"Stop apologizing, you're allowed to get sick. Apparently, you don't like to be fussed over," Katie said. "I made hot tea and toast. It's on the coffee table." She walked into the kitchen and returned with a pitcher and glass. "Drink some water. You're probably dehydrated."

"Thank you." He pushed himself into a sitting position and gulped down the water.

She refilled his glass. "The coffee pot is set up, push the button if you want coffee later."

A horn beeped outside. Katie glanced out the front window. "There's my cab." She kissed Nick's forehead. "I'll call later to check on you. Feel better. Love you."

"Thanks."

A wave of relief washed over him when Katie closed the front door. He picked up the water pitcher and drained it dry. Easing himself up from the couch, he walked to the bathroom to urinate. Katie had draped his clothes over the shower door. They were still soaking wet. He wandered into the kitchen in a daze and slammed the lid closed on the case of knives.

Across from the kitchen, a flashing orange light on his printer caught his eye. It signaled an empty paper tray. He didn't remember printing anything. He hurried to the laptop and cleared the screen saver.

As he read the text on the screen, his heart beat sped. These weren't his words.

The story began with a man peering into a woman's window and fantasizing about killing her. He was someone the woman knew, and she let him into her home. From the detailed descriptions, he knew immediately the female character was Katie and the setting, her apartment. He scrolled quickly over the graphic paragraphs detailing how the man attacked, tortured and then eventually killed her. Each bloody knife thrust was described in gory, yet gleeful, adjectives. The torture scene continued for pages.

More pages described the blood. The scent of it, how it pooled on the white linoleum kitchen floor and splattered across the walls and the furniture. *Pools of blood glimmered like huge rubies on the white tile floor.* Nick's stomach quaked. Had he eaten anything he would have vomited. He selected all the text and hit the delete key. He kept punching the key long after the page was nothing more than a blank window and a blinking cursor. Shaking, he slammed the laptop closed.

Ruby's card lay on the desk next to his wallet and laptop. Everything had started after he read the phrase on the back of the card. He stared at the card as if it were an insect. He flipped it over. The back was blank.

The computer's digital clock displayed seven-thirty. He ran to the kitchen and called Stephanie.

"Hey," she answered. "I'm in line at Starbucks, what's up?"

"I'll be there at eight when the office opens. I have to see Ruby," he said.

"I don't know what his schedule is today. I'll call you when I get into—"

"No! I'm leaving now." Nick ended the call even though Stephanie was still talking.

He rushed to the bedroom and dressed. He knelt on the floor and strained to reach the fillet knife under the bed. His cell rang, he jumped up and ran to the kitchen to answer it.

"I called Mr. Ruby. He's at the office now, but said he'd be leaving in a few minutes. He'll be gone all day," Stephanie told him.

Nick hit the end button as he ran to his desk, grabbed his wallet, keys and Ruby's card. On the way out the door, he scooped up his grandfather's knife case.

Nick stormed past Stephanie at her desk and strode straight to Ruby's office door. He grabbed the handle, but it wouldn't turn. He banged on the door. "I have to talk to you. Now!"

Stephanie held the phone to her ear staring at him. "Please hold." She pressed a button on her console. "Nick? What–?"

He leaned across her desk. "Where is he?"

"Mr. Ruby left ten minutes ago." She rolled her chair back.

He banged his fist on her desk knocking over a pen holder. "Where did he go?"

Stephanie stood, her eyes darted from Nick to the outer door. "I, I don't know. He didn't say."

He moved around the desk, blocking her path. "Call him. Tell him I need to see him."

"Okay. I'll tell him . . . if he calls in."

"What do mean if he calls in? Don't you have his cell number?"

"Y-yes."

"Then call it. Now. Let me talk to him."

"I'm not supposed to call his cell unless it's an emergency. I'll get in trouble—"

Nick grabbed her arm. "This is an emergency. Call the sonofabitch."

"Nick, you're scaring me."

He released her arm and took a step back.

Stephanie's hand shook as she dialed the phone. "It's ringing," she said.

He snatched the phone from her hand and listened. "Damn it. His mailbox." He paced as far as the phone cord would stretch while he waited for a signal to leave a message. "This is Nick Teravelli. I have to see you today. It's urgent. Call me."

Stephanie jumped as he slammed the receiver down.

He continued to pace around the waiting room, rubbing his hands over his face.

Stephanie stood frozen in place, gaping. "What's wrong Nick?"

He whirled to face her. "The other night, you said Ruby had Chris killed. And that you had seen and heard stuff. What did you mean?"

"Uh, I, I don't know. I was drunk. Upset about Chris." She cowered against the wall as Nick loomed over her.

"What was it you saw and heard?"

She cringed and shielded her face with her hands when he raised his arm and reached for hers.

"I wasn't going to hit—" He ran his raised hand through his hair and sighed. "I'm sorry, Steph." He backed away and sat on the corner of her desk.

"I only meant stuff like Ruby always called Chris horrible names. And how they fought all the time." Stephanie's voice quivered and tears shone in her eyes. "Now he makes horrible jokes about Chris's death."

"When Ruby calls, tell him to call me right away, understand?"

"Yes."

Nick opened the door to leave. "What time did he say he'd be back?"

"Late. After five."

He sat in his car in the parking lot of Ruby Promotions, next to the empty space with a sign that read Victor Ruby, CEO. If Ruby wasn't returning until after five o'clock, he would have an eight hour wait. Yet, he didn't know who else he could turn to for answers. He slipped Ruby's card from his wallet and examined the back. Blank. The strange words that he read had to be related to what he experienced last night.

He remembered standing by the bed holding the knife. It wasn't a dream, yet he had felt like a horrified observer, trapped within his own mind and body, unable to control either, and forced to watch as his own hand stabbed Katie to death. The business card fluttered in his trembling hand when he thought how close he had come to plunging the blade into Katie. Then he remembered the filet knife. "Shit. I left it under the bed." He had locked the case of knives inside the trunk of his car to get them out of the apartment. He needed to retrieve the knife.

As he slid Ruby's card back into his wallet, he saw Joseph Cullen's card. Ruby said Cullen recited the Latin phrase all the time. Cullen must know something. Nick straightened up in the driver's seat and turned the ignition. He had wanted to pay Cullen a visit after the way he'd treated Katie at the VIP party. Old man or not, if he had to, he'd beat the truth out of Cullen.

Nick eased the Mustang into a space in front of a rundown, six-story brick tenement. He climbed out of the car and checked the address printed on Cullen's card. It must be a mistake. A famous author like Joseph Cullen wouldn't live here. Tall weeds grew up through the trash-littered, narrow strip of dirt that posed as a lawn between the sidewalk and the building. Obscenities, initials and symbols were scrawled in spray paint across the building's red brick facade.

He pulled on the horizontal steel bar to open one of the grimy double doors. The rusty protest of its hinges echoed inside the dank-smelling entrance.

As his eyes adjusted to the dim hallway, he found a row of doors to his right and a metal staircase to his left. A bank of mailboxes faced him on the narrow wall separating the hall from the stairs. Some of the mailbox doors were missing and most had no names. The box marked 3-C sported a shiny black label with *J. Cullen* printed in raised white lettering.

Nick took a few tentative steps down the hallway. Cigarette butts littered the worn mosaic tile floor. Beer cans, food wrappers and other trash drifted into piles in the corners and a foul-smelling puddle lured a cloud of buzzing flies. The first battered metal door had no identifying numbers. The second door had a tarnished gold 1-B on it. Cullen's apartment number, 3-C, must be on the third floor.

Nick sprinted up the staircase. The second-floor landing and corridor looked equally as filthy as the first. A sour, vomit-like stench hung in the air. Down the hall, behind one of the closed doors, a man and woman argued, their angry shouts punctuated by the piercing screams of a baby.

Footsteps descending above him drew his attention. Clear acrylic stacked heels attached to skinny white legs walked down the third-floor staircase. The woman stopped a few steps above the second-floor landing where Nick stood. Excruciatingly thin with stringy hair, she wore a wrinkled, red mini dress. Her dull blue eyes studied him cautiously.

"Looking for some action, honey?" she asked.

"No." Nick climbed the stairs, staying close to the wall to keep his distance from the prostitute.

"Ah, don't fly away, pigeon," a deep male voice called from above. His laughter boomed in the hollow stairwell.

The woman turned and looked up the stairs. "Crazy ass freak!" The loud clopping of her plastic heels on the metal steps faded to light taps as she descended. The sound disappeared with the metallic squeal of the bar on the front door.

The laughter stopped. A slim, grey-haired man in a navy-blue bathrobe stood at the top of the stairs. His robe appeared hastily tied, gaping open above his waist and revealing a thick mat of gray chest hair. The hem grazed his bony knees above pale shins. Although his hair looked unwashed and stuck out at wild angles, Nick recognized him immediately.

"Cullen!" Nick yelled. "I came to talk to you."

"How nice." Cullen spun around on his bare heels and sauntered down the hallway. "I don't wish to talk to you."

"Wait!" Nick ran up the remaining steps and followed Cullen down the hall. "I met you at the VIP party. I'm Nick. You told me to call you."

Cullen stopped. "I said call, not come to my home."

"There's no phone number on your card, only this address," Nick said.

"Exactly. So, when someone tells you to call them and gives you a card without a phone number . . ." Cullen's voice trailed off and he waved his hands above his head. He turned and faced Nick. "Besides, I distinctly remember giving my card to your blond lady friend." He flicked his tongue between his thin lips and gave a lewd grin. "The luscious nurse."

Nick lunged at him.

"Don't step on my bread crumbs!" Cullen shouted, pointing at the floor. Nick stopped, his fingertips grazing the collar of Cullen's robe. He looked down at the floor and saw crumpled balls of paper money scattered among discarded liquor bottles and trash. Denominations of twenty and fifty dollars were visible on some of the bills. The money trail led down the hall and into an open doorway.

"Bread crumbs? You mean the money?"

"Money is bread crumbs for my little birds." Cullen spun around and disappeared through the open door.

Nick followed, stepping over the trash on the floor, but then stopped in the doorway. The apartment's interior was dark and the only sound, a steady, rhythmic, whirring noise he couldn't quite place. Odors of cigarette smoke and stale liquor barely masked an ammonia stench of urine. Thin rays of sunlight sliced through openings in the bent slats of the window blinds on the far wall, illuminating the gray haze of smoke hovering in the air.

"What is it you want, Nick?" Cullen called out. "I'm a busy man." He giggled. It disintegrated into a low, growling sound which made Nick's scalp crawl.

As his eyes adjusted to the darkness, he saw Cullen seated in an upholstered chair a few feet away to his right. "What do you know about the writing on the back of Ruby's business card? He said you recite the words every time you start a new book."

A click and then a small flame illuminated Cullen's face. The glowing orange ember on the end of his cigarette bobbed when Cullen spoke. "Drink?" He held up a liquor bottle and wiped his mouth on the sleeve of his robe.

"No. Tell me what the phrase on the card means."

Cullen hoisted himself from the chair. He drained the bottle as he walked toward Nick. "What do you think it means?"

"Ruby said it was an old Latin quotation. Something about opening your mind to inspiration. But that's not true, is it?"

Cullen brushed past Nick and tossed the empty bottle out the front door into the hallway. It hit the floor with a loud clunk and rolled across the tile until a pile of trash swallowed and silenced it. Cullen crouched down and peered around the edge of the doorway. "Pigeon? Is that you?"

"The girl left, Cullen. I heard her go out the front door."

"They always come back. They can't resist my bread crumbs." He cackled as he plucked a balled-up bill from the threshold. "See? One hundred. They know they have to come closer for the bigger crumbs. Then, I—" He made a quick snatching motion in the air with his hand.

"You sick sonofabitch. Tell me what those words on the card mean."

Cullen stood and skirted around Nick into a small kitchen across from the living room. He flipped on a light switch. Nick recoiled in disgust. Hordes of cockroaches scuttled across the counter tops and floor. They burrowed under stacks of dishes crusted with the molding remains of unidentifiable foods. More roaches tunneled into the putrid-smelling mounds of garbage which had overflowed the trash can and spilled onto the floor. Cullen appeared oblivious to the crawling landscape surrounding him. He opened a cabinet door above the stove and selected a Jim Beam bottle from the well-stocked shelf.

He strolled to the living room and flopped into his chair. The bare bulb on the kitchen ceiling threw a harsh yellow light across the foyer into the living room. With the exception of the chair Cullen sat in, stacks of white paper covered the floor and the furniture. Some piles nearly touched the ceiling. An old computer monitor flickered on a desk in one corner of the room. Text appeared on the screen line by line as if someone were typing it. The steady whirring sound came from a printer next to the computer. It spat out sheet after sheet of paper. The collection tray full, the excess pages fell in a disheveled heap on the floor.

"Stay away from my books!" Cullen shouted. "You came to steal my ideas, didn't you?"

"I don't give a damn about your books, or you." Nick stood over him with clenched fists. "Tell me about the words."

"Tell you what? About the demons?" Cullen's voice cracked. He let out a shrill cackle, higher pitched than his previous laughter. "So, Victor told you it was an old Latin quotation!" He doubled over in his chair, shrieking with laughter, clenching his stomach and the whiskey bottle.

Nick shook Cullen by the shoulders. "What does it say? What does it do?"

"Have you tried saying it out loud, Nick?"

"Y-yes, only once."

"Ah, only once. Well, Nick, once is all it takes. Mammon, father of all lies, he is clever."

"What the hell are you talking about? Who's Mammon?"

Cullen stood and paced around the tight maze of paper stacks. "Victor Ruby. Also known as The Devourer, fallen angel, Lucifer, Beelzebub, the Son of Perdition, the Great Deceiver, and my personal favorite, Ol' Scratch." He dragged on his cigarette and cocked his head sideways to peer up at Nick. "You're not very informed for a horror writer, Nick. How about we just keep it simple and call him Satan? Or perhaps, you'd prefer the devil?"

"You're telling me Victor Ruby is the devil?"

"No, Nick." Cullen winked. "*We're* telling you Victor Ruby is the devil."

Cullen's body shivered and convulsed. His head twisted at an odd angle atop his neck and his shoulders and hips jerked in violent spasms. His bones shifted, stretching Cullen's skin as they poked beneath it with dull, clicking noises. His arms twisted and writhed at his sides like two thick snakes, into positions human arms couldn't form. Cullen's mouth opened; stretching wider and wider, as if invisible hands pried independently at his upper and lower jaws. A chorus of voices, some deep, some shrill, some in odd-sounding languages, screamed obscenities. All of the voices joined together and screamed simultaneously, "Hail Satan!"

Heart pounding, Nick backed toward the open door. "You're fucking insane."

Cullen leered at him with glittering red eyes. Nick stepped back into the hallway.

"Wait." The voice sounded tired, hoarse and old. "I'll tell you."

Nick inched his feet across the threshold.

Cullen collapsed into his chair. His eyes glassy, but no longer red. Beads of sweat dotted his forehead and upper lip. "The phrase is from an ancient satanic ritual. Sumerian devil worship. An invitation for demons to enter your body. To allow them to see through your eyes, use your mind and hands to perform whatever disgusting depravities they wish." Cullen took a long swig of whiskey. "Of course, ol' Victor has his people ready to clean up the mess. He prefers his demons have access to free and prominent citizens. They can do the most damage that way." He swept a limp arm in the air. "And in return, you get all of this."

Nick recalled finding himself at the foot of the bed, clutching a knife. He shuddered. Something vile and evil had controlled him. Had he been possessed by a demon? It had taken every ounce of his will to suppress the overwhelming desire to kill Katie. And the disturbing writing on his computer screen, he hadn't typed those words. He glanced over at Cullen's printer. The steady hum had stopped. A red light blinked on the front panel.

"They write my books for me now." Cullen struggled to his feet. "They need my body for . . . other things." He placed a new ream of paper in the empty tray. The whirring sound resumed. More sheets cascaded in rapid succession and joined the chaotic paper carpet covering the floor.

Nick stared at him. "I only said the phrase once. I'll never say it again. I'll burn the damn card. That will stop it, right?"

Cullen shook his head. "Too late. You opened a portal in your soul. Victor has so many souls trapped in hell. The worst of the worst. He's promised them a way to wreak havoc on earth again. We're their fleshy puppets. Their means to inflict pain, to rape and to murder. You can't stop them, Nick. They wait and overtake us when we are weak. They slip into us during our anger, exhaustion, fear . . . even in the throes of an orgasm." Cullen trailed off into laughter. His hunched shoulders shook, and he clamped his hand over his mouth to muffle the piercing squeals. "They use your vices against you. Mine are women and alcohol. First, it's one or two demons, but then others follow. Soon a never-ending deluge of filth floods your soul and controls your body, your mind, your will. They're relentless. They'll find a way into you. They *always* find a way."

"Why would Ruby turn people he can make money with into criminals?"

"Why does a snake bite?" Cullen made a snorting sound. "Victor doesn't care about money. He thrives on creating chaos. And if one of us is destroyed in the process, so be it. He has a thousand others to take our place. The demons have tired of my old, worn-out body. But, now they have you, my younger, stronger replacement."

"How long have you been . . . possessed?"

"Ever since I signed with Ruby. I wanted best-selling books, fame, money, and women. Especially women, after my wife . . . left me." Cullen bent and picked up his whiskey bottle.

"There's got to be a way to stop it."

The weariness in Cullen's eyes faded leaving a hard, red-tinted gleam in its place. A gruff voice bellowed from deep within him. "Get the hell out! I have work to do." He shuffled to a closed door between the living room and kitchen. As he opened it, Nick glimpsed a woman's body draped across a bed. Streaks of dark red stained the sheet hanging over the edge of the bed. Cullen slipped inside and slammed the door. The lock clicked.

The woman's sudden, raw scream jarred Nick. His dry throat contracted, and his heart raced. He banged on the door with his fists. "Cullen! Open the door!"

He backed up and then lunged forward, heaving his shoulder into the door. Searing heat scorched his shirt sleeve and burnt his skin. His feet lifted off the ground and his body hurled backwards. He landed in the kitchen doorway, his head slamming against the door jamb. He lay dazed, terrified by the unseen force that had flung him across the room.

He scrambled to his feet and bolted out the front door. He saw the top of the blond prostitute's head. Her pale, bony arm snaked through a gap in the bars of the railing. She stood on the steps below straining to reach the wadded balls of money. Nick kicked some of Cullen's bread crumbs closer to the railing as he rushed past. The girl snatched them up and stuffed them into the neckline of her dress.

"Get out of here! He'll hurt you," Nick yelled. He ran past her down the stairs.

"Wait!" the girl called out.

Nick paused on the second-floor landing and looked up at her.

"You're cute. I'd do you for half price." Her cracked lips parted in a lop-sided smile, revealing stained teeth.

He ran down the remaining two flights of stairs. Shoving open the front door, he gulped in the fresh air. Sunlight hurt his eyes. He jogged to his car, relieved to find it still intact where he had parked it. After several attempts, his trembling hand finally fitted the key into the ignition and started the Mustang. He threw the gear shift into drive and floored the gas pedal. A fantail of smoke and gravel flew from the rear tires as he sped away.

He drove to a more familiar neighborhood. At a corner gas station, he found a lone, operational pay phone. Dialing 9-1-1, he anonymously reported a murder in progress at Cullen's address. When the dispatcher asked for his name, he hung up and prayed the police would hurry.

Nick drove around the city in a daze, trying to process what he had seen and heard at Cullen's apartment. He finally pulled over on a small side street and parked. A neon sign beckoned to him. It flashed Do Drop Inn.

It was dim and cool inside the shot-gun style building. A long bar ran down one side and empty tables and chairs lined the other. A handful of middle-aged men sat at the far end of the bar under a cloud of cigarette smoke watching a baseball game on a large screen television.

Nick sat on a stool at the other end, near the front window.

"What'll it be, honey?" The woman behind the bar smiled at him as she ran a rag across the lacquered bar top.

"Bud. Bottle." He peeled bills from his wallet and laid them on the bar. The woman returned and placed a coaster and an icy bottle of beer in front of him. She picked a five-dollar bill from the stack. After ringing the sale on the cash register, she placed his change on the bar.

"We got lunch specials if you're hungry." She offered a folded paper menu.

"No, thanks."

She leaned forward displaying a maze of crinkly lines radiating from the deep crevice where her breasts slammed together inside her tank top. "Let me know if you change your mind. Big Dave's a decent cook." She nodded her head toward a pass-through in the wall at the end of the bar. A large man in a white tee shirt with a bandanna tied around his bald head flipped burgers on a grill. The bartender turned and strolled to the other end of the bar. She plucked a burning cigarette from an ashtray and turned her attention to the television.

Nick checked his cell phone. Ruby hadn't called, but there was a voice mail from Katie.

"I didn't want to call and wake you in case you were sleeping. Hope you're feeling better. I changed my rules. It hasn't been 24 hours, but I couldn't wait to tell you. My answer is yes, I'll move in with you. I love you. Call me when you get this."

He put his phone down on the bar and cradled his head in his hands. There was no way he could allow Katie to move in with him now. He picked up the phone and called Stephanie.

"Ruby International Promotions. How may I help you?"

"Has Ruby called in yet?"

"Nick? No, not yet. But if he does, I'll—"

He ended the call.

"Ready for another?" The bartender stood smiling in front of him. Sunlight from the front window turned the white-blond frizz on her head into a misshapen halo. He finished the first beer in one long gulp and nodded yes to another.

Rush hour traffic crawled. His mind muddled after hours of drinking beer in the dim bar. Nick cursed, slammed his foot on the brake and sat through another red light. The trek was painfully slow. At ten past five he finally staggered into the elevator in the lobby of Ruby's office building.

The outside office door stood open. Stephanie was gone. He went straight to Ruby's door and pounded on it. "Ruby!" No answer and the door was locked when he tried the knob. He punched the door and then stumbled around the reception room kicking over chairs and cursing.

Ruby's door swung open, startling him. "Problem, Mr. Tera?"

"You never called me back!" Nick shouted. He followed Ruby into his office.

"You're obviously drunk and also confused. I don't answer to you, Nick."

"Your card. Your damn card with those damn words." Nick grabbed Ruby's silver business card holder and dumped the cards onto his desk. He shuffled through them, frantically turning each one over, but all of the backs were blank. "The words. I know what they do."

Ruby sat and clasped his hands behind his neck. He grinned, showing white, perfect teeth.

"Damn you! You fucking sonofabitch! You think it's funny? I almost killed Katie last night!" Nick lurched across the desk and took a swing at Ruby's face. Before his fist could make contact, a sudden pressure on his chest shoved him back. He landed hard in the chair facing Ruby. The chair didn't move, and the impact knocked the air from his lungs. He struggled to catch his breath and stand but couldn't move. Something held him in the chair.

"Having trouble with your inner demons?" Ruby sneered.

Nick gasped. "What the hell is happening to me? It's true, isn't it? Cullen's not crazy. Y-you are the devil, aren't you?"

"So you talked to ol' Joe?" As Ruby stood, his body grew larger and taller until he towered over Nick. The skin on his face and hands deepened from his normal ruddy complexion to a fiery red with the texture of coarse-grained leather. Horns sprouted through the skin on his forehead and spiraled outward and then upward until the pointed tips scraped the ceiling. "So, I have you to thank for Cullen's arrest today."

Nick stared, stunned by the apparition before him. Words tumbled from his lips. "Cullen's a twisted pervert. I had to stop him. He lures prostitutes into his apartment and . . . and kills them."

"Everyone has their vices, Nick. I don't judge people." Ruby's voice thundered inside the office. "Of course, with Cullen in jail, or a mental hospital, and Slaughter dead, I'll be expecting so much more from you."

Nick tried to stand, but invisible hands held him tight to the chair. The air temperature rose. His nostrils burned when he inhaled, and his skin felt as though he were inches from an open fire. "What the hell do you want from me?"

"The same thing I want from all my clients. To honor your end of the contract."

"Honor? You lied about the words on the card."

"I didn't lie. You were inspired, were you not?"

"Inspired to torture and to murder."

"Well, if you want to split hairs." Ruby chuckled as he moved around the desk. "I kept my end of the contract. You're a published author. A rising star in the literary world with more money than you've ever seen in your entire pathetic life. That is what you wanted, isn't it?"

"Not like this! Forget the book. Take back the money, the car and the damn apartment. Just make whatever it is inside me stop."

"It's too late. You signed a contract."

Paralyzed in the chair, Nick stared up at the horrific creature looming over him. The heat radiating from it dried the sweat pouring from his forehead before it reached his eyes.

"The contract. All that fine print. I sold you my soul?"

A rumble grew deep inside Ruby's chest and exploded from his mouth in deafening peals of laughter. "This is always my favorite part. *The devil took my soul!* All of you humans are the same." He walked back to his chair and sat. "Your precious little souls."

Nick blinked his eyes. Ruby had transformed back into his human form.

Ruby leaned forward. "Screw your soul. Why would I waste so much time and effort for one soul when I can use you to get thousands. Maybe millions."

"What are you talking about?"

"Listen." Ruby waved his hand toward his computer station. A steady *ding, ding* filled the room. "Do you know what that sound is, Nick?"

Nick shook his head.

"It's the sound of lust-struck women joining your fan club. We posted it yesterday on your website."

"You're going to take their souls?"

"First their minds and bodies, eventually their souls. Of course, it's only an experiment. He's bound me by certain rules." Ruby glowered up at the ceiling. "But the Internet is a marvel. The ability to reach out and influence so many. I'm not certain if an impersonal electronic signature is enough. There's still that elusive human element missing. The minuscule piece of DNA left behind as a hand holds pen to paper." Ruby lit a cigar and leaned back in his chair, smiling. "It's a numbers game, Nick. He has so many, and I have so many. All I need to do is tip the scales in my favor."

He thought of Tara bragging how she'd joined his fan club online. "What happens when they join this fan club?"

"Ideally if they express enough desire, one click of the mouse and they'll be mine. They'll be emailed a membership with a phrase inserted. Not too worry, there's also plan B, a bit slower than I'd like, but workable. They sign up and we send them a slick little package in the mail. Very Madison Avenue. Glossy. Full color. The Nick Tera official fan club packet. They'll receive your signed photograph, a coupon toward the purchase of your books or poster. And a membership card with a secret phrase."

"The same phrase you gave me?"

"There are many phrases, Nick. Once they recite the words, another portal opens. Another opportunity for one of my poor, tortured souls to take human form again. Eventually, the world descends into chaos. And, I am the ruler of chaos." Ruby waved his arms in the air as if directing an orchestra. "Chaos is a beautiful rhapsody. I'm its conductor."

"I won't have any part of this."

"You will play a big part in this, Nick. I chose you."

"Why? Why me? Was it my book?"

Ruby grinned and tapped his cigar into the ashtray. "Your book? Hardly. Horror writers are a dime a dozen. There are hordes of amateurs clamoring to be published. Ah, don't pout Nick, your writing is acceptable, and even if it were pure drivel, I have a staff of professionals to rewrite it. I didn't choose you for your writing."

"Then why?"

"You're a handsome young man, Nick. You possess both sex appeal and that certain X factor. I knew you'd attract female fans. Slaughter was supposed to lure in the females. But who knew a writer would outperform a rock star? You also expressed genuine desire. And despite your Catholic upbringing, I sensed you have a conflict with God. Am I right?"

"No, you're wrong. I believe in God."

"Do you remember your answer when I asked you if you were a Roman Catholic?"

"I said yes."

"No. You said you were raised a Catholic. I bet you began doubting God's existence when your mother became ill. When she died, you must have been furious at Him. Disillusioned. All your prayers unanswered. How could God let this horrible thing happen? Does He even exist?"

Nick strained to move in the chair. He couldn't break the invisible ties that lashed him down. "I still believe in God."

"Of course, you do. The same way you once believed in Santa Claus or the Easter bunny." Ruby scraped his long nails across the desktop as he gathered up his business cards. He stacked them neatly into the holder. "When's the last time you went to church? And carrying boxes of cannoli to a charity event doesn't count." Ruby's upper lip rose exposing long, pointed teeth.

"How do you know about that?"

"Relax, Nick. My instincts about character are excellent, however I can't read minds. I hire people to investigate my prospective clients. Standard practice."

Nick's mind reeled. "Janis Ford?"

"She's one. The girl was devastated when I didn't choose her. Her writing is excellent, but she has no physical appeal. Too plain to attract a male fan base. But she's proven herself useful." Ruby blew out a long stream of cigar smoke. "Her jealousy has motivated her to dig deeper into your personal dirt."

"I don't have any dirt."

"Well, maybe nothing the tabloids are interested in publishing. Your frequent school yard fights told me you have anger issues. Quite a temper. And all those amorous encounters you had as a teenager. You were a horny little bastard. I liked that. You possessed the tendencies necessary to become a tabloid sensation."

"I was a kid then. I've changed."

"Really? I think you've merely buried those traits. Perhaps the right demon can bring them out again."

"You have to stop this demon from possessing me. I can't live my life knowing this evil can overtake me at any time."

"You mean Artie?"

"Who?"

"Artie. Arthur Mosley. A wretched little man. Product of a broken home, abusive childhood, no friends, the proverbial loner, blah, blah, blah." Ruby chuckled. "A thin, sickly character. Socially, he was a train wreck, especially with women. Impotent as well. But Artie turned it all around. He really made something of himself."

"Made what? He's a sick, sadistic—"

"There you go again, Nick. Judging. I applaud the success Artie achieved. The challenges he overcame. He started out with a cheap pocketknife slaughtering stray cats. Sloppy at first. But with practice, he became quite the artist with his blade. Ask the women who rejected him."

"I can't. He murdered them."

"A rhetorical question. The point is, Artie rose above the crappy hand his Creator dealt him. Had they known of DNA evidence in his time, they would have connected him to dozens of killings. Sadly, he was convicted of only one murder and never received his due credit for the rest. They executed poor Artie in the electric chair."

"Why are you doing this?"

"Well, Nick, you tell me, what is the devil supposed to do?"

Nick licked his dry lips. "The devil presides over the souls damned by God in hell."

"So, that would make me, what, God's pit bull? That doesn't sound like much fun. Think about it. If that were true, wouldn't that put me on His side? Keeping the damned confined in an eternal prison?"

"But that's—" Nick stammered.

"Yes, yes, I know, that's what you learned in catechism class. But, it's not true. I seek ways to reward damned souls. The endless torture, eternal flames, the screaming, the wailing and gnashing of teeth, it gets old after a few millennia. He allows me to roam the earth. Free will, you know. This is my playground. I want to share it with the other condemned souls. At the risk of sounding cliché, I wish to create hell on earth."

Nick pushed against the force holding him. It relented and allowed him to move.

"Don't try to attack me, Nick. You'll only get hurt." Ruby waved his hand. "Run along home. Get yourself sober and cleaned up. You look like shit. I have a book signing scheduled for you tomorrow at two o'clock."

"Book signing? I don't care about my book." Nick shifted forward in his chair and gripped the edge of Ruby's desk. "Please, I'm begging you. Make the possession stop."

"I have my obligations. Promoting you, as well as a host of damned souls. It's a delicate balance. Artie is so excited to have a body like yours at his disposal. Strong, good-looking and able to attract women. The opposite of everything he was in life. The poor bastard had to sneak in while they were sleeping. It was the only way he could approach a woman. Sad, don't you think?"

"Sick."

"What it is, is a real dilemma for me. Artie is fascinated with Katie. I hate to disappoint him."

Nick jumped up and leaned across the desk. "You bastard. Leave Katie out of this. She didn't sign a contract, I did."

"So selfish. I ask you to give up one little thing. I'll give you all the women you want, plus wealth and fame."

"So, I end up like Cullen? A twisted, murdering pervert living in some rat hole?"

"That's Joe's choice. I've given you everything you wanted. I even tried to rid you of your personal albatross at the VIP party, but Katie only drank enough champagne to get a nasty tummy ache." Ruby's lips twisted upwards and he winked at Nick.

Nick's eyes widened. "You poisoned Katie?"

Ruby shrugged. "Poisoned is such a strong word. I only made her ill. She's holding you back. If you had dumped her like I advised, Artie wouldn't be fixated on her now."

"You're the fucking devil! You have the power to stop it—Artie. I-I'll stay away from Katie. Just promise me you won't let him take over my body again."

Ruby drummed his nails on his desk. "So noble, Nick." He stood and let out a long sigh. "I'll see what I can do. Stay away from Katie. She should be safe."

"No. You swear to me. She has to be safe or I won't do anything you ask."

"Yes, you will. Of course, if you want to initiate a pissing match with the devil, we can go that route. It would be a pity to see your poor, old grandmother run over by a car on her way to church, or your scrappy little brother have a fatal accident in the boxing ring." Ruby's voice trailed off into ugly sounding laughter. "There is another reason I chose you, Nick."

"What?" Nick spat the word between his clenched teeth.

"Your sanctimonious diatribe about good always having to win over evil. You pissed me off. *You* made it personal. Now I'm going to prove to you that evil will win."

Nick sat slumped in his car in the Ruby International Promotions parking lot. Dusk settled over the city and the last wave of rush hour traffic hummed around him. Was he really possessed by a demon? Would he end up like Cullen? Until today, the surreal images he'd witnessed only lived in horror films; products of a writer's imagination, confined to a screen with no chance of becoming reality. The hazy hours he had spent drinking inside the dive bar offered a brief respite and dulled his senses. But seeing Ruby transform into a seven-foot beast had shocked Nick into sobriety.

His cell phone rang, and Katie's picture displayed on the screen.

"Hi, how are you feeling?" she asked.

He rolled up the driver's window to block the noise of traffic. "Not good."

"You sound exhausted. Listen, I get off work in fifteen minutes. I asked Julie to drop me off at your apartment."

"No!" He held the phone away and drew a deep breath. "I-I mean, I don't want you to catch what I've got."

"It's probably the same stomach bug I had last week. I should be immune."

He wished it were simply a stomach flu. "Maybe, but I feel like crap. I just want to sleep."

"Have you eaten anything? I could pick up soup for you on the way."

"Please, don't bother, babe. I'm not hungry."

"Did you get my message this morning?"

Morning seemed like a lifetime ago. "Oh, yeah. You're gonna move in. That's great."

"You don't sound very happy about it."

"Sorry—"

"No, I'm sorry. You're sick. I remember how God-awful I felt."

"I meant to call you when I got your voicemail, but I must have passed out."

"Are you sure you don't want me to come over?"

"Positive." He forced a short laugh. "I prefer to be alone when I'm puking."

"Okay." Katie sighed. "Call me later. Hopefully you'll feel better tomorrow, and we can make plans for me to move in."

He could hear the disappointment in her voice. "I hope so. Yeah."

"I'll sort through my old nursing books tonight. Maybe I can sell some or give them away. It will be less stuff to have to pack."

"Um, yeah."

Katie chuckled. "You're obviously too sick for conversation. Get some rest. Love you."

"I love you." Nick swallowed hard. "So much."

He threw the phone into the passenger seat. Last night he had vowed never to lie to Katie again. Not only did he lie, but Ruby was forcing him to break up with her. How could he tell her she couldn't move in? He longed to hold her, to salvage some sense of normalcy. But he couldn't risk being near her for fear a depraved murderer would take over his body. He banged his fists on the steering wheel until his hands hurt. "How do I fight the devil?"

The traffic had thinned, but it still took Nick forty minutes to drive to Katie's apartment. He coasted slowly past her building. Her kitchen and living room lights were on. Knowing she was safely at home made him feel better, although his stomach knotted at the thought of her packing. He would have to lie again; find a plausible excuse why she couldn't move in with him until he could figure out a way to rid himself of the demon, and Victor Ruby.

He continued his meandering drive past his family's restaurant. His grandmother's church group sat around the large table by the front window. Nick wished he were back working in the restaurant.

The light turned green and he started to turn left to head to his apartment when the tall spire of Saint Michael's church caught his eye. On an impulse, he veered right, swerving across two lanes and cutting off a yellow cab and a small sedan. The taxi driver yelled, "Hey watch it, moron!" and leaned on his horn as Nick turned into the church parking lot.

The front entrance of the church was locked after dark. The pastor, Father Santore, left one side door open, close to the Rectory, so local parishioners could enter after hours.

It had been over two years since Nick had stepped inside the church. Even when he walked his grandmother to Sunday mass, he waited in the outer vestibule or on the front steps, much to her very vocal disappointment.

The heavy, wooden door swung shut behind him with a muffled thud. About a dozen people sat scattered in the front pews close to the altar with their heads bowed in prayer. None looked up when he entered. The dimly lit air smelled of incense and burning candle wax. Tall stained-glass windows lined both sides of the huge cathedral. They looked a drab, opaque gray at night. In the sunlight, the bible scenes depicted in the glass blazed to life and bathed the smooth stone floors and plaster walls in mosaics of colored light.

The silence in the church calmed him. A quiet so deep, it felt as though a thick blanket covered his head and shielded him from the noise of the city outside, as well as the din of his own thoughts.

He reached over to dip his fingertips into the holy water font mounted on the wall, and then hesitated with his hand poised above the glass bowl, wondering if the blessed water would burn his hand. He plunged his fingers in anyway. The water felt cool on his skin. He made the sign of the cross as he genuflected by the corner of the altar and turned down the side aisle. The leather soles of his boots made a soft, scuffling sound on the polished floor. He walked until he reached an arch-shaped niche midway between the main entrance at the back of the church and the altar at the front. A rack of votive candles stood in front of the alcove, next to a confessional booth. A familiar spot he had visited often before his mother died.

The single kneeler in front of the votives creaked as he knelt, the sound echoed up to the vaulted ceiling. His mother's candle burned brightly on the bottom row of the gold filigree rack. He reached out and touched the glass holder. The name ROSE was printed in black marker on the glass in his grandmother's handwriting. She insisted on printing her daughter's name on the candle holder and Father Santore had allowed her to do so.

The candle's straight, black wick peeked above the top of the glass holder. His grandmother must have replaced it today. She'd touch a new candle's wick to the dying one and then replace it in the glass holder. The flame never died.

The array of tiny, flickering flames mesmerized him. Each one symbolizing a spark of divine light fueled by a loved one's whispered prayers. The tiers of candles climbed upward like bleachers in a football stadium. The last two rows at the top held tall pillar candles. Behind the votive rack, a statue of Saint Michael the Archangel stood on a stone pedestal inside the alcove. As a boy it had been Nick's favorite statue. Unlike the other saintly-posed statues, Michael's face held a fierce, defiant expression. Dressed in armor and brandishing a long sword, he stood guard over the votives.

Nick bowed his head and prayed, repeating the same words over and over in a silent, desperate, chant. *Please, God. Please help me.* He took a deep breath and tried again. *God, help me find a way to remove this demon from me.* Victor Ruby's scowling face interrupted his prayers, followed by the chilling vision of his transformation into the devil and his mocking words about Nick's wavering belief in God.

It's true, Nick thought. I hated You for letting my mother suffer with cancer. I prayed every day for You to cure her. When she died, I stopped believing. Nick opened his eyes. "I'm a hypocrite," he muttered. "Running back to God because I'm scared." He wondered if God was laughing at him, too, the same as the devil.

The sound of the confessional door opening and then closing distracted him. An old man shuffled past, up the aisle and then exited through the side door. Nick looked up at the three lights on top of the confessional booth. The priest's white light shone above the center compartment. Green lights above the two doors on either side indicated they were unoccupied.

Nick stood and entered the closest door. As he knelt, a small door in front of his face slid open, revealing a tight lattice-work screen back-lit with soft yellow light and a shadowy silhouette of the priest on the other side.

He automatically recited the words he had memorized in elementary school. "Bless me Father, for I have sinned." He paused. "It's been a long time since my last confession."

The priest answered in a hushed voice, "May the Lord, Jesus Christ be with you, my son, to help you confess your sins. Begin whenever you are ready."

He didn't know what to say. His sins seem trivial now, angry thoughts or speaking the Lord's name in vain. His worst sin had to be losing belief in God. Should he admit to the priest he questioned God's existence? Or ask the priest how to fight off the devil and remove the demon inside him? Certain the priest would label him a mental case who drifted in off the street, he decided to simply confess his sins. Once he confessed, the priest would bless him, and the blessing might expel the demon.

Nick cleared his throat. Invisible hands closed around his neck and choked off his voice. He coughed, gasped for air and rubbed his throat.

"Are you all right, son? Take your time," the priest said.

Red-hot claws dug into his flesh and tightened their grip around Nick's neck. He couldn't breathe. His heart raced until he feared it would burst. The cramped space grew sweltering hot and the warm yellow glow behind the screen glared a deep, sinister red. Everything inside the dim space took on a red cast, as though he were looking through blood-stained lenses. He fought back the urge to scream obscenities at the priest behind the wall.

He jumped to his feet, jerked open the door and ran up the aisle to the exit. He glanced over his shoulder to see if the priest had come out of the confessional, but the center door remained closed. He paused with his hand on the door handle and stared at the holy water. The blessed water might suppress the demon raging inside him.

Yelping in pain, he yanked his fingers from the water. Clouds of steam rose from the font as the water bubbled and hissed. It turned from clear to crimson, boiled up and over the edges of the bowl and streamed down onto the floor. Blood-red puddles writhed and sizzled on the stone floor around his feet. Nick heard a creaking sound. Father Santore stood outside the door of the confessional. The priest craned his neck and squinted in his direction. Nick ducked out the door.

He vaguely remembered the drive to his apartment. By the time he exited the elevator and walked to his door, the choke-hold on his neck relented and the red haze obscuring his vision cleared.

A white envelope hung, taped to his front door. He ripped it off as he entered. Inside, he found a note from the building manager telling him the mirror in the bedroom had been removed and the ceiling had been patched and painted. It said they left the balcony doors open to air out the paint fumes.

Nick crumpled the note in his fist as he walked into the bedroom. Covered in a fresh coat of white paint, the ceiling looked naked and huge. Whether the mirror hung on the ceiling or not, no longer concerned him.

He looked at the rumpled sheets he and Katie had made love on last night. Lifting her pillow, he buried his face in the soft folds and breathed in the faint, sweet scent of her.

Throwing the pillow down, he walked into the living room, flipped on the television and lay on the sofa. The low murmur of a newscast provided background noise. The flickering images on the screen blurred. None of it held his interest. Last night he'd made love to Katie a second time on the floor by the fireplace. Afterward, they'd laid naked on the big throw pillows and made plans for their future together.

Tears coated his tired eyes. Through the liquid blur, a familiar image on the television screen jolted him upright. He watched two police officers escorting a handcuffed, wild-eyed Joseph Cullen to a patrol car. Cullen wore the same ratty, navy blue robe. His hair stuck out in absurd, greasy points and he had something red smeared on one side of his face. One of the cops pushed down on Cullen's head as he put him into the back seat of the police cruiser.

Nick turned up the volume. The camera panned to a male reporter standing on the sidewalk in front of Cullen's building.

". . . has been taken into custody. Police have not said what Cullen is charged with, if anything. He appeared to be in shock and had blood on his face. We don't know if he was injured or if the blood belongs to someone else. Minutes ago, an ambulance arrived and EMTs rushed into the building . . ."

The scene switched to a female news caster sitting at a desk.

"That was correspondent Ed Davis earlier today at Cullen's residence where this bizarre story began. We have since learned from police sources that Joseph Cullen has been charged with first degree murder. The identity of the victim is being withheld, pending notification of the family. Stay with us for complete coverage of this breaking story.

For those of you who don't know, Joseph Cullen is the best-selling horror author, known as the king of horror . . ."

Nick muted the television and slumped back onto the sofa. His call to the police had been too late.

Chapter 13

Nick awoke to a distant ringing and staggered, groggy with sleep, from the sofa into the kitchen. He grabbed his cell phone from its charger. "Yeah?"

"Nick, are you awake?" Victor Ruby asked.

"Am now," Nick grumbled.

"Drink some coffee and then get down to my office. I want my stylists and Wardrobe to work on you before your book signing today. I need you to look your best."

Nick squinted at the wall clock. It was almost ten.

"Did you hear me?" Ruby bellowed.

"Yes. I heard you."

"Good. Be here at eleven sharp." Ruby hung up.

Nick had forgotten about the book signing. After learning he was possessed by a demented serial killer, the thought of smiling at strangers and signing books seemed ludicrous. Ruby demanded he play along with the author charade in order to entice more fans.

He started a pot of coffee to brew and then opened his laptop and typed NickTera.com into the url field. A banner on the Home page announced the book signing at two o'clock in the Volumes Book Store, an enormous new store in an upscale shopping mall. A muted ding and animated movement drew his eyes to the lower right corner of the page. The Nick Tera Fan Club counter boasted over four hundred thousand fans. Nick clicked on the Join the Fan Club button and was re-directed to an electronic form. The instructions said to type out the form and sign it electronically before submitting it. The form also included a line for a physical address, Ruby's backup plan. He slammed the lid of his computer in disgust.

After gulping three cups of black coffee, he headed into the bathroom to shower. The hot water left him feeling sluggish and tired. He dressed, picked up his phone, keys and wallet and trudged out the front door.

Stephanie smiled when Nick entered the office. "Hey, Nick!"

He ignored her greeting. "Is he here?"

"Yes." Her smile faded into a worried frown. "Are you feeling okay?"

"Buzz him and tell him I'm here, will ya?"

Stephanie pressed a button on her console and told Ruby that Nick had arrived.

Ruby's door swung open. "Follow me, Nick." He strode past Stephanie's desk, out of the office and down the hallway. Nick lagged several steps behind, wondering where Ruby was leading him.

Ruby waited at the elevator. "Nick, let me make this clear. Your full participation is key to fulfilling your contract. Dragging yourself in here looking like dog crap is unacceptable."

Nick's lethargy turned to anger. "What the hell do you expect from me? Some psycho murderer takes over my body at will and tries to kill Katie! You've forced me into breaking up with the woman I love. Then you blackmail me into attracting fans so they can be possessed by demons. For what? Money and a book deal." He slammed his hand against the elevator door. "Fuck you!"

The doors slid open and Ruby pushed Nick inside. "Fuck me? Ian Slaughter said those exact words. You saw how he ended up."

"So what, now you're going to throw me out a fucking window? Go ahead. I'd rather be dead than live like this."

Small flames licked at the bottom of the silver walls forming a bright orange, yellow and red border around the elevator floor. With a sudden whoosh, the flames erupted into an inferno and raced upward, consuming all four walls and the ceiling. Trapped inside the tiny burning room, Nick whirled around in panic. Intense heat and a strong odor of sulfur sucked the cool air out of the elevator. Nick gasped to draw a breath. His legs weakened from lack of oxygen and he dropped to his knees on the floor next to Ruby's feet.

"I have no intention of throwing you out a window, Nick. I think it will be far more fun if you are responsible for the deaths of your loved ones. And be assured they will be particularly long and painful deaths. Imagine if your family's restaurant caught fire one night? Your family lives above it, they would all burn to death."

The fire on the back wall faded and changed to an image of Rosa's Ristorante. The front plate glass window exploded spewing glass and flames like fireworks. The fire quickly engulfed the building. Nick saw his grandmother, father, and brother trapped inside the raging flames. They yelled his name as their skin blistered and melted away, reducing them to grotesque manikins of blood-red tissue laced with white muscle. They continued to burn into charred, blackened bones. Still, the hideous skeletons called out to him. Nick closed his eyes, but couldn't stop the stomach-turning smell of burning hair and flesh from invading his nostrils. Worse than the horrific images and nauseating odor, were their shrieks, begging Nick to save them.

He crouched on the floor with his eyes squeezed shut and his hands clamped over his ears. The screams grew louder. "It's not real. It's not real," he shouted over them.

"It's not real *yet*, Nick. But it could become quite real." Ruby grabbed him by the throat with one hand and lifted him effortlessly until he was standing. "Watch this," he said.

On Ruby's command, Nick's eyelids shot open. The roaring fire disappeared, replaced by a familiar street scene. Katie walked alone on the sidewalk near her apartment. A battered, windowless van pulled up beside her. Two men jumped out, grabbed her by the arms and dragged her into the back. The doors slammed shut, muffling her screams for help.

"No! Stop this! Stop it now!" Nick shouted. "I don't want to see this." He tried to close his eyes, but his rigid eyelids refused to close.

Ruby's laughter rumbled inside the elevator along with Katie's desperate pleas. She screamed for Nick to help her. The terror in her voice wrenched his heart. The scene abruptly changed to inside the van. One of the men pinned Katie down on the floor, kneeling over her and pressing a knife to her throat. A thin line of red blood stained the shiny blade. The other man tore at her nursing uniform. Two more men with ugly grins watched from the front of the van.

"God damn you!"

"He already did, Nick."

"Stop this!"

"They're just getting started. It gets so much better. Shall I fast forward to the good part?"

"No! I'll do whatever the fuck you want. Just stop." Nick's voice cracked. "Please." He collapsed to his knees and covered his open eyes with his hands. Katie's raw, wrenching sobs tortured his ears. "Please, make it stop."

The images rippled and then faded until nothing but the silver walls remained. Ruby leaned down and whispered into Nick's ear. "I have a special treat planned for your book signing today. I expect your full cooperation, or I promise you, what you just saw, will happen tonight." The elevator stopped and the doors opened. Ruby shoved

Nick out into the hall. "You know where Wardrobe is. Get yourself cleaned up, Nick. You look like shit." The doors closed on Ruby's laughter.

Nick clutched the wall as he made his way down the hall. Feeling like he might vomit, he stumbled into the men's room. He dry heaved over the sink and then threw cold water onto his face. His hands shook as he took out his cell phone and called his friend, Ray.

"Ray, I need your help."

"Name it, buddy."

"Pick Katie up from work tonight. Saint Mary's hospital. Make sure she gets home safe."

"Yeah, sure. What time?"

"Seven. Do you remember what she looks like? I'll send you her picture from my phone."

"Send me the picture. I saw her at your mom's funeral. But that was a while ago. What's going on, Nick? You sound stressed."

"I can't explain now. Please Ray, please make sure she gets home okay."

"No problem. After I drop her off, let's grab a beer. You can tell me what's going on."

"I can't talk about it. I just need Katie to be safe. You're the only one I trust—"

"Hey, relax, Nick. I said I'd drive her home."

"Ray, could you take her home for the next few nights? I can't be there for her until I . . . until I work out some stuff. She's in danger. You should carry some protection on you."

"Geez, Nick. What the hell's going on? Does Katie know she's in danger?" Ray waited and then let out a long, low sigh when Nick didn't respond. "We have to talk later, all right?"

"Yeah, okay. Thanks, Ray. Thank you."

"Considering how you looked when you came in, I think we did a fantastic job," the stylist said. Nick murmured a thanks. He knew one of the blondes was named Lise and the other either Kendal, or Kendra, but he couldn't remember which was which.

The shorter of the two women stood behind him and massaged his shoulders. "You're so tense, honey." She walked to the mirror and grabbed her handbag from a cabinet beneath the counter.

"Here." She held a small blue pill in the palm of her hand. "This will take the edge off."

The tall woman handed him a cold, canned energy drink. "Take it with this. Or else you'll be sleeping on your books instead of signing them." The two women laughed and high-fived each other.

"Mr. Ruby just left." Stephanie handed him a printed sheet with directions to the Pine Castle Mall and Volumes Book Store. "He said to go in the back employee entrance." Stephanie touched his arm. "Nick, are you okay?"

"No." He shoved the paper into the pocket of the leather blazer that Wardrobe provided.

"What's wrong? You've been acting so weird lately. Like the way you barged in here yesterday and—"

"Steph, do you know who Ruby is?"

"Depends who you ask." Stephanie smirked. "Some people love him, and others, not so much. He can be a real pain in the ass, I know that."

"No, I mean who he *really* is."

"I'm not following you."

"Remember the night Chris died? You said Ruby was pure evil."

Stephanie stood and walked around the desk. "I was wasted. I blamed Ruby for Chris's death. All the pressure he put on him. I thought that's why Chris jumped."

"Do you believe Chris committed suicide?"

"Yeah. Well, maybe." Stephanie lowered her eyes. "It could have been an accident. The autopsy showed he had a lot of drugs in his system. Maybe he was stoned and lost his balance on the balcony."

"Did Chris do drugs?"

"Not around me. But it was a heavy metal party, there were booze and drugs everywhere."

"I didn't know Chris very well, but I know Ruby. I think your first instinct is right."

Stephanie lowered her voice to a whisper. "Nick, be careful, Mr. Ruby can be—oh, Mr. Ruby, I thought you had left."

"Still here, Mr. Tera?" Ruby stood glowering at them from the outer doorway. "You'd better get going. Don't want to be late for your first book signing, do you?"

"I was just leaving," Nick said.

Ruby turned his glare to Stephanie. "Don't you have work to do?"

"Yes, sir." She hurried to her seat and focused on her computer screen.

"I'll see you at the book store, Nick." Ruby slammed the door behind him as he left.

Nick whispered, "You're scared of him. Has he ever threatened you?"

Stephanie kept her eyes on her screen. "What I'm scared of is losing my job. I need it. You'd better go. He looked really pissed."

Nick sighed and held his hand out with the blue pill. "Do you know what this is?"

Stephanie picked up the pill and examined it. "It's a Xanax. For anxiety."

"How do you know?"

"Cause, I know." She pulled a prescription bottle from her purse and shook out a pill, identical to the one in Nick's hand.

"You take them?"

"Sometimes, when I'm stressed out. Where'd you get it?"

"One of the stylists gave it to me. She said it would take the edge off my nerves."

"It will. But you should take it now. It takes about twenty minutes before you feel the effects. Are you that nervous about your book signing?"

"Yes. Ruby is going to be there watching me." He stared at the pill. "I never take drugs. What if I can't function?"

"Don't worry, you'll be able to function. It will just make you feel calm and relaxed."

Nick popped open the energy drink & tossed the pill into his mouth. "Does everyone who works for Ruby take drugs?"

Stephanie shrugged. "I wouldn't be surprised."

Nick knocked on a metal door marked Volumes Book Store Employees Only. A pale, balding man in a tweed jacket opened the door.

"Hi, I'm Nick. Nick Tera. I'm here for the book signing."

"You're late." He tsked as he opened the door wider to let Nick enter. He stuck his head outside and looked in both directions before closing and locking the door.

The large room was a combination storage and break room. One side held cardboard boxes stacked on tall steel shelving units, the other side contained a round table and chairs and a small kitchenette. Victor Ruby sat in one of the chairs drumming his long fingernails on the table.

He narrowed his eyes and said, "Nice of you to join us, Nick."

"There's a traffic jam at the mall entrance," Nick said. "I was stuck half a block away for almost twenty minutes."

"You should have left when I told you to," Ruby commented.

The bald man wrung his hands and paced. "I should call Mr. Barrows. There are too many people." He peered at Ruby over thick, round lenses in his wire-rimmed glasses.

"Relax, Wendall. A large turnout is good for Barrow's business."

"There are laws about maximum occupancy. If the fire marshal—"

"I said relax. I talked to Barrows. He wants a big show and we're going to give it to him." Ruby stood up. "Ready to meet your adoring fans, Nick?" He slapped Nick on the back and nudged him toward the doorway into the book store.

Wendall led the way up the wide main aisle. Their footsteps echoed on the laminate flooring inside the cavernous store. Rows of tall bookcases extended about a hundred feet on either side of the aisle. Reading areas with comfortable chairs and specialty displays were sprinkled among the book aisles. Nick wondered why there were no customers in the store. As the three neared the front of the store he heard a muffled roar. The crowd gathered in the mall outside the store stunned him. Bodies filled the mall as far as he could see in all directions. The impatient throng appeared to be all female, and all ages. They pressed their faces and hands against the glass storefront and peered inside. The floor to ceiling glass vibrated from the pressure.

"I insist on an orderly and dignified event," Wendall said. "Mr. Barrows put me in charge and that is what he expects." He squinted at Nick over his glasses with an expression of disgust. The few thin hairs combed across his scalp were slick from sweat.

"Of course," Ruby said. He grasped Nick's elbow. "Full cooperation or Katie will be taking a ride in a van tonight, understood?"

Nick's mouth was dry, and he felt light-headed. He wasn't sure if nerves or the Xanax were to blame. "What is it you want me to do exactly?" Nick asked.

"Sign books. Chat. Flirt with the ladies. This is all about building your fan base." Ruby said. "You can start by smiling, Nick. You look like you're at a damn funeral."

Nick forced a smile.

"Here's the signing table." Wendall motioned to a square wooden table and matching chair near the front of the store. Nick's novels lined a display case near the front counter. Two easels with board-mounted posters of Nick and the models stood by the table.

"Very dignified, Wendall." Ruby slapped him on the back. Wendall blinked and took an involuntary step forward.

"It's sixteen minutes past two." Wendall tapped his wristwatch. "The sign on the door specifically says closed from one thirty until two, and then will reopen at two for the book signing." His voice climbed an octave and droplets of perspiration sprouted on his forehead.

"We're building anticipation." Ruby smiled. "Nick, sit." He waved an arm toward the entrance. "Open the doors, Wendall."

Nick sat at the table. Sales clerks standing behind the counter stared at him; two young men and a woman who looked to be in their late teens. Three more young girls stood behind a coffee counter in the corner. One smiled and waved at Nick.

"Good afternoon. Please enter slowly. Single file. You may purchase your book at the front counter and then have it signed." The crowd of women pushed through the double doors. Chatter and excited squeals drowned out Wendall's orders. "Ladies, no pushing. Please!"

The throng of women crammed into the front of the store. Wendall waved his arms to get their attention. Soon, only his fingers were visible wriggling in the air at the back of the crowd. "You must show your receipt before getting the book signed," he yelled.

Ruby patted Nick on the shoulder. "You're on, Mr. Tera." He stepped back as the swarm of women converged on the table.

Two teen-aged girls were first in line. "Oh, my gawd! It's him!" One girl pointed her cell phone camera at Nick while the other jumped up and down with her hands clasped together under her chin.

Nick felt Ruby's presence behind him. He stood, smiled and held out his hand to one of the girls. "Hi, I'm Nick. And you are?"

The girl grasped his hand. "Jennifer. Um, Jenny."

"Jenny. Great to meet you. Have you read my book?"

Both girls nodded and giggled. Her friend grabbed a book from the stack on the table. "I'm Serena. Can you, like, write, 'to Serena,' on it?"

"I'd love to." Nick picked up a pen from the neat row on the table. He opened the book and scrawled, 'To Serena, from Nick Tera' on the title page. Serena hugged the book against her chest while Jenny handed her book to Nick. She ran around the table with her cell phone held high, leaned close to Nick and snapped a picture.

"Here ya go." He winked as he gave Jenny the signed book. "Pay for them up there." He pointed to the counter. Serena hesitated, and then ran to Nick's side with her phone poised. "I wanna picture, too." The two girls walked a few steps and stared down at their phones comparing photos.

Nick made small talk, shook hands, signed books and smiled until his cheek muscles hurt. Ruby's threat weighed on his mind. He flirted with the younger women and tried his best to charm the older ones. The Xanax calmed his nerves. For a while, he even forgot about Ruby's ominous presence and enjoyed answering questions from the fans about his story and characters.

"Wendall, we need more books!" Ruby called out.

Wendall squeezed his way through the dense crowd. He took a utility knife from his pocket and slit open a cardboard box and then neatly stacked the books on the empty shelves by the front counter.

"Mr. Tera, you are checking their receipts before signing, aren't you?"

"Get some more cases from the back," Ruby said.

"But there's fifty per case. That's one hundred books."

"And there's four hundred or more customers," Ruby said. "The line goes through the mall all the way to the outside entrance."

"I don't like this. Too many people. And so noisy." Wendall crossed his arms. "Our maximum capacity is two hundred and twenty-four. If it exceeds—"

Ruby glared at him. "This is a gold mine for the store. Shut up and get more books."

"Sir! I'm the manager in charge. I don't appreciate your tone."

"Mr. Barrows won't appreciate losing sales. Now, get your ass in the back and get more books."

Wendall yanked on his jacket lapels and stalked off toward the back of the store.

Ruby leaned and whispered to Nick. "Keep smiling, Nick. The press is here."

Nick looked up and saw two arms holding a video camera high in the air making their way through the crowd. Janis Ford and a tall, lanky camera man emerged from the front of the crowd. Janis moved to the small opening behind the easel on the side of the table. Nick heard her commentary as she spoke into the video camera. "We're here at Volumes Book Store in Pine Castle Mall where new horror author, Nick Tera, is signing his premiere novel, *Thirst*, for a record number of fans. Local police are on scene directing traffic, while mall security is attempting to control the crowds of fans inside the mall. This is truly an unprecedented turnout for a new author's—"

A woman's shrill scream stopped Janis's report in mid-sentence. Nick jerked his head up from the book he was signing.

"Don't cut in front of me, bitch!" A dark-haired woman shoved a tall, blond woman. The blonde fell against the table. She straightened up, drew back her arm and then punched the dark-haired woman in the face. The woman stumbled backwards holding both hands over her face. The blonde spun around and smiled at Nick. "How about signing these?" She stripped her tee shirt off above her head and then leaned forward dangling her bare breasts over the table. She offered a black marker to Nick.

Although Ruby wasn't in sight, his voice whispered in Nick's ear. "Full cooperation." Nick pasted a smile across his face. "Yeah, sure." He took the marker and signed *Nick* on top of her left breast and *Tera* on the right. The blonde turned toward the crowd with her arms in the air. She jumped up and down and yelled, "Nick signed my boobs!"

Pandemonium broke out. Women elbowed and clawed each other as they fought to get near the table. Screams rang out as several fell to the floor. He heard Janis Ford's voice off to his right yelling above the din. "Are you getting this? Turn the camera over there!"

Something flew through the air, grazing Nick's cheek. A bra landed on the table.

"Sign these Nick." A plump, topless woman stood grinning at him.

"Get out of my way, you fat cow!" A teen-aged girl with long curly hair crawled up on the table. She knelt, yanked down her low-cut jeans and exposed her pelvis. "He'd rather sign this, wouldn't you Nick?"

The plump woman grabbed the teenager by the ankle and dragged her off the table. The girl landed on top of an open case of Nick's books. She scrambled to her feet clutching a book. She swung, smashing it into the side of the large woman's head. The woman fell backwards into the crowd, knocking three women down behind her.

"My word! My word! What is happening?" Nick turned to see the store manager standing behind him with a handcart and two more cases of books. Beneath his thick lenses, Wendall's eyes bugged from their sockets. His open mouth sagged downward at the corners in a grimace of horror. "Good Lord! They're undressing! I knew you looked like trouble. Make them stop!"

Hands grabbed Nick around the neck and a woman pressed her mouth against his while his head was turned toward Wendall. He pried the woman's hands away and spun around. Two women, one topless, climbed up on the table while more rushed around the sides. An easel displaying the poster toppled over onto Wendall.

Nick held up his hands and shouted, "Calm down, ladies! Please!"

The front of the store turned into a full-blown riot with women screeching, pulling at each other's hair, kicking and wrestling on the floor. Others huddled on the sidelines and screamed. Outside the store entrance, the overflow crowd banged their fists against the window. The sales clerks shielded their heads with their hands as books and novelty items displayed on small shelves inside the window rained down. They ducked under an opening in the counter and ran to the back of the store.

Nick struggled to extricate himself from the women who clutched at his arms and clothing. He backed down the main aisle, stunned by the chaos in front of him. The chunky, topless woman staggered after him. She had bright red scratch marks on her cheek and blood oozed from a gash on her right temple. The curly-haired girl leaped onto her back and grabbed fistfuls of her hair. They fell on the ground punching and kicking each other.

Wendall hopped backwards to avoid the wrestling women. He stood a few feet from Nick shrieking into his cell phone. "What is my emergency? We have a riot, that's what!"

Ruby appeared at Nick's side. "Let's go out the back, Nick."

Ruby tapped his long fingernails on the tall oak book cases as he strode down the aisle. The heavy units lurched forward in slow motion. Books cascaded from the upper shelves. Each bookcase toppled over and slammed into the one in front of it. Like enormous dominoes, the cases thudded to the floor and avalanches of books spilled into the aisles. Nick sprinted for the back door. A piercing whistle sounded and a man's voice bellowed over a bull horn, demanding order.

He slipped out the back door and found Ruby outside, lighting a cigar.

"That went well, don't you think?" Ruby asked.

Nick stared. His heart still pounding from the chaos he had escaped "You planned this circus, didn't you?"

"I simply provided a catalyst. People are sheep. Their herd mentality did the rest."

Sirens wailed on the other side of the plaza.

"Why would you want to cause a riot at a book signing?"

"Controversy entices more fans. After Slaughter's death, and Cullen's sordid little mess, I needed to make sure your event got the media's attention." He threw his head back and laughed. "I believe it did. You're done for today, Nick. Come by my office tomorrow at ten o'clock, sharp."

"Mr. Ruby," Nick forced a polite tone as he followed Ruby to his car. "I cooperated. My family and Katie will be safe, right?"

Ruby ground the cigar under his heel and opened the door of his red Jaguar. "For now, yes."

"No, wait. You have to promise me they'll be safe forever. I'll stop seeing Katie. But I have to talk to her. As myself. Without any demons taking over."

"Come now, Nick. I can't allow that." Ruby slid into the low-slung sports car.

"But I have to talk to her, so I can . . . so I can break up with her."

"You can barely say the words. I don't believe you have any intention of breaking up with your precious Katie."

"No! You said if I cooperated, she'd be safe. All I'm asking is to talk to her. One last time."

Ruby studied Nick with a thin-lipped smile. "We'll see." He started up his car.

Nick placed his empty beer bottle in line with five others on the table in front of him. He checked the time on his cellphone again. Nine-seventeen. More than enough time for Ray to pick up Katie at seven, take her home and then meet him here at the bar. Yet, Ray hadn't shown up and he wasn't answering his cell phone. Nick stood and pulled money from his wallet for a tip. A hand slapped his back.

"Sorry I'm late, buddy," Ray said.

"What took you so long? I've been calling you."

"Yeah, sorry, I left my phone in the car." Ray signaled to a waitress walking past. "Bud Lite."

She collected the empty bottles from the table. "Another one?" She smiled at Nick.

He nodded, sat down and waited for Ray to settle in the chair opposite him.

"Is Katie all right?"

"She's fine," Ray said. "Home safe and sound. It was weird at first. I assumed you had told her I was picking her up."

Nick looked down and shook his head.

Ray grunted. "Yeah. Well, once I showed her my identification and answered all her questions to prove I was really, Ray, your friend, she finally agreed to accept a ride."

The waitress put their beers on the table. She took part of the tip money Nick had put on the table and waited while Ray dug out his wallet from his jeans pocket.

"Here, I got it," Nick said, pushing more bills toward her. "I owe you for tonight."

"Thanks, but you don't owe me nothing."

"So, did Katie say anything?"

"On the drive to her place she asked me if you were still sick." Ray shook his head. "I didn't know you told her you were sick. Sorry man." Ray held up his hands in a sheepish shrug "I think I blew your alibi."

"Is she pissed?"

"Yeah, but not about that so much. I walked her to the door. She invited me in for coffee."

Nick scowled.

"What's with the look? You don't trust me? Besides, I said no thanks. Then her roommate runs over and said we needed to come look at the news on TV. The riot at your book signing today was one of the top stories." Ray grinned. "They had to blur out an awful lot of tits for television."

"Shit."

"Yeah, that's when I accepted the coffee. Katie insisted. She wanted to talk. It was awkward, man. I didn't know what to say. I've hardly seen you since I've been home."

"Katie must be furious. What did she say?"

"Most women would want to hang you by your nads, but she seemed to think it was the promoter guy you work for who set it all up. She stayed pretty calm, considering. Of course, her roommate, what's her name, Clara?"

"Tara," Nick said through clenched teeth.

"Yeah, she's a friggin' trip. Katie defended you, but Tara ripped you a new one. There's a lot of tension between them. Katie told me she can't wait to move in with you. She's over Tara's bullshit. After being around her for an hour, I can understand."

Nick rubbed his hands over his face. He had been agonizing over how to tell Katie she couldn't move in with him the entire time he had waited for Ray.

"What's going on, Nick? You're not sick. You say Katie's in danger. The poor girl is worried about you. Then she sees women throwing their tits in your face on the news. Is that normal at a book signing?"

"No, it's not normal. Nothing is freaking normal anymore. And yeah, it's my agent. He sets up these stunts to get publicity. More book sales, or more fans. Whatever."

"So, you lied to Katie about being sick?"

"No. I was feeling sick. But I had to go to the book signing today. I have a . . . very strict contract."

"And asking me to carry a gun, what's that all about?"

Nick glanced at Ray and then turned away. "I can't talk about it." He turned back and looked Ray in the eyes. "Katie is in danger. But I don't want to scare her. I need her to be safe and I can't protect her right now. It's making me crazy, Ray. Time. I need time to work it all out."

"You owe somebody money?"

"No, it's nothing like that. Drop it, all right?" Ray's penetrating gaze and pointed questions irritated Nick. The atmosphere inside the bar agitated his nerves. The older patrons who had quietly sipped their after-hours drinks had left. A swarm of younger people now filled the bar. Loud voices and rowdy laughter replaced the low murmur of conversation. The juke box blared, and dancing bodies gyrated all around them.

"Hey, look man, you asked me to pick up your girlfriend *and* carry a gun. I think I have a right to know what's going on."

The bar felt like an oven. Sweat made Nick's shirt stick to him under his jacket. A reddish haze covered his friend's face. Nick looked around and realized everything had taken on a bright red tint.

"I asked you to drive her home, not spend two hours drinking coffee and talking to her. It wasn't a fucking date." The harsh words shot out of his mouth.

"You're accusing me of hitting on Katie? You asked me to help you and I did." Ray stood and gulped his beer. He flipped bills onto the table and turned to leave.

The sudden heat and red-tinted vision dissipated. "Wait, Ray. I'm sorry. I didn't mean it." Nick stood and swayed on his feet. He grabbed his friend's arm both to stop him and for balance. "I apologize, okay? I'm pissed about shit I can't control. All I want to do is see Katie. But I can't. I worry about her, all the time. I'm not . . . myself anymore."

Ray looked at him, shook his head and sat. Nick motioned to the waitress.

She put two more bottles on the table. Nick handed her money.

"I can buy my own," Ray grumbled.

"I know." Nick squeezed Ray's shoulder. He held onto the table and eased himself back into his chair. "I do owe you. More than I can ever repay. I appreciate you taking Katie home. I really do."

"Katie wants you to call her or come see her. She wants to talk to you tonight."

"I don't have a freaking clue what to say to her."

A young brunette with a bare midriff bumped against Ray as she danced with a group of girlfriends. She touched Ray's arm and shouted an apology over the loud music. Ray smiled at her. She smiled back, spun around and then wiggled across the dance floor in rhythm to the music.

"Hey Nick, think I'd have a shot with her?" Ray turned to Nick and sighed. "You're lucky. I wish I could find a girl like Katie. Beautiful, smart and sweet as hell. She's the perfect package."

Intense heat rose in Nick's face. He squeezed his eyes shut and fought to control the jealous rage simmering inside him. He wanted to punch Ray, but instead chugged down the beer in front of him and stood. "I gotta go." He took one step, bumped into a couple dancing and staggered backwards.

"You're wasted, my friend." Ray stood and pressed his hand against Nick's back to stop him from falling onto the table. "I saw all your empties when I got here."

"I'm fine." He stumbled into the crowd toward the front door. Ray followed beside him, pushing and pulling him to the right or left to avoid crashing into the dancers.

Once outside, the quiet brought some relief, but in spite of the cool night air, a burning heat consumed him. Nick zigzagged across the parking lot to his car.

"Nick, you can't drive. I'll give you a ride. We can pick up your pony tomorrow morning."

"I can drive."

"Don't be an asshole, man. You can't even walk."

Nick jammed the key into the door lock. "I said I can fucking drive. I need to see Katie."

"Like this? Not a good idea. Why don't we get some coffee first? Then I'll drop you off at Katie's."

Nick half fell, half sat in the driver's seat and closed the door. He struggled to find the ignition keyhole. Ray opened the door and grabbed for the keys. Nick shoved him back, slammed the door and then locked it. Ray banged on the window. Nick started the car, put it in reverse and floored the gas pedal. He saw Ray in his side view mirror running toward his old fifty-seven Chevy parked across the lot.

Nick sped up, but couldn't shake Ray, tailing him in the big two-toned Bel Air. He jammed on his brakes at a red light, rolled down his window, and waved for Ray to go away. Ray shot him the bird. Angry, he stomped on the gas pedal and then slammed his foot on the brake as a panel truck honked its horn and sped past, inches in front of him. The traffic light overhead still shone red.

Ray blared his horn and yelled, "Pull over!" Nick gunned the gas and shot through the intersection leaving Ray sitting at the red light.

After three attempts, Nick maneuvered his car into a parking spot in front of Katie's building. Ray's car rolled past and pulled into an open space half a block up the street.

Ray got out and leaned against the trunk of the cream and turquoise boat-sized car with his arms crossed, glaring and shaking his head.

Nick staggered up the path to Katie's front door. He tripped up the front stoop and pounded on the door. "Katie! Katie!

Katie opened the door and stared up at him. "Nick? What's the matter?"

Stacks of books and cardboard boxes filled the small kitchen. In the midst of them, Jon Gerber sat at the table sipping coffee.

"What the hell are you doing here?" Nick pushed past Katie and glared at Jon.

"Nick!" Katie grabbed his arm.

"B-Buying books from Kate." His head swiveled from Katie to Nick.

Nick jerked his arm from Katie's grasp. A red transparent film covered his vision. Jon's blond-streaked hair and wide blue eyes looked red. He lunged across the table knocking a pile of books to the floor. "Get the fuck out!"

Jon jumped from his chair and flattened his back against the refrigerator.

"Nick! What do you think you're doing?" Katie stepped in front of him with her hands on her hips. She turned to Jon. "I'm so sorry, Jon."

"No problem." He skirted around the table and picked up a stack of books. Hesitating, he held the books up as if to get Nick's approval. "Thanks again, Kate." He turned sideways to squeeze past Nick and then hurried out the front door.

Nick slammed the door behind him and then whirled around to face Katie. "What the hell is going on with you and that guy?" He moved toward her with his hands raised.

"Jon came to buy some of my books." She gave Nick a withering look. "I don't have to explain having a friend over. God, what is wrong with you?" Katie stepped back. "Your eyes, they're so red."

Nick's vision cleared and he saw his outstretched hands reaching for Katie's neck. Dropping his arms, he backed away. "Katie, I'm so sorry."

"Sorry? You barge in here like a maniac and chase Jon out! I can see you're drunk, but what, are you on drugs, too? And your eyes . . . uh . . . they're normal now."

"I'll go." He turned and opened the door.

"You're just going to leave?" She grabbed his arm. "Nick?"

His temper raged at her touch. "I need to go *now*." He shook off Katie's grip and jogged down the path toward the street.

"Nick, wait!" Katie ran after him.

Ray stood blocking the end of the path. "What's going on?"

Unsteady on his feet, and blinded by the unexplained rage, Nick stopped short and swung. His fist grazed the top of Ray's crew cut. He swung again. Ray side-stepped the sloppy round-house punch, and then straightened up with both fists cocked in front of him. Nick landed a right hook on Ray's jaw. Ray stumbled backwards, shaking his head but stayed on his feet. Ducking under his friend's long reach, Ray charged, rammed his head and full weight into Nick's chest and bulldozed him backwards. Nick landed hard on his back on the lawn.

"Stop it! Both of you!" Katie yelled.

Nick rolled onto his stomach and then pushed himself up on all fours. Grass, trees, lights, and faces spun in a blur around him. Two Katies scowled at him and two Rays loomed over him in a fighting stance. Without warning, an arc of liquid shot out of his mouth and splattered onto the cement path.

"Oh, God," Katie said.

A window raised and a woman's voice called out, "Are you all right, Miss Harrington?"

Katie rushed up the walk toward her front door. "Yes. Thank you, Mrs. Neil. I'm fine."

A man's voice yelled, "What the heck's going on out there? Break it up or I'll call the cops!"

"Sorry, Mr. Gretzski. Everything's fine now." Katie ran into her apartment.

Still on his knees, Nick sat back on his heels and closed his eyes to stop the spinning images.

"Need a hand, buddy?"

He looked up at Ray's outstretched hand and smiling face. Nick leaned his weight onto one knee and then bent his other leg to get one foot on the ground. He grabbed onto Ray's forearm and felt himself hauled upward. He stumbled. Ray gripped his arm and stopped his fall. Nick turned his head away, bent at the waist and threw up again.

Katie hastened down the path carrying a plastic pail with water sloshing over the sides.

Ray jogged across the lawn and took the bucket from her. "I got it." He poised the bucket over the path. "Geez, Nick, looks like somebody spilled a friggin' keg out here. It's even got a head on it."

He tossed the warm, pine-scented water and washed the foamy, pale yellow vomit into the grass.

"Now you're best friends again?" Katie glared at Nick. "Go inside. Clean yourself up." She motioned to Ray. "Come in, Ray. Help me get him off the street before someone calls the cops."

Ray and Nick followed behind Katie. She waited and then closed the door after they entered.

Nick glanced sideways at her. "I'm sorr—"

"I swear, if you say you're sorry one more time—just go and wash up."

Nick went into the bathroom and closed the door. He peeled off his jacket and sweat-soaked shirt. Leaning over the sink, he splashed water on his face and upper body. He loaded the toothbrush he kept at Katie's house with toothpaste and scrubbed his mouth to remove the beer and bile coating. For the moment, he felt in control. The demon, whom Ruby called Artie, had overwhelmed him with thoughts of torture and murder, but tonight, intense flushes of heat and red-tainted vision brought on erratic fits of rage and jealousy. The thought that yet another demon had emerged inside him both sickened and terrified him.

He heard a soft knock at the door. Katie entered carrying a folded bath towel and a tee shirt.

"Here." She handed him the towel and sat on the closed toilet lid while Nick dried his face and torso. "It's one of the shirts you gave me. My favorite sleeping shirt." She offered a weak smile. "I want it back."

He reached out and ran his hand over her cheek. She shrugged away from him. A sudden rush of heat and then Artie's angry whisper, *Reject me? Bitch. You'll be sorry*. The demon's voice in his head sent a chill down his spine. He turned away and pulled the shirt over his head.

"I saw your book signing on the news. Seventeen women hospitalized, three seriously injured, and dozens more treated at the mall. My God, Nick, what happened?"

Nick shook his head. "Victor Ruby happened. Bastard planned it all. He wanted the publicity to draw attention away from Cullen's arrest and Chris' death."

"I figured Ruby set it up. But what I don't understand is why you went along with it?"

"I–I had no choice."

"No choice?" She stood, her arms crossed and anger glinting in her green eyes. "It didn't look like you were forced into signing that woman's breasts."

"Look, Katie, I didn't want to do it, but I had to—"

"You had to? Oh, please! You're acting like Ruby put a damn gun to your head."

Nick blew out a long breath, leaned on the counter and stared down into the sink.

"You heard Chris at the VIP party. Ruby's publicity stunts ruined his marriage. Maybe even caused his suicide." She sighed as she wrapped her arms around his waist and leaned her head on his back. Her voice softened. "I'm so worried about you. About us."

Nick turned and leaned his chin on the top of her head. He hugged her and whispered, "Nothing Ruby does will ever make me stop loving you."

"I hardly see you anymore. I miss you," she murmured into his chest.

He lifted her chin with his fingers and kissed her. Tension melted from her shoulders and she pressed her body against him. A pleasant heat radiated through his body. Fearing his arousal might turn into something darker, he gently pushed her away.

Katie sighed and leaned against the wall. "Why were you fighting with Ray?"

He avoided her gaze, staring into the mirror as he ran a comb through his wet hair. "Just drunk."

"I've seen you drunk. I hate it, but you've never acted violent before." Reaching up, she massaged his shoulders. "You acted like you were on drugs or something."

Nick put the comb down. "I took a Xanax today."

"A Xanax? Why?"

"Ruby said he had something planned for the book signing but wouldn't say what. One of Ruby's hair stylists gave it to me. Said it would calm my nerves."

Katie rolled her eyes and threw her hands up in the air. "Of course, a hair salon, where else would you go to get prescription drugs?"

"It was one pill, one time."

"And then you drank. A lot. Do you know how dangerous mixing Xanax with alcohol is?"

Nick opened the bathroom door. "I'm fine."

Katie followed him into the kitchen. Ray sat at the table holding a mug. The smell of fresh-brewed coffee hung in the air. She poured a mug for Nick and handed it to him. He nodded and put the coffee on the table while he bent to pick up the medical books he had knocked on the floor earlier.

"How long ago did you take it?" she asked.

"Take what?" Ray asked, looking from Katie to Nick.

"A Xanax," Katie said.

"I've heard of it," Ray said. "What is it?"

"An antidepressant. Relieves anxiety," Katie said.

Ray looked at Nick. "You're taking drugs?"

Nick flushed with heat. He squelched the surging anger, but it invaded his words. "What is this, a freaking intervention? I took one pill. Around one-thirty this afternoon. Stop treating me like a damn drug addict."

"It stays in your system for two days. With all the beer you drank, you could have ended up in Emergency getting your stomach pumped. Plus the combination makes your heart rate and respirations slow down. Or stop." She slammed the books together as she stacked them on the table.

"I pumped your stomach for you," Ray said. "Saved you a hospital bill."

Nick grinned at Ray's goofy smile. At least Katie blamed his behavior on the pill and alcohol.

Ray rubbed his jaw. "It sure didn't feel like a depressed dude hit me. It friggin' hurt."

"I'm sorry." Nick glanced at Katie after saying the words.

"It's rare, but some people react the opposite. Become violent." She packed books into a box. "Please, promise me you won't take anymore pills."

"Yes, I promise, I won't take any more pills, all right?"

Ray stood and put his empty mug into the kitchen sink. "I'm gonna take off. Thanks for the coffee, Katie." He gripped Nick's shoulder. "Call me tomorrow."

"I need to get going, too." Nick stood.

Katie dropped the books she held onto the table. "But I thought you'd stay here tonight?"

"I can't, babe. I, uh, have an early meeting. With the publisher. I have to do some work on the computer tonight." He hoped she believed the lie.

"Give me five minutes to pack. I'll go home with you." Katie hurried to her bedroom.

Another flash of heat accompanied Nick's panic. "Shit."

"What's the matter?" Ray whispered. "You don't want her to go to your place?"

Nick shook his head. "It's not safe."

Ray sucked on his upper lip, studying him. "You got people after you, too?"

"Something like that, yeah."

"Crap." Ray opened the door. "I'll wait outside. Let me know what I can do to help."

Nick walked into Katie's bedroom. A small pile of clothes sat on the bed. She pulled a canvas bag from her closet shelf. "Two more minutes," she said.

He sat on the end of her bed, his nerves tensed. "Katie . . . you can't move in with me."

She stopped packing and stared at him. "Why not?"

"It's complicated." His mind sifted through the various lies he considered while waiting for Ray at the bar. "I talked to Ruby about you moving in. He has this insurance plan. If you're not a client or an employee, you can't live in his building. Some legal, liability stuff. It'd break my contract if you moved in."

Katie sank down on the bed next to him, her shoulders slumped forward. He turned away from the battered look in her eyes, stared at the floor and rattled off more excuses. "Plus, the rent's astronomical. Over three grand a month. I know, I should've checked all this out before I asked you to move in. But, tomorrow, I'll start looking for another apartment for us. Okay? It shouldn't take too long."

Katie let out a long sigh. "Nick, I can't stay here. After we made up the other night, I confronted Tara about her lies and trying to break us up. She acted crazy. She said you wanted her, not me. Ranted some nonsense that she was the first to sign up online for your fan club. And then tonight, after Ray left, we got into another fight. She stomped off into her room. I followed. Her closet door was open. She had pictures of you and news clippings taped inside the door. Like some sort of creepy shrine. She's obsessed with you. I can't believe I never knew it before."

"I've never liked Tara, but I didn't know either." Nick put his arm around Katie's shoulders.

She cuddled against him. "Ruby's not going to know if I spend the night at your place. I really need to be with you tonight." She ran her fingers over his chest and brushed her lips against his neck.

Desire flooded over him and then something darker stirred within him. The thought that Artie felt aroused by Katie's touch disgusted Nick. He shifted his weight away from Katie. "What if I tell Tara to move out? I'll pay your rent here until we find another place together."

"It's not the money. We have a joint lease. For a year. Tara refuses to move. Legally, I can't make her. So, I told her I'd move out." Katie's eyes watered. "Or at least I thought I would, until now."

Nick swallowed the lump swelling in his throat. "Please, hang in there, just a little bit longer—"

"Why can't I stay with you tonight? Or, you stay here? Something's wrong, Nick. Something you're not telling me. What is it?"

He slid his arm from around her and stood. "I can't explain now. But I swear I'll straighten everything out. I just need time. Please, Katie, trust me."

Katie hung her head. Her tears fell, leaving dark dots on her faded blue jeans. He wanted to hold her, comfort her, stay with her, but redness colored his vision and a sudden anger grew inside of him. A new voice growled in his head, *give her something to cry about.* He rushed out of the room and left her crying on the bed.

Ray stood waiting by the Mustang. "What about getting the cops involved?"

Nick brushed past Ray, choking back his own tears after leaving Katie crying in her bedroom. "Cops can't help me. I have to work it out myself." He opened the car door.

"Bullshit." Ray grabbed Nick's arm and stopped him from getting into his car. "Tell me exactly what's going on. We'll figure out something together."

His simmering anger bubbled over into rage. Nick ripped his arm from Ray's hold. "Just make sure Katie's safe. Pick her up from work and take her home."

"Nick, c'mon man, it's me. Talk to me. Let me help you."

He clenched his fists and fought the urge to lash out at Ray again. "You wanna help? Leave me the fuck alone. That's how you can help." Nick got into his car and drove away.

As he stared at the television screen, all Nick saw was the image of Katie crying on her bed. His gut twisted thinking about it. He shuffled mindlessly though the stack of junk mail building on his coffee table. At the very bottom he found a brown padded envelope addressed to Stephanie. She had left her demo CD behind the other night. He held it for a moment, thinking he shouldn't open it, but then ripped open the flap anyway. Steph wouldn't mind. A CD slid out encased in a folded sheet of paper.

He slid the CD into his laptop and turned up the volume. Leaning his head back on the sofa, he closed his eyes and listened to the series of country songs and ballads. The soothing melodies distracted him. Stephanie's voice sounded sweet and clear. On the ballads she sang with Chris, their voices blended in a natural harmony. After the CD had played through, he got up and ejected it.

He started to call Stephanie and offer to bring the CD upstairs to her apartment but stopped when he saw it was after one in the morning. He opened the folded paper to re-insert the CD. It was a letter from Chris. The words 'Victor Ruby' caught his eye.

> *Stephanie,*
> *As promised, here is your demo CD. Your voice is a true gift, and a delight to listen to. Follow up with the contacts in Nashville I gave you. I have no doubt you will become the star you've always dreamed of being.*
> *More importantly, you must get far away from Victor Ruby. I've told you what he is, though I'm sure you don't believe me. A year ago, I doubt I'd believed it. I have found myself trapped inside a true hell on earth. But I refuse to let Ruby win. I'm sorry, Love, I know I promised to help you with your career. The enclosed CD is really all you need. It speaks, or sings, for itself. You are a sweet girl. If you stay, Ruby will destroy you, your dreams and everyone you love.*
> *There is only one sure way to break a contract with a devil. I want you to know, I have no regrets about my*

decision. Without me, he cannot threaten my daughter and wife or countless other innocents whose only sin is to be a fan of my music. Don't waste tears on me. Get away from Ruby. Pursue your dreams.

I have a favor to ask, but only if you can find a way without putting yourself in danger. Locate my contract and burn it. I never gave much thought to an afterlife, until recently. If I do possess a soul, I don't want Ruby to have it.

Be safe, Chris

The paper shook in Nick's hands. The sentence, *there is only one way to break a contract with the devil,* made his scalp crawl and his heart pound. It was a suicide note.

Chapter 14

Stephanie's desk stood vacant when Nick arrived the following morning. He paced the waiting room until Ruby opened his door at precisely ten o'clock.

"Where's Steph?" He tried to keep his tone neutral as he sat in the chair opposite Ruby.

"Downstairs in Publicity. We're announcing Talon as the new lead singer for Blood Lust. I'm planning a world tour." He slid a check across the desk to Nick. "Not bad, hey Nick? Half a million dollars for a couple of hours of signing girls' tits. I knew the publicity would positively impact your sales."

Nick slipped the check into his pocket without looking at it. "So, now what?"

Ruby clasped his hands behind his neck and leaned back in his chair. "Another book signing. Maybe some interviews. And, I have a surprise. I'm working on a movie deal for your trilogy series. Quite impressive, considering you're a newbie on the horror scene."

Nick nodded his head. He felt numb, empty. None of the news Ruby told him mattered. His thoughts centered around Katie. Ruby used her and his family as pawns to force him to do his bidding. Even if he broke up with Katie, Ruby knew he still loved her. She would always be in danger.

"You're quiet today, Nick. Tell me, any ideas for future novels?"

Nick shook his head. He'd play along with the author charade so as not to anger Ruby and to buy time to figure out a way to get away from him. "I emailed your publisher about doing a book of short stories. He's interested."

"Short story collection? Hmm, yes, Cullen did a few of those. But you need to start working on your next best-selling novel, since Cullen won't be publishing any more books." Ruby stood and tapped his long nails on the desk. "Because of you, Cullen will spend the rest of his life locked up in a lunatic asylum. My demons are quite unhappy, they want to be free, not locked away in a padded room."

"I had to try and stop him from murdering the girl."

"Why? She was nothing to you. If you hadn't interfered, 'ol Joe would still be pumping out books and providing a playground for a host of my deserving demons. His most important work."

Nick stood and scowled at Ruby. "Murder is important work?"

"Murder without consequences. I protect my clients. One call, and much like that catchy television commercial, it's like it never even happened." Ruby flung his head back, laughing at his joke.

"You're a liar. Cullen's going to rot in a mental hospital. You're not protecting him."

"You called the police, what could I do? No time to spirit away the body, clean up the mess, or pay off witnesses." Ruby sighed and waved his hands in the air. "I've lost count of the messes I've cleaned up for Joe. Starting with his wife's sudden . . . disappearance." The corners of Ruby's mouth tugged up into a smug, evil smile. "Joe chose not to heed my advice. Much like you with Katie. The curse of love! No matter, Joe's time is over. My demons crave a new host. Tell me Nick, have you had any visitors besides Artie?"

Nick looked away. Ruby's glittering black eyes widened along with his malicious grin. "So, you have! Cullen's a dead end. They're always drawn to a newly opened portal."

"What do I have to do to make it stop?" Nick slammed his fist down on the desk. "I refuse to end up like Cullen, do you hear me?" Shaking with rage, he grabbed Ruby's jacket.

Ruby flicked his thumb and forefinger.

The force hurled Nick across the room. His body slammed into the wall next to the door and then slid onto the floor. Stunned by the sudden impact, he rubbed the back of his head and gaped at Ruby.

"You have no right of refusal in your contract, Nick. That frustrates you, doesn't it? Standing here, muscles taut, veins bulging, panting through your mouth like a damn baboon. So predictable. When all else failed you before, you've always resorted to your fists, didn't you? Now, run along. Go write a book. Or not. I have thousands of Cullen's unpublished pages. Just think Nick, your idol's stories published under your name. You said you wanted to be like Cullen. And now you shall be. Exactly like him."

Nick scrambled to his feet, glared at Ruby. He stalked out and slammed the door.

Stephanie jumped in her chair. "Nick, what's wrong?"

"Nothing," he grumbled. He focused on Stephanie's wet, puffy eyes. "Why are you crying?"

She sniffed into a balled-up tissue clutched in her hand. "Ruby's made Talon lead singer of Blood Lust. I–I hate her. She even can't sing. It's not fair. If only Chris. . .."

Nick leaned across the desk and whispered. "Steph, I opened your demo CD last night and listened to it. Chris enclosed a letter. I'm sorry, I didn't mean to snoop. But it was a suicide note."

Stephanie gasped. "Suicide note?"

"Call me as soon as you get home tonight. We have to figure out a way to get the contracts—"

Stephanie's gaze panned up and over Nick's shoulder. Her mouth dropped open and her pink cheeks paled to a waxy white.

Nick followed her petrified stare. Ruby stood in his open doorway.

"Whispering secrets to my secretary, Mr. Tera?" His upper lip curled into a snarl, exposing his pointed, unnaturally white teeth. "Get out, Nick. And you," he hissed, pointing a claw-like finger at Stephanie, "Get back to work."

Nick called Stephanie at five fifteen that afternoon and continued to call on every half hour. His calls went straight to her mailbox. At seven o'clock he ran upstairs and knocked on her apartment door. No response. He went back downstairs to his apartment.

His own cell phone teemed with messages from Ray, Katie, and his family. Ray's curt message reported he drove Katie home. Katie's pleaded for Nick to call her. His grandmother ranted on about his book signing which she had seen on the news. Sal's message warned him Nonna was pissed. Nick erased all of them and tried Stephanie again. Still, no answer and her mailbox was full. As he hung up, a text message from Katie displayed. *I Luv U. Plz Call Me.* He hesitated and then texted back *I Luv U.* Frustrated, he grabbed a beer from the refrigerator. Ruby had him trapped. Unless he and Stephanie could find and destroy the contracts in Ruby's office, he'd end up like either Cullen or Chris. He didn't know which would be worse. Five more beers smothered his fears under a murky blanket of alcohol-induced numbness.

Chapter 15

As soon as he awoke the following morning, Nick called Stephanie. Her overloaded mailbox rejected his message. After a quick pit stop, he washed his face and then ran upstairs and banged on her door. No answer. He ran downstairs to the parking garage and jogged through all six levels searching for Stephanie's yellow Volkswagen. Not finding her car, his worry turned to a cold, heavy dread. He returned to his apartment, dressed, and then drove to Ruby's office.

Stephanie's desk had been stripped clean. Her silly leopard-print high heeled shoe tape dispenser and cup of purple, fuzzy-topped pens, gone. The freshly polished top held only a computer and a phone.

Nick knocked on Ruby's door.

"Come in," Ruby called out.

Nick stormed inside. "Where's Stephanie?"

Talon stood in front of Ruby, naked. He lay sprawled on the black leather couch on the far side of his office. She puckered her lips and blew a kiss to Nick and then took her time sliding one long leg at a time into a red satin thong.

"I need to talk to you. When you're done."

"We're done. Have a seat, Nick." Ruby patted the couch cushion. "What's on your mind?"

Talon adjusted her breasts in the cups of a lacy, red bra. She smiled at Nick as she reached behind her back and fastened it.

"I need to talk to you. Alone," Nick said.

"Don't be shy. Or, is this the wrong ratio? Your preference is two females, right?"

Nick grunted and sat on the arm of the sectional across from the two. "Where's Stephanie?"

"She took a personal day," Ruby said.

Talon winked at Ruby and giggled. Her tan skin glistened with sweat from the heat in the office. Strolling over to Nick, she ran her long red fingernails through his hair.

He brushed her hand away. "Why did she need a personal day?"

"How should I know?" Ruby shrugged. "That's why it's called a personal day. It's *personal*."

Nick swiped Talon's hand from his thigh and stood. "Why is Steph's desk empty?"

"Maybe she cleaned it, for once." Ruby said. "More importantly, something has come up we need to discuss." Ruby stood and embraced Talon. Even barefoot, she towered over him. "Run along now, my dear. I'll see you at the press conference." She paused and patted Nick's cheek on her way out.

"Stunning, isn't she?" Ruby walked to his desk. "I can arrange a date with her if you'd like."

"No, I wouldn't like. What did you want to talk about?"

Ruby buttoned his shirt and slipped on his tie and suit jacket. "Someone tried to blackmail you."

"What? Who?"

"One of the workmen who removed your bedroom ceiling mirror. Seems the mirror had quite a sophisticated video system built into it. Activated by a motion detector and recorded onto a DVD."

Nick sat down hard in the guest chair, a stunned expression on his face.

Ruby laughed and wagged his long-nailed finger at him. "Trying to remember what took place under the mirror? This might jar your memory." He aimed a remote at his television. The seventy-two-inch screen burst into a video of Nick and the two models in his bed. The audio of the two women moaning streamed through the speakers mounted around the office.

Nick jumped up. "Turn that down. Turn it off!"

Ruby muted the sound, but left the video playing. "I understand your concern. Your performance is a bit lackluster. I told Ebony drugging you was a bad idea. You appear unconscious. The poor girls had to do all the work."

"What else is on that DVD?" His stomach churned, knowing the answer.

Ruby nodded as if reading his thoughts. "There's a lovely segment with Katie." He fast forwarded. "I must say, you are much more vigorous here, Nick." Ruby turned his head from side to side as he leered up at the screen. "A shame it's so dimly lit. Was she opposed to having the lights brighter?"

"Turn that damn thing off!" Nick grabbed for the remote in Ruby's hand only to find himself knocked back into the chair and unable to move.

"Your Neanderthal displays are getting tiresome. You can't hurt me." Ruby smiled up at the video. "Katie is a beautiful girl. If this video got out, she'd be humiliated, don't you think? Or, perhaps, I could launch a new career for her. The Naughty Nurse, what do you think, Nick?"

Nick strained to move in the chair. "You sonofabitch, that's my fiancée. Turn it off!"

Ruby paused the video. "The two models expose your lie to Katie. You did lie to her, didn't you?" His mouth twisted into a wicked grin. "Of course you did. And the segment with Katie, well, it literally exposes Katie. Very nicely, though, I must say. But frankly, as your devoted agent, it's the last segment that worries me." Ruby fast forwarded to Nick kneeling over Stephanie, pinning her down on the bed.

"That's not what it looks like," Nick said.

"What it looks like is you overpowering a little girl in your bed. How old does she look in this video? Twelve, maybe fourteen?" Ruby left the paused scene on the screen. "This is the kind of thing that destroys careers. Ruins lives. Didn't they recently find some poor pedophile crushed to death in a garbage truck?" Ruby tsked and shrugged his shoulders. "For some reason, people just detest pedophiles."

"I am not a fucking pedophile! Go to the end of the video. Nothing happens."

"Unfortunately, the DVD ran out of space. Right as you're threatening to tie her to the bed if she tries to run away, I believe."

"Steph was drunk, I was—"

"So, you plied an underage girl with alcohol, and then raped her when she wouldn't cooperate?"

"No! I wouldn't rape anybody. Steph will tell you. Ask her."

"That's my dilemma. I already have." Ruby pressed a button on his phone console. "Bring her in."

"Who did you call? What's going on?" He struggled to stand but couldn't.

"You'll see. I'll let you loose but don't be stupid, Nick. Stay in your seat."

Ruby's door opened and an older woman in a business suit entered. Stephanie shuffled in behind her with her head down. Her long, wavy hair obscured her face.

"Come in. Sit." Ruby pulled his chair to the side of his desk facing Nick. Stephanie sat down.

"Nick, this is Patricia from Human Resources," Ruby said, motioning to the woman.

Patricia stood behind Stephanie with her hands on the back of the chair and glared at Nick.

"Stephanie, look at me," Ruby ordered.

Nick gasped as she slowly lifted her head. Ruby pushed back her hair, exposing the left side of her face. Swelling forced her left eye closed. A deep purple bruise surrounded it. Blood seeped from a deep split in her bottom lip. Smaller cuts and red marks covered her cheek. Dark bruises in the shape of finger prints marred both of her arms.

"My God! What happened, Steph? Who did this to you?" Nick slid forward in the chair.

Patricia huffed. "Victor, is this really necessary? Making her face this deviant, after what he did to her?"

"What *I* did? I didn't do anything. Steph, tell them."

Ruby held up his hand motioning for Nick to be quiet. "Stephanie, who did this to you?"

Stephanie dropped her head down and whimpered. Ruby grasped her chin and forced her head up. "Who beat you, Stephanie?" Ruby asked.

Her fingers dug into the ends of the chair arms. "Nick," she whispered.

"Louder," Ruby commanded.

Tears flooded down her face. She gulped them back. "Nick." She met Nick's shocked stare for an instant and then ducked her head down.

"And what did he do after he beat you?" Ruby asked.

Stephanie stared at the floor shaking her head back and forth. She squirmed sideways in the chair and shielded her face with both hands when Ruby leaned close to her ear. "Answer me," he hissed.

"H-he raped me."

"Steph?" The air drained from Nick's lungs. His body fell limp against the back of the chair.

"You lied about your age to get a job here. How old are you really, Stephanie?" Ruby asked.

"F-fourteen," she answered in a hoarse whisper.

Ruby walked to the door and opened it. "You may go now."

Stephanie pushed herself up from the chair with shaking arms. She kept her eyes trained on the floor as Patricia put her arm around her shoulders and led her out of the office.

After shutting the door, Ruby turned to Nick. "So, Nick, do you see my dilemma?"

Jumping to his feet, he jabbed his finger in front of Ruby's face. "You did this, you bastard! I didn't beat or rape her. You forced her to lie. How could you hurt Steph? She's only a kid. You've already threatened Katie and my whole family. What the hell more do you want?"

"Easy, Nick, I'm on your side. I'm simply protecting my client. The blackmail threat has been eliminated. The worker took a nasty fall from a ladder. Broke his neck. And Stephanie will go away. The problem is handled." Ruby held out both arms and flashed his toothy smile.

"Handled? You murdered a man and beat Stephanie! And you have a DVD with my fiancée on it."

"The video will be kept safely in your file." Ruby shrugged and then added, "As long as you cooperate. I don't protect uncooperative clients."

"What did you mean by Stephanie will go away?"

"Just that. Back to whatever cornfield or haystack she came from. She's underage, she can't work here. Especially looking as ugly as she does now. Bad for my business."

Nick leaned across the desk, his voice shook with rage. "Somehow, I'm going to find a way to kill you. You . . . you fucking piece of shit!"

"Sticks and stones, Nick." Ruby's laughter followed Nick as he stalked out the door.

Nick punched the elevator button and paced the hallway while he waited. His anger churned like molten lava fueled by his helplessness to retaliate against Ruby.

The elevator doors opened, and Janis Ford stepped out. "Well, well, picking up a paycheck for feeling up your fans yesterday?"

Her sarcasm ignited Nick's temper. "You're the witch who writes all the lies about me. And you're too much of a coward to answer my calls." He took a step toward her. "Why were you at my girlfriend's apartment?"

Janis jerked her head back and blinked. She stepped sideways and pulled a can of pepper spray from her purse. "Back off." She held it at arm's length in front of her.

Nick threw his hands in the air. "Yeah, it figures. You need to carry that with all the trash you print about people."

"Oh, that's rich, coming from the poster boy of morality," Janis sneered. She turned and sauntered down the hall toward Ruby's office.

Nick knocked on Stephanie's apartment door. "Steph, it's Nick," he called, his face pressed close to the door. He thought he heard a sound. "Steph? Open the door, please."

He turned to go downstairs as the dead bolt clicked. The door opened as far as the secondary chain lock allowed. Stephanie peered out with her right eye. Although red and swollen from crying, the battered left side of her face stayed hidden behind the door.

"I'm so sorry, Nick. Please forgive . . ." Her words disintegrated into ragged sobs.

"Can I come in?"

"Are you going to hit me?"

"No, of course not. I only want to talk to you."

The door closed and the chain slid in the track. It fell and rattled against the inside of the door. When Stephanie didn't open the door, Nick turned the knob and pushed it open.

She stood in the living room with her arms wrapped around herself, peering at him through the tangled mat of hair laying across her face. When he closed the door behind him, she backed away.

"Steph, I'm not angry at you. And I'm certainly not going to hurt you." He walked over and put his hands on her shoulders. Her body trembled. She kept her head down and stared at the floor.

Nick gently lifted her chin with one finger. He winced at the sight of the left side of Stephanie's swollen and bloodied face. The red marks, bruises and cuts, were emphasized by her milky complexion. Her left eye was still swollen shut, the purplish-black color had deepened and spread, encircling her eyebrow and underneath her eye. Her split lower lip looked more than twice its normal size.

"Don't look at me." She turned her head. "I'm so ugly."

"You're not ugly. It's looks bad now, but your face will heal, and you'll be as pretty as before."

She hung her head and cried.

Nick walked into the kitchen and rummaged through her freezer. He found a tray of ice, a frozen dinner and a carton of Ben and Jerry's ice cream. "Do you have any bags of frozen veggies or fruit?"

Stephanie ventured to the edge of the kitchen. "No. Are you hungry?"

Nick smiled and shook his head. "Not to eat. To put on your eye. Looks like you don't cook much." Bottles of beer and wine lined the otherwise pristine, white refrigerator shelves.

He found a plastic bag and filled it with ice cubes. After tying it closed, he handed it to Stephanie. "Here, hold this on your eye. It'll bring down the swelling."

She gingerly put the bag against her face. "Ow."

"I know, it hurts at first. Keep it on there. The cold will help numb the pain."

"You've had a black eye before?"

"Yeah. A few."

He took two glasses from a cabinet and an open bottle of wine from the refrigerator.

"C'mon sit down. Try to relax." He walked into the living room and poured the wine. "Here." He handed Stephanie a small glass.

The wine inside the glass trembled in her hand. "Aren't you afraid I'll get drunk and do something stupid? That's what started this whole horrible mess."

"This wasn't your fault. Besides, it's only half a glass. If you were older, I'd say you're entitled to get drunk." He took a long sip from his glass and looked around the apartment. "What's with all the boxes?" He hadn't noticed the stacks of folded, cardboard boxes lining the living room walls when he first entered.

"Ruby fired me. Told me to move out."

Nick cursed Ruby under his breath. "When?"

"By tomorrow." She put the ice bag on the coffee table and lightly dabbed at her left eye with a tissue, then wiped her right eye and blew her nose.

"Tomorrow? Shit." Nick scanned the shelves of electronics, stacks of DVD's and CD's, books, stuffed animals and too many other novelty items to count. "Where are you going to go?"

Stephanie shook her head and curled up in the corner of the sofa. Sobs racked her slight frame.

"Steph?" Nick sat and put his arm around her. "Calm down. Sit up." He placed the ice bag back on her eye. "You have to be out of here by tomorrow?"

She nodded her head and opened her mouth to talk, but only gasps came out. After a deep breath, she blurted, "I-I don't have anywhere to go."

"You can stay in my apartment until you find another job. I sleep on the couch anyway. You can have the bedroom." Under his present circumstances, it probably wasn't a wise offer, but Stephanie's sobs wrenched at his gut.

Her uninjured eye widened. "Oh, no. Mr. Ruby ordered me out of his building. If he found out I moved in downstairs . . . he'd . . . he'd kill me."

"Have you called your family? Can you go back home?" Nick picked up a framed photograph. A woman with wavy, red hair and warm eyes stood with her arm around an athletic-looking man. In front of them, two small children; a young girl with an unruly mop of red hair and a small boy with a crooked, gap-toothed grin. "Cute. Is this you when you were little, or your kid sister?"

Stephanie took the picture from Nick and flipped it over. She pried up the metal clasps on the back of the frame and slid out the thin sheet of printed paper with the frame company's logo on the back.

"The print came with the frame. I bought it 'cause the woman had the same color hair as mine," she murmured.

"What about your real family?"

"Don't have one. I've been in foster homes since I can remember. Nine all together, I think."

"You don't know who your parents are?"

"When I was ten, I was in a car with one of my foster mothers. She pointed at a skinny red-haired woman standing on a corner. She said, there's your mother, I went to high school with her. She's a heroin addict and a whore and she doesn't even know who your father is."

"Jesus, Steph, that's awful. I had no idea."

Fresh tears dripped from her eyes. "At least I got to see my mom, once."

Nick squeezed her hand. "Is it true you're only fourteen?"

"No, Ruby made me say that. I'm sixteen. I'll be seventeen tomorrow."

"Tomorrow's your birthday? Helluva birthday present, getting evicted."

"He saw my birth date in my personnel file. He laughed and said it was appropriate I get thrown out on my birthday. Said it was just like my real birthday, when my mom . . . threw me away." Her face crinkled as she broke into more sobs.

"How did Ruby know about your mom?"

She grimaced and covered her neck with her hands. "H-he made me tell him everything."

Nick stroked the tear-soaked hair away from her face and saw deep red bruises in the shape of finger marks on her neck. "Oh, Steph."

"How did you get out of foster care if you're still a minor?"

"I ran away. The last family they placed me with, the father was weird. Came into my bedroom at night and sat on my bed. Stared at me. I stole money from his wife's purse and bought a bus ticket. I was going to age out in two years anyway." Her voice dropped to a whisper. "I didn't want to get raped."

He put his arm around her. "Steph, did Ruby do this or did he have someone else beat you up?"

She shook her head hard and whimpered from the pain. "He said I-I can't tell anyone."

"You can tell me. It's okay."

"Ruby did it," she whispered. "I hate him so much. Please, Nick, you can't ever let him know him I told you. He'd kill me."

"Beating up a girl. Fucking coward." Nick's voice softened. "Did he rape you?"

"No. He hit me. Choked me. He said if I didn't say you beat me and raped me, then. . . .."

"Then, what?"

She shuddered against him. "He showed me this movie, but it wasn't a real movie. It just started playing on the wall. Four horrible-looking men in an old van . . ."

"You don't have to say anymore."

She gripped Nick's arm. "I don't know how he did it. But it was me in the movie. Getting beat up . . . and raped. Over and over. He forced me to watch it. Then they stabbed me and threw my body into a river. Ruby said it would all happen tonight, exactly like the movie . . . unless I lied about you. I'm so sorry, Nick. I didn't want to say those terrible things about you, but I was so scared."

"I know, it's okay. I've seen Ruby's movies."

Stephanie stared up at him and whispered, "Ruby's the devil, for real."

"Yeah, he's the devil for real, all right. He tortures all of his so-called clients. Cullen. Me. God only knows how many others. And Chris. I wanted to talk to you about Chris, and his suicide note."

Fresh tears spilled down her cheeks. "Poor Chris, please, I-I can't deal with that right now."

Nick handed her a tissue. "Steph, do you know where Ruby keeps his client's contracts?"

Stephanie bolted upright. "Nick, don't even think about—"

"You have to tell me where he keeps them."

She sighed and shook her head. "The big, bottom drawer in his desk. But he never leaves his office unlocked. He'd kill anyone if they tried—"

"Let me worry about that." Nick stood and looked around the room. "Right now, we need to figure out where you can go. I guess a hotel? I doubt we can get a moving company on such short notice. I'll help you pack up your stuff. Rent a U-Haul. You can put everything in a storage unit until you find a new place."

Stephanie stood and paced around the room. "How much is a hotel? And a storage unit?"

"We can check online. Find a hotel with weekly or monthly rates. I don't know what storage units cost, I've never used one."

She leaned her head against the wall and stared out the front window. Tears dripped from her chin.

"I'm sorry, losing your job and having to move, it all sucks."

"It's not that," she said. "I-I don't have any money."

"I thought you said you made good money?"

"I did. Fantastic money. But . . . I spent it all." She waved her arms around the room. "Clothes, shoes, make-up and all of this stuff. I kept buying things. I'm such an idiot."

"You've got nothing saved up?" He thought of how Katie deposited most of her paycheck in the bank every two weeks like clockwork.

"I have, maybe, three hundred and seventy something dollars. I didn't get a pay check yesterday, Ruby refused to pay me."

"That's illegal—"

Stephanie grunted and laid her head back on the wall. "What am I supposed to do, sue the devil?"

"I have money," Nick said. "Money's about all I do have, since I signed with Ruby."

"I can't let you pay for a hotel room and storage for all this stuff."

"Why not? What else can you do?"

"I don't know how long it will take for me to find a job. A good job, that pays enough to afford an apartment in the city. I'm seventeen. Only stupid fast food places would hire me. Ruby burned my fake ID. It cost me a lot of money to get it made."

Nick poured himself more wine and thought while he sipped it. "Let me talk to my grandmother. I bet she wouldn't mind if you stayed at my house. It's a big, two-story apartment. There's a guest room plus my old room. Maybe you could even work at the restaurant, until you get back on your feet."

Stephanie walked over to him. "Why are you helping me after the horrible stuff I said about you?"

"Ruby forced you to say it. Probably because he heard me ask you about the contracts. I'm so sorry he hurt you to get back at me." Nick smiled and wiped a tear from her cheek with his thumb. "You're my friend, Steph. I'm not gonna leave you stranded."

He picked up a packing tape dispenser lying near the boxes. "I'll put these boxes together so we can start packing. I'll talk to my grandmother and rent a truck tomorrow morning."

Chapter 16

Early the following morning, Nick drove to the U-Haul rental. The closest one happened to be located on the same street as Ray's auto restoration shop. He found Ray inside wiping down an antique coupe.

"Hey, Ray do you mind if leave my Mustang here? The lot at U-Haul doesn't look very secure."

"Sure. Pull it into bay three. U-Haul, huh? You moving Katie in with you?"

"No." Nick scowled. "I'm helping a friend from work move."

Ray threw the rag down on the workbench. "You need a hand?"

"Seriously? You want to huff boxes around all day?"

"We haven't hung out much since I got back. I planned to spray the twenty-two coupe today. But the paint I ordered never came in. I thought about going to the gym, but, hell, moving's a work-out."

"Yeah, it is. Especially when you see all the boxes this girl's got."

The two walked down the street and rented the largest truck available. As Nick pulled out of the rental truck driveway, he told Ray he needed to stop by his family's apartment. Ray settled into the cushioned seat and adjusted the radio. "No problem." He bobbed his head and moved his torso in rhythm with the music as they drove.

Nick parked in the alley between the restaurant and the dress shop next door. He laughed at Ray singing along and moving in time to Santana's *Smooth* on the radio. "I'll leave it running for you, *Carlos*. Just be a minute."

"Hey, you gotta admit, I got the moves. You might be taller, but you dance like a white boy."

The restaurant was closed on Mondays. He found his grandmother upstairs in the apartment kitchen mixing bread dough. She wiped her hands on her apron and rushed to hug him when he entered.

"You finally come! Sit, Nickie. We talk."

"I only have a minute Nonna, I came to ask you a favor. A friend of mine from work needs a place to stay. She's had some bad luck and has no family or money and nowhere to go. Kind of like some of the girls at the Shelter. I wanted to ask you if she could stay here, just for a little while. Maybe she could help out in the restaurant."

"I don't know this girl, Nickie. I don't like strangers in my house."

"She's not a stranger, Nonna. She's my friend."

"She's got no family?"

"No. She was in foster care. I don't think she'd be any trouble. You'd like her."

His grandmother scowled. "First, I meet her. Then, I see. I don't like the people I see you work with on television. We need to talk about this work of yours. How you act. And on the TV, for everyone to see!"

"Hey, Nick." Sal strolled into the kitchen. He opened the refrigerator door and stood studying the contents.

"You let the cold out!" Nonna chided. "Close the door."

"But, I'm hungry," Sal whined.

"You always hungry. Get something and close the door."

"Sal, what are you doing home today?" Nick asked.

He grinned at his brother. "No work and a teacher's day at school. Gonna grab a snack and fire up a new video game."

"Want to help me move a friend?"

"On my day off? No, thanks."

Nonna scowled and rapped the side of his head with her hand. "Salvatore, how you raised? Your brother ask you for help. You help."

"I don't want to spend my day moving, Nonna."

Nick gripped Sal's shoulders. "I'll pay you. C'mon, between you, me and Ray, we can do this in a few hours. You'll have the rest of the day to yourself plus some extra cash."

"Salvatore, go help him," Nonna said.

Sal sighed and rolled his eyes. "Fine. Let me put my shoes on."

"When are we gonna talk, Nickie? You never come by. Don't answer your phone. Then I see you on TV acting like a . . ." She threw her hands up the air. "I don't know what. What does Katie say? Does she know this girl you want to live here?"

Nick wasn't in the mood to discuss the disastrous book signing with his grandmother. "Yes, she does. And Katie and I are back together, Nonna. Your idea to cook her dinner worked. Thank you." He leaned and kissed her on the cheek hoping the good news would distract her. Technically, he wasn't lying. He and Katie were back together, but for how much longer was the true question.

"Of course it work. That's good Nickie, I'm happy for you both."

Sal trudged into the kitchen. "Ready."

Nick opened the front door. "We'll be back later, Nonna. You can meet Stephanie then."

"I don't forget, Nickie. We still need to talk."

"I gotta go." He pecked her on the cheek. "Ray's waiting in the truck."

Sal leaned against the hallway wall with his hands in his pockets while Nick knocked on Stephanie's door. Ray stood with a hand cart behind the two.

Stephanie opened the door and looked distressed when she saw Ray and Sal with Nick. "I'll be right back." She ran into her bedroom and closed the door

Sal grabbed Nick's arm. "When you said a friend, I thought you meant some dude. Why didn't you tell me it was a hot girl?" He pulled a comb from his back jeans pocket and ran it through his hair.

"Mother . . ." Ray looked at the piles of boxes stacked in the living room and hallway. "How many people live here?"

"One," Nick answered with a grin. "She has a lot of stuff."

Stephanie weaved through the boxes piled in the hall. She had arranged her hair to hide the bruised left side of her face and put on a bright pink ball cap studded with rhinestones to hold it in place.

"Steph, this is my friend, Ray and my brother, Sal."

Ray nodded and said hello.

Sal stuck out his hand and stood with his shoulders back and his chest puffed out.

"Nice to meet you, Sal. Thanks for helping," Stephanie said taking his hand.

"You're really hot! So, what happened to your face?" Sal asked with a big grin.

Nick elbowed him in the ribs.

"What? She is hot." He looked at Nick with a hurt expression.

"Start moving stuff," Nick hissed at him. He turned to Stephanie. "The building manager's a nice guy. Let me park the truck out front." He pushed the hand cart at Sal. "Grab some of the boxes by the front door and take them down to the truck."

"I'm almost done packing up the bedroom." Stephanie said.

"You've done a ton since last night." Nick said. "Go finish packing. We'll start loading."

Stephanie walked back into the bedroom. Sal stepped into the doorway and called out, "You need any help? I can lift any heavy stuff. I'm really strong. I'm a boxer."

"You're an idiot," Nick whispered as he slapped him in the back of the head. "You don't ask a girl what happened to her face. What the hell's wrong with you?"

Ray stood with his arms crossed grinning at the two brothers.

"I didn't mean it bad. I only wanted to know. Hey, does she have a boyfriend? Is he the one who beat her up? Maybe the three of us should go talk to this guy, you know?" Sal smacked his fist into his open hand.

"Mind your own business, Sal. Grab some boxes."

Sal mumbled under his breath as he hefted four cartons onto the cart. He wheeled it out the door toward the elevator keeping one hand on the teetering top carton to steady it.

Ray secured the other full boxes with tape. "Not that I feel like getting shot by some asshole, but what Sal said wasn't wrong. If somebody beat up one of my sisters, or Katie, we'd go visit the guy."

Nick looked at his friend and sighed.

When Sal returned for a second load, Nick pulled him aside in the living room. "Steph doesn't have a boyfriend. Some guy, not important who, attacked her. Plus, she lost her job and this apartment came with it."

Sal frowned and looked around the apartment. "Damn, that sucks. This is a nice place."

Ray called out he was taking a load down on the cart. Sal and Nick each grabbed two boxes and followed.

After five trips, the three were happy to see the living room and hallway emptied of boxes.

"We're actually making progress," Ray said.

Stephanie stood in the bedroom doorway. "Everything's packed. I just need to tape up the boxes."

"I'll do it." Sal grabbed the tape gun and jogged into the bedroom.

"What about the furniture? You'll need another friggin' truck," Ray said.

Nick shook his head. "Nope, the place came furnished. It all stays."

"Good."

They walked into the bedroom. Sal kept up his non-stop chatter as he worked. "I know this guy at the gym who got punched in the face. Real hard. Kinda like you. Except his eyeball was hanging out and they had to shove it back in. His face was all black and purple, too, for a long time. Then it turned green and yellow. It went back to normal, eventually. Except his one eye is still kinda jacked-up. You know, if the messed up side of your face heals up and looks as good the right side you'd be super hot."

Stephanie kept her head down, her face hidden behind a thick curtain of red hair and wrote the contents of each box on the top flaps while Sal talked.

Nick whispered to Ray, "Did we sound that freaking stupid when we were seventeen?"

Ray laughed. "Yeah, we did."

Stephanie's vast collection of clothing and shoes took up another twenty-five boxes and several large plastic trash bags. Nick, Ray and Sal made trip after trip hauling as many boxes as they each could carry. They were surprised to see a pizza delivery man standing at the front door when they exited the elevator.

"Steph, you shouldn't spend your money—" Nick started.

"It's the least I can do. If it weren't for you guys, I don't know what I'd have done."

Stephanie handed the man money and took the two pizza boxes from him. "Lunch is here." She put the boxes on the kitchen counter. "There's beer and wine in the fridge. Help yourselves."

Nick reached in the refrigerator and handed a bottle of beer to Ray and took out one for himself. Sal stood looking at him with pleading eyes. "C'mon Nick, don't make me look like a jerk in front of Stephanie. Lemme have a beer," he murmured.

Nick smiled and poked his brother in the chest. "And explain to Nonna why I let you drink when we get back to the house? No way."

Sal glanced over his shoulder at Stephanie and then back to his brother. "One beer? How's Nonna gonna know? C'mon, Nick, please?"

Ray grinned when Nick finally handed his brother a bottle and said, "Just one."

Sal took the beer, strutted to the counter and sat on the stool next to Stephanie. Nick and Ray each grabbed a slice of pizza, walked into the living room and sat on the couch.

"So, what happened to her?" Ray asked in a low voice.

"Some guy beat her up."

"She know him?"

"Not really." Nick took another bite of pizza. He couldn't remember the last time he had eaten and all the heavy lifting had made him hungry.

"So, is she the reason you're avoiding Katie?" Ray asked.

"Huh?" Nick asked with his mouth full.

"You and the redhead. Are you two, ya know . . . involved?"

Nick shook his head. "Not at all. Steph's just a friend. She was in a bad position and I wanted to help her out. That's all."

"And this guy that she doesn't really know, are you afraid he'll do the same thing to Katie?"

Nick swallowed and then took a long drink of beer. He picked at the label on the bottle with his thumbnail and avoided Ray's pointed stare.

"All right, I get it." Ray sighed and bit into his pizza. "I'll carry my gun when I pick up Katie."

"Thanks, Ray. I appreciate you looking out for Katie." Nick turned toward the kitchen when he heard Stephanie giggle. He hadn't heard her laugh in days. She picked a long thread of melted mozzarella from Sal's chin.

▲

Stephanie closed the door of the apartment. "I'll drop my key and security card off at the manager's office," she said. "Guess I'll follow you guys to the storage unit?"

"Okay," Nick said. "Which one?"

Stephanie stared at him and bit her lower lip out of habit. "Ow!" She touched her fingers to her red, swollen lip. "I forgot to look online. I'll check now." She pulled out her phone before they entered the elevator. She swiped the screen for a few moments and then read off the address of a nearby storage facility. When they reached the ground floor, she said, "Give me a minute to get my car and I'll follow you."

"I'll keep you company," Sal said. He walked with Stephanie toward the parking garage. Ray and Nick climbed into the U-Haul and waited until Stephanie's yellow bug pulled down the driveway.

▲

The attendant at the storage complex scratched his head and surveyed the huge U-Haul. "You'll need at least four units, if that truck's full," he said. "You want climate-controlled spaces?"

Nick looked at Stephanie and shrugged. "How much?" he asked the man.

"It's three hundred a month for regular units."

"Not too bad, I guess," Nick said when he saw Stephanie frown.

"That's for one," the man said. "Times four, is twelve hundred. If you want temp-controlled units, they're four hundred and fifty each. If it all fits into four, that is."

Stephanie's shoulders sagged and her swollen lip trembled. "No. Forget it. Sorry." She ran back to her Volkswagen and buried her head into her folded arms on the roof.

The man shrugged and returned to his office. Sal and Nick walked over to Stephanie. "This is the first place we tried. There's got to be cheaper places," Nick said.

"It's Thrifty Storage. It's advertised as the cheapest. And the others are even farther away." Tears dripped down her face. "Give it all to charity or the city dump. I don't care anymore." She opened the door, sank into the driver's seat and covered her face with her hands.

Ray poked his head out the truck window as it sat idling in the driveway. "We unloading?"

Nick shook his head no.

Sal held his cell phone to his ear and walked away. A few moments later, he motioned to Nick. "Let's go to Eddie's."

"Eddie's? What for?" Nick asked.

He followed Sal around the car to Stephanie's open driver's door.

Sal squatted down beside the car and grinned up at her. "Hey, it's okay. I found a place. And it's free. The top floor of Eddie's Gym is empty. He's been talking about expanding and making the second floor a women's workout place. Knowing Eddie, that ain't gonna happen for a while, if ever. He's fine with us putting your stuff up there. No charge."

Stephanie climbed out of her car. "Really?"

Sal stood, beaming at her. "Yeah. It's safe and close to our house if you need any stuff."

Stephanie touched Sal's arm. "Thank you, Sal."

Old Eddie shuffled out when the U-Haul and Stephanie's Beetle pulled into his parking lot. He eyed Stephanie as he pressed a key into Sal's hand. "There's nuthin' illegal in the truck, right?"

Sal smiled and shook his head no. "Nope. Just clothes and stuff."

"I'm holding you responsible," Eddie said, poking a gnarled finger into Sal's chest. "You leave the door unlocked and somebody breaks in, I break your head. You lose the key, you pay to get the locks changed." He turned and walked back into the gym.

For the next three and a half hours they hauled Stephanie's belongings up the outside metal staircase into the second story. Three quarters of the upstairs space stood empty except for some broken gym equipment at one end. The other side of the huge space housed a small studio apartment.

"It's a little dusty, but I could clean it up and paint it for you. It could be kinda nice." Sal said. He led Stephanie by the hand, pointing out the tiny kitchenette area and a bathroom with a shower stall. "Eddie used to let guys from outta town stay here before a match. But he hasn't used it in years. I could ask him if you can stay here, if you want me to."

"I can't live here. I'd have to pay rent and I don't have a job." Stephanie said.

"Eddie's been talking about hiring someone to help with the memberships and bookings. It's a lot of paperwork and phone calls. He hates that stuff. Maybe you could work here." He flopped onto the single bed, the head pushed up against the only window in the studio. "Bed's comfortable." He grinned at Stephanie, rolled to one side and patted the mattress. "Wanna try it?"

Nick cleared his throat. "We need to get back to the house. I want Nonna to meet Steph."

"Nick! What's the matter with you? Give beer to children? Don't shake your head. I smell it."

"Just one beer, Nonna." He glared at Sal who stood smirking next to Stephanie in the doorway between the kitchen and living room.

Ray pretended to cough and covered his smile with his hand.

"It's no different than drinking a glass of wine, Nonna," Sal said.

Nick shook his head knowing what was coming next. His grandmother crossed the kitchen and wagged her finger in Sal's face.

"No different than wine, eh? Do they have beer in church? No! They have wine. Jesus drank the wine. Not the beer!"

Sal's face flushed pink. He asked, "What're you cooking Nonna? It smells good."

"Chicken and pasta," she said. "Don't tell me, I know. You hungry!"

"It smells amazing," Stephanie said in a meek voice. She had been staring wide-eyed around the apartment since they arrived.

"You hungry, too?" Nonna asked.

"I'm always hungry," Stephanie said with a nervous giggle.

"Dinner be ready soon." Nonna squeezed her arm. "You need to eat. Look how skinny she is!"

Sal gave Nick the thumbs up sign behind his grandmother's back.

"After dinner, I show you the guest room, okay?" Nonna asked Stephanie.

"Thank you," Steph said. "I really appreciate you letting me stay here. I promise I'll look for a job as soon as, um, my face looks better."

"It's okay, sweetheart. Everything will be okay." Nonna patted Stephanie's unhurt cheek. "Salvatore, take her into the living room until dinner's ready. Go watch TV. All of you. I can't cook with a crowd in my kitchen."

"Hey, you wanna play a video game? Or listen to some music?" Sal asked. "I have a killer gaming and sound system in my room." He took Stephanie's hand and led her toward the staircase.

"Keep your door open, Salvatore. You hear me?" Nonna shook a wooden spoon in the air. "Boys!"

Savory aromas of fresh-baked bread, Parmesan and Romano cheeses, tomato sauce, garlic and basil filled the kitchen. Heaping dishes of food covered the table. Stephanie and Sal sat across from Nick at the large oval table chatting and smiling as they ate. Even his father seemed amiable tonight. He talked about his time in the Navy and asked Ray questions about his recent stint in the Army. The cozy dinner scene reminded Nick of when his mother was alive. He missed seeing both her, and Katie, seated at the table.

Nonna made another trip around the table spooning more food onto everyone's plates.

Ray held up his hands. "No thanks, I'm stuffed, Nonna. I forgot how good your cooking is." Ray looked at Nick. "We need to take the rental truck back. Katie gets off work in forty-five minutes."

Nick and Ray walked from the U-Haul rental back to Ray's shop, moaning about how full they felt from dinner. Ray unlocked and raised the bay door so Nick could pull his Mustang outside. Then Ray backed his old Chevy out and parked it behind Nick's car on the street.

"Nick, I can't pick up Katie forever, ya know. She wants you, not me. She's worried about you, man. So am I."

Nick stood by his car kicking at the curb. Today had been the first good and sober day he had in a while. Focusing on helping someone else took his mind from his own troubles. He felt relieved knowing Stephanie had a safe place to stay and grateful for an entire day without any bursts of rage or red-tinted vision. But Ray's words brought reality crashing down on him. He wanted to pick Katie up from work, spend the evening making love to her and then wake holding her in his arms. Thanks to Ruby's demons, he was terrified to go near her. The thought of returning to his apartment alone, and worse, having to deal with Ruby in the morning, made him feel sick and hopeless.

"I offered to help today so we could talk about this shit. Figure something out. But between Sal and Steph and then your family around . . ." Ray waved his hand in front of Nick's face. "Nick! You hear me?"

Nick swiped his sleeve across his eyes. "Yeah. I hear you." He blew out a long breath. "I need more time." He slid into his driver's seat, started the car and pulled away.

Chapter 17

Seeing the new girl seated at the receptionist's desk in Ruby's office the next morning both angered and depressed Nick. Stephanie had been a familiar, friendly face and his only ally in the office. Her replacement fit all of Ruby's criteria for his female employees—young and attractive. Glossy black hair framed her smooth, golden complexion and dark, almond-shaped eyes. She offered a rehearsed smile when Nick entered. He told her his name and she dutifully pressed the intercom and announced his arrival. She motioned for him to sit with a graceful wave of her hand and then sat with her head bowed, rapidly tapping on her computer keyboard.

He chose to stand and pace. The photographs hanging on the walls of Joseph Cullen and the Blood Lust band that had awed him on his first visit to Ruby's office, now made his stomach knot.

Ruby summoned him from his doorway. The wave of heat inside the office reminded him of the flush of rage he experienced when one of the demons took over his body. He perched on the edge of the guest chair and waited for Ruby to speak.

"What do you think of Kim, my new receptionist?"

Nick shrugged and sat nervously tapping his feet.

"No opinion? I find her so much easier on the eyes than Stephanie. She's smarter, too."

A fiery sensation quivered inside Nick's gut, but he bit his tongue.

"What's wrong?" Ruby flashed his signature toothy grin. "Kim's twenty-two, is that too old for you to pin down on your bed, Nick?"

The fiery ball inside him intensified. He spat his words. "What did you want to see me about?"

"Ah, busy schedule, hey Nick? Do you have a new book in the works or are you simply itching to carve up your fiancée?"

Nick squeezed his hands into fists. Ruby enjoyed goading him into a fit of anger so he could flick his finger and fling him across the room like a rag doll. "No book right now," he answered in a low, measured voice. "I simply wanted to know what you have planned next."

"A book signing. Today at one o'clock. I won't be able to join you. I'm launching Talon's world tour promotion. Think you can handle it alone?"

He glared at Ruby. "Did you hire more strippers to show up?"

Ruby laughed. "No. We'll see how the herd reacts on their own today."

"Where is it?"

"The Book Shelf, it's downtown—"

"I know where it is." He jumped up from the chair, eager to leave.

"Afterward, I promised Janis Ford an exclusive interview with you. She'll meet you at the bookstore."

Nick rolled his eyes and kept walking toward the door.

"One more thing, Nick."

Nick paused with his hand on the doorknob and turned. Ruby curled his finger indicating for him to come back.

"Tonight, there's a cocktail party. Seven o'clock. The penthouse of the Grande Plaza. Same hotel where I hosted the VIP. I want you there."

"Why?"

"So, I can introduce you to the movie producer I've chosen to make the film version of your books." Ruby's eyes narrowed into dark glittering slits and his lips pressed into a tight smile. His expression made the sweat running down Nick's back turn cold.

"What else do you have planned at this cocktail party?"

Ruby held up his hands, palms outward and smiled. "Drinks, hors d'oeuvres. Polite conversation."

The Book Shelf was a small, local book shop located five blocks from Ruby's office. A line of mostly women stretched all the way down the street. A small group of reporters stood at the front door. They shouted questions and snapped pictures as Nick entered the store.

The set up inside the store was more organized than his first book signing. A team of cashiers sold books and then directed customers to the back of the store where Nick sat at a table and signed them. The event proceeded smoothly, and the press left early, seeming bored with the large, but orderly crowd.

Near the end of the two-hour scheduled signing, Nick heard a woman scream and then sounds of a scuffle. He stood and watched as police led two women out the front door with navy blue blankets draped around them.

Janis Ford strolled to the table with her camera in her hands. "Looks like I snagged an exclusive photo. Two more of your crazed, topless fans." She glanced at her cellphone. "How much longer will you be?"

"Until I'm done." He nodded toward the women patiently waiting in line.

Janis heaved a loud sigh. "I'll be in the coffee shop."

The signing officially ended at three o'clock but Nick stayed until after four to accommodate the fans waiting at his table. He found Janis Ford sitting in a booth in the coffee shop typing on her laptop.

"Your legions of panting, under-aged groupies finally have enough of you?" Her brown eyes fixed on him in a cold stare.

"I don't want to talk to you either, Janis." He slid into the booth opposite her. "But since I'm forced to, let's start with why you were nosing around my fiancée's apartment last week?"

"Maybe you're not bright enough to understand how this works, pretty boy. I ask the questions, you answer."

Nick moved to the end of the seat and stood. "Screw you."

"Not if you were the last man on earth." She waved a packet of typed pages. "Besides, Mr. Ruby already gave me your interview to publish."

Nick grabbed for the papers, but Janis snatched them away.

"So, why even bother with this damn interview?"

"I'm allowed to add my personal observations to the piece. Which right now are an arrogant, conceited asshole in need of anger management classes." She sneered at him.

He sat and leaned across the table. "I need anger management? What is your deal? Are you that bitter because I won Ruby's contest and you didn't?"

Janis studied her laptop screen. "Let's just say if I had won, I would have accomplished a hell of a lot more than getting shit-faced drunk and screwing everything that walked in front of me."

"You don't know jack shit about me or Ruby. You're so gullible and desperate for a story, you take whatever crap he hands you and then run with it. If you knew the truth, you'd be celebrating that you lost his fucking contest."

Janis's head snapped up. "What truth?" Her tone, while cold, sounded civil for once.

"Publish whatever trash Ruby gave you. I don't give a shit." He stood and walked away.

"Wait! What do you know about Ian Slaughter and Joseph Cullen?" She hurried to catch up with him. "How about Bethany Grant or Lee Woods? Do you know anything about them?"

Nick quickened his pace and shouted over his shoulder. "You're Ruby's lap dog. Ask him."

Ruby had reserved the penthouse of the Grande Plaza hotel for the cocktail party. A smiling young woman dressed in a black and white uniform greeted Nick as he entered the luxurious suite. She offered a silver tray of hors d'oeuvres.

"No, thank you," he said, waving his hand.

Scanning the spacious room, he immediately spotted Talon. She stood a head above everyone else in the crowd. Her skimpy, red sequined gown molded to her body like scales on a snake. The fabric shimmered with her every movement under the dim lights in undulating shades of red. She dwarfed Victor Ruby, who escorted her with his arm around her waist. The two stopped and greeted a slender, middle-aged man with a clean-shaven head and narrow-framed, tinted glasses.

Nick maneuvered through the small groups of elegantly dressed guests who stood talking with drinks in their hands and wound his way to the closest portable bar. Fortified with a drink in his hand, he reluctantly joined Talon and Ruby.

"Nick. Right on time," Ruby said with a smile. Talon wound her arm through Nick's. He could feel the sinewy muscles in her arm flex against his forearm like a boa constrictor, tensed and ready to tighten its suffocating grip at will.

"This is Jason Myriad," Ruby said, motioning to the bald man. "Myridian Productions. I trust you've heard of it, Nick."

Nick shook Jason's hand. "Yes, of course." He had seen the Myridian logo at the beginning of almost every horror movie he'd ever watched.

"Victor has me intrigued about this epic vampire story of yours, Nick," Jason said. "He tells me it would translate quite well to film. Of course, I hope you're not one of those writers who's convinced a movie will never capture the true essence of their work." Jason's lips jerked up at the corners in a feeble attempt at a smile. His eyes remained fixed and cold, shielded behind amber-colored lenses.

"Not at all," Nick said. "In fact, I admire how much visuals and special effects add to a story. Especially in the horror genre. Those are the kind of things an author can only hope a reader envisions in their minds when they read the book."

Jason raised his eyebrows and nodded at Ruby. "I'll look forward to reviewing the screenplay."

"We'll have it to you next week," Ruby said.

"Are you writing the screenplay, Nick?" Jason asked.

Before Nick could respond, Ruby answered, "Nick's overseeing the project. I've hired a screen writer to expedite the process. I'd like to see the film in theaters by this time next year."

The corners of Jason's mouth twitched again. "Victor, even if I decide I want to produce this film, that's optimistic, but, not at all realistic. There's casting and—"

"I have investors eager to spend money, Jason. A shit-load of money. If not with Myridian, then with another production house. After our long and fruitful relationship, I wanted to give you first pick. Nick is making a big impact in the industry. A movie based on his books is a guaranteed box office hit." Ruby winked at Nick. "Especially with my unique promotional skills behind him."

Jason bowed his head and stared into his drink. "I do appreciate our relationship, Victor. But, as you know, I've been branching out beyond horror movies. I have several serious projects in the works."

"If it weren't for my films, you wouldn't have the money for your so-called serious projects." Ruby craned his neck, looked past Jason and waved. A young girl of fifteen or sixteen in a short, baby blue dress waved back from the other side of the room.

"I so enjoyed talking to your daughter this evening, Jason." Ruby grasped Jason's arm, his claw-like nails dug into the sleeve of the suit jacket. "She's blossomed into a real beauty. And, she told me she has aspirations to be an actress. It can be a rough industry for a young, innocent girl. I've offered to represent her. And, as a personal favor to you, I promise to pay extra special attention to her."

Jason's Adam's apple moved up and down in his throat. "She's only sixteen. Still in high school. She doesn't know what she wants. I planned for her to attend college. I don't want. . .." A thin sheen of sweat coated Jason's bald head and face.

"Of course, you don't. But it's so difficult for a single father to keep tabs on a teenage girl. They can be quite impetuous, can't they?"

Jason gulped his drink and glared at Ruby. "I'll read your screenplay as soon as it arrives. I'll make it my priority."

"I'm so glad you're enthusiastic about the project." Ruby smiled and held his hand out to Jason. "I'm positive it will be quite lucrative for everyone involved."

Jason accepted the handshake, excused himself and then hurried off toward his daughter.

Talon withdrew her arm from Nick's and wrapped both arms around Ruby, drawing his face close to her breasts. "You were spectacular, Victor!" She bent at the waist and planted her mouth on Ruby's. Nick turned away from the two when Ruby's long tongue flickered from between his lips.

"Nick, stick around," Ruby said. "I hired several photographers. I want your picture taken in the Hollywood circle. It'll be great PR for your transition from print to film."

Nick ordered another drink and strolled to the expansive wall of floor to ceiling windows with double French doors leading outside to a tiled balcony. Holding his glass, he leaned on the iron railing, and looked out across the city. Shit, all I need is a freaking cigarette and I'm Cullen, he thought.

His cell buzzed indicating a message. Ray texted he dropped Katie off at her apartment. As usual, the text ended with *we need to talk*. Nick pocketed his phone, turned and studied the crowd while he sipped his beer. A few couples, arms entwined, stood gazing out over the balcony admiring the colorful array of lights glimmering in the night sky. They spoke in hushed tones and smiled at each other. Some kissed. He missed being part of a couple. He missed Katie.

A young woman stood a few feet away, alone, with her back to him. His eyes drifted from her long, slender neck down her bare back. A voice, not his own, whispered, *let's get a piece of that*. He averted his eyes and focused his thoughts back on Katie. Ray had seen her safely home. Nick ached to be making love to her in her bed and far away from Ruby's lurid world of parties and publicity. His mood darkened as he dwelled on how Ruby had destroyed his relationship with Katie and ruled his life.

Classical music provided by a solo pianist drifted outside. Above the din of conversation and tinkling notes, he heard Ruby's distinctive laughter. He watched him lead Talon around the crowded suite like a jockey showing off his prize filly. He glowered at Ruby through the glass wall and fantasized about choking him to death with his bare hands.

The young woman in the backless gown stared at him.

Nick shook off his murderous thoughts and forced a smile. "Hi, I'm Nick," he said, holding out his hand.

"Mary, uh, Bethany." She barely touched his fingertips and then withdrew her hand. She clutched a small purse in her arms which she kept folded tightly across her chest.

"I saw you at the VIP party. You're a movie actress, aren't you?"

"Yes." Her gaze dropped to her feet. "You're that writer. I saw your book signing on the news."

Nick grunted. "Yeah, well, Ruby stages a lot of things for the publicity."

"Yes." Her light blue eyes blazed with anger. "I'm familiar with Victor Ruby's tactics."

"So, your real name's Mary. Ruby changed it, right?"

"Victor despised my name. Said it reminded him of someone he hated. It was the first thing he changed about me."

"The first thing?"

She shook her head and turned away. "Nice meeting you," she said over her shoulder. She stood with her back to him again. He noticed thin dress straps dangled from the material at her waist, the ends frayed.

Nick leaned back against the railing. A young, blond man sneaked up behind Mary and grabbed her roughly around the waist. She let out a short scream. People turned to look. The man laughed and waved off their curious stares. "It's nothing. A joke." He whispered into Mary's ear.

Mary whirled around to face him. "I told you, I'm not doing it."

"And I'm not gonna let you screw up my future." The man jerked Mary's wrist. "Let's go."

"Stop it, you're hurting me."

He wrenched her right arm away from her body. The bodice of her dress drooped on the right side.

Nick walked to Mary's side. "Is everything all right?"

"No, it's not," she said, using the interruption to free her arm from the man's grasp. She yanked up the bodice of her gown and crossed her arms to hold the material in place.

"Mind your own business," the man said to Nick. "Who the hell are you, anyway?"

A blaze of angry heat shot through Nick. He instantly disliked the cocky, little man. "Nick Tera," he said, not offering his hand.

The man rubbed his smooth-shaven chin. "Oh, yeah, that new writer. You've got a sweet deal. Naked girls throwing themselves at you all the time, huh?" His mouth formed a leering grin and he moved his eyebrows up and down as he jutted his thumbs in the air.

"Who are you?" Nick asked.

He stuck his chin out when he answered. "Lee Woods, Bethany's co-star in *Night Birds*, the new vampire movie."

It explained Lee's pale, powdered face and black eyeliner. His hair swooped upward from his forehead into a tall, platinum-streaked pompadour.

"You and Mary having a problem?" Nick asked. She stood a few feet away watching them. Lee snorted and pointed at Mary. "Her name's Bethany, and she's the damn problem. We've got about a week left to promo the movie before the big premiere." He moved closer to Nick and lowered his voice. "The tabloids and cable have been running stories about her and me having this hot, kinky affair. Mr. Ruby arranged a special photo op tonight. We get caught naked in a bedroom." Lee snickered and slapped Nick on the back. "I'm a method actor, know what I mean? But she refuses to play along." Lee squinted his eyes and his upper lip twisted into an ugly snarl. "That icy bitch is going to ruin—"

"Maybe she's just not that into you." Nick smirked back at Lee, aware he towered over the actor and outweighed him by at least fifty pounds.

Lee cocked his head back, eyeing Nick through half-closed lids. He held out his hands, palms up, flipped his fingers inward and taunted Nick to come closer. "C'mon, big man. You wanna get into it? I'm a state kick-boxing champion. I'll chop you down like a fucking tree." Lee circled around Nick, kicking the air and striking various martial arts stances. The guests standing near them backed away and stared.

Nick's anger flared into a fiery rage. He waited until Lee circled back to face him and then threw one hard punch. His fist made a sickening, crunching sound when it smashed into the actor's face. Lee let out a high-pitched scream and fell backwards. He rolled and moaned on the patio floor with both hands clamped over his face.

Blood seeped between his fingers, dripped down his neck and dyed his white shirt with bright red.

A chorus of 'oohs' rose from the people on the balcony. Reporters and photographers swarmed in, shoving Mary and Nick closer together. Flashes of light punctuated their chorus of rapid-fire questions.

"Nick, are you and Bethany having an affair? Is that what the fight's about?"

"Bethany! Is it over between you and Lee?"

Nick grasped Mary's elbow. "You wanna get outta here?"

She nodded. Nick put one arm around her and used the other to push his way through the clinging throng of press. When they cleared the balcony, he grabbed her hand and they ran for the exit. As they entered the elevator, one of the reporters caught up to them and wedged his foot in between the doors. Nick shoved the man back and the doors slid closed.

Mary crouched in the corner of the elevator, catching her breath.

"Where's your car?" Nick asked.

"I don't have one."

"I'll drive you home, if you want?"

"No. I already have enough scandals. If I'm seen with you—"

"You've already been seen with me. The reporters will follow us downstairs. You can either come with me or deal with them."

The elevator bell rang, and the doors opened. "Oh, fine." Mary ran alongside Nick until they reached his Mustang. Bursts of camera flashes blinded them as he sped out of the parking garage of the Grande Plaza Hotel.

"The tabloids and television will have a field day with this," Mary said.

"It's a set up. Either with that asshole Lee, or me. Ruby probably planned it."

"I know what Ruby planned for me with that disgusting pig, Lee." She tightened her arms around her chest and stared out the window. "Where are you going?"

"I don't know. Where do you live?"

"The Grande Plaza. At least until after the premiere. Ruby said he'd find me an apartment. But . . ."

"But what?"

"I can't take any more of this charade. I just want to go home. To Florida. Would you drive me to the airport?"

"Um, yeah, sure." He braked at a red light and turned to face her. "Don't you have a contract with Ruby?"

Tears leaked from the corners of her eyes. "Y-yes."

They snaked through the heavy downtown traffic without speaking.

"Would you pull over?" Mary asked. "I need to buy clothes. I can't get on a plane like this."

Nick slowed, pulled past a space on the right side of the street, shifted into reverse and then steered into the spot.

Mary opened the door and got out. "Thank you. I'll call a cab from here. I appreciate you helping me get away from that party."

"I thought you wanted a ride to the airport?"

She glanced up and down the block. "No offense, but you work for Ruby. I can't trust you. At the least, you're hoping for another conquest, at the worst, you'd take me right back to him." She turned, ran down the street and disappeared into a department store.

Nick waited in case she changed her mind. He didn't blame Mary for not trusting him. God only knew what evil Ruby had threatened her with and his new tabloid reputation with women didn't exactly inspire trust. Twenty minutes later, a yellow cab double-parked a few car lengths in front of him. Mary sprinted from the store, dressed in jeans and a tee shirt, and slid inside the cab.

Good for you, he thought. Get as far away from Ruby as you can.

Chapter 18

Victor Ruby's call, demanding Nick come to the office right away, awoke him the next morning. Nick checked his cell phone. Although he hadn't returned Katie's previous calls, finding no messages or texts from her left him with a hollow, empty feeling.

Ruby escorted him into his office. "You certainly have a knack for promoting yourself, Nick. The media is all abuzz about your affair with Bethany." He chuckled and added, "Lee's nose is broken. He's livid. He'll probably have two black eyes at the premiere." Ruby lit a cigar, layering a cloud of thick, pungent smoke onto the stifling air in his office. "We need to keep up the momentum until your own movie debuts. How do you feel about switching from author to actor?"

He wondered why Ruby hadn't mentioned Mary's disappearance. Perhaps he wasn't aware she had fled the city. Could it be that simple to end this nightmare, just pack his things and leave?

Ruby's long nails tapped on the desktop. "Well?"

"I'm not an *actor*," Nick grumbled.

"One could argue you aren't a *writer* either," Ruby said with a sneer. "Other than your fairy tales about vampires, ghosts and witches."

"You've certainly shown me a new definition of horror."

"See Nick, I knew you'd come around. Some people have to experience it in order to understand what real horror is. Girlfriends slashed to pieces. Families burned alive. Nuns, children, little old ladies and war heroes make the best victims. When terrible things happen to them, people find it so much more horrifying, don't you agree?"

"What are you getting at?"

"Our first conversation. What is horror, remember? Thanks to me, you have a new perspective." Ruby grinned and blew a plume of smoke into Nick's face.

Nick waved the smoke away. "Evil doesn't always win. God does exist and I believe He's more powerful than you."

Ruby clapped his hands in mock applause. "Well, well, the fallen Catholic has spoken. Tell me Nick, did God comfort you on your last visit to church?"

Nick envisioned the steaming, blood-red holy water writhing like a bloated eel on the church floor. He stood to escape Ruby's piercing eyes. As he walked past, he glanced down at the deep bottom drawer in Ruby's desk, adorned with a silver handle and no visible lock.

He pointed to Ruby's blank, silent computer monitors. "So, how's the Nick Tera Fan Club doing?"

Ruby's lips and eyes squeezed into straight lines.

A rush of confidence emboldened Nick as he met Ruby's angry stare. "The last time I visited that cesspool you call a website, I noticed fans had to sign up and receive an application and then mail it back to you. What happened to one click delivers your soul to the almighty devil?"

Ruby spoke in a low, jagged tone. "I said it was an experiment. A few kinks came up. I'll work them out."

"So, in the meantime, the devil has to wait for snail mail to deliver his signed contracts." Nick threw back his head and laughed. "I bet only a small percentage actually print, fill out the form and then mail it back. Shit, does the age group you're targeting even know how to mail a letter?"

"We're done for today, Mr. Tera." Ruby ground his cigar into the ashtray until the butt end shredded from the pressure of his pointy fingernails. "Leave."

Nick smirked at him as he exited his office.

His small victory in Ruby's office quickly faded to despair. Another day had passed, and he was still trapped in Ruby's hellish web. He drove around the city thinking about Katie until his gas tank neared empty. After filling up at a gas station, he bought a hot dog from a stand and sat in a small park to eat. His appetite waned after two bites; he threw the rest to a flock of hovering pigeons.

Later that evening, the ringing of his cell phone jarred him from his half sleep and half alcohol-induced daze. He pulled himself up from the couch, focusing his bleary eyes on his phone. His family restaurant's number displayed on the screen. He didn't want to talk to his grandmother in his condition. But she had taken in Stephanie at his request, the least he could do was answer her call.

"Hi, Nonna."

His father's voice answered, "Nick, come to the restaurant right away."

The urgency in his father's voice sliced through his drunken fog. "Why, what's up?" He heard voices and a woman crying in the background. "Pop, what's wrong?"

"I don't want to say on the phone. Hurry, Nick."

Dread stuck in his chest like an icy knife. His father never called him. Something must have happened to Nonna or Sal. Did his sarcasm cause Ruby to retaliate? He drove as fast he could, running two stop signs and swerving around the slower traffic. Cars lined the street in front of the restaurant. Turning the corner, he parked in the only space next to the yellow-painted curb.

Inside, his grandmother's church group huddled around their usual table by the front window. They cried and passed tissues to each other. Nonna sat at the head of the table. She looked up at him with wet, grim eyes, stood and wrapped her arms around his waist.

"Nonna, what happened?" He hugged her and then pulled back to look into her face.

"Maria and Ray," she gasped. "Someone shot them."

A cold numbness drizzled down Nick's body. He let go of his grandmother and staggered backwards.

His father and Sal rushed from the kitchen. Their lips moved, but all Nick heard were the words *little old ladies and war heroes* replaying in his mind, punctuated by Ruby's wicked laughter.

"Nick, did you hear me?" His father pushed down on his shoulders. "Sit."

Nick dropped down into the chair. "Ray and Mrs. G, are they . . . dead?"

"No," Sal said. "But, Ray's hurt real bad."

"When . . . how did this happen?"

Nonna dragged a chair next to him. "Three hours ago. Captain Brannigan called us. Poor Maria. God help her. Her mind is not so good anymore. She asked Ray to walk to the shelter with her. She thought today was Thursday, the day she brings cookies to the kids."

"It was still daylight. There were witnesses. Some thug jumped out of an alley and pointed a gun at them," his father said. "Grabbed Maria's purse and then fired. Ray pushed Maria out of the way. She fell and banged up her arm." He paused and his face paled. "This scumbag starts to run away, then stops and shoots Ray in the back as he's helping Maria up." His eyes misted and his voice thickened. "He might be paralyzed, Nick."

Nick sat stunned, looking from his grandmother, to his father, to his brother. All three stared back with bleak expressions.

The small hanging bell on the front door jingled and they all turned. Father Santore walked inside, bowed his head to the group of ladies and then hurried across the room to Nonna. He placed his hand on Nonna's shoulder. She patted it and stood.

"We go to the church now to pray for Ray and Maria. And we light a candle." She nodded at the priest. "Nickie, go to the hospital. Represent the family."

He stood. His legs quaked and he couldn't focus his thoughts. Only two days ago he'd joked with Ray about his dance moves inside the U-haul truck. Before that, he had punched Ray in one of his red-tinted rages. Now Ray lay shot and possibly paralyzed. Nothing made sense anymore.

Father Santore squeezed his arm. "Are you all right, son?" His dark eyes peered from beneath bushy black and grey eyebrows that knitted together as he frowned.

"Yes, Father." The priest's steady gaze unnerved him. Had he recognized Nick running from the confessional the other night? He turned to his grandmother. "I'll drive you to church. You shouldn't be walking at night."

"Father Jonathan drove the church van here," Santore said. "There's room for all of the ladies. We'll drive each home to their doors when we're done. Don't worry, Nick. Go, see your friend."

The priest held the door while the somber line of women shuffled outside. Nonna wrapped a moss-green cardigan around her shoulders and followed. Nick walked her to the van where a younger priest held out his hand and helped her into the vehicle.

"Go now, Nickie," Nonna called through the open window. "We pray for Ray and Maria. God will heal them. Have faith."

Ray's family filled the hallway outside his room in the Intensive Care Unit. A nurse allowed two at a time inside the room and cautioned them to stay only a minute.

Nick offered his condolences to Ray's brothers, sisters and their spouses as they exited the room.

Ray's older brother, Louis, thanked one of the nurses for the pillow and blanket she handed to him. With tears running down his face, he told Nick, "I'm gonna stay in the waiting room tonight."

Ray's parents were the last to leave. Ray's father held his wife up as they made their way down the hall. Nick hugged them both. Ray's mother tried to speak but couldn't find words. She clutched Nick in a tight embrace, her warm tears bled through his tee shirt.

Ray's father shook his hand. "He's gonna need you, Nick," he said. "You're like a brother to him."

Nick swallowed hard. Guilt gnawed at his stomach. This was his fault. He goaded Ruby and Ruby attacked his best friend. Who would be next? He hadn't acted like much of a brother to Ray recently. "How's Mrs. G?"

Ray's father sighed. "She has a sprained wrist. A few scrapes. They're keeping her overnight on the second floor to monitor her. They gave her something to make her sleep. She's worried sick about Ray. We haven't told her he might not walk again. And she's upset because the thief took her purse, with her mother's rosary beads inside."

Nick waited until the family boarded the elevator. He asked the nurse if he could see Ray.

She hesitated, then smiled. "Only for a minute," she said.

He slipped inside the door and stood at the foot of the bed. The bed didn't look like a normal hospital bed. It sat higher, tipped forward at a slight angle and had hydraulics beneath it. Ray lay with his eyes closed, wearing a strange open helmet of metal bars attached to a thick collar around his neck. Tubes ran from both of his arms up to intravenous bags hanging on stands. A mass of colored wires taped to his chest led to metal boxes with digital displays mounted on the wall behind the bed. Nick stared down at him. Ray lay so still Nick feared he had stopped breathing.

He moved on heavy legs to the bedside and touched Ray's forearm. "I'm so sorry, Ray. So sorry. This is my fault. I shouldn't have taunted Ruby. I deserve to be in this bed, not you."

A warm hand patted his arm and startled him. Katie smiled. "This isn't your fault, Nick." She squeezed his arm and then walked around the bed, checking the tubes and wires.

"What's the thing on his head? And the strange bed?" Nick asked.

"The device is called a halo. It keeps his head and neck rigid to avoid further spinal damage. There's a bullet lodged near, or possibly in, his spine. With the swelling and tissue trauma, they can't be sure. The bed's a Stryker frame, it keeps him stable and lets us care for him without having to move him."

"They'll take out the bullet, right? Then he'll be okay?"

"There's a neurosurgeon flying in tomorrow morning from Chicago. He's going to try." Katie stroked Ray's cheek through an opening in the halo. "If the bullet struck his spinal cord, removing it may cause more damage. They can't get a clear picture until the swelling subsides. He's on an anti-inflammatory, an antibiotic, pain meds and drugs to induce a coma state."

"A coma?" Nick covered his face with his hands. "Oh my God."

"It's to keep him still so he doesn't cause more damage." Katie's voice was calm, reassuring. She adjusted the blankets and gently moistened Ray's lips with a medicated swab. Watching her comforted Nick. He understood why so many of her patients sent her gifts and cards long after they were discharged.

She took Nick's hand. "We should go now. There's nothing anyone can do until the surgeon arrives."

Nick touched Ray's arm. "Hang in there, buddy." He reluctantly followed Katie.

They walked down the hall in silence, their arms encircled around each other's waists.

"You must be furious with me after I ran out on you the other night. I'm sorry, I—"

"I was furious, until Nonna called and told me about Ray . . . this puts things into perspective. I wanted to be here when you first saw him. It's a shock."

When they stepped into the elevator, Nick pulled her close and kissed her. "I love you so much."

Katie snuggled into his embrace. They kissed until the doors slid open.

"Did you walk here tonight?" he asked.

"Yes."

His heartbeat sped up. What if Ruby had sent the men in the van after Katie just as he was certain he'd sent the gunman after Ray and Mrs. Gonzalez. "I'll drive you home." Ray wouldn't be able to pick up

Katie from work anymore. The thought made him feel guilty and terrified at the same time.

They drove to Katie's apartment without talking. Nick couldn't erase the image of Ray wearing the halo from his mind. He steered with his left hand and gripped Katie's hand with his right.

Inside, Katie brewed coffee for Nick and fixed herself a cup of tea. She placed a mug in front of him on the table. An envelope lying on the table addressed to Tara with the Nick Tera Fan Club in the return address caught his attention. "What's this?"

Katie rolled her eyes. "Tara brags that she's your biggest fan. Apparently now she has an official card to prove it."

Nick ripped open the letter and found an application to join his fan club along with a small card. A strange phrase was printed on the card. He recalled Tara telling him she joined his online fan club but signing up electronically mustn't have worked or Ruby wouldn't need to mail out printed cards. The knowledge provided a small comfort as he tore the envelope into pieces and stuffed it into the kitchen trash can.

"That's Tara's mail, you really shouldn't—"

"Trust me, I'm doing her a favor. Doing us all a favor."

Katie shrugged and sat at the table. "Do you want to talk about Ray?"

Nick cleared his throat. "His chances of being paralyzed are pretty high, aren't they?"

"Yes," Katie answered softly. "But until the neurosurgeon examines him—"

Nick pounded his fist on the kitchen table. "This fucking sucks!"

Katie's tea splashed over the sides of her mug and formed a puddle around the bottom. She pulled a paper towel from the holder and folded it under her cup to sop up the spill. "Yes, it does."

"All the shit he went through in Iraq and Afghanistan, he survived. Then he comes home and gets fucking shot in the back in his own neighborhood. Not to mention this piece of crap tried to shoot his grandmother, too. I wish I could have five minutes with the bastard who shot him."

Katie reached over and placed her hand on top of Nick's clenched fist.

"I've known Ray my whole damn life. He's like my second brother." Nick rubbed his eyes and looked away. When he turned back to face Katie, he forced a weak smile. "Did I ever tell you how we became friends?"

Katie returned the smile. "No, how?"

"We were six years old. First day of first grade. The bell hadn't rung, so we were running around the playground. Ray and I tried to climb up the ladder to the slide at the same time. He grabbed onto the rungs and wouldn't let go, no matter how hard I punched him. He was six inches shorter than me but charged at me like a damn bull. Rammed his head into my stomach and knocked me on my ass. We rolled around fighting on the grass until a couple of teachers pulled us apart. I remember thinking, 'this kid's fearless'."

Nick ripped off a paper towel and blew his nose. "That same day, after the last bell rang, he came up to me outside and stuck out his hand, like an adult. He said, "My name's Ray." We started hanging out at each other's houses after school. After that day, we both had second families.

"I didn't realize you two were friends for so long," Katie said.

"Nineteen years. When we weren't getting into trouble, we were altar boys together. Served all the Sunday masses for Father Santore. Talk about a hard-ass priest. He caught us drinking the wine one day after mass. Made us get buckets and brushes from the janitor's closet and scrub the church vestibule floor on our hands and knees." Nick grinned. "The whole time we were altar boys, the church had really clean floors." Nick's grin faded. He shook his head and stared into his coffee.

Katie squeezed Nick's hand. "Being paralyzed is a terrible thing, but it's not death. Ray's a fighter. There are so many things now to help people be independent. With therapy and time—"

"No. No–for Ray, it would be the same as death. Worse." Nick stood and threw the wet, crumpled paper towel into the trash can. Tearing another from the roll, he turned his back to wipe more tears from his eyes before sitting down.

"Ray is fearless. The only thing that ever scared him was girls. Not scared, but he was shy and tongue-tied around them. He used to have me ask girls out for him."

Katie smiled, rolling her eyes. "I bet you excelled at that."

"I never had a problem talking to girls. Except for when I first met you." He paused and turned the mug around in his hands. "I guess that's how Ray felt all the time."

Katie moved behind Nick and rubbed his shoulders.

"I'd be here all night telling you the crazy shit we did." His eyes brimmed with new tears. "At my mom's funeral, Ray happened to be home on leave from the army. If he weren't . . ."

Nick couldn't say the words out loud, but the scene played vividly in his mind. Ray had insisted on being one of the six pallbearers at his mother's funeral. Four of his uncles and a cousin manned the other five handles on the casket. Nick carried the front right corner. His legs shook during the final procession down the aisle of the church after the funeral mass. Exiting the church, his knees buckled just as they descended the steep, concrete stairs leading to the sidewalk. His sudden lurch threw the other men off balance. For an instant, which had felt like an eternity, he pictured his mother's casket tumbling down the steps and crashing into the black hearse parked on the street below. Yet, his corner of the casket never dropped. When he stood up, he saw Ray in his Army uniform holding his handle of the casket.

"I remember." Katie wrapped her arms around his shoulders and pressed her cheek against his. "Up until the last few days, your mom's funeral was the only time I had ever seen Ray."

Katie straightened up and retrieved a brown paper bag from on top of the refrigerator. "Are you hungry? I'm starving. I never ate dinner." She unwrapped the package. "One of my patient's moms baked loaves of zucchini bread. I hid it so Tara wouldn't scarf it all." She placed the loaf on a plate and then rummaged through a kitchen drawer and pulled out a long carving knife.

The glint of silver caught Nick's attention. He stared, fascinated by the way the overhead light played on the long, tapered blade.

Katie smiled at him. "I know what you're thinking, Mr. Chef. It's the wrong kind of knife to use for bread. It's the only sharp one I have, so it'll have to do." She cut two thick slices, put them onto a plate and placed it between them on the table.

Sweat beaded on Nick's forehead caused by the rising inferno inside him. Then something darker stirred. Mesmerized by the knife, Artie's perverse thoughts invaded his mind and his body like a swarm of stinging wasps. His body trembled as he fought to push back the emerging demon.

Katie broke off a corner of bread and popped it into her mouth. "Mmm, delicious. Do you want some butter?"

"Huh?" Nick stared at her. Her hair and face had a crimson tinge.

"Do you want butter for your bread?"

"N-no. Not hungry." He wiped his sweaty forehead with the paper towel he clenched in his fist.

Katie swallowed the mouthful of bread, stood and hugged him. "The surgeon they're flying in is the best in the country. All we can do right now for Ray is to pray."

"I gotta go." Nick jumped up from his chair and pushed Katie aside.

"Nick, no. You look exhausted. My place is closer to the hospital. We'll go see Ray first thing in the morning." She scooted in front of him blocking his exit, stood on her tiptoes and kissed him. "I hoped you'd stay here tonight. It's been days since we—"

"I can't." He backed away from Katie and rushed to the front door. Artie clawed beneath his skin. Katie threw her arms around him. He squeezed his eyes shut and willed the demon to leave. White-hot pinpricks peppered his body and images of the shiny carving knife jabbing into Katie's flesh made his eyes shoot wide open.

"If you're too upset to make love, I understand. Stay here tonight. Please."

"It's not that I don't want to . . ." He pulled away from her embrace and faced the door.

"Every time I get close to you lately, you push me away. I don't understand." Katie's voice quivered. "Tell me what's going on. We've always been honest with each other. You owe me that much." She wrung her hands. "Is there someone else, Nick? That actress on the news, Bethany Grant?"

Nick turned, his hands clutched the door knob behind him. Tears mixed with sweat rolled down his cheeks. "Do you remember the night you called me? You saw a black shadowy figure—"

"And you said it was only a nightmare. That has nothing to do with how you're acting now."

"Yes, it does. Katie, I was wrong. It wasn't a nightmare, it's real. And it gets worse. So much worse. I-I'm that shadow now. It's inside me. Steph was beaten because of me. And now, Ray's paralyzed because of me. I love you so much, but if I stay here, I'll hurt you. Or worse." Artie's perverted whispers throbbed in his head like a relentless toothache.

"You're not making any sense. And your eyes, they're so red again. Did you take more pills?"

Artie's whispers rose into shrill shrieks. The knife glistening under the light on the table beckoned. He wanted to feel the weight of it in his hand and caress the silvery blade with his fingers. He wanted to draw Katie's blood with the knife.

Sobs strangled his words. "I couldn't . . . live with myself if I . . . I can't see you anymore, Katie."

"You're breaking up with me?" Tears welled in her eyes.

"Y-yes." He jerked open the door and ran down the path.

"Don't come back here," she yelled. The rest of her words dissolved into her sobs.

Nick ran to his car and fumbled to fit the key into the ignition. He sped away, trying to put distance between Katie and the depraved force commanding his thoughts. As he neared Ruby's office building, he focused his murderous urges on Ruby. He had no plan, only the knowledge that Ruby lived on the top floor of the building and he had to destroy him in order to end this nightmare.

The building's windows looked dark. The front doors were locked. Ruby's Jaguar wasn't parked in the lot.

Nick sat in his car while Artie chewed at his thoughts. Visions of the carving knife on Katie's table taunted him. He gripped the steering wheel and gritted his teeth as he fought the desire to return to her apartment. The demon's seductive whispers described the long, sharp blade slicing into Katie's soft flesh. Aroused by the images, Nick moaned and licked his fingers imagining the salty taste of her still-warm blood. He jumped out of the car, furiously wiping his hands on his shirt and spat out the imaginary blood. In the dark, deserted lot, he screamed curses at the sadistic killer inside him and fought to regain control of his thoughts. When Artie finally retreated, the other unnamed demon took his place, bringing feverish waves of rage and violent tremors that wracked Nick's body. He channeled the demon's fury toward Ruby.

He paced around his car and planned his attack, scene by scene. When Ruby stepped from his sleek, red Jaguar, he would ram him with the Mustang. He'd pound his fists into Ruby's maddening smile, shattering his white teeth. Then he'd grab his ponytail and slam his head into the pavement, again and again until his face became an unrecognizable, bloodied pulp and his mocking laughter stopped forever. A low growl deep inside his chest burst from his lips into bouts of maniacal giggling. Between the spasms of laughter, he chanted, "Kill Ruby. Kill the devil. Kill the devil." His laughter turned into gleeful shrieks, barks and then howls. "Die. Die. Die. Die." He stomped his boot heel into the asphalt, over and over, imagining Ruby's skull crushed into splinters beneath it. He stamped his foot until he collapsed across the hood of his car in exhaustion.

The night dragged on, but Ruby never came. Fatigue overwhelmed Nick. He crawled into his car and fell into a fitful sleep. Vivid nightmares of Ray withered in a wheelchair and Katie's bloodied body jolted him awake. At sunrise, the demons finally released their grip. Like barbed wire embedded into his flesh, they slowly tore their claws from him, leaving him bone-weary and trembling with pain.

Chapter 19

Ruby's new secretary, Kim, arrived an hour later. Nick followed her into the building and stumbled into the elevator before the doors closed. Kim stared at him, her hand hovered over the control panel. "Mr. Ruby is out of town today," she said in a polite but curt tone.

"When's he coming back?"

"Sometime tomorrow."

"He left an envelope on his desk for me," he lied.

The girl raised her eyebrows. "He didn't mention any envelope to me."

"Just unlock his door, I'll grab it and be outta there in a minute."

"I don't have a key to Mr. Ruby's office. And I wouldn't allow anyone inside without his express permission." The doors slid open. Kim punched a button, bolted out the door and raced down the hall.

Nick struggled to stop the doors from closing and then ran after her. He reached the outer office door just as she slammed it in his face. The lock clicked.

"If you don't leave, I'll call the police!" Kim yelled through the door.

Nick cursed his clumsy, hastily planned attempt to get into Ruby's office. He trudged to the elevator. The reflection of his wild hair and scruffy beard in the shiny doors startled him and explained Kim's reaction. The dark circles under his eyes reflected in the distorted, silvery image. His damp T-shirt reeked of sweat and stuck to his body.

Exhausted and defeated, he left the Ruby building and drove to his apartment. He called the hospital to check on Ray. The nurses' station transferred him to a phone in the Neurosurgical waiting room. Ray's older brother, Louis, answered.

"The surgeon's here. He's decided to operate. Ray's in OR. They said it could be hours. I'll call you as soon as we know anything."

He ended the call and started to text Katie from habit, but then stopped. He broke up with her. Nothing he could type in a text could erase last night.

Nick dropped his cell onto the charger and wandered into the bedroom. He fell onto the bed. Every muscle in his body ached. He stared up at the ceiling and realized the raw, gasping sobs he heard came from his own mouth and matched the rhythm of his heaving chest.

The ringing persisted until he pried open his eyes and recognized the sound of his cell phone. He hauled his sore body from the bed and hurried into the kitchen.

"He's in Recovery," Louis said. "They got the bullet out, but there's still swelling. The doctors can't tell yet if it nicked his spinal cord. It'll be a while before they know if he can walk."

"At least they got the bullet out," Nick said. "Is he awake?"

"No, they're keeping him drugged for another day or two."

"Ray's strong. He'll walk." His heartbeat pounded in his ears as he tried to convince himself.

"God, Nick, I hope so."

Nick put down the phone. He took a long drink from a bottle of beer in his hand, though he didn't remember getting it from the refrigerator. The clock on the wall read five forty-seven. Ray had been in surgery all day while he slept.

He scrubbed his hands through his hair and downed the rest of the beer. His shirt stunk and a stale film coated his teeth. The cold beer quenched his dirt-dry throat. He drank four more.

Restless and buzzed from the alcohol, Nick paced the apartment. Katie would be leaving work at seven and walking home alone now that Ray lay helpless in a hospital bed. If Ruby sent someone after her, she'd have no protection. Katie could be brutally raped and murdered.

Anger surged through him, turning everything in his sight a bloody red. He guzzled another beer and slammed the empty bottle on the counter. I should have knocked down Ruby's door. He knew Kim would have called the police before he could break through both doors and retrieve his contract from the desk drawer. He would have ended up in a jail cell, unable to protect Katie from Ruby's van of murderers.

As he glared up at the wall clock, frustration fanned his anger into a full-blown rage. Six twenty-six. He couldn't risk anything happening to Katie. She must hate him after last night. He doubted she would accept a ride from him. Even if he drove alongside her as she walked, at least she wouldn't be alone. After last night, he knew he was as much of a threat to her as the thugs in the van. He would have to suppress the demons as best he could. Either way, Katie was in danger. He hurled an empty bottle against the kitchen wall. Shards of brown glass rained down on the tile floor. Grabbing his car keys, he ran out the door.

🕯

The rear tires of the Mustang smoked when he slammed on the brakes and jerked the steering wheel to make the turn into the driveway of Saint Mary's hospital. Katie would be coming out the doors any second.

He jogged to the wide staircase leading to the front entrance and scanned the people walking up and down the steps. From the corner of his eye, he saw a flash of pale blond hair. He spun around and saw Katie, her long ponytail hanging down her back, as she rounded the corner of the building.

He chased after her, running past the old security guard sitting in his golf cart. He stopped and searched the packed lot. Two rows away, he spotted Jon Gerber holding open the passenger door of his light blue Camry as Katie slid inside.

Jon closed the door and then turned his smiling face into the full force of Nick's fist. He yelped in pain and fell sideways, landing on the hood of the car. Nick grabbed him by his blue scrubs and punched him in the face again. Katie screamed from inside the car. Jon reeled from the second vicious blow and rolled down the hood of the car onto the pavement. Nick knelt on top of him and hammered Jon's head and torso with both fists.

Katie scrambled out of the car and grabbed Nick's left arm. He flung his arm back, throwing her into the side of the car. She gripped the door handle to steady herself and screamed, "Stop it! Nick, stop!"

Nick's fists were slick with Jon's blood. The red haze he glared through filtered out the bloodied mess of Jon's face and shirt. Jon's mouth worked, gasping, gurgling, and begging Nick to stop. Blood leaked from his nostrils, mouth and one ear. He crossed his arms above his face to shield his head from the relentless volley of blows.

"For God's sake Nick, stop!" Katie's screams turned to sobs. "Please, you're killing him!"

Nick stood, straddling Jon's prone body. He stared at his bloody hands and then down at Jon, who curled onto his side, groaning and coughing.

"My God, what's happened to you?" Katie whispered.

Nick stepped over Jon's legs and lunged at Katie. Flattening herself against the side of the car, she slid sideways to avoid his grasp.

Fear shone in her eyes. A dark, predatory urge clawed inside him as he watched her cower at the trunk of the car. He licked his lips, savoring her terror.

Running footsteps approached. Three policemen and the security guard in his cart raced toward them.

"Don't move! Put your hands behind your head," an officer yelled.

Nick froze at the sound of guns cocking and slowly raised his hands.

The guard pulled Katie by her arm over to his cart. "Stay here, Miss, let the officers do their job."

Two cops grabbed hold of Nick's raised arms. He yanked one arm free and swung wildly. His fist grazed one policeman's jaw. The cop recovered and then landed a solid, hard blow into Nick's stomach, causing him to double over and struggle for a breath. The two pushed him face down onto the hood of the Camry. They wrestled his arms behind him, handcuffed him and then patted him down. The third officer knelt on one knee by Jon. Emergency Room orderlies, one pushing a gurney, ran across the lot.

The two cops dragged Nick past Katie, shoved him into the back of their cruiser and slammed the door. Dazed and still gasping for air, he stared out the window at Katie. The red vision faded, leaving his sight clear but his mind muddled. He couldn't remember how he had gotten to the hospital or what he had done to end up handcuffed inside a police car.

The policemen talked to Katie and the security guard. The old guard pointed his finger at Nick. Katie's head swiveled back and forth, looking over at Jon and then back at Nick. The orderlies lifted Jon onto the gurney and then rushed him toward the Emergency Room entrance.

Rotating lights atop the cruiser turned Katie's face and hair a bright blue with each sweeping turn. The fast spinning lights made Nick dizzy. He couldn't focus his scrambled thoughts.

As the cops slid into the front of the car, Nick strained his neck to peer over his shoulder. Katie stood with both hands covering her mouth, watching the car drive away.

Chapter 20

Nick's right hand throbbed. His body ached. A strong smell of pine disinfectant filled his nostrils. Overhead he saw a white plaster ceiling with brown water stains. He looked down at his feet hanging over the end of the hard cot and struggled to sit up. A wall of steel bars faced him. Grabbing the bars with his left hand, he eased himself up into a standing position. The knuckles on his right hand were swollen and covered with dried blood. Beyond the bars, he saw two more cells on the other side of the narrow room. Loud snoring came from one of them. Light filtered in through a narrow rectangle of glass in a gun-metal gray door to the right.

He shuffled over to a toilet and small stainless basin in the corner of the cell. After urinating, he splashed water on his head and used his filthy tee-shirt to wipe his face. Sitting on the cot, he leaned his aching head against the cold block wall and tried to remember how he ended up in a jail cell.

The sound of a lock turning startled him. The metal door swung open and his grandmother bustled in, followed by the tall, hulking form of Police Captain Brannigan and another younger officer. Brannigan and his grandmother had been friends for years. The captain was a regular guest at the police functions his family's restaurant hosted. Nick also knew him from some of the scrapes he and his friends had gotten into when they were teenagers. Brannigan was a tough man, but fair.

"Nickie, you all right?" Nonna gripped the bars, her small face pressed against the rungs.

Nick hung his head, too ashamed to meet his grandmother's eyes. She shouldn't be in this place, he thought. Though he had little memory of last night, the twisting in his gut told him he had done something terrible. He remembered seeing Katie from the window of the police car. At least he hadn't killed her.

"Let him out." Nonna motioned to Brannigan.

"I can't, Rosa, I told you. I'm not even supposed to let you see him."

"Humph, some captain you are."

Brannigan shook his head. "These are serious charges, Rosa. It's not like when he was kid smoking cigarettes in the park or egging a house on Cabbage Night."

His grandmother turned back to the cell. "Nickie, what happened? They say you beat up someone? Is this true?"

Nick mumbled, "I don't remember, Nonna." He leaned forward on the cot and covered his face with his hands.

"See?" Nonna turned to Brannigan. "I told you. He's sick. Nickie wouldn't do this thing you say he did. Let him out. He needs to see a doctor. Maybe he's hurt."

The younger officer snorted. "The other guy's the one who's hurt, lady."

Nonna spun around and shook her finger in the patrolman's face. *"Chiudi la bocca! Idiota!"*

The cop stepped back and shrugged at Brannigan. The captain stood with his arms crossed, one hand covered the smile on his face.

"The lady asked you to bring the chair over to the cell, Lepkowski," Brannigan said.

The officer picked up the single straight-backed chair and placed it next to the cell. Nonna settled into it, clutching her floral-print, brocade bag in her lap.

"Five minutes, Rosa. That's all. And no passing anything into the cell, you hear me?"

Nonna straightened her shoulders and lifted her chin. "Bring my grandson something to eat."

Lepkowski grinned at Brannigan. "Pushy old lady, huh?"

"She's right, by law we need to feed him. His arraignment isn't until after noon. Go make a take-out run," Brannigan said.

"Asino di cavallo," Nonna waved her hand at the young cop.

"What did she say?" Lepkowski asked.

"Get him a burger and fries." Brannigan grinned.

"I didn't know you spoke Italian, Cap." The two left the room and closed the door behind them.

"Nickie, come here," Nonna said.

He slowly stood and took the two short steps to the bars. Nonna reached into her purse and pulled out a gold cross on a long chain. "Take this, Nickie. I had Father Santore bless it this morning especially for you." She reached a thin arm through an opening in the bars and pushed the medal into Nick's hand. "Put it on."

He dropped the chain over his head. The cool, metal cross slid under his tee shirt.

"Tell me what happened. I can't help you if you don't talk to me," Nonna said.

Nick laid his forehead against the steel bars. "I can't remember, Nonna. Please, go home. I feel terrible seeing you in this place. I'll be all right.

They both looked up when the metal door opened.

"Rosa, you'll have to leave now." Brannigan held out his hand to help her up. "Nick has a visitor across the hall."

"What visitor? Who?" Nonna asked.

"Katie?" Nick asked.

"An attorney." Brannigan unlocked the cell and held up a pair of handcuffs.

"What you doing?" Nonna grabbed Brannigan's arm. "He's my grandson, not some criminal!"

The captain eyed Nick. "Do I need to cuff you?"

Nick shook his head. The captain kept a strong grip on his arm as he escorted him across the hall to a room with tables, chairs and two barred windows. Nonna followed and squeezed her way into the room past the uniformed officer standing guard.

Inside, a slender, brunette woman dressed in a white blouse, black skirt and jacket sat at a table sorting through the contents of her briefcase.

"Take a seat, Nick." Brannigan motioned to a metal table with two chairs tucked under it. Nick dragged out one of the chairs and sat.

"Rosa, c'mon, let's go," Brannigan said.

"No! Not until my grandson tells me his side of the story." Nonna crossed her arms and turned her back to the captain.

"Don't say anything, Mr. Tera." The brunette stood and walked across the room. Her high heels rapped like small hammers on the tile floor and echoed in the low-ceilinged room.

Nonna moved between Nick and the woman. "Who are you?"

"Lydia Cambridge." She held out her hand. "Ruby International Promotions retained me to represent Mr. Tera." Lydia arched one manicured eyebrow. "And you are?"

"Rosa Cipazzio, Mr. *Teravelli's* grandmother." Nonna ignored the woman's outstretched hand and turned to Nick. She gestured over her shoulder. "You know her?"

Nick shook his head. "The agency must have hired an attorney."

"That's a good thing, Rosa. He's going to need a lawyer," Brannigan said. "Let me take you home so Ms. Cambridge can do her job."

Nonna looked the attorney over from head to toe. She cupped Nick's stubble-covered chin in her hands. "She don't even know your name. If this *puttana* doesn't get you out, I find you a real lawyer. Don't worry, eh?"

"Rosa." Brannigan took her arm. "She needs to talk to him before the arraignment. Maybe they'll post bail and get him released, I don't know."

"Nickie, you come home as soon as you get out." She poked her head back inside the door as Brannigan tried to close it. "Come home!"

Lydia settled into the chair across from him, holding a silver pen and a yellow legal pad. "So, Mr. Tera, tell me everything that happened last night." Her ice-blue eyes studied him over narrow, dark framed glasses.

"I don't remember much. I tried, but all I remember is being at my apartment. Then being roughed up by some cops, shoved into a patrol car and brought here."

"Were you drinking or doing any drugs at your apartment?"

"I don't do drugs. I might have had a beer or two."

"Might have had, or did have, Mr. Tera?"

"I told you I can't remember."

"Well, did you consent to a Breathalyzer or blood alcohol test?"

"I *don't* remember!"

Lydia pursed her thin lips and stood. "All right. I'll check with the front desk to see if they administered a sobriety test." She walked to the smaller table and shuffled through a manila folder in her briefcase. "According to the police report, you assaulted a Mr. Jon Gerber in the parking lot of Saint Mary's Hospital." She paced around the room holding the report. "Do you know a Jon Gerber?"

"Sort of," Nick mumbled. "He works with my fiancée."

"Mr. Gerber is currently in Saint Mary's Hospital, listed in serious condition. Concussion, broken nose, dislocated jaw, one dislodged tooth, multiple facial lacerations, two requiring stitches, two blackened eyes, one broken rib and multiple contusions on his upper body."

"God." Nick pressed his palms against his temples. "I did all that?"

"According to the eyewitnesses, yes. And they are, Andrew Walker, a security guard at the hospital and Katherine Harrington, a registered nurse, also employed at the hospital. Do you know either of them?"

"Katie, um, Katherine Harrington, is, or was, my fiancée." Nick sank lower in the chair. "Katie's pressing charges against me?"

"No," Lydia said. "Actually, she refused to press assault charges against you. The security guard, Mr. Walker, told the police, quote 'when Ms. Harrington attempted to pull you off Gerber, you violently shoved Ms. Harrington into a parked car, then proceeded toward her in a menacing way', end quote. However, when questioned by police, she denied the statement. Said she tripped. But she is still an eyewitness to Mr. Gerber's assault." Lydia looked at Nick. "You don't recall any of this?"

"No, I swear I don't. Is Katie hurt?"

"There's nothing in the report about any injuries to Ms. Harrington. And she declined offers for medical evaluation." Lydia continued to read from the document. "Three officers already at the hospital escorting prisoners for medical treatment responded to Mr. Walker's 9-1-1 call. All three confirm in their report they saw you standing next to Mr. Gerber with bloodied fists. In addition, they claim you resisted arrest and struck a police officer." She paused and turned to the second sheet of the report. "An Officer Lepkowski wrote in the report, and I quote, 'appropriate force was used to restrain the suspect'. Do you recall being hit by any police officers?"

Nick stood. "Don't I get a phone call? I need to call Katie and make sure she's okay." His mind swam with thoughts of Katie alone and vulnerable, while he was locked up, helpless to protect her.

"As your attorney, I would strongly advise you not to contact Ms. Harrington."

"But I have to—"

"Mr. Tera, *you have to* appear at an arraignment at the courthouse in less than two hours. We have a lot of work to do." She pulled a cellophane-wrapped package from her case. "First things first," she said, tossing the package onto the table.

Nick grabbed the new, white dress shirt and hurled it across the room. "What the hell is it with you people? I'm in a damn jail and you're still obsessed with how I'm dressed!"

Lydia clasped her hands behind her back and rocked on her heels. "Personally, I don't care how you dress, Mr. Tera. I do, however, prefer my client not appear in front of a judge with the blood of the man he's accused of assaulting splattered all over his tee shirt."

She opened the door and signaled to the uniformed policeman standing outside. "This officer will escort you to a washroom. Clean yourself up. Change your shirt."

"So, what did all that mean in there?" Nick asked Lydia as they climbed into her car in the courthouse parking lot.

"You've pled not guilty to the charges and you've been released on bail. Mr. Ruby posted the one-hundred-thousand-dollar bond."

"Hundred grand? Shit."

"Aggravated assault is a serious charge in this city." Lydia backed her navy-blue BMW out of the parking space. "Depending on the judge, and prosecutor, it could carry up to a seven-year prison term."

Nick sat stunned. "I-I'm going to prison?"

Lydia smiled for the first time since Nick met her. "Not if I can help it."

"What happens now?"

"Well, the bond stipulates you can't leave the city. There's usually a series of hearings to determine the exact level of charges against you; motions will be filed on either side, and then a judge will set a trial date."

"Trial." Nick leaned his head back against the head rest and closed his eyes. "Seven years, I'm screwed."

"I don't plan to let this go that far, Mr. Tera."

"What are you going to do?"

"Well, right now we're heading to Mr. Ruby's office to discuss our options."

"It doesn't seem like there are any options."

"There are *always* options, Mr. Tera."

Lydia led the way down the hall to the conference room, located at the opposite end of the corridor from Ruby's office. Through the large glass window, Nick saw Victor Ruby seated at the head of a long, rectangular conference table. A half dozen men and women sat around the table scouring through papers and typing on laptop computers.

"Lydia," Ruby said, rising from his chair as the two entered. "Lovely to see you." They embraced and then Ruby escorted her to an empty chair on his left.

"Nick, sit." He tapped the chair on his right with his nails. "Looks like you've had a rough night."

Nick sank into the chair and scowled at Ruby. After what Ruby had done to Ray, he wanted to grab his throat and squeeze until Ruby's eyes protruded from his skull and he took his last gasping breath. But he had to play along or end up in prison. "I'll pay you the hundred grand you put up for bail."

"No need, I'm sure we'll resolve this, and my bond will be refunded. It's all part of my job." He winked and flashed his toothy smile. "This is the entertainment industry, you're not my first client who's gotten into a bit of a mess."

Nick snorted. "A big mess. I seriously injured Gerber."

"Allegedly," Lydia said.

"You read the list of his injuries on the police report," Nick said.

"And police reports never lie," Ruby said. He and Lydia looked at each other and laughed. Ruby thumbed through folders on the table. "Now that you're both here, let's see what we have."

Nick read Katie's name on one of the folders. "Why do you have a folder with Katie's name?"

"I have a file on all parties involved," Ruby replied. He slipped Katie's file to the bottom of the pile. "Phillip, what have you found?" Ruby stared at a balding man with wire-rimmed glasses.

"Still checking, Mr. Ruby." Phillip's voice quivered and his bald head shone with sweat.

"You've had three hours. I need information now," Ruby said.

"Well, sir, uh–I–uh—"

A knock on the glass window interrupted Phillip's labored reply. Ruby strode over and opened the door to a young man with spiky dark hair. His faded red tee shirt looked a size too small, with That's How I Scroll printed in white block letters across the front. He carried a tablet and spoke in a low voice to Ruby.

"Phillip!" Ruby barked. "You're done. Go."

The bald man's head jerked up. Sweat trickled from his forehead "A little more time," he pleaded.

"I said get out." Ruby flipped his thumb toward the door. Phillip started to close up his laptop.

Ruby placed his hand on the lid. "Leave it."

Phillip shuffled to the door. He turned and opened his mouth to speak, but then exited. The others at the table kept their heads down and their eyes intent on their work.

"What did you say your name was?" Ruby asked the young man.

"Justin. Justin Gray," he answered.

"Have a seat, Justin," Ruby motioned to Phillip's empty chair. "Is this machine suitable?" He tapped a pointed fingernail on Philip's abandoned laptop.

"Sweet. More powerful than my tablet." He fingered the keyboard as he slid into the chair.

"How long do you need?" Ruby asked.

"A minute or two to get set up," Justin said.

Ruby smiled and elbowed Lydia. She looked over her glasses at the young man who busied himself plugging USB cables into a remote console in the center of the table.

"There're refreshments if you're hungry, Lydia, Nick." Ruby pointed to a table in the corner laden with wrapped sandwiches, bags of chips, soft drinks and a silver coffee urn.

Nick took one of the black ceramic mugs adorned with a metallic red Ruby International Promotions logo and filled it with black coffee.

A hulking man dressed in a grimy denim jacket and black knit cap walked in the door without knocking. Ruby greeted him with a smile and immediately led him to the food table. The man bypassed the stack of plates and napkins and grabbed two wrapped sandwiches and a can of soda. He settled into an upholstered chair in the corner of the room, jammed the soda can between his knees and ripped open a sandwich.

Ruby helped himself to a small bag of potato chips.

"Ready, Mr. Ruby," Justin said.

"Excellent." Ruby flicked off the light switch. A large screen lit up on the wall.

It displayed a grainy, black and white picture of a parking lot. Seconds later, Jon Gerber and Katie appeared in the image.

Ruby sat next to Nick and ripped open his chip bag. His dark eyes glittered, intent on the video, as he shoved a handful of chips into his mouth.

Gerber opened the passenger door of his sedan and Katie slid inside. A third figure bolted across the screen and swung his fist into Gerber's stunned face.

"Jesus, that's me," Nick whispered.

Ruby chuckled, leaned back in his chair and crunched the chips between his teeth. Tiny flakes flew from his mouth onto the table.

Although thankful the video had no sound, Nick cringed when he saw himself fling Katie into the side of the car. His stomach knotted at the sight of the dark stains on Gerber's face and shirt. Three policemen ran into the scene with their guns pointed at Nick's chest.

Lydia asked, "Is it possible to get a closer view of these next few frames?"

"Sure," Justin said. The screen froze as Nick took a swing at one of the police officers. Justin tapped a key and the image enlarged in increments before continuing. The same cop turned and punched Nick in the stomach.

"Police brutality?" Ruby asked with a grin. He ran his long tongue around his mouth collecting the chip fragments and then smacked his lips.

"Possibly, although Tera swung first," Lydia said.

They watched until the cops loaded Nick into a cruiser and the orderlies rushed Gerber away.

"That's enough, Justin." Ruby stood and turned on the lights.

"Without audio, I can't be certain, but I'm thinking these cowboys never read him the Miranda," Lydia said. "Do you remember hearing your rights read to you in the police car, Mr. Tera?"

Nick shook his head. "I don't remember."

"That would be too easy," Ruby said. "Justin, what kind of security system is this?"

"The cameras are an older analog system converted to download the video onto a PC. I hacked into their mainframe and then into the video feed. It's all kept on one dedicated server. Not smart."

"Can you erase this portion?" Ruby asked.

"Yeah, sure. Or, if we have time, I can edit it. Add or delete people or fill in the time block with images from another night."

Ruby stood behind Justin and patted him on the shoulders. "Congratulations, Mr. Gray. You've just been promoted. Head of IT."

Justin tipped his head back and grinned up at Ruby.

"Experts could tell the video was tampered with, couldn't they?" Lydia asked.

Justin cocked his head and smiled. "I used to fool my instructors in school all the time,"

"I appreciate your talents, but just make it disappear this time," Ruby said.

"Without video, that leaves the witnesses and the victim," Lydia reached for the manila folders.

Ruby bent and whispered in her ear. He sat and gathered up the folders.

"Andrew Walker," Ruby read, "retired cop, seventy-four years old. Medical records indicate he had a triple bypass six years ago. And he's a smoker." Ruby flashed a wide, white smile. He nodded to the man in the knit cap. The man rose from his chair holding the second partially eaten sandwich in one meaty fist, adorned with crude tattoos of letters, dots and spider webs. He reached in front of Lydia's face, and grabbed the folder from Ruby's hand.

Ruby passed Katie's folder along with the security guard's.

Nick jumped up. "Hey, wait! That's Katie's file."

"Calm yourself, Nick. A simple mistake," Ruby said. "Give me back the second folder."

The man tossed Katie's folder on the table. Two sheets of paper slid out. One with text and another with an enlargement of her hospital identification photo. His mouth twisted into a leer revealing tufts of chewed bread poking between yellowed teeth.

A sharp jolt ran up Nick's spine. He recognized the man's ugly, grinning face from the vision of the men in the van Ruby had projected on the elevator walls. He slammed his hand down on Katie's folder. "Who the hell is this guy?"

"Easy, Nick," Ruby said. "Mr. Jones is a private investigator I employ."

Jones grunted and returned to his seat. He glared stony-eyed at Nick, ripped off a chunk of sandwich and chewed with his mouth open. One corner of his mouth hiked up in a taunting sneer. A knife sheath strapped to his ankle stuck out above one dirty work shoe. The zipped hoodie he wore under his jacket thinly concealed the gun-shaped bulge at his waistband.

Lydia cleared her throat. "What about Gerber, do we have any intel on him?"

Ruby waved his hand in disgust. "That's what Phillip was working on." He looked around the table. "Anyone?"

A woman raised her hand. "He's an ER tech. Hired in the Emergency Care Department one month ago at Saint Mary's Hospital," she said.

"We already know he's a fucking ER technician!" Ruby glowered at the woman. She dropped her gaze and bit her bottom lip.

"Who are we looking for info on?" Justin asked.

Ruby slid Jon's folder across the table to Justin. "Jon Gerber, the victim." He rapped the table with his knuckles. "We need a publicity angle for Mr. Tera. Ideas?"

Another younger woman spoke up. "Obviously it's a crime of passion. Jealous rage, over the woman in the video, I presume. It fits Tera's image."

Nick stood and paced back and forth behind Ruby, annoyed that they spoke as if he weren't in the room.

"Sheer genius, Paula," Ruby sneered.

"Well, um, until we find out more—"

"Shut up, Paula." Ruby banged his fist on the table. "I have a lot of time and money invested in Nick Tera. One of you had better come up with a way to make this work to my advantage. Fast. The media already has the police blotter info."

"I don't think the jealous rage angle will work, Mr. Ruby," Justin said.

"Why not?" Ruby asked.

"I found Gerber's Facebook page. He goes by Jonny Gee online. His real name's hidden in his profile. According to this, Jon Gerber's gay." Justin frowned at Nick. "Unless, Nick Tera's gay, too?"

"Gay? Fucking wonderful!" Ruby pointed a tapered fingernail at Nick. "The press simply adores crucifying celebrity gay bashers."

"Gay?" Nick asked. "But I thought . . . shit."

"Shit is correct, Mr. Tera. And if it hits the media fan, it will destroy everything I've built for you. What else did you find, Justin?"

"His partner is a guy named Lyle Ross. Owns a fancy salon on the Upper East Side. They have a townhouse nearby. Exclusive neighborhood. It looks like Ross's business isn't doing well. He filed chapter eleven papers two weeks ago."

"There's our in," Lydia said. "Pay Gerber's medical bills and pay off the boyfriend. I know a real estate agent in Hollywood. Maybe we can relocate them to an upscale salon on Rodeo Drive? If he agrees to drop the charges, that is. Fresh start for them, no victim for us."

"I like it." Ruby patted Lydia's hand. "Now, how do we handle the PR on Tera?"

"Spaghetti press?" a slim, grey-haired man called out.

Ruby blew out a long breath and nodded. "Probably our only way out. I've already called Janis Ford to meet me here for an exclusive. The rest of you, start working on the releases for the other media outlets. I want to review them in one hour."

"What's spaghetti press?" Nick asked.

"We send out several versions of the incident simultaneously. There's so much confusion conflicting information, and media speculation, the truth never surfaces. Politicians do it all the time. Eventually, our sanitized version will stick. I'll give Janis Ford the lead. *The Entertainer* has the lion's share of print and cable news. People will believe them. In the meantime, buy off the victim, massage the witnesses, and erase the video evidence. The police will have no choice but to drop the charges."

"Leave Katie out of this," Nick said. "Lydia said she refused to press charges. I'll talk to her."

Lydia nodded. "That's true. It's in the report."

"Very well, Mr. Tera," Ruby said, baring his teeth in something between a smile and a snarl. "I'll leave Ms. Harrington as your responsibility. I'm positive she won't pose any problems, correct?"

A chill crawled across Nick's scalp. "No, Katie won't be any problem at all." Nick glared at Jones and then Ruby. "I'll take her folder."

Ruby raised his eyebrows, shrugged and then slid the folder to Nick.

"Excuse me," Nick said. "I need to use the rest room,"

"My office is the closest," Ruby said. "You really need to do something about that nervous stomach of yours, Nick."

Nick sprinted down the hall to Ruby's office. His cell phone was dead. It had been in a police evidence envelope all night. He picked up the receptionist's desk phone and dialed his brother.

"Sal, it's Nick. I need you to do something important for me."

"Shit, oh man, are you calling from jail?"

"No, I'm out on bail. I need you to walk Katie home from the hospital tonight at seven o'clock."

"I'm supposed to be helping Dad in the restaurant—"

"Screw the restaurant! This is life and death. I'm depending on you, Sal."

"Yeah, yeah, okay, Nick. What's going on? Why can't you pick up Katie?"

"I can't talk now. Make sure she gets inside her apartment and locks the door. Promise me."

"All right, geez, I promise."

As Nick hung up the phone, he saw the door to Ruby's private office stood slightly ajar. He glanced down the empty hallway and then hurried to Ruby's door. Nick eased the door open a few inches and peeked inside. The green glass shaded banker's lamp on the desk illuminated the desk. The rest of the room silent and shrouded in shadows.

Nick laid Katie's file on the desk and pulled open Ruby's bottom file drawer. The drawer kept rolling outward as Nick walked backwards. The length extended three times the width of the desk and emitted a luminous red glow. "This isn't possible," he whispered. He crouched as his fingers frantically combed through the thousands of files crammed into the drawer.

"What are you doing?"

Nick jumped. He stared up at Janis Ford, dumbstruck, his heart thumping in his throat.

Not waiting for an answer, Janis shrugged off the strap of her over-sized shoulder bag. She knelt on the floor and searched through the opposite end of Ruby's drawer.

"Are the files alphabetical?" she asked.

"No." He struggled to grasp the tabs of the tightly packed folders and slide them up to read them. Ruby leaving his door open was an amazing stroke of luck. If he could only find his contract and destroy it, Ruby would have no power over him. He searched for Chris Turner's file as well. He would destroy it to honor Chris' last request in his suicide letter.

The eerie red light lit Janis' face. "I can't make any sense of his filing sys—"

"I hear Ruby." Nick leaped to his feet and ran to the door.

Janis shoved papers into her bag and then pushed the drawer closed. She grabbed her shoulder bag and rushed over to Nick, who stood with his ear against the door.

"He's down the hall talking, but coming closer," he said in a low voice. "What files did you take?

"If you say one word to him about this . . ." Janis shot Nick a wicked stare and then grabbed the knob and let herself out.

He grabbed Katie's file and then slipped out, quietly pulling the door shut.

Janis ran into the bathroom and Nick leaned against the receptionist desk with his arms crossed. He pulled in a deep, shaky breath to calm his racing heartbeat.

As Ruby entered the door, Janis burst from the rest room and confronted Nick, waving her hands in his face and shouting, "Asshole!"

Ruby looked from Janis to Nick. "Problem?"

"He barged into the rest room without knocking."

"It never occurred to you to lock a public bathroom door?" Nick shot back at her.

"Enough!" Ruby held up his hands. "Nick, in my office. Now." He strode to the door and slipped a key into the lock. He hesitated and glanced over at Nick before pushing open the door. "Janis, give us a minute."

She flopped into a chair in the waiting area.

Ruby shut the door and faced Nick. "You're in luck, Mr. Tera. Unless there's any other unexpected details, I believe the charges will be dismissed. Needless to say, don't leave the city." He walked to his desk and examined the items on it, touching each one. Then he stared down at his desk drawers.

Nick held his breath when Ruby leaned to open a drawer. In their rush, he feared they may have left papers sticking up from the folders.

Ruby pulled a package of cigars from his top drawer and lit one.

"I'm negotiating your movie deal. I don't need your jealous antics screwing it up." He exhaled a stream of smoke into Nick's face. "Are you striving for the celebrity-death knoll trifecta? First, pedophile, now homophobe. All we need is a racist slur and you'll be finished in the public eye."

"Fuck you and fuck your movie deal! You had Ray shot and tried to shoot his grandmother. He's probably fucking paralyzed! War heroes and little old ladies, that's what you said!"

"I saw the news report. How unfortunate. They were friends of yours?"

"You know damn well who they are, you heartless bastard!"

"Perhaps you'll heed my advice, before more people get hurt." Ruby's lips pressed into an ugly smile. "Girlfriends and grandmothers."

"You have me trotting to all of your events. That sick freak Artie and God knows what else takes over my body and my mind. You got what you wanted. Leave my friends and family out of this!"

"Sometimes my demons get overzealous. I'm helping you out of this incident."

"What if I'd killed Gerber? Then what? I'd rot in a cell with Cullen while you destroy someone else's life?"

"You didn't kill him, Nick." Ruby sat on the edge of his desk. "What concerns me is this jealous rage over Katie. It's time to remove her, so you can focus on more important things."

"I broke up with Katie. Your demon attacked Gerber. I don't even remember driving to the hospital."

Ruby eyed him, twirling his cigar between his fingers. Whips of smoke swirled around his head. "The movie premiere for *Night Birds* is in ten days."

"So what."

"So, you will be there. You're my hottest property at the moment. We're announcing your film debut next year."

"My best friend is paralyzed. I don't give a shit about a damned movie."

"It's not all about you, Nick. There are others to consider. Artie has graciously stepped back and allowed the others to use you. Apparently for drinking and fighting. So base, so unimaginative. It's not fair to poor Artie. I made him a promise."

"What the hell are you talking about?"

"On premiere night we'll announce the winner of the Dream Date Contest with Nick Tera."

Nick rubbed his hand over his mouth. His forehead was slick with sweat and his hands trembled with pent-up anger. "Once again, I have no choice but to go along with this or you'll threaten me with . . . what?"

"On the contrary, Nick. I'm giving you a choice. Free will. Isn't that what He touts?" Ruby pointed to the ceiling with an ugly sneer. "You see, the date is for Artie, to fulfill my promise. But I'll let you choose. Either a girl from a random drawing, or Katie? The decision is yours."

Nick stared as Ruby's words sank in. "You're picking a girl from a drawing for Artie to torture and murder? And you expect me to let him use my body to do this sick—"

"You catch on fast, Nick." Ruby sank into his chair, leaned back and grinned. "So, tell me, who do you choose? A random stranger, or your darling Katie?"

Nick's breath caught in his throat and his mouth turned bone dry. "Neither. You can't force me to commit murder."

"Actually, yes I can. Ask Joe Cullen. Although you've done surprisingly well in suppressing your demons. So much so, Artie has appealed to me for help. You can't stop both of us, Nick."

"I refuse to let you or, that . . . deviant use me to murder anyone!" Nick kicked over the guest chair and headed for the door.

"Don't be so selfish. I've kept all of my promises. It's time for you to fulfill your contract. I'll give you some time to think it over. I don't give everyone choices. But I like you, Nick."

Peals of Ruby's vicious laughter followed him out the door. He slammed it behind him.

Janis started in her chair at the sound. "What happened?"

Nick stormed past her and headed for the door.

"Oh, Nick," Ruby called from his doorway.

Nick whirled around.

Ruby dangled a set of keys in his hand. "Your Mustang is in the lot. I had it towed for you. I take excellent care of my clients." He tossed the keys to Nick.

Nick's hands shook as drove to his family's restaurant. A faint glow of light shone from the open kitchen door at the back of the closed restaurant. He found Sal dumping the mop bucket in the fenced grassy area.

"How's Katie? You did walk her home, right?"

Sal put the bucket down. "Yeah, she's fine. Well, she's upset about you beating up that guy. She cried a lot. You all right? You look like hell. Nonna's going bat-crap crazy worrying about you."

"Tell her I'm out of jail and not to worry. I'll call her. Nothing happened on the walk to Katie's apartment?"

"No," Sal paused. "Well, some assholes in a van slowed down and whistled and stuff, but they kept on going. Katie's cute. Guys probably whistle at her all the time."

Icy fingers choked Nick's heart making it skip a beat and then race. He gripped his brother's shoulders. "What did the van look like?"

"Some old, green, beat-up van. A Ford, I think, why?" He shrugged off Nick's grasp.

"The men in that van are rapists and murderers. They're after Katie."

Sal's eyes widened and his mouth gaped open. "Holy shit. How do you know that?"

"I just know!" He paced around the enclosure, clenching his fists. "Dammit."

"I wouldn't ever let anybody hurt Katie," Sal said.

Nick spun around to yell at Sal for sounding so naive, but when he looked into his little brother's eyes, he saw the same fearless, sincere expression he'd seen in Ray's eyes many times. He hooked his arm around Sal's neck and sighed. "I know you wouldn't, Sal."

"I'll walk Katie home until you guys work out whatever's going on between you two."

Nick pictured Jones' blank, evil eyes and despised himself for even considering his brother's offer. Sal could end up like Ray, or more likely, dead. "No, Sal. It's too dangerous."

Sal straightened his shoulders, pushing his chest and chin out in his signature cocky stance. "I can take care of myself. And Katie."

Nick sighed. Frustration and fear twisted in his gut. He had no other options. "All right. But I'll follow you in my car and stay out of sight. Don't be a hero, understand? These bastards have guns and knives. It's not a boxing ring, Sal, they don't play by any rules. If you see that van again, or anything suspicious, call 9-1-1 right away."

Sal slapped him on the back. "Don't worry. Nobody's gonna mess with Katie when I'm around."

Chapter 21

Nick woke late the next morning and fixed a pot of coffee. He sat at the kitchen counter rubbing his temples to ease the throbbing pain. Empty beer bottles from the previous night cluttered the counter. He had to stop drinking, but alcohol numbed his frustrations and sent him into a dreamless black void. Drinking himself into a stupor had become his nightly ritual. Worse, he wasn't sure if the whispers encouraging him to drink came from the demons or his own mind.

He jumped when his phone rang. Ray's older brother, Louis, sounded encouraged on the other end. "Ray's coming out of it. He should be fully conscious by this afternoon. You can visit him then."

"Can he walk?" Nick asked.

"They still can't get a clear picture. The surgery caused more swelling. They're gonna tell him about the possible paralysis when he wakes up."

Nick choked back a sudden flood of tears as he thanked Louis for the call and hung up. The thought of Ray in a wheelchair for the rest of his life tore at his gut. Ruby had him shot because Nick asked him to protect Katie. Now, he'd put his little brother in the same danger.

His cell rang again. He sucked in a ragged sob before answering.

"Good news, Nick," Lydia said. "Jon Gerber was discharged this morning. He's not pressing charges. He and his partner accepted our offer. They're relocating to the west coast."

"Thank God. Is Gerber gonna be okay?"

"He'll heal. The money Mr. Ruby paid him will go a long way to ease his pain."

"What about the cops? And the guard?"

"This morning, the police discovered the security camera in that sector of the parking lot isn't recording. There's no video evidence. All they have is three cops who saw you standing near Gerber. Our story is, you injured your hand when you fought off his attacker. He fled the scene. You tried to help Gerber and came in contact with his blood. Plain and simple, they arrested the wrong man. I'm filing to have the case dismissed. I don't expect any blow back. If they do, we'll counter with you don't recall being read your rights and the police used excessive force when they falsely arrested you."

"But the security guard saw everything."

Lydia paused. "I'm told he no longer works at the hospital."

"What do you mean?"

"Have you spoken to Ms. Harrington? If we have to push back, her testimony as the only eye witness is key. She's not going to contradict our story, is she?"

"No. Don't worry about Katie."

"Then, it's settled, Mr. Tera. The media thinks you're a hero. Try to stay out of trouble." Lydia hung up.

Nick didn't understand why Lydia said the media considered him a hero. He turned on his laptop. The home page of his website touted new headlines of how he intervened in a robbery and assault while visiting a sick friend at a local hospital.

He Googled 'Nick Tera' and found two other versions of the story. In one, he beat up a female friend's abusive boyfriend, and the other stated he had a confrontation with an unnamed man over an unnamed woman. He was relieved that neither article implicated Katie. The second version rumored Bethany Grant, the movie actress, as the woman in question and her co-star, Lee Woods, as the man. Photos of him and Bethany leaving the cocktail party were splashed across the page, along with a picture of Lee Woods sporting a bandaged nose and two blackened eyes.

Returning to his website, he saw the space which had previously advertised The Nick Tera Fan Club was conspicuously missing. A new animation of a cartoon cupid shooting an arrow at a throbbing red heart took its place. Bold red text appeared, 'Win A Dream Date With Nick! Enter Contest Here! The winner of the contest will be chosen in a random drawing at the upcoming premiere of the movie, *Night Birds.*'

He tapped the back arrow and returned to his browser's default page with local news. The top story headline read, Three Officers Gunned Down In Drug Bust. The name Lepkowski leapt out at him. He had been killed at the scene and the other two officers were in guarded condition. The three policemen pictured in the article were the same three who had arrested him.

His stomach spasmed and he spat the sour-tasting bile that rose in his throat into the kitchen sink. Leaning against the refrigerator door he downed a bottle of beer in one long gulp, and then reached in and grabbed another. He pushed the coffee mug away and huddled on a kitchen stool clutching the bottle. His hand trembled as he brought it to his mouth. He wasn't going to jail because everyone involved had been paid off, wounded, or dead. All, except Katie. How many more innocent people would end up dead or hurt because of his contract with Victor Ruby? He had to find a way out.

A voice told him to have another beer.

Nick staggered down the hospital hallway toward Ray's room. The nurse sitting at the station desk looked up from her computer screen.

"Can I help you? Sir?"

"Wanna shee my friend." He pointed to Ray's room door.

"Are you all right, sir?" she asked, standing.

"Juss hard to shee im like dis." Nick wavered on his feet as the nurse studied him.

"Five minutes only." She gestured toward Ray's room as she made a note on a pad.

Ray's eyes fluttered open when Nick dragged a chair across the linoleum floor to the side of the bed and dropped heavily onto it.

"Nick," Ray said in a hoarse whisper.

Nick swallowed hard. "S'how ya doin', buddee?"

Ray grunted and closed his eyes. Nick sat, watching him breathe.

"Promise me," Ray whispered.

Nick leaned over the side rail of the bed. "P-promish what?"

"If what they say is true," Ray paused and opened his eyes. "If I can't walk. I'll need your help."

"Anythin, man, anythin. You don havta ask." Nick swiped his sleeve across his face to catch the tears.

"My bedroom's on the third floor." Ray's voice deepened. "I won't be able to get up the stairs. My guns are up there."

"Whadda ya shaying?"

"I'm not living in a goddamn wheelchair. Promise me." Ray's steely gaze fixed on Nick.

Nick shook his head. "No, Ray, I c-can't. Pleash, don' ask me ta—"

"You're the only one I can ask."

"But dey don even know for shure if you're pa-paralysed." Tears streamed down Nick's face. "Even if . . . ya can't give up. Ya juss can't." Acid burned his throat as beer roiled in his stomach.

"Time's up," the nurse announced from the doorway. She scowled at Nick, grabbed a plastic pan from a cabinet and rushed to the bedside. She positioned it under his chin just in time to catch the vomit.

Nick nodded at the nurse as he exited the rest room and walked past the station.

She shook her head. "Did you drive yourself here?"

"No, my ride's downstairs," he lied and then mumbled, "I'm really sorry about, um, thanks."

The numb sensation from the alcohol had worn off leaving a hollow feeling in his stomach and head. He leaned in the corner of the elevator as it descended. Ray's desperate words played in his mind.

He walked down the hospital steps and rounded the corner to the parking lot. Sal had told him Katie had the day off. He wanted to at least drive past her apartment to check on her as best he could from the road.

A small group of people and a security golf cart blocked the narrow sidewalk. Flowers and candles filled the cart. Propped in the driver's seat, a framed picture of a smiling, white-haired man.

Nick excused himself as he edged past the group. An older woman standing in his path turned and offered a sad smile. "Did you know Andy?" she asked.

"No, ma'am."

"He was a security guard here for eleven years. Someone broke into his house last night. Killed him. Poor dear." She blotted her eyes with a tissue. "Bludgeoned to death in his own bed. So horrible."

Cold pin pricks ran down his spine. "I-I'm so sorry." As he cleared the crowded corner, he broke into a run, remembering Lydia's terse comment about the guard no longer working at hospital. Inside his car, Nick laid his head on the steering wheel. The old man was only doing his job, like the cops who arrested him. Now they were dead and two other cops in critical condition. He sat until his tremors calmed and then started the car with a shaky hand.

His cell rang as he waited to pull out of the hospital driveway. Rosa's Ristorante displayed on the screen. He hit the button and before he could talk, a deep, somber-toned voice on the other end spoke, "Nick, there's trouble at the restaurant. Your family needs you. Hurry."

An anxious flutter caught in his throat. "W-who is this?"

"Father Santore. Rosa asked me to call. She wants you to come home right away."

A horn beeped behind Nick. He ignored it. "What is it, Father? Is Nonna all right?"

"Yes, but please, come as quickly as you can, son." The call ended.

Nick threw the phone down and hit the gas pedal. He gunned the Mustang into a narrow gap in the traffic and then braked hard when the rear lights of the car in front of him suddenly flashed red. Sirens wailed and two ambulances sped around the corner in front of them, headed in the opposite direction toward the hospital.

He broke from the slow, heavy traffic and turned onto the same side road the ambulances had exited. Taking a short cut to the restaurant, he ran stop signs and swerved through the narrow residential streets at twice the posted speed.

Spinning red, yellow and blue lights blinded him when he turned the corner onto his street. Police cars and a fire truck blocked his view of the restaurant. He pulled into the alley next to the corner florist shop, jumped out and ran down the street.

A fireman in a yellow coat swept broken glass from the sidewalk. Bright yellow police tape cordoned off the sidewalk in front of the building. Groups of people stood gawking on the other side of the road. A policeman yelled for him to stop just as Nick's waist breached the tape.

"I live upstairs. This is my family's restaurant."

The cop raised his palms. "Step back, sir."

"What happened? My grandmother. My brother and my father—are they okay?" Nick shouted at the cop.

"I called him, officer. He's the eldest son." Father Santore's shoes crunched over remnants of glass glistening on the wet sidewalk.

The cop nodded at the priest and then raised the tape so Nick could duck under it. "Go ahead."

Father hurried him to the door leading upstairs to the apartment. Nick stopped. The front picture window of the restaurant had been shattered. Jagged shards of glass dangled precariously from the top of the window frame. Wisps of acrid-smelling, white smoke drifted out the gaping black hole.

"Father, what happened? Where's my family?"

"Upstairs." The priest jogged up the steps at a rapid pace for a man of his age.

Nonna stood in the kitchen grasping a handkerchief. "Nickie!" She ran into Nick's arms.

"Nonna what happened? Where's Sal and Pop?'"

"The ambulance. It take them away." She sobbed into her wet hanky and shook her head.

Nick looked at the priest, his heart thumping in his throat. "No, Nonna. Are they—?

"Someone drove by and shot out the front window," Father said. "They threw firebombs inside. Molotov cocktails, the police called them."

"Sal? And Pop?" Nick stood, searching the priest's dark brown eyes for answers.

Father Santore grasped his arm. "Flying glass hit Salvatore. He has cuts on his face and arms. He'll be okay. Your father, one of the bullets hit him. Here." The priest patted the left side of his chest.

"Is he—?"

"No, but he lost a lot of blood." He glanced over at Nonna and then whispered. "It's serious."

Nonna grabbed onto Nick. Her small frame shook in his arms.

The priest waited a few moments and then laid his hand on his shoulder. "Nick, you should go to the hospital. I'll stay with your grandmother." He pulled out a chair. "Please, sit down, Rosa."

She sank into the chair. Nick squatted in front of her. "Do you want to come with me?"

Nonna nodded and rose. Nick gripped her shoulders as she keeled sideways. He helped her back onto the chair.

"She's too upset, Nick. Better if she stays here." He leaned down and spoke in her ear. "We pray, okay Rosa?" He repeated it in Italian. *"Preghiamo, si?* Tomorrow morning, we will light a candle."

"*Si, si.*" Nonna's glassy gaze fixed on Nick. "Nickie, you come home after? Please, I need you here."

Nick bent and kissed her cheek. "Yes, Nonna. I'll come home."

A nurse directed him to a curtained alcove in the Emergency Room where he found Sal lying on an examination table. Stephanie stood next to him holding his hand while a nurse cleaned and dressed his cuts. Black thread held a deep gash on his forehead closed. The nurse dabbed antiseptic on the shallower wounds on his cheeks and arms with a gauze pad.

Sal bolted upright when he saw Nick. With wide, frightened eyes he asked, "Nick, how's dad?"

"In surgery. It'll be a while. How are you doing?" Nick walked over to his brother.

Stephanie smiled at Nick. "He's going to be fine." She stroked Sal's hand.

Sal sat with his legs dangling over the edge of the cot and stared at the floor. The nurse handed him a plastic bag with gauze pads and medication. "There's instructions inside. Follow up in about a week with your doctor to have those stitches removed, all right?"

Sal nodded. Fat tear drops splashed onto the bag he clutched in his hands. "Is dad gonna die, Nick?"

"Pop's a tough guy, Sal." Nick stopped short of reassuring him their father would be fine. Every nerve in his body vibrated with his own fears. Ruby was intent on killing everyone he loved, and Nick couldn't stop him. Only his grandmother and Katie remained unscathed from Ruby's wrath, so far.

The nurse made notes on a clipboard. "We have all of Salvatore's information. Will you be taking him home?"

"Yes," Nick said. "Thank you, nurse."

She nodded and hurried off to another curtained room.

The three walked through the hallway connecting the ER to the main hospital building. Stephanie and Sal embraced for several minutes in the front lobby. The tenderness of their exchange surprised Nick. Their relationship had obviously deepened since the last time he observed them chatting at the kitchen table. Stephanie gave Sal a long kiss, waved to Nick and then exited the glass doors.

The two brothers rode the elevator to the fourth floor. Nick walked with his arm around Sal's shoulders to the OR waiting area, a small room with mint green walls, mismatched furniture and white linoleum floor tiles worn to a dull grey. He paced the perimeter of the room, stopping every few minutes at the double swinging doors to peer through the tiny windows. Fingerprint smudges and crosshatched wire embedded in the glass offered a murky view of the hallway leading to the operating suites. Sal slumped in a chair with blue vinyl cushions and dabbed at his eyes with one of the gauze pads from his bag. A dozen other men and women sat huddled in small groups; some held Styrofoam cups, others stared blankly at a muted television on the wall or talked in hushed tones while they waited for news of their loved ones.

Two hours passed before a thin man in green scrubs and mussed gray hair entered the room. All eyes in the room turned toward him. "Anyone here for Dominic Teravelli?" he asked.

Sal jumped to his feet.

Nick strode across the room. "We're his sons, Sal and Nick," he said. "How is he?" His heartbeat quickened as he waited for the doctor to answer.

"Your dad's a lucky man. The bullet missed both his heart and left lung by barely two centimeters. I removed it. Stitched him up. He's in Recovery, until the anesthesia wears off. You boys should go home and get some sleep. You can see him in the morning. They'll have him settled into a room by then. Barring any unseen complications, I'd say he's going to be pretty sore for a while, but he'll recover."

"Thank you, doctor," Nick shook his hand and then patted Sal on the back. "See, I told you the old man's tough." He forced a weak smile for Sal's benefit, yet his insides quaked.

Sal gulped back a sob as he attempted to smile. Tears poured from his eyes and he rubbed his shirt sleeve across his face.

Father Santore met them at the kitchen door when Nick returned home with Sal.

"Your nonna's finally asleep in the living—"

"Salvatore! Thank God!" Nonna rushed into the kitchen and threw her arms around Sal. "Come, sit." She pulled out a chair, hugged him again and then turned to the refrigerator and began pulling out casserole dishes, plastic-wrapped platters and bowls. She stared at Nick with red-rimmed eyes. "Your papa?"

"Pop's gonna be okay," Nick said. "They operated and got the bullet out. It missed his heart and lung. He's resting now. I'll go see him in the morning."

Nonna put down the dish she held and blessed herself. "Thank you, God."

"Yes, thank God." Father walked to the door. "It's a miracle everyone is all right. At least there were no patrons in the restaurant."

"Stay and eat, Father," Nonna said.

"No, thank you, Rosa. It's been a long night. You and your grandsons be safe. I'll come by for you tomorrow morning and we'll go to the church. Get some rest."

Nonna's eyes locked onto the priest's. "*Si, si,* tomorrow. *Accendiamo la candela.*"

Nick walked Santore downstairs to his car. He wanted to inspect the damage in the restaurant. Several business owners from the block approached hauling ladders, hammers and sheets of plywood to board up the gaping hole where the plate glass window once stood. They told Nick the police had given them permission to cover the window and start the clean-up. Each man shook Nick's hand and expressed their concern for his grandmother, dad, and brother before going to work on the window.

Father Santore waved from his small, compact sedan as he pulled away. Nick helped the four men install the boards over the opening and then invited them inside for a drink.

He opened the breaker box and flipped on the lights. Broken glass crunched under their shoes as they walked through the restaurant. A harsh burnt odor hung in the air and black soot stained the cream-colored stucco walls and ceiling. Smoke and the water from the fire hoses caused most of the damage. Many of the heavy wooden tables and chairs showed scorch marks. They can be sanded and refinished, Nick thought. The stone tiles on the floor had charred areas that rubbed off when Nick scraped them with the toe of his boot. Water from the force of the fire hoses had toppled chairs and tables, shoving them into jumbled clusters. Soaked, blackened table linens, silverware and broken condiment containers lay strewn among the shards of plate glass on the floor.

Nick picked up the framed photograph of his grandmother and grandfather from the grimy, wet floor. The picture was taken over fifty years ago on their grand opening day. The smiling couple stood in front of the now demolished front window with Rosa's Ristorante painted on it in curly red and green letters. He wiped soot and droplets of water from the glass with the hem of his tee shirt and set it on an upright table.

At the back of the dining room, Nick stopped short at the corner of the pizza counter. A large puddle of dark red with smaller puddles surrounding it dotted the tile floor. Blood. Some of the blood had seeped into a wad of raw pizza dough on the floor turning the edges a sickening pink. The light dusting of flour on the floor contained the blood in neat, oval-shaped pools.

He pictured his father standing behind the counter putting on his usual show, throwing a spinning circle of dough in the air and then deftly catching and twirling it as he stretched and kneaded the pliable disk with his fists before tossing it high above his head again.

One of the men looked down at the floor where Nick stood. "Holy Jesus," he muttered and gripped Nick's shoulders with both hands.

"Who would do this to Rosa and Dom?" another asked, shaking his head.

Nick stepped around the blood to get to the cooler. He passed bottles of beer over the counter. He felt no desire to drink tonight. While the men righted a table and chairs and sat, he went into the kitchen and filled the mop bucket with hot water, soap and disinfectant.

He sopped up the blood on the floor and then dipped the long, red-stained tendrils of the rag mop between the rollers to wring out the bloody water. The sudsy water turned a deep crimson.

Carrying the bucket out the back door, he dumped and refilled it. He scrubbed the same few feet of floor until the men finished their beers, stood and said their good nights. Nick thanked them and locked the front doors behind them.

Retrieving a broom from the back, he pushed large swaths of the wet, sooty, glass shards into a pile at the front of the store. He squelched down the rage he felt for Ruby and focused his fury on sweeping the debris. He vowed to deal with Ruby later.

His grandmother touched his back, startling him. With the sound of the glass scraping across the stone floor, he hadn't heard her come in the side door.

"We clean it up. Make it nice," she said. Her voice sounded strong. She walked the dining room silently surveying the damage while Nick herded the green-tinted glass chunks and debris to the front of the room. She paused to touch the portrait of her and her husband and then walked to the back counter.

Nick joined her and put his arm around her shoulders. She bowed her head and said a short prayer as she stared at the shiny wet, tiles behind the pizza counter and the bucket of soapy water.

"I'm so glad you're home, Nickie." She patted his hand. "It's late. Come upstairs. Rest. We start to fix this in the morning."

Upstairs, Sal sat at the kitchen table with a full plate of food in front of him.

"Why you not eating?" Nonna clamped her hand on his forehead. "You feel all right?"

"I'm full, Nonna. This is the third plate you gave me. I can't eat anymore."

"Then go to bed. Sleep. You stay home from school tomorrow."

Sal kissed her and then turned to Nick. "Dad's gonna be okay." He nodded his head up and down as if reassuring himself. "I'll help you fix up the restaurant." He threw his arms around Nick and held him in tight embrace. "I'm glad you're here." He released his hold and gave Nick one of his big, crooked grins. "Your old room's empty. Did Nonna tell you I got Steph at job at Eddie's? She's living in the studio apartment over the gym. I painted it for her."

"Better she not under the same roof with him," Nonna said, jerking her head at Sal.

Nick knew Sal could spend unchaperoned time with Stephanie if she were not staying in the same house. He winked at his brother. Sal climbed the stairs to his room.

While Nonna made coffee, Nick cleared the table and put the leftovers into the refrigerator.

"I do this. You sit," she said.

"No, Nonna. You need to sit and rest." He took the coffee pot from her hand, poured two cups and carried them into the living room.

Nonna settled into her chair and sipped her coffee. She put the cup down on the end table and rested her head against the back of the chair. With her eyes closed, she pulled her rosary from her apron pocket and rolled the small baby-blue beads between her thumb and forefinger.

Nick sat on the big, overstuffed ottoman at her feet with his legs stretched out in front of him. He had sat there countless nights as a boy listening to her recite the rosary. A calmness filled him as he cradled the warm coffee cup between his palms and listened to his grandmother's whispered prayers. The cross she had given him felt cool against his skin beneath his tee shirt. He closed his eyes and mouthed a Hail Mary along with his grandmother. Demons didn't plague him here, but the guilt of knowing Ruby attacked his family and best friend to manipulate him, consumed him.

His grandmother had always tried to instill in him her unshakable faith in God and the power of prayer. But his faith hadn't been simply shaken, it had shattered when his mother died. An insidious darkness had taken root in the very cracks of his soul. The demon seeds Ruby planted flourished into vines in those inky crevices, and nourished by his weakened faith, they grew stronger each day.

Overwhelmed by guilt and shame, he covered his face with his hands and blurted, "It's my fault. Pop and Sal. Your restaurant. I'm so sorry, Nonna. I-I don't know how to stop him."

She didn't reply. Turning, he saw her head tilted to one side and her eyelids closed. Her hands lay still in her lap with the rosary beads entwined through her thin fingers. Stress had deepened the lines in her face. Despite her dominant personality, she was a frail, old woman. Guilt dragged on his heart until the heavy weight felt as though it would crush his entire body. He could never bring his grandmother into a fight with the devil. This was his battle and he could never let her know. He stood and picked up the soft, crocheted afghan from the sofa and tucked it around her.

Entering his old bedroom felt both strange and comforting. The wooden floorboards squeaked when he walked to the desk. He found an old phone charger in a drawer and plugged in his cell. Sitting on the bed, he pulled off his boots. The soft, white cotton sheets had the familiar, clean scent of his grandmother's favorite detergent. He stretched out, his feet hanging over the end of the bed, and allowed the tears that had bit at his eyelids all evening to finally flow. Ruby ruled his life and his demons controlled his mind and body at will. He thought about the deaths of the police officer and security guard. Ray's grandmother hurt, and Ray most likely paralyzed. Jon and Stephanie, both beaten. Now, the restaurant destroyed and his father and brother narrowly escaping death. All of it because he wanted Ruby to make him rich and famous. Becoming a best-selling author meant nothing to him now, he was consumed with figuring out a way to destroy Ruby.

A warm glow from the streetlight below the window illuminated the figure of Jesus as He hung on the bronze cross on the wall, His head tilted to one side and His eyelids closed.

Chapter 22

The man lying in the hospital bed looked gaunt-faced and pale. He wasn't the burly, robust man Nick had locked horns with for seemingly his whole life. Thin, clear tubes attached to his father's left arm ran up to plastic bags hung on an intravenous stand. Colored wires taped to his barrel-shaped chest led to a digital monitor on the wall. The machine emitted a steady, muted beeping sound. The blue hospital gown, partially opened and pulled to one side, revealed a large white bandage around his father's chest. A pinkish stain surrounded a small drainage tube inserted through the bandage.

Nick pulled a chair to the right side of the bed so as not to disturb the tubes and wires. Leaning forward, he placed his hand on his father's forearm. Beneath the coarse, curly hair, the skin felt cool and dry. He studied the tattoo on his father's upper right arm, a permanent tribute to his mother, Rosemarie. Although the colors had faded over the years, the word "Rosie" stood out in black ink on a red heart. Two roses framed each side of the heart, their long stems curved downward and then formed into crossed dark green swords under it.

Nick looked up to find his father gazing back at him through half-closed eyes.

"Hey, Nick," he croaked.

For a moment, Nick wished he would yell at him in the deep-chested bellow he had heard so many times. "Hi Pop. How ya feeling?"

His father's laugh sounded more like a wheeze. "Peachy."

"They removed the bullet. You were lucky, it missed both your heart and lung."

"Good," Dom said as he struggled to push his body upward in the bed.

Nick pressed a button on the side of the bed raising his father to a sitting position.

"How's that?"

His dad nodded and cleared his throat.

"Water?" Nick held a plastic cup with a straw to his father's lips. He watched as he sucked in the cool liquid, coughed and then drank some more.

"Sal and Rosa, are they . . .?" His father's eyes widened with fear, an expression Nick had never seen on his dad's face.

"They're fine. A bullet grazed Sal's arm here," Nick pointed to his left upper arm. "And he has cuts on his face and arms from the flying glass. They patched him up and sent him home. Nonna's shook up and worried about you, but not hurt. She's at the church now with Father Santore. She wanted to light a candle for you."

His father closed his eyes. "Thank God they're all right. How long has it been?"

"The shooting was last night."

"Helluva thing," his father said. "Flipping dough one minute, shot the next." His laughter turned into a coughing spasm. He pressed his hands to his chest and winced. "Have they caught the bastards that did this?"

"No, not yet." Nick stood. "I should go, you need to rest. They told me not to tire you out."

His father grasped Nick's hand. "Could ya stay a little longer?"

"Sure." Nick lowered himself back into the chair.

"I hate to ask you, Nick," his father paused, "The restaurant—"

"I got it, Pop. Don't worry. I'm staying at home with Nonna and Sal."

"Thank you." His father closed his eyes and sighed. "I know you hate the restaurant. But just until I'm back on my feet. How bad's the damage?"

"The front window's being replaced tomorrow. There's a lot of smoke and water damage inside. I'll get it fixed."

"Insurance should cover it. Ask Rosa . . ." His father's eyelids drooped shut.

Nick waited. Sure his father had fallen asleep, Nick eased his hand from under his father's limp fingers.

Dom's eyelids fluttered. He squeezed Nick's fingers. "Love ya, Nick."

The cleanup in the restaurant progressed faster than Nick had expected. Sal wheedled three days off from school but worked each day from early morning until late into the night helping with the restoration.

The number of neighboring business owners and residents who streamed into the restaurant amazed Nick. Each were happy to share stories of how Nonna had helped them over the years, and eager for an opportunity to repay her kindness.

The owner of the hardware store down the block brought over electric sanders and helped Nick strip down the charred tables and chairs. Then, he and Sal stained and lacquered them.

A quiet, high school-aged girl arrived and set up her paint case on the floor by the one unmarred wall in the restaurant. Using an old photograph Nonna had given her, the girl spent days creating a *Trompe l'oeil* of a weathered trellis leading into a vibrantly colored vineyard on the wall behind the hostess table. Amazed by her talent, Nick stared at the detailed painting and wished he and Katie could vanish into the beautiful Italian countryside and escape Ruby.

Loretta, the florist on the corner, presented Nonna with two life-sized, silk Cypress trees potted inside Mediterranean-style stone urns. They flanked the small reception area wall near the mural.

Each evening at seven, Nick and Sal took a break to drive to the hospital. Sal walked with Katie, and Nick followed, unseen in his car a block behind them. Thankfully, the green van didn't make a reappearance.

Sal relayed messages to Nick that Katie wanted to talk to him. She called Nick's cell several times, but he let her calls go to his mailbox. Afraid to be alone with her and at a loss to explain his bizarre actions, he avoided calling her and only texted short apologies that ended with *I Luv U.*

Katie didn't reply to his texts. Her latest voice mail message sounded angry. "If you do love me, then you would at least speak to me in person."

Nonna pushed to have the restaurant reopened by the time his father came home from the hospital. She orchestrated the cleanup and redecorating, negotiated with the insurance company, and called Captain Brannigan twice a day demanding information about the people who had attacked her restaurant.

Nick threw his energy into the work and blocked out his growing frustration over Katie and his dread of Ruby's looming premiere movie event. He rolled a second coat of paint onto the restaurant walls. The pale, coppery color Nonna chose looked unimpressive in the can, but once on the walls, it gave the large dining room a warm, cozy glow. The refinished tables and chairs stood in the middle of the polished floor until the walls dried.

Captain Brannigan arrived at the restaurant the fourth morning following the attack and greeted Nonna. He walked around shaking his head and then patted Nick on the back and complimented his hard work.

"We believe the people who did this are all dead," Brannigan told Nick and his grandmother.

"You say a man named Jones was the ringleader. Why he do this to us?" Nonna asked.

Nick stopped painting when he heard the name Jones.

"So far we've only positively ID'ed the one I told you about, Rosa," Brannigan said. "Frank Jones, the driver of the van. Witnesses gave us his license plate number."

"A van?" Nick asked.

"Yes, a 1986 green Ford. Two of my officers spotted it and attempted to pull it over. Jones sped up and a chase ensued. The van plunged off an overpass at over eighty miles per hour. Jones and his three passengers were pronounced dead at the scene. We recovered guns, same caliber as the bullets we dug out of your walls, though we'll have to wait for ballistics to make an exact match. But from what witnesses described and the incendiary materials we found in the van, we're fairly certain they were they perpetrators."

"His name was Frank Jones?" Nick asked.

Brannigan nodded. "He went by Mr. Jones on the street. Had quite a record. Rape and murder, among other things. He'd only been out of prison a couple of months. Still can't figure a motive for the attack." Brannigan studied Nick's open-mouthed expression. "Did you know this Jones character?"

"No. Only curious about who'd do this." Nick turned his back to the captain and continued painting. A sigh of relief escaped his lips. Jones and the infamous green van were no longer a threat to Katie or Sal, though he had no doubt Ruby kept a never-ending supply of depraved thugs on his payroll.

Nick finished up the painting and left his grandmother thumbing through a catalogue of restaurant linens while he went to pick up the wrought iron wall sconces she had ordered. Sal would be home from school when he returned and would help install them. Once the sconces were on the walls, they could move the tables and chairs back in place and let Nonna dress the tables in new linens.

Nick called out, "Hey, Sal, I'm back," as he entered the front door.

Nonna and Katie embraced in the kitchen. Both looked at him with teary eyes.

His surprise to see Katie dissolved into fear at the sight of her stricken expression. His throat tightened. "What's wrong?" Nick tossed a paper bag of screws from the hardware store onto the table as he hurried toward her.

Nonna glared, waved him away, and mumbled something in Italian. She cupped her hands around Katie's face, kissed her forehead and then both of her cheeks. She left the kitchen, pulling the door shut behind her.

"Are you okay?" Nick took a tentative step toward Katie and held out his hands. "I was going to call you. I-I was so busy working on the restaurant."

Katie turned away from him and laid her fist on the kitchen table. As she opened her hand, Nick heard a dull, metallic thunk. Katie's engagement ring wobbled on the wooden table, the diamonds caught the overhead light, projecting a moving pattern of tiny sparkles across the walls. She looked at Nick with tears streaming from her eyes, opened her mouth to speak but then shook her head and ran out the door. Her footsteps running down the staircase grew fainter. The door at the foot of stairs slammed.

Nick's heartbeat pounded in his ears. He leaned on the back of a chair to steady himself and told himself it was better this way. Katie would be safe if she weren't in a relationship with him. He repeated the words in his mind, but his heart ached.

Nonna burst into the kitchen wagging her finger and yelling, "*Stupido, stupido, stupido*! You go after her, Nickie. You fix this—"

A thin, high-pitched ringing in his ears obliterated the rest of her words. The room dimmed, as though he viewed it through a foggy, rain-soaked windshield.

Nonna covered her mouth with her hands as Nick sank into a sitting position on the kitchen floor, his back against the cabinets. He hugged his knees to his chest and laid his forehead on his crossed arms. Nonna hovered over him, patting his head. "*Mi dispiace*, I'm sorry, Nickie, *mi dispiace*."

Sal walked into the kitchen. "Did Nick call me?" He stared down at Nick. "What happened? He hurt?" He looked at his grandmother.

She pointed to the table.

Sal picked up the ring. "This is Katie's ring, right? What's it doing here?"

Nick raised his head and looked at his brother with dulled eyes.

Sal paused open-mouthed. "Oh, crap."

Nonna snatched the ring from Sal's hand and shooed him away. "Leave Nickie alone."

Sal shot his grandmother a defiant glance and crouched down next to his brother. He gripped Nick's shoulder. "I'm really sorry, Nick."

Nick jumped up and brushed past his grandmother and brother. They were both talking, but he didn't hear what either said. He ran down the stairs, through the restaurant, out the back door and into the fenced rear yard. In the corner behind the dumpster, he leaned his head against the rough, wooden fence. Katie returning his ring shouldn't be a surprise. He had told her he didn't want to see her anymore. He lied to her, ignored her calls and acted irrationally the last few times he had seen her. All she knew was the Ruby-manufactured persona from the newscasts, the website or tabloid articles which bragged about his fictional exploits with other women. Thinking he could rid himself of Ruby and the demons before his relationship with Katie imploded had been a fantasy. He wiped his eyes and drew in a deep breath of fresh air. If telling Ruby that Katie had broken their engagement would protect her from harm, it would be worth it. But he knew better. Ruby would continue to threaten Katie, or worse. She'll always be in danger because he'd never stop loving her and Ruby would use his love for her against him.

He punched the fence, and then cursed, cradling his bloodied knuckles with his other hand. Deep down he knew Katie loved him. If he told her the truth, she would forgive him—if she believed his fantastical story. But Nick couldn't chance putting her in more danger.

"You okay?" Sal ran toward him. He touched the fresh blood stain on the fence slat. "I did that once. Flippin' hurts. This old wood's harder than it looks. Like ol' Eddie says, never punch anything harder than your fist."

Nick grunted at his brother's simple wisdom. He crooked his arm around Sal's neck. "Ain't that the truth."

"Everybody knows you guys belong together. Katie loves you, Nick. You want me to talk to her for you?"

"No. Leave it alone." Nick released his hold on Sal. "There's some things I need to do. Can you finish up here, hang the sconces and move the tables back into place?"

Sal straightened his shoulders. "Sure, I can handle it. What do you have to do?"

"Some stuff." Nick walked beside his brother into the kitchen. "Sal, even though Katie broke our en–" He paused, the words stuck in his throat. "I still need you to walk her home after work, understand? I'll try to follow in the car."

"Geez, Nick. What if she gets pissed or tells me to get lost?"

"Then follow four feet behind her. Swear to me you'll make sure she gets home every night."

"All right, if you want me to. But it's gonna be weird, now that you guys are broke up."

"I'm counting on you, Sal. She's still in danger."

Sal nodded his head and stared with solemn eyes at Nick's grim expression.

Nick pulled his car keys from his jeans pocket. "Thank you, Sal. For everything."

"Hey, wait, when will I see you again?"

"I'll call you." Nick hurried out the door to his car.

The luxurious apartment felt like a prison cell and depression enveloped Nick the minute he entered. He immediately checked the refrigerator for beer and found it had been well-stocked with six-packs of Budweiser. He stopped his hand from grabbing the nearest icy bottle and slammed the door, refusing to let Ruby keep him in a drunken haze. He snooped around the other rooms to see if anything else had been added or removed.

A black suit bag hung on the bedroom closet door. Pinned to the bag, and dated for two days from today, he found an invitation to the premiere for *Night Birds*.

Grabbing his gym bag from the closet, he stuffed it with clothes and toiletries. By tomorrow, he planned to be far away from the city and Ruby. Perhaps the distance might sever the hold the demons had over him. Vague thoughts flitted through his mind. He had restaurant experience or maybe he'd land a job as a stringer at a newspaper. Money, for once, wasn't a problem. He'd deposited all of Ruby's six figure checks into his bank account. Once settled, he'd convince Katie to join him. He'd find a city with a large hospital so she could continue her nursing career.

The cowardly plan gnawed at his stomach. He didn't want to leave his family and spend his life running, but reasoning with Ruby had failed and fighting him proved futile. He remembered the night he watched as Bethany Grant fled the city in a yellow cab. She had escaped Ruby. He would, too.

On an impulse, Nick sat at the desk, opened his laptop and typed a letter to Katie. Starting with the night of VIP party, he detailed everything about Ruby. He confessed the lies he had told Katie to protect her from the truth. He wrote how he witnessed Cullen's gruesome possession, his own demons, Ruby's transformation into the devil, Chris's suicide note, Ruby beating Stephanie, Ray's shooting and finally the attack on his family at the restaurant. He told how Bethany had escaped Ruby, and his own plan to flee the city.

He told her about Artie and how he prayed leaving the city would release him from the clutches of the twisted murderer inside him who was hell-bent on killing her.

He typed non-stop for an hour, pouring out his frustrations, fears and hopes for their future. At the end, he told Katie how much he loved her and how deeply sorry he felt for not being able to stop Ruby or control the demons inside him. He begged her to join him once he was certain he was free of Ruby and the demons who controlled him.

Hitting the print button, he stood, paced the room and finally flipped on the television to break the suffocating silence in the apartment. He brewed coffee for his road trip. Searching the kitchen cabinets for a thermos, he froze when he heard a reporter's words on the television.

"The mysterious disappearance of young actress, Bethany Grant, has reached a tragic and gruesome conclusion this evening. We now join Rob Taylor live at the grizzly scene in Ocala, Florida."

Rushing into the living room, he watched as rescue workers hauled two black body bags from a deep, overgrown ravine. The reporter on the scene said Bethany's mutilated body, and the body of her fiancé, were found today in a wooded area, sixteen miles from her home in Florida. The rest of the reporter's words were lost. Nick kept on punching the screen until the sputtering electronic flashes of light stopped and it turned black and silent. It dangled by one bolt, swaying against the wall with a raspy, scraping sound.

That evening, he sped into Ruby's parking lot and screeched the Mustang to a stop. A few employee's cars remained. Lights burned in the windows of the lower floors and the front doors were unlocked. He rode the elevator to Ruby's office suite on the eighth floor. The locked door sported a shiny, new sticker, Protected by Ace Alarm Company. The police would arrive before he could break down two doors and locate his contract in Ruby's ominous file drawer.

He strode to the far end of the hallway to a small, private elevator. He stepped inside and rode up the one floor to Ruby's living quarters.

The elevator doors slid open revealing a framed painting of Dante's Inferno adorning the wall of a small foyer. Floor-length burgundy velvet drapes covered the window to his left and two massive, mahogany doors stood to his right. The entrance, with its intricate carvings and stout iron hardware, looked like it belonged in a medieval castle rather than a modern high-rise.

He gripped the heavy metal ring in the lion's mouth knocker and slammed it against the door three times. Sweat coated his body from the heat radiating through the ornate doors.

The doors swung open, revealing Ruby, dressed in a black satin robe with a red collar and sash. His dark eyes glistened, and his lips parted in an ugly facsimile of a smile. "Good evening, Nick. What a pleasant surprise." Ruby gave a little bow and an elaborate hand flourish. "Do come in."

A wave of hot air hit Nick's face, sucking his breath away. His eyes immediately fixed on a floor to ceiling, twenty-foot wide glass wall with flames raging behind it. Ruby's fireplace. There were no visible windows in the suite. The polished black marble walls and floor of the foyer opened into a expansive room in front of the immense, glass-enclosed inferno. A blood-red carpet covered the living room floor and statues of grotesque horned creatures with stony eyes stared from various perches around the room.

Talon lounged on a black leather sectional, her long, lean body, barely covered in a sheer bra and panties, her tan skin oiled with sweat. She ran her red tongue over her redder lips and patted the seat cushion beside her. "Join us, Nick."

Nick ignored her and jabbed his finger into Ruby's chest. "I came to talk to you about the shooting."

Ruby's eyes narrowed as he brushed Nick's hand away. "I'd prefer you make an appointment during office hours. But, since you're here, don't be so rude, Nick. I don't believe I've ever formally introduced you two." He beckoned to Talon.

She walked to Ruby's side with the confident stride of a runway model, her chin high and her black, stiletto heels drummed a slow staccato beat on the marble floor of the foyer.

"Talon, meet Nick Tera, horror writer and soon to be serial killer." Ruby's low giggle grew into a rant of maniacal laughter that filled the room. The ruddy skin on his face vibrated as he howled, flickering between his human form and a black, reptilian-looking image lurking beneath. His outburst stopped as abruptly as it started. "And, Nick, let me introduce you to my dearest daughter, Talon."

Talon seized Nick's hands and pulled him toward her.

He wrenched his hands from her vice-like grip and stepped back. Glaring at her, and then at Ruby, he spat, "Your daughter? You disgusting—"

"Tsk, tsk," Ruby turned to Talon. "Seems we've offended Mr. Tera's delicate morals." He snapped his fingers, his long nails clicking against each other. "Run along, my dear."

Talon stuck out her bottom lip in a mock pout, swiveled on one skinny heel and sauntered off down a long, dim hallway.

"I invite you into my home and you insult me?" Ruby pointed a polished nail at Nick's chest. "Those are not allowed in my home."

The cross tucked beneath Nick's tee shirt heated against his skin, the red-hot metal singed his chest hair. Fumbling to grasp the chain, he yanked it over his head. Searing heat shot up the chain, burning his fingers. He dropped it on the floor.

Ruby turned his back and walked to a corner bar, well-stocked with liquor bottles and decorative decanters. He poured red liquid from a cut-glass decanter into a silver chalice.

"Why are you here, Nick?"

"You tried to kill my family. Now I'm going to kill you." Nick leaped onto Ruby's back, knocking him to the floor. A brilliant-red rage blinded him. He pounded his fist into Ruby's stunned face. Grabbing Ruby's satin collar, he slammed the back of his head into the marble floor.

Nick's back hit the heavy front doors just as he realized he had been blasted through the air. He dropped onto the hard floor, dazed, and stared at his burning hands until his brain made sense of what his eyes saw. He screamed and held up the two flaming torches at the end of his arms. Trying to smother the fire, he beat his hands against his torso and the door. The flames flared higher, blistering his flesh with excruciating pain. His screams turned to desperate, raw gulps as he watched his skin char and then drift away in black ashy, sheets. Burning chunks of tissue dropped from his bones with sickening soft plops and lay smoldering on the shiny floor. He smelled his flesh burning and saw the skeletal remains of his hands silhouetted inside the two ferocious blazes.

Ruby climbed to his feet, straightened his robe and smoothed back his hair.

Nick whimpered, "Make it stop." He curled into a fetal position on the floor with his arms stretched out. Flames covered the blackened bones of his fingers.

Ruby strolled across the foyer humming a bar of 'Happy Birthday.' "Shall I make a wish first?" He puckered his lips, bent at the waist and then blew out each flaming hand.

Nick squeezed his eyes closed and tucked his body tighter. The super-heated air didn't allow tears or sweat to flow. "Kill me," he gasped. "Take my soul. End this."

"Stop your whining." Ruby kicked Nick's ribs. "Get up!"

Nick panted short, ragged breaths as he opened his eyes. He turned his hands over and over staring at both sides, shocked to see his flesh intact and unscathed from the fire.

"You can't wield a knife with bones for fingers, now can you?" Ruby swiped his hand across the blood trickling from a cut under his eye. His long, tapered tongue lapped the red smear from his fingers. Nick crawled to the door, grabbed onto the knobs and pulled himself upright. He flattened his battered body against the oven-hot wood and gulped in air that burned his mouth and nostrils.

"You will go to the premiere tomorrow night," Ruby said. "You will smile and be charming when I present the winner of the contest. The press will document your date. It will appear the girl was driven home, instead, you will bring the young lady back to your apartment and let Artie have his fun." Ruby strolled to the bar and picked up his untouched drink. "My people will do the clean up the following day. Nick Tera, horror writer, will continue to enjoy wealth and fame. And Artie will be satisfied . . . for now at least."

"Kill me! You still get a soul. I won't murder any—"

"If you refuse to cooperate, I'll send Artie, via your body, to slaughter Katie instead. I don't care either way, but Artie has expressed a strong preference for your fiancée." Shrugging his shoulders, he took a long drink from the chalice and then smacked his lips. "He's quite smitten with Katie."

Ruby kicked the cross with the toe of his leather slipper. "Leave my home."

Nick bent and scooped up the chain as it slid past his feet. The metal had cooled, and he jammed it into his pocket. "Please, I'm begging you, don't you have any mercy?"

As he pleaded, Nick saw faces form inside the huge fireplace behind Ruby. A mass of pale, distorted heads writhed in the flames. Their eyes, blank white ovals, and their mouths, black and gaping open in tortured screams, yet emitting no sounds. Elongated fingers stretched from misshapen hands pressed and clawed against the glass. Icy terror tightened around his pounding heart. He tore his gaze away from the horrific sight of Chris Turner's and Bethany Grant's tormented faces among the frenzied mass.

"I'm being quite merciful, Nick. I'll overlook your intrusion into my home, your insult to my daughter and your pathetic outburst. But I won't kill you tonight, or anytime soon for that matter. If you don't show up at the premiere, or are one minute late, you'll live on for decades in a prison cell with Artie's fond memories for company. Katie's dying screams and the vision of the knife you held in your hands as you very slowly slashed your beloved to death. And of course, her blood." Ruby smiled, his teeth coated in a crimson sheen. "And that's only the beginning of my plans for you. When you finally die of old age, I'll see you in Hell."

Chapter 23

The morning of the premiere, Nick woke from a nightmare-filled sleep, soaked in sweat. For the first time in weeks he didn't suffer from a hangover, but instead, ached all over from the body-slam Ruby delivered last night. Limping into the kitchen, he glared at the beer stocked inside the refrigerator. The bright white interior turned to red as his anger grew. After a short but violent bout of rage, his vision cleared. Broken brown glass covered the floor and sudsy puddles of beer sloshed around his bare feet.

He gathered his letter to Katie and Stephanie's demo CD he had hidden in his desk drawer. While coffee brewed, he aimed the shower head onto his back and let the hot water beat against his sore muscles. Clutching a bar of soap in his hand, he shuddered at the memory of seeing his charred finger bones.

His cell phone rang as he finished dressing. He picked it up, not recognizing the number.

"Hello, Nick? It's Janis Ford. I need to talk to you."

He hit the END button and slammed the phone down on the kitchen counter.

It rang again. Seeing Janis' number, he let it ring until the mailbox picked up. He poured coffee and as he took a sip, the phone sounded again. He finally answered it to stop the ringing, "What the hell do you want?"

"We need to talk. Maybe we can help each other."

"What has Ruby put you up to now?"

"Ruby doesn't know I'm calling you. Can I come to your apartment?" Janis blew out a long breath. "I understand why you don't trust me. I don't blame you. Please, give me a chance. I can explain."

A glimmer of hope flickered in Nick's mind. Janis had stuffed papers from Ruby's file drawer into her bag. By some miracle she might have his contract, though he worried what she would demand in return.

He sighed into the speaker. "When?"

"I can be there at eleven."

Nick glanced at the wall clock. "All right."

He gulped down his coffee and then packed his laptop into his gym bag. Grabbing the letter and CD, he hurried out of the apartment.

The bank presented him with a long succession of papers to sign in order to close out his account. He slid a cashier's check in the amount of two-million, nine-hundred and ninety-seven thousand dollars into the envelope with Katie's letter and sealed it.

At ten-fifteen, he waited inside his car in the parking lot of Eddie's Gym and called Sal's cell for the third consecutive time.

Sal ran down the outdoor staircase from Stephanie's apartment, shirtless, barefoot and buttoning his jeans. He shoved his uncombed hair back with both hands as he approached Nick's car.

"What's the big emergency, Nick?"

Nick passed the envelope out the window. "Give this to Katie tonight."

"Um, listen Nick, Katie's *really* pissed off. She told me last night not to dare show up and walk her home anymore."

Nick got out of the car and slapped the envelope into Sal's hand. "You have to meet Katie at the hospital tonight and make sure she gets home safely. Especially tonight. Do you understand me?" He gripped his brother's arms and shook him.

Sal stared at Nick's fingers digging into the flesh on his upper arms. "Nick, what the hell?"

Nick released his grip. "Swear to me you'll be there tonight and give her this envelope."

Sal rolled his eyes. "I swear, okay?" He glared at Nick through the hair which had fallen over his eyes and rubbed his hands over the red finger imprints on his arms.

"I'm sorry," Nick threw his arms around his brother. "I love you, Sal. You know that, right?"

Sal's tensed body relaxed. He hugged Nick back. "I know. I love you, too."

Nick reached into the car for the padded brown envelope. He had taken Chris' suicide note out and left only the compact disc inside. He handed it to Sal. "This belongs to Steph."

"What is it?" Sal examined the slim package, flipping it over in his hands.

"Her demo CD. She left it at my place."

"Whaddya mean a demo CD?"

"A CD of her songs. It's what singers send to music studios to get recording deals."

A smile tugged at the corners of Sal's mouth. "I didn't know Steph was a singer."

"Yeah. A good one, too. Mostly country songs, some ballads."

Nick hurried to the trunk of his car and unlocked it. He motioned to Sal.

Sal approached as if expecting to see a dead body stashed inside. "What's that stuff?"

"Grandpa's chef knives. Take them to the restaurant." Nick laid the leather case in Sal's outstretched arms. He slung the strap of an overnight bag on Sal's shoulder. "This is Katie's. Give it back to her, okay?" He left his gym bag inside and slammed the trunk lid.

Sal adjusted the strap on his shoulder. "Why don't you take the knives to the restaurant? You haven't even seen it since it's all finished. The whole neighborhood's talking about how awesome it looks. And, Pop's coming home tomorrow. Nonna's been trying to call you. She wants to have a big grand reopening party—"

"I'm glad Nonna's restaurant is all fixed up. Thanks for finishing it." He grasped Sal in a bear hug. "Please, don't let me down, Sal. Stay close to Katie tonight. And watch your own ass, too, you hear me?"

"You're freaking me out, Nick. What's going on?"

Nick slid into his car. "Be good to Steph, she's a sweet girl. I'm glad you two are together."

Sal stood holding the two cases as Nick pulled his car into the street and drove away.

Nick greeted Janis at his apartment door with a terse, "What do you want?"

"I need to ask you some questions."

"I'm in no mood for one of your fucking interviews," he said, slamming the door behind her.

"You wanted to know why I was at your girlfriend's apartment. I'll tell you, if you tell me some things. Deal?"

He sighed, trudged into the kitchen and poured himself a mug of coffee.

"Yes, please, I'd like a cup." Janis smiled for the first time that Nick had ever seen.

He handed her an empty mug.

She inspected it to see if it was clean and then poured coffee into it. "Got any milk?"

"In the 'fridge." He sat at the counter.

She rolled her eyes. "Fine, I'll get it." Janis tiptoed through the beer and broken glass on the floor, giving Nick a curious sideward glance. She pulled a carton from the refrigerator and opened it. The stench of spoiled milk made her gag.

Nick jumped up, took the carton from her hand and dumped it down the sink drain. He ran the hot water to dissolve the curdled mass in the strainer.

"Black's fine." Janis fanned away the lingering sour odor with her hand. She looked down when a piece of glass crunched under her shoe but didn't comment.

He studied Janis while he sipped his coffee. Her facial expression looked pleasant but guarded. "You knew about Ruby's contracts. Do you have a contract with him?"

Janis ignored his question and strolled into the living room. "Nice place you—" She frowned at the busted, big-screen television dangling from a bolt on the wall. "Humph, maybe you do need an anger management class."

"I heard on the news Bethany Grant was found murdered in Florida. I-I just lost it."

"Yes, I heard about that, also. Brutal scene. You whisked her off from the cocktail party last week. Does that make you a suspect, or simply a person of interest?"

"I didn't kill her."

"Maybe you punched out your TV because she dumped you for her fiancé in Florida?"

"Everything's a lurid headline to you, isn't it?" Nick slammed his mug down on the coffee table. "I knew Bethany, or Mary, for all of twenty minutes. I gave her a ride downtown. She wanted to get away from Ruby. I offered to drive her to the airport, but she didn't trust me after reading all the lies printed in that piece of trash you work for. She got into a cab and drove away." Nick glowered at Janis. "Another decent human being is dead. Two, including her fiancé. I guess me having feelings doesn't fit your sleazy tabloid stereotype, does it?"

Janis sucked on her upper lip and looked down at the coffee mug in her hands. "I'm sorry."

Nick snorted, picked up his mug and stalked back to the kitchen to refill it.

Janis followed. "Victor Ruby hired me to interview your girlfriend. He wanted to know anything that might present a PR problem. Relationships, police records, financials, drug habits, etcetera. Lots of employers do it. It seemed like a reasonable request, considering the money Ruby planned to invest to promote your book."

"You talked to Katie? When?"

Janis stared at him with her mouth open. "Well, duh—you said you saw us talking outside her apartment. You've badgered me with phone messages ever since. Has alcohol impaired your short-term memory?"

"No-o-o. I said I saw you talking to her roommate, Tara."

Janis pulled her phone from her blazer pocket and scrolled her finger on the screen. "Here. Look. This is the woman I interviewed at the apartment, Katie Harrington." She held up the phone.

Nick took the phone. "This is Tara. I don't know her last name. She's Katie's roommate."

Janis snatched her phone back and jabbed her finger at the screen. "She said she was Katie, your fiancée. Dated you since high school. She knew everything about you. Answered all my questions without hesitation."

Nick sneered at her. "Nice work, Lois Lane. Katie didn't go to my high school. She only moved to the city when she got the job at Saint Mary's. That's when I met her."

Janis' cheeks flushed red and her eyes glinted with anger. "I'm a professional journalist—"

"Yeah, right, *The Entertainer* is a real Pulitzer Prize winner."

"Damn it! I worked at the *Daily Record* for six years as their top Breaking News Reporter. And at the Glen Haven *Journal* for five years before that. I always check my sources. I don't understand how she could have lied, and I didn't catch it."

"Tara's nuts. Every word she says is a lie. I can only imagine the shit she told you about me." Nick sighed and poured more coffee into Janis' cup. "So how did you go from the *Daily Record* to a rag like *The Entertainer*? That's a big step down the journalism ladder."

Janis's hands shook as she tore through the pages of a small spiral-bound notebook. "Here. Tara Burns." She drummed her fingers on a page of scrawled notes. "Katie said you were sneaking around having an affair with her roommate, Tara." She yanked folders from her over-sized bag and riffled through them. She held up a page. "The nurse in this picture, isn't she Tara?"

Nick stared at the photograph of a group of young women dressed in nursing uniforms. Hand drawn red arrows pointed to two women in the photo, one was labeled Katie and the other, Tara.

"This is wrong, you have their names switched," Nick said.

"Are you sure?"

"Of course, I'm sure. She's my fiancée. Or, was." Nick tossed the photo on the counter. "Who gave you this picture?"

"Katie, or now you're telling me it was Tara, gave it to me the day I spoke to her at her apartment. This is a copy of the photo I gave to Ruby in my report."

"Ruby knows what Katie looks like. He met her at the VIP party. Didn't he question it?"

Janis shook her head. "No . . . but I'm not sure he even looked at it. His snotty girlfriend Talon grabbed the file and snooped through it the day I delivered it. She was half-naked and draped across his desk like a cheap coat. Ruby was distracted, to say the least. He shoved the file into a drawer, handed me a check, and told me to go."

Janis flung the folder on the counter. Papers slid out and fluttered to the floor. Nick stared down at a paper copy of *The Entertainer's* front page. A close-up of Stephanie's battered face with a black rectangle superimposed across her eyes stared back. The headline loomed in huge block type, Nick Tera: Pedophile! Fourteen-Year-Old Victim Tells All.

He snatched up the paper and crumpled it. "This is a fucking lie! This is going on your front page?"

"No, relax. It's a mock-up. A fake. I put it together myself to show Ruby. He told me to have it ready."

"Ready for what?" He swooped down and scooped up the other papers from the floor.

He unfolded another tabloid-sized page showing a collage of pictures of himself and Bethany at the cocktail party running from reporters. The headline, Jilted Nick Tera Slaughters Bethany And Her Fiancé In A Fit Of Jealous Rage. He threw his hands in the air. "I'm screwed. Ruby's got me tied to every dirty—"

"Shush. Listen to me, Ruby gave me the Bethany story three days ago."

Nick sat with his elbows on the counter and his head in his hands.

"Did you hear me? That's two days before Bethany's murder was even discovered."

"That's your big revelation? I know Ruby's a killer. And God only knows how many other killers he has on his payroll." Nick lifted his head. "What do you want from me? And why were you snooping in Ruby's contracts?"

"Can I trust you?" Janis asked.

"I don't care if you trust me or not. I know I don't trust you."

She gripped the edges of the counter, her fingertips white. "This is what Ruby wants. He creates distrust, paranoia. He isolates people inside their own fear. Until they feel like they have no one to turn to, no way out."

"You think I'm paranoid? Slaughter's dead, Steph's been beaten, my best friend's probably crippled for life and my father's been shot. He also tried to kill Ray's grandmother and my little brother. They're alive by sheer luck. He murdered a security guard and a cop. Two more cops are in critical condition. Now, Mary and her fiancé are dead. And Ruby is threatening Katie and my grandmother. He's systematically destroying everyone I care about. It's not paranoia, it's the fucking nightmare my life has become."

Janis stared down at her fingers squeezing the edge of the countertop. "My girlfriend, Casey. I was searching for her contract." She glanced up at Nick and let out a long sigh.

"Where is she?"

"Dead. Three years now. She was twenty-three. Wanted to be a rock star. Infuriatingly stubborn. Talented, beautiful, and . . . I loved her more than anything on this earth. I've been investigating Ruby ever since."

"So, that's why you wanted to win his contest so badly."

"I'm a journalist, not a fiction writer. I plagiarized a horror story I found online in order to enter his damn contest. When that didn't pan out," she shot a burning glance at Nick, "I went to work for the tabloid trash. It gave me an in with Ruby."

"You didn't answer me. Did you sign a contract?"

"No. So far I've managed to fool Ruby into believing I'm loyal. That I'll write up whatever crap he hands me. As for *The Entertainer*, well, shit, they'll print anything. The more shocking and salacious the better. But my real story will be published someday."

"Your real story?"

"Yes. Exposing Ruby for the murdering, despicable, evil bastard he is."

"You know he's the devil, don't you?"

"Like any sane person would believe that." Janis scowled at Nick and then turned away. "I know exactly what Ruby is. My editor at the *Daily* thought I'd lost my mind when I showed him my notes. I quit because they were going to fire me after that."

"Do you know how to destroy Ruby, or at least get to his contracts again?"

"He's immortal, I think. As for the contracts, I don't know. Ruby's suspicious. He had an alarm and a camera installed at his office. And his new secretary is a bitchy, little watch dog. I almost conned the dumb redhead into letting me into—".

"Hey, Steph's a friend. She's not dumb, just young and trusting. She got hurt for trying to help me."

"Sorry."

"So, you didn't steal any of the contracts?"

Janis picked up the folder on the counter. Nick ripped it away from her hold.

"Hey!"

As soon as he opened the folder, he recognized it. "You got it." His heart pounded as he flipped though the papers to the last page containing his signature. "Yes! Oh my God. I can finally end this."

He ran to the living room and opened the fireplace door.

Janis rushed after him. "It won't work."

He pressed the button to ignite the fire. "Why, did you plan to use this to blackmail me?"

Janis pointed to the stack of papers he tossed into the hearth. "Look."

Small flames lapped at the edges of the papers, singing them brown and curling the corners. The small, black type had faded away to white on the top page. The word COPY in large red letters replaced the text.

Nick opened the door and hastily lifted up the burning stack. He shuffled off each burning page back into the fire. All of the pages were blank, except for the word COPY printed on each.

"No." He stared at the fire which now engulfed the papers and leaned his forehead on the mantle. "No, no, no. This can't be happening."

Janis touched his arm. "I'm sorry. I tried to burn Casey's contract. The same thing happened. It was a copy. I swear to you, Nick, it if were your real contract, I would have given it you. I'm not out to get you. I only want Ruby."

He looked at Janis with glassy eyes. "What now?"

Janis threw her hands in the air. "Hell if I know. Every time I get any of his clients to trust me, they turn up dead. I tried to meet with Bethany. You know what happened to her. I had a meeting set up with Ian Slaughter, too. When I pulled into the parking lot of his hotel that evening, I saw someone falling from a balcony. I ran over. It was Slaughter. Dead, obviously, with black feathers sticking out of his mouth."

"Feathers?"

"Similar, or the same, as Talon's winged costume at the VIP party. What do you know about her?"

"Just that she's Ruby's daughter and from what I can see, as evil and twisted as he is."

"Daughter?" Janis wrinkled her nose and grunted. "They act like lovers."

"I know. It's perverted." Nick jabbed the button and turned off the fireplace, then stalked into the kitchen. "Talon killed Chris? I thought he committed suicide."

"Ruby told me Chris was suicidal. As cold a bastard as he is, that seemed to anger him for some reason. I've heard suicide breaks the contract, but I don't know if that's true."

"Destroying my contract was my only hope. Now, I'm screwed."

"There's got to be a way to stop Ruby. Between the two of us—"

"Look, I don't have a lot of time left. Ruby's forcing me to do something after the premiere tonight. If I refuse, he'll kill my fiancée."

"What's he forcing you to do?'

"Commit murder."

Janis scooped up her papers and stuffed them into her bag. She backed toward the front door.

"I'm not a murderer. I won't do it. No matter what." Nick sighed and shook his head. "I'm sorry about your girlfriend. But, writing a story won't stop Ruby. It's hopeless. God's the only one who can destroy the devil." He laughed, a short dry sound. "I don't think He's a fan of mine anymore."

Janis stood with her hand on the doorknob eyeing Nick. "I don't believe in God."

"Yet you believe in the devil. That makes no sense."

"Occupational hazard. I believe in facts. Things I can see, prove and verify."

"Like you verified Tara was Katie?"

Janis huffed and then stomped out of the apartment, slamming the door.

Nick sank onto a kitchen stool, the tiny flicker of hope he felt earlier, extinguished. Either Janis was out to revenge her girlfriend's death as she said, or she was a spy for Ruby. Maybe Ruby had sent her to check up on Chris, too. Everything she said could be a lie. The contract, a fake and the mock-up front pages, real.

He stared at the clock. None of it mattered anymore. The premiere started in seven hours. His heartbeat revved up and vibrated in his dry throat.

After taking a deep breath, he pushed open the door to Ray's room in the physical therapy wing of the hospital. As much as he tried to mentally prepare himself for the sight of his best friend sitting in a wheelchair, the actual image unnerved him.

"Hey, Nick!" Ray grinned, pointed a remote at the television set and clicked it off. The muscles in his biceps worked as he wheeled himself across the room toward Nick.

Ray's grin disturbed Nick. He prayed Ray wouldn't ask him to get his gun again.

"I'm sorry I didn't come to see you sooner, how are you feeling, buddy?"

"I'm good. Be even better when they discharge me next week." He turned his head when the door swung open and a petite, young woman dressed in a pink golf shirt and white slacks entered. His smile broadened and he winked at Nick. "Now, I'm feeling excellent."

The woman nodded at Nick and then addressed Ray. "Ready for your session?" Her smile brightened her entire face, especially her expressive brown eyes.

"I'm always ready for you," Ray said. "Nick, meet Alona Vargas, my physical therapist and future girlfriend."

Alona's cheeks flushed a rosy pink. "Ray, you're going to get me fired."

"Nice to meet you." Nick shook her dainty hand.

"Why? It's true. We've got a date to go salsa dancing in sixty days," Ray said.

Her dark eyes sparkled. "I agreed to a date in ninety days. Now it's sixty?"

Nick stared from one to another. Ray's talk of dancing and his carefree manner confused him.

Alona rolled an aluminum walker from a corner of the room and stood it in front of Ray's wheelchair. "Remember, slow and easy, use your arm and leg muscles to lift up and . . . oh, Ray."

He stood up before she finished her instructions. The only indication of pain, a wince as he straightened his back.

Nick stepped back, his eyes wide. "Y-you can walk?"

Ray and Alona both looked at him. "Yeah, didn't Louis call you?" Ray asked.

Nick gave a sheepish shrug. He had kept his phone turned off most of the time since Katie broke their engagement and hadn't checked his messages.

"He still has some swelling, muscle and nerve damage," Alona said, "If he slows down and focuses on his therapy, he should be back to normal in about ninety days."

Ray leaned over the walker and pecked her on the cheek. "Thirty days."

Alona shook her head and then smiled at Nick. "Would you please watch him for a minute? I left his chart on my desk. I'll be right back."

"Ray, this is fantastic." He wrapped his arms around Ray's shoulders and hugged him. "I'm so relieved—so happy—you can walk."

"Me too. Man, it gave me a whole new respect for people in wheelchairs. That takes superhuman strength to deal with. I don't have that kind of strength."

"Looks like you've gotten over your shyness with girls, too."

Ray's grin widened. "Guess I had to find the right girl. Alona's it. She has so much positive energy, like a tiny bundle of dynamite. Said she loves to dance, too." Ray laughed. "She's so petite, she makes me feel tall. And, when she smiles at me, her eyes . . . well, you saw her, she's incredible."

Nick grinned. "You've fallen hard, buddy. So, which is it, thirty, sixty or ninety days until you're back to one hundred percent?"

"The doctors say ninety, but I'm shooting for thirty." He took a few steps and grimaced. "Shit, maybe forty." He grunted and rubbed his lower back. "Are you and Katie back together?"

Nick walked to the window and gazed outside. He slid his finger back and forth in one of the open spaces between the slats of the blinds. "We're taking a break."

Ray stopped moving the walker. "Taking a break? What the hell does that mean?"

"What it sounds like."

"Sounds like bullshit. Is your situation worked out?"

"Should be settled by tomorrow. One way or the other."

"You never did tell me what was going on. Are you all right, Nick?"

Nick turned to Ray and smiled. "Much better, now that I see you up and walking."

"I feel shitty that I pressured you about the gun, Nick."

Nick gripped Ray's shoulder. "Forget it, I probably would have felt the same way."

Ray made his way across the room. "Did you hear the asshole who shot me is dead?"

"No, what happened?"

"Weird shit. Cops matched the bullet they dug outta me to a gun used in other armed robberies. They tracked the guy down yesterday. Lamar Evans. Belonged to some gang, Hell's Hounds, I think. He stole my grandma's purse that night. Only valuable thing in it was her mother's rosary beads. Real old and made of semi-precious stones. She was sick over losing them."

"Yeah, I remember them. They were unique, multicolored. Did the cops get them back?"

"Yup. This ass wipe was wearing them around his neck like some sort of trophy. When the cops chased him, he climbed out a second story window and then jumped from the fire escape to get away. The beads got caught on a broken rail. Dumb prick hung himself before they could get him down."

"Holy crap. The beads didn't break?"

"Probably would have, except my old man got tired of fixing the chain every time Grandma snagged it on something. He reinforced the chain with fishing line. Heavy test."

Alona walked in carrying a clipboard. Her eyes lit up when she looked at Ray. She touched his arm. "How's your back feeling, Ray? Fatigued yet?"

Ray brushed his fingers against her cheek. "Nope. Just getting started."

Nick left Ray to finish his physical therapy session with Alona. Discovering Ray could walk lifted a heavy burden from his mind. He rode the elevator to the second floor to check on his father.

"You're looking a lot better today, Pop," Nick said as he entered the room.

Dom sat upright in bed with a partially eaten tray of food on the adjustable table in front of him. "Damn bullet didn't kill me, but this lousy food will," he grumbled.

Nick smiled. "You'll be home tomorrow."

"I hope! They've been talking about letting me out for days now." Dom shook his head. "Goddamn doctors never give you a straight answer. Just like when your mother was here."

Nick remembered the heated arguments between his father and his mother's doctors. Despite her aggressive breast cancer, his father still blamed them for her death.

"Nick, sit for a minute." His father cleared his throat and took a sip of water. "I wanna talk to you."

Nick pulled a chair near the bed. "What's up?"

"Sal came by today. He's worried Nonna changed her mind about letting him box."

"She's upset about the shooting. Nonna gets overprotective, especially with Sal."

"Ya know why your grandmother feels the way she does about boxing?"

Nick shrugged. "I guess she doesn't like fighting."

"No. She hates boxing 'cause of me," Dom said.

"What do you mean?"

"You're old enough to know the truth." Dom's attempt at laughter came out as a deep guttural sound. "And one more reason to hate your ol' man."

Nick shook his head. "I don't hate you, Pop, I just—"

His father held up his hand. "Let me get this out, okay? When I first met your mother, I was a high school dropout working at Eddie's gym. I'd quit school for dreams of being a big-time boxer, just like my father, Ol' Joe the Hammer. All I wanted was my photo hanging next to his on the wall at Eddie's. My father wanted it even more than me. He couldn't take on the younger guys in the ring anymore and he expected me to continue his . . . legacy." His gaze drifted from Nick to the open window.

"I worked my ass off, training every day in that damn gym. But the reality—I just wasn't that good. I had the muscle but didn't have the moves. A boxer needs agility. Eddie tried to tell my father I should give it up. Find something else to do. Boy, did that ever piss off my ol' man. He pushed me even harder. Against Eddie's advice, he found people to promote me. Local fights. Small time stuff, but with a lot of betting. I got my ass kicked in the ring three times a week. Then kicked again at home by my father." Dom grunted. "He'd give me a hard shot to the gut. Then he'd shout, 'learn to take a punch' and walk away."

Nick's head snapped up. His father nodded as if he could see the memories playing in his son's mind.

Nick at three years old, play-boxing on the living room floor with his father. Dom would land a punch every now and then in Nick's stomach. Even though he pulled his punches, they still hurt and knocked young Nick to the floor. If he cried, his father would yell, "Ya gotta learn to take a punch, Nick".

"I hated it when my father did it to me. Then I did the same to you. I'm sorry, Nick. More sorry than you'll ever know."

Nick rubbed his chin. "Go on."

"These two low-level wise guys, Jimmy Grazziano and Big T, Tony Borrelli, were making good money taking bets against me. One night they came to me and told me what round to fall down in. Ordered me to throw the fight! For once, I was sure I could take the guy. He was a rookie, a skinny, little Irish kid." Dom balled his fists, anger flashed in his eyes.

"What happened?" Nick asked.

Dom snorted. "Pride happened. I wouldn't throw the fight. Ironically, it was the one and only knock-out in my career. Round two. A body shot and then a solid right hook to the jaw. The kid hit the mat like a rock. Stayed down for the full ten count and then some."

"What about the guys who wanted you to throw the fight?"

"Yeah, them. Well, my high of winning lasted as long as the walk from the ring into the locker room. The SOBs jumped me. Beat the be-Jesus outta me. Told me I had one week to come up with fifty grand."

"Shit! What did you do?"

"Nuthin' I'm proud of," Dom closed his eyes and pushed back against the pillows.

Nick leaned forward, waiting for his father to continue.

"I already told ya I was a high school drop-out and a lousy boxer," Dom said. "I was also a husband and a new father. You were about eight months old. I'd lost the crappy little apartment we were living in 'cause I couldn't pay the rent. Why the hell your mother stayed with me, I don't know. I kept telling her my big purse would come at the next fight. Never did. When we got evicted, your nonna, Rosa, took us into the apartment over the restaurant. Gave us the whole second floor." Dom rubbed at his eyes with his knuckles.

"I was desperate for money. Big money. Nothing I could earn at a regular job in a week's time. Those guys weren't messing around. So, one day when everyone was downstairs in the restaurant, I went through Rosa's jewelry box. When I got to the pawn shop, they offered me twenty-grand for it. I was screwed. A failure and now a thief. I left the shop with the jewelry. The thought of facing your mother . . . I couldn't. So, I laid low at a buddy's house. Stayed shit-faced drunk for a week."

Dom wiped his eyes before continuing. "Then I heard when they couldn't find me, they roughed up . . . your mother." Dom's voice broke and he buried his face in his hands. "I swear to God, Nick, I didn't know they knew where she lived or that they'd dare go by the restaurant. Please, I need to know you believe me, son."

Dom's eyes were wet. He reached out toward Nick with both arms.

Nick's jaw muscles worked. He swallowed hard and pushed back in his chair. "What did they do to Mom?"

His father held his hand over eyes. "She was walking back to the restaurant one evening pushing a baby carriage with you in it. These two scumbags, they came up to her and one grabbed her arms. The other started flashing a knife around. Threatened to cut her. They held the knife on you . . . a baby, for Christ's sake. They told Rosie they'd slit your throat right then if she didn't tell them where I was hiding. The tip of the knife cut you." Dom pointed to his throat. "Here."

Nick fingered the scar on his neck. "Mom said it was from a soup can lid . . ."

"Your mother didn't want you to know. She didn't want you to think bad of me." Dom reached over, grabbed tissues from a box and blew his nose loudly. "That was real important to her."

"Then what happened?"

"Your mother saw the blood on your neck. She broke loose and grabbed for the blade. It cut her hand, bad. Some guys from the neighborhood heard her screaming. They ran over and the two thugs took off." He dabbed at his eyes. "All the commotion brought Rosa outside. She saw blood all over the baby carriage. Rosie and you both crying . . . bleeding."

Nick touched the scar again. His stomach churned, pushing a sour taste into the back of his throat. He looked at his father's tear-streaked face, then down at the floor.

"I came clean, Nick. When I heard what they did, I sobered up and went to the restaurant that same night. Rosa demanded to know the truth. I told her everything. She laid into me good. Cursed me up and down, first in Italian and then in English. Slapped me across the face a few times, too."

Dom sighed and shook his head. "I deserved it and more. I took her jewelry out of my pocket and put it on the table. I headed for the door, but she stopped me." Dom managed a weak smile. "Here's Rosa, all four feet, ten inches of her standing between me and the door. She told me I had two choices. I could walk out the door and never come back, or I could be a man and take care of my family. She said if I stayed, and swore off boxing for good, she'd help me. Give me a job at the restaurant."

"You chose to stay," Nick said.

"The thought of leaving your mother, you . . . I couldn't. I needed to make things right."

"What about the guys who wanted the money?"

Dom didn't answer for several seconds. "Rosa said she'd take care of it. I figured she'd pay them and then I'd work off the debt at the restaurant, but. . .." Dom trailed off and looked away.

"But what?" Nick asked.

"Look, Nick, I'm not saying your grandmother had anything to do with this, okay? But, two days later they found both of those guys, dead. Throats slit and their bodies dumped in the river. The cops didn't look into it very hard. Everyone figured they were killed by their own kind. No big loss, ya know?"

"You're not saying Nonna put a hit on those guys, are you?"

"No! No. Like I said, it was a coincidence. They were bad guys. Had a lot of enemies," Dom licked his lips and averted his eyes from Nick's hard stare.

"What is it?" Nick asked.

Dom spoke in a whisper. "I always wondered, ya know, I mean, Rosa is from Sicily."

"Oh, c'mon, Pop!"

"I know, I know. Forget I said it. God forgive me for even thinking it," Dom made a quick sign of the cross. "I owe my life to that woman. If it wasn't for her, I don't know where I'd be now. She made me work hard. Mopping floors. Washing dishes. Waiting tables. She also taught me to cook, and then, after your grandpa Vincente passed, she taught me how to run the business. Rosa gave me my pride back. My life and my family back. I love her and I love the restaurant more than I can say."

"So, Mom forgave you?" Nick asked.

"It took a while." Dom's eyes glossed with tears. "We worked it out. She saw I was serious about turning my life around. I loved your mother with all my heart." Dom traced his fingers over the tattoo on his arm. "The heart is for your mom. The two roses, you and Sal."

"Why are you telling me this now?"

"Laying here, shot, it makes ya think. We've always butted heads, you and me. I wanted you to understand . . . you're my oldest son. I'm so proud of you, Nick. I love you."

Nick stood and walked around the room trying to process what his father had told him.

"Nick, I don't know what's happened between you and Katie. She sneaks in to check on me, but I know something's wrong. She's an angel. A keeper. Like your mom. You have to do whatever it takes to make things right with her."

Nick looked at his father sitting in the hospital bed. A jumble of thoughts and emotions swam through his head. He was taller and stronger than his father now. Dom still had large biceps, but his once rock-hard stomach had drifted southward into a soft paunch. Nick wanted to punch him in the gut and then scream at him to learn to take a punch. Hearing his father say he was proud of him, made him want to cry after all the years of frustration and fighting. He hated his father for putting his mom in danger. And yet, he also admired him for staying. His last thought made him sink back into the chair and hold his head in his hands.

"What is it, Nick?" his father said.

"I'm the same as you. That's why we never got along. Too much alike."

Dom snorted. "Nah, you was always smarter than me, even as a kid. You did good in school. Went to college. You ain't nuthin' like me. I let your mother handle your writing stuff. The only time I ever felt like your father was when you were in jail. Pretty sad, huh?"

Dom reached under the blanket. He pulled out a copy of Nick's book. "Hell, you're twenty-five and you have a best-selling book. Sal brought it to me. Told me while I'm laying around here doing nuthin' I should read it. I am. I'm not fast at reading, so it might take me awhile. What I read so far is good, real good." Dom patted the book cover. "You have a new life outside the restaurant. You're famous. On television and all, like a movie star. I guess you changed your name cause you're ashamed. I'm not educated—"

"I didn't change my name, Pop. The agent did. I'm not ashamed of you, or our name."

"Why'd he'd change it?"

"That bastard changes everything. Twists everything. He says it's marketing, sales, always some bullshit reason to manipulate and torture people. He's the fucking dev—he's . . . evil." Nick stood and paced the small room again. "It's the same as you wanting your picture on Eddie's wall. Me wanting my damn stories published. I can't pay the price either. Not without doing things I don't want to do. Hurting people. The people I love the most. Especially Katie."

"Nick, tell me how I can help you, son."

"You can't, Pop. Nobody can. I got myself into this, I have to get myself out, one way or the other." Nick clenched his jaw and his fists. "I have to take the punch."

Chapter 24

Admittance to the world premiere of *Night Birds* was by invitation only, yet it didn't stop the hordes who gathered around the movie theater to gawk at the celebrities attending. The air crackled with energy and anticipation. For three blocks surrounding the iconic Majestic Cinema, the city took on a carnival-like atmosphere. Street vendors hawked everything from T-shirts to Italian ice. Savory aromas of roasting chestnuts, hot pretzels and sausage and peppers drifted on the cool evening breeze.

Nick gave up trying to find a parking space near the traffic-choked theatre. He parked in a closed dry cleaner's lot and sprinted three blocks to get to the theater on time.

A handwritten sign hanging over the ticket booth window announced the public midnight showing of *Night Birds* had been sold out. Still, long lines formed for advanced ticket purchases.

Police directed traffic at the busy intersection by the theater. More uniformed officers stood on the sidewalk guarding a line of wooden barricades which separated the premiere guests from the onlookers.

Nick pushed through the crowd toward the theater entrance. A woman screamed out, "Nick". He turned in the direction of her voice. More women waved and yelled to him from behind the barricades. The commotion drew a group of reporters. They rushed over, snapped pictures and shouted questions. He recognized Janis Ford in the fray.

Nick jogged along the barricades to escape the press.

"There you are." Ebony grabbed Nick's arm.

He felt the pressure of her long, curved nails through the sleeve of his leather jacket.

"C'mon, sweetie. You're a star. You don't have to wait in line." She led him around the corner of the theater building into an alleyway. Halfway down, a stocky man stood in front of a metal door. His shoulders extended a good inch past the doorway on either side. Squinting at Nick, he nodded to Ebony and then opened the door. The movement exposed the 9mm Glock holstered beneath his suit jacket.

The door opened into a long hallway with closed doors along either side. The corridor ended at the massive lobby inside the front entrance. The theater, recently restored to its original splendor of the early nineteen-hundreds, featured an enormous chandelier that hung from the high, gilded ceiling. Its dazzling array of lights reflected in the polished marble floors.

Celebrities and VIPs mingled in the lobby, the men dressed in tuxedos and the women in glittery evening gowns. Their dress shoes shuffled and clicked on the shiny floor. Laughter and the clinking of glasses echoed through the lobby. Small round tables dotted around the front entrance held trays of canapés and pyramids of champagne-filled glasses.

Ebony pressed her cat-like claws into Nick's arm. "Over here." She led him to a table on the left side of the lobby. "Sit," she said. Her eyes flashed an eerie yellow-green.

Rich, red velvet cloth draped the table. Behind it, copies of Nick's book and poster were displayed inside a glass concession case. Rachel leaned on a brass-trimmed wooden lectern with a thick, open book displayed on top.

"What is all this?" Nick asked.

Rachel smiled. For a split second a black skeletal shadow hovered beneath her skin and her irises gleamed red with black slits for pupils. "You'll sign your novel and then I'll direct the women to sign this book in order to join your fan club." She winked at Nick, her upper and lower eyelids flicked together. "Each page has an invisible contract. They'll sign away their souls and open more portals for Mr. Ruby's demons."

"Later, you'll draw the ticket for your big date." Ebony pointed to a large barrel-shaped metal cage filled with ticket stubs. It sat on the gleaming glass counter which ran the length of the wall behind them. A black-carpeted, square platform and microphone stand stood next to it.

"Don't try anything stupid," Rachel hissed into his ear. "We're watching you." Her long, forked tongue flicked Nick's cheek.

An identical corridor, on the other side of the lobby, mirrored the one he had entered. The tall, wooden, double doors leading into the movie theater were closed. Nick stood and walked toward the opposite corridor.

Rachel hurried after him and grabbed his arm. "Where do you think you're going?"

"I gotta piss. Do you mind?"

She hesitated, then loosened her grip. "Hurry up."

The men's room was a long, narrow, room with urinals and stalls lined along one tiled wall and sinks on the opposite mirrored wall. Nick ran to the end of the room and looked up at the only window. His fingers gripped the tile sill as he climbed up on a covered radiator to peer outside. Even if he could manage to squeeze himself through the tiny window, a heavy steel grate covered the outside.

A toilet flushed, startling him. He jumped down as Lee Woods exited a stall. Woods stopped short when he saw Nick.

"Trying to escape from all those girls out there, Nick?" Lee sneered. He sauntered to the counter and admired his image in the mirror, smoothing his hair with his fingers. He took a small spray bottle from an inner pocket and misted his rock-hard pompadour. "Wanna spritz, Nickie boy? Or do you prefer your cave man look?"

"Shut the fuck up." A demon-fueled rage simmered inside Nick at the mere sight of Woods.

Lee stepped sideways. "Big night, huh? Of course, tonight *I'm* the main attraction, not you." He pulled another smaller bottle from his jacket pocket, tilted his head back, and squeezed a drop of liquid into each eye. "Fuck! Damn, that burns!" He squinted at his reflection. The whites of his eyes turned bloodshot and tears rolled down his pale, powdered cheeks. He laughed and looked at Nick. "I gotta look all broken up about my murdered costar and lover."

"You're an asshole." Nick splashed cold water on his face and then pulled paper towels from the holder to dry himself.

Lee chuckled. "I'm glad Bethany the ice bitch is dead. She was a drag. Did you at least get to nail her the night of the cocktail party?"

Nick grabbed Lee by the jacket collar and cocked his arm back.

"No! No! Not in the face." Lee shielded his face with both hands and ducked his head down. "My nose isn't healed from the last time."

Nick wasn't sure if the tears flooding from Lee's eyes were real or from the drops. He released his jacket and shoved him into the counter.

Lee grabbed the edge of the sink for balance. "Ruby said after tonight he'd hook me up with some hot models. I'm gonna convince him to let me kick your ass in public! I'll be the new king of the bad boys." He jumped backward as Nick lunged for him.

"Problem, gentlemen?" Ruby glared at them from the doorway, his arms crossed.

"This big turd was trying to climb out the window, Mr. Ruby," Lee yelled.

Nick punched Lee in the stomach as hard as he could. Lee made a gurgling sound, doubled over and stumbled backwards. He landed on one of the urinals.

"Enough, Mr. Tera." Ruby walked over to Lee. "Compose yourself, Lee. Remember your role tonight—grief-stricken over Bethany's death. Now, get out there and act."

Lee struggled to stand and yanked at the hem of his jacket. He limped to the door with his arms crossed and pressed against his stomach. "You gotta let me kick his ass, Mr. Ruby."

Ruby opened the door and pushed him outside. "Do as I said. I'll have a reward for you."

Fiery heat radiated from Ruby's eyes as he turned and faced Nick. "What's this about climbing out the window, Nick?"

"I was only trying to open the window. I'm burning up from the rushes of heat," he lied.

Ruby studied him through narrowed eyelids. "That's to be expected. Artie's excited about his date. He should calm down after tonight, for a while." He glowered at Nick. "Of course, if you were trying to climb out the window, your loved ones will pay." A black haze swirled on the mirrored wall. A splattering of liquid sounded and ribbons of bright red streamed down the silver surface.

Ruby smiled, baring his pointed white teeth and then exited.

Nick turned away from the blood-drenched mirrors and rubbed his sweaty face. Panic welled up in his throat and he sucked in deep, rapid breaths to calm his racing heart and trembling body. Artie stirred inside of him, sending a new shock wave of intense heat throughout his body. He had to find a way out of this nightmare before Artie took complete control of him and forced him to murder an innocent girl.

🕯

Nick signed his books and posters while Ebony hovered over his shoulder. Rachel escorted the girls to the lectern. With a wicked smile, she handed each a silver pen and instructed them to sign a page in the fan club book. Ruby's plan to capture millions of souls via the Internet had failed. Yet tonight, the ancient-looking book would steal hundreds of women's souls and offer as many demon portals.

Anxiety coupled with feverish heat and red-tinted vision plagued Nick. The pen shook in his hand. His self-control weakened each time one of the demons surfaced. One minute he envisioned stabbing the young girls who lined up, mooning over him with wide, innocent eyes; the next, he felt horrified and sickened by the thoughts.

Across the lobby, the guests chatted in small groups and sipped champagne. Lee Woods wiped tears from his eyes and looked soulfully into a young brunette's eyes. She touched Lee's hand. Nick regretted not re-breaking his nose in the bathroom when he had the chance.

Ruby stepped onto the platform next to him and tapped the microphone sending a series of hollow, metallic raps throughout the lobby. Everyone turned. The vibrant chatter dulled to a low, expectant murmur.

"Before we start our main event, the world premiere of *Night Birds*, we must draw a ticket and see which lovely young lady has won a date with our infamous horror writer, Nick Tera."

Nervous titters and excited giggles swept through the crowd of young women gathered near Nick's table. The double line of women snaked around the lobby, out the entrance and overflowed into the plaza in front of the theater. Ebony turned the crank on the metal cage. The ticket stubs tossed and tumbled inside, mimicking Nick's stomach.

Ruby motioned to the cage. "Mr. Tera, please do the honors."

Ebony stopped turning the handle and opened a small door as the tickets settled inside the cage.

Nick reached in and pulled out a ticket. He glanced at it before Ruby snatched it. Turning to the expectant sea of female faces, Ruby bellowed, "And the lucky winner is, number seven-eight-two-five."

It wasn't the number on the ticket. A chilling inner voice told Nick that Artie had preselected a girl. Voices swelled as the contestants checked their stubs. Ushers repeated the numbers to the crowd gathered outside the lobby.

A squeal rang out. "That's me!" A hand holding a ticket flew up in the center of the crowd.

The crowd shuffled aside, revealing a slender, young girl with long blond hair making her way toward the platform. She ran the last few steps and presented her ticket to Ruby.

Ruby jammed her ticket into his pocket. "Congratulations, my dear. What's your name?"

"Kathleen Sommers. Everyone calls me Katie."

"Katie. A splendid name." Ruby shot a sideward glance at Nick as he took the girl's hand. A surge of photographers crouched, their cameras poised. "Katie Sommers, meet your dream date, Nick Tera." He placed the girl's hand into Nick's.

Nick gaped at the petite girl. She looked like *his* Katie might have looked at age sixteen, only instead of green, this girl's eyes sparkled a bright sky-blue.

She peered up at him between a center-parted curtain of pale blond hair. "Hi, Nick." Her smooth cheeks flushed pink.

"Hello." He squeezed her hand, involuntarily. The demon's red haze veiled his vision, turning her hair a deep, strawberry color. An image of her naked body bathed in blood flashed in his mind followed by a shudder of anticipation. Bursts of camera flashes interrupted the sadistic thoughts. Nick loosened his hold on Katie's hand. She smiled, her glossy lips framed perfect teeth.

A reporter asked, "Katie, how does it feel to win a date with Nick?"

She clasped her hands together under her chin and bounced on her heels. "I can't believe it! I'm so excited—I could just die!"

Ruby waved his hands, signaling the end of the photo shoot. "We've given the press your itinerary. I ask our media friends to allow these two some private time. There will be photo-ops throughout the evening. Nick and Katie, enjoy your romantic evening." Ruby bowed his head and made an elaborate hand flourish. Applause filled the lobby.

Nick excused himself from Katie and grabbed Ruby's arm as he strutted away. "Please, you can't do this. Look at her. She can't be more than eighteen, if that."

Ruby smiled. "The contest rules clearly stated twenty-one or older. Besides, I thought you liked them young, like Stephanie." He leaned closer to Nick. "Call me in the morning. I'll arrange the clean-up."

Ruby nodded to Rachel and Ebony and then walked to the theater doors. Raising his arms high above his head, he boomed, "Ladies and gentlemen, please enter the theater for your exclusive showing of *Night Birds*! And be sure to stay seated after the credits, I have a special announcement about Nick Tera's upcoming movie."

The guests filed into the dimly lit interior of the theater. Reporters flocked after them, shouting questions and snapping photos until the ushers closed the massive, double doors.

The press and young women who had lost the contest were ushered out the front entrance. Nick paced in a circle around Katie as the lobby emptied. She texted on her phone.

She grinned and asked, "Where are we going, Nick? I'm posting everything on Facebook."

Rachel slid an arm around Katie's shoulders. "It's a surprise. We have a limo waiting on the side of the building." She nudged Katie toward the corridor where Nick had entered. "Go on." Slithering around to Nick's side, Rachel whispered. "Walk. If you keep Artie waiting any longer, we'll be mopping up blood on the lobby floor."

Something hard pushed against his arm. Rachel slid a long, sheathed knife inside his jacket sleeve. Her eyelids twitched in a reptilian wink. "A party starter."

"I've never ridden in a limo." Katie said as she trotted alongside Nick.

He watched Ebony close the fan club book. With his heart pounding, he darted to the lectern and ripped the book from her hands. The force sent Ebony stumbling backwards and she fell against the glass counter.

She scrambled to her feet and screamed, "He's getting away!"

Nick sprinted across the lobby to the opposite corridor.

"Wait for me!" Katie ran after him and grabbed his sleeve.

"You won't get far, Nick." Rachel's high heels banged on the marble floor close behind. Nick knocked over tables as he ran, sending avalanches of champagne glasses and hors d'oeuvres crashing to the floor. Rachel shrieked. Her scream ended abruptly when her forehead hit the marble floor.

A neon exit sign shone at the end of the long corridor. The hundred feet looked like a mile. Nick ran faster, dragging Katie on his arm.

Twenty feet before they reached the door, it opened and a tall man in a dark suit blocked the doorway. Nick stopped short and grabbed Katie's arm to keep her from falling. The man scowled and slid his hand under his jacket. A door swung open next to Nick. Hands pulled him and Katie inside. The door slammed behind them and a lock clicked.

Nick froze until his vision adjusted to the darkness. "What are you doing?"

"Trying to help you, asshole." Janis Ford jerked her head to the left. "Follow me. Hurry." He hesitated, but then heard a heavy weight slam against the outside of the door. They followed Janis through another door. She locked the second door behind them and then hurried around a corner into a dark hallway.

"This is part of our date, right?' Katie asked, breathless from running. "My friends said they might do some cool, horror stuff."

Ignoring Katie, Nick glared at Janis. "Where are you taking us?"

"To the walkway the movie ushers use."

Nick stopped and gripped Janis' shoulder. "You're leading us into the theater where Ruby is? I knew I couldn't trust you."

"Ruby has all the other exits guarded. It's the only way out. It's dark and the curtain will hide us from view. It leads to the front of the theater. Next to the screen there's an exit. My van's parked outside."

She slipped through a doorway with a black wall on one side and a satiny red curtain on the other. Dim yellow lights recessed in the floor gave a faint, eerie glow to the long, dark corridor. The narrow ramp sloped gently downward.

"Stay close to the wall and be quiet," Janis whispered. The soundtrack from the movie vibrated around them as they crept down the walkway.

They finally reached a metal door with a red exit sign glowing in the darkness above it. Janis grabbed the knob.

"Shit, it's locked." She dug inside her shoulder bag with both hands.

"Let me try," Nick said. He shook the long knife from his sleeve and pulled off the sheath. The curved, wooden handle felt good in his hand. The light from the sign bathed Katie and Janis in a red glow. Artie's murderous thoughts bubbled in his mind. He squeezed the knife grip and fought the urge to plunge the long blade first into Katie and then Janis. A blood-curdling shriek from the movie filled the theater followed by a deafening crescendo of ominous music.

"Where'd you get that?" Janis whispered.

Nick forced himself to focus on the lock. "Never mind." He worked the skinny tip inside the keyhole while he jiggled the door handle. The lock clicked. He eased the door open and peered outside. A white van with *The Entertainer's* logo printed on its side stood parked in the dark alley. The three rushed out. Nick tossed the knife into a pile of cardboard boxes.

They all crammed into the front seat. Janis started the ignition and flicked on the headlights. Two men ran toward them. One aimed a gun and fired. The bullet pinged off the edge of the van's roof. Katie screamed and pressed her face against Nick shoulder. Janis ducked her head, shifted into reverse and floored the gas pedal.

Nick leaned out the passenger window. "Watch out!" A man ran toward the rear of the van.

"If he wants to play chicken with a six-thousand-pound van that's his problem." Janis pressed harder on the gas pedal. The van shot backwards down the long driveway. The man leapt to the side of the alley, flattening himself against the brick wall as they sped by. The rear of the van ran over a police barricade, bumped across the sidewalk, and then swerved into the busy avenue. Brakes screeched and horns blasted. Katie screamed again. Janis spun the steering wheel and shifted into drive. She raced up the street, zigzagging through the downtown traffic.

Nick pointed to a side street. "Make a right. My car's two blocks over."

Janis jerked the wheel to the right. The van rocked and its tires squealed as it rounded the corner. Seconds later, she pulled into the dry cleaner's lot and jammed on the brakes.

Nick jumped out. "Thank you, Janis." Katie slid her legs out. He pushed her back inside and slammed the door.

"What about our date?" she called out.

"There is no date." Nick leaned into the open window. "Janis, take her home, please?"

"No! We have a date. I won. It's on my Facebook page. What'll I tell my friends?" Katie's face scrunched into a pout and tears welled in her eyes.

"Shut up, Blondie. Keep quiet and I'll buy you an ice cream." Janis nodded to Nick. "What are you going to do?"

"End this once and for all." Clutching the thick book under his arm, he sprinted to his car.

♦

The demons battled for control of his mind and body. A furious Artie cursed and clawed at Nick's insides while the other demon tormented him with surges of heat. Not wanting to wait for the elevator, he ran up the stairs two at a time until he reached his apartment. He slammed the door and locked it. His cell phone rang, and he saw Victor Ruby's name displayed. Rushing to the fireplace, he pushed the button to ignite it, opened the glass door and tossed the heavy book into the fire.

Small yellow flames licked at the leather binding. The book writhed as flames took hold. Growls and shrieks rang out. Then, a whooshing sound as the flames enveloped the book. Thick, black smoke billowed from the flames and reeked of sulfur.

Nick ran to the bedroom closet. He pulled his gun from the top shelf and then sat on the edge of the bed. Gulping in deep breaths, he squeezed his eyes shut and pictured a line of Chris's suicide note; *There's only one way to break a pact with the devil.* He knew now that Ruby had Talon murder Chris before he could kill himself. Suicide would destroy the demon's host. He didn't want to kill himself, but he had run out of time and options. Katie's face flashed in his mind. Without his body, Artie couldn't kill Katie, or anyone else. It was the only way he knew to save her. If Ruby owned his soul, there was nothing he could do about it now.

Sweat trickled down his forehead, stinging his eyes and dripping down his neck. His hand shook as he jammed the gun under his chin. The barrel tip skidded across his wet skin. Cursing himself for not pulling the trigger, he wiped his sweaty palms on his pants legs and repositioned the gun.

His cell phone rang. He jumped and jerked his finger on the trigger. The close gun blast deafened him on one side. Plaster, dust and debris rained down from the ceiling. It was Ruby calling. He flung the phone on the floor and stomped it with his boot heel. It still rang. Kneeling, he hammered the phone with the butt of the gun until it lay in pieces on the carpet, silent.

He sat back and braced his back against the side of the bed. Tears and sweat streamed down his cheeks. His left eardrum throbbed from the first shot and he needed two hands to steady the gun under his chin. The phone rang. He stared at the crushed battery and plastic splinters ground into the carpet. Ruby's voice boomed from the shattered speaker. "You won't die tonight, Nick. But Katie will." Ruby's laughter filled the room.

"No!" Nick pressed the gun to his right temple. Searing heat from the handle burned his hand. He dropped it on the carpet. Thin wisps of smoke rose from the gun. He crawled closer, covered his hand with his shirt tail and grasped the handle. The hot metal scorched the material.

He let go. The gun barrel glowed bright red and then dull white. It dissolved into a puddle of molten metal.

Nick collapsed on the carpet staring at the melted gun. Enraged, Artie scratched and tore at his insides. The pain and incessant heat felt like it would either rip him to shreds or burn the flesh from his bones. Rage grew inside him. The room turned a deep crimson color and his right arm lunged out, his hand flat on the floor. His fingers inched along the carpet until they touched the cold, familiar steel hidden in the shadows under the bed. He gripped the handle of his grandfather's fillet knife. Raising to his knees, he grinned at the long, razor sharp blade, threw back his head and laughed. His maniacal whoops grew louder, ending in a triumphant shriek.

Nick willed his hand to drop the knife but instead his fingers tightened in a white-knuckled grip around the handle. He tried to pry the knife from his right fist with his left hand, but only sliced his fingers on the blade. His muscles strained as he forced his left arm to bend his right arm and angle the knife toward his heart. He heaved his body into the long blade.

He lay in a silent vacuum, his vision blurred by a deep red veil. Artie's voice commanded, "Stand up". Nick crawled to the bed and pulled himself up, leaving bloody smears on the white sheets. Cradling the knife in both hands, he staggered out of the apartment and then rode the elevator down to the parking garage.

He steered his car with one hand along the familiar route to Katie's apartment. In the other, he clutched the knife. Tremors of excitement rippled through his body as he listened to Artie's hushed promises of the bloody pleasures to come.

"Stop where you are!"

"He's got a knife."

"Drop the knife! Do it now! Put your hands behind your head."

Spinning red, yellow and blue lights blinded Nick. Footsteps pounded nearby. Four policemen surrounded him on the lawn outside Katie's apartment, their guns leveled at his chest.

"I said, drop the knife!"

Confused by the command, he looked down and saw a fillet knife clutched in his right hand. A slick red liquid coated the blade up to its hilt. He flung it into the grass.

The cops edged closer. "Get down on your knees. Put your hands behind your head."

Ragged breaths caught in his throat. He spun in a circle, the constant strobing of multi-colored lights slicing through the darkness made him dizzy. His clothing felt heavy and stuck to his body. He ran his hands down his torso and stared at the red covering his palms. Blood soaked his shirt and pants.

A police officer's silhouette stood in Katie's open doorway. Nick stumbled toward him. The officer aimed his gun, ordering him to halt. Nick stopped a few feet from the door. Under the fluorescent kitchen light, puddles of red shone on the white linoleum floor.

"Sparkling like red rubies. Rubies. Ruby." His giggles turned to screams and then raw sobs. "Ruby. No. No. Oh, God, no. Not Katie. No. I killed her." He collapsed to his knees, rubbing his bloody hands over his face and through his hair.

Rough hands grabbed his arms, yanking them behind his back and then forcing his head down into the moist, cool grass. A loud click. Hard metal cuffs bound his wrists together. Katie's voice screamed from far away, "Nick, no!" Her voice sounded tinny, a memory replaying in his mind accompanied by the vision of the silvery glint of a knife blade. He rolled onto his side. Katie's screams faded into Ruby's sadistic laughter.

"No. Please. No." He sobbed as he rolled onto his back and dug his fingernails into the dirt. Two cops stood over him, staring down at him.

"Sonofabitch looks like he took a bath in blood."

"You saw that poor girl."

The toe of a shiny, black shoe jabbed Nick's side. "Did he pass out?"

"Get the EMTs over here. Damn, I hope we don't have to carry this bastard. Better get some gloves on."

Their voices faded, overpowered by Ruby's, "Evil won. Katie's dead. Evil won. Katie's dead. Evil won." The singsong rant played over and over.

Numbness crept over Nick as the realization of what he had done penetrated his daze. His limbs turned leaden. He couldn't move or open his eyes. Breathing became too much effort. He begged God to let him die and slipped into a deep, silent, black pit.

Chapter 25

Demons whispered in the blackness beneath him. Claws clicking as they skittered about. Above, Nick saw a brilliant white light with one glittering gold star, twirling and twirling.

He floated between the darkness and the light. Was this Purgatory? God surely knew he deserved to burn in hell after what he had done.

Cool hands touched his face. An angel hovered over him. The bright light behind her illuminated the pale, golden halo surrounding her sweet face. Her eyes shone a liquid green with tears. Katie's eyes cried for him even after he had killed her.

As he reached up to touch the angel, her image dimmed. Darkness obliterated her. A chorus of raspy whispers swelled into a deafening buzz. Demons' mouths spewed out blackness. It covered him in a massive, droning swarm of hornets.

His mother set a steaming bowl of soup on the coffee table. She sat on the edge of the couch, placed her hand on his forehead and then kissed him. "You're burning up." She cuddled him in her arms. "You're burning up, Nick. Burning. Burning." Blood oozed from deep, jagged cuts on her palms. Warm blood flowed over his face and arms as she caressed him.

He reached up to touch the blue flames dancing under the sauce pot on the stove. Nonna whacked his hand with a wooden spoon. "No!" she scolded. "Never touch the fire!"

"I have to touch it, Nonna." He reached into flames. The fire raced from his fingertips, up his arms and engulfed his body in a billowing inferno of red and yellow. There was no ground, only fire and above his head, more flames. His father dragged him from the fire by his feet, yelling, "Do as I say!" Nick kicked his father's legs and punched his hairy arms.

His heart beat faster, and his breath quickened into short huffs. Exquisite spasms wracked his body. Katie gasped and shuddered beneath him, their arms and legs wrapped around each other. Suspended in air, they floated. He couldn't tell where his body ended and hers began. A warm, sultry breeze blew against their skin. He tightened his grasp, drawing her closer. The gentle breeze billowed into hot, gusts of wind. The scorching-hot gale buffeted their naked bodies. It flaked their flesh into a fine powder and swept it away like ashes in the wind. He held her until there was nothing left of either of them but minute, glittering particles swirling in the air.

Kneeling on the ground, he groped through flesh-colored sand as fine as talcum powder. It sifted through his fingers and lifted into the wind. He couldn't separate the tiny specs into what was Katie and what was him. Panic rose in his chest. His desperate gasps blew the precious dust into the wind.

A thin ribbon of bright red trickled through the dust. More scarlet ribbons appeared, flowing faster through the sand. They joined into one gushing torrent. He stood neck deep in blood. A red wave washed over him, knocking him down. He struggled to push his head above the suffocating sea, kicking his legs and pushing back the thick, salty current with cupped hands. With his lungs burning for air, he swam upward until his hands broke the crimson surface, and then his head. He gasped to draw in air but instead sucked in flames that burned his nostrils and mouth and raced down into his lungs. An inferno spread throughout his body. Victor Ruby's laughter vibrated around him in thunderous rolls.

Blinded by flames, he stretched his arms to grope in front of him and staggered through the fire. The air stank of sulfur and burnt flesh and beneath his bare feet, black, jagged rock laced with lines of roiling, red lava. Moans, shrieks and gut-wrenching wails deafened him. He glimpsed shadowy figures in the flames. In a blink, naked bodies surrounded him, twitching and lurching in stop-motion alongside him in a macabre march. Anguished faces with white eyes, devoid of pupils, stared straight ahead. Nick's outstretched hands collided with a barrier. The throng of bodies crushed against him, their hands clawing at the barrier. Pinned against the invisible wall, Nick pressed his face to the searing hot glass and stared into Victor Ruby's living room. A scream welled up from deep within his soul, but his open, gaping mouth delivered no sound.

Katie's mutilated corpse lay on a low, stone table. Her blood-stained hair hung in tangled mats over the edge. Blood seeped from countless slashes in her flesh. It pooled around her body and drooled over the edges of the table to the floor. Ruby and Talon filled their silver goblets with the dripping blood. Smiling, they tapped their cups together, turned toward Nick and drank.

God decided. He was in hell.

Chapter 26

A blurry hand hovered over his eyes. He blinked to focus. The face above him looked down at him with kind, blue eyes surrounded by tiny crinkles of pink flesh.

"You had another panic attack. Try to relax." The nurse adjusted a clear plastic mask over his nose and mouth. "Good, now just breathe normally."

Nick closed his eyes and inhaled the sweet, cold oxygen. The pressure in his chest subsided and his rapid heartbeat slowed. *Not in hell. A hospital.* He opened his eyes.

"You're going to be fine." She removed the mask from his face. "Stay calm. Even breaths."

He tried to bring his hands to his face and couldn't. It must be a trick, he thought, Ruby had him lashed down. He yanked at the bonds holding his hands, pulling as hard as he could until he heard a rattling, metallic sound.

"It's all right. You're in Saint Mary's Hospital. Once you're calm and coherent, I'll remove the restraints." The nurse walked away from the bed. "I'll be right back."

Nick strained to lift his head and looked around. A window with partially opened blinds to his right revealed skinny slices of a night sky. To his left stood machines and an intravenous stand. A deep throbbing pain in the left side of his abdomen forced him to drop his head back onto the pillow.

The nurse returned with a young man dressed in dark blue scrubs. He stood close, watching, as the nurse approached Nick. "Can you tell me your name?" she asked.

His mouth and throat felt parched. "Nick Teravelli," he answered in a hoarse whisper.

"Very good," she cooed. She made notes on a clipboard while she asked him a series of questions.

"I'm going to remove the restraints. Stay still." She nodded to the man in scrubs and then loosened and removed the strap on his right wrist. She waited a moment and then took the strap off his left wrist.

He slowly raised his arms and ran his hands over his face. White bandages wrapped his left forearm and hand. His beard felt thick and scruffy.

"Why am I here?" He lifted his head and looked down at his body.

"A puncture wound to your small intestine. Left side. You lost a lot of blood and were in shock when they brought you in. You had surgery last Friday night to repair the intestine. It's healing nicely, no infection and no internal bleeding, in spite of all your thrashing."

"A puncture?"

"A stab wound from a knife. Don't worry, it's normal to have no memory after a trauma. Give it some time."

"How long have I been here?"

"Four days. It's Tuesday, May second." She checked her watch. "Ten twenty-three at night. A few more days and if you continue to do well, you'll be discharged." She lowered the blanket and raised his gown to check the wound. "We'll change the bandage tomorrow morning."

She positioned an attached tray table over the bed. "I'm going to raise the bed a bit." As the top of the bed lifted, Nick had a better view of the wall with the door and large window. Outside, he saw a man standing with his back to the window. He wore a policeman's light blue shirt and navy-blue hat.

The nurse and the man in scrubs left the room. The nurse returned alone a minute later carrying a clear plastic cup. "Ice chips. Take tiny sips. You have fluids in your IV. Maybe tomorrow you can start on a soft diet. We'll see what the doctor says in the morning." She slid a second pillow behind his shoulders.

Nick sat propped in the bed staring out the window into the hallway. He struggled to clear the thick fog clouding his memory. His body felt heavy, his muscles sore and stiff. The cop outside his room stood and spoke briefly to the nurse when she exited. He turned, peered at Nick, then adjusted his hat, and sat with his back to the window.

Nick closed his eyes. A flash of a knife blade and Katie's shrill scream jolted them open. The pain in his side quickened from a dull throb to a deep, sharp sting. He tried to recall what happened after the premiere, but his memories muddled together with Artie's. He remembered the melting gun, Ruby's laughter and finding his grandfather's fillet knife. Artie had taken control of his hand and forced the blade away from his heart. It must have penetrated his abdomen instead. After that, his memories were disjointed, surreal. A series of fragmented images and sounds. Katie's screams, blood—so much blood, flashing lights, blackness and then hellish nightmares. An intense dread overwhelmed him, then a blood-chilling revelation. "Oh, God, no. I killed her. I killed Katie." Panic swelled in his chest, his breathing turned to rapid gasps and his stomach tightened into a rock-hard knot. "I'm a murderer. That cop is guarding my room. As soon as they discharge me, he'll take me to jail. Just as Ruby predicted, I'll spend the rest of my life in prison reliving Katie's murder." He didn't ever want to recall the details of what he had done. Yet he knew Ruby would make sure the memories surfaced to haunt him for the rest of his life. Bits and pieces of that night danced at the edges of the black fog shrouding his memory, jabbing red-hot daggers of recollection into his brain. The terror of regaining his memory brought cold droplets of sweat to his forehead and acidy bile bit the back of his throat. Of everything Ruby had done to torture him, this was the most sadistic. Without Katie, life no longer mattered. Silent sobs wracked his body. He pulled the blanket to his face to smother his sobs and wished he had bled to death on the cool grass outside her apartment.

Chapter 27

"Blood. Katie's blood!" Nick awoke from another blood-drenched nightmare to two nurses struggling to pin down his arms. A plump young nurse stared, her eyes wide. The older woman had smooth mahogany skin and spoke in a crisp, firm voice. "Calm yourself, Mr. Teravelli. There's no blood. You're fine."

He wrenched his arm free from the plump nurse's grasp and rubbed his hand across his chest. His gown was soaked.

"It's water," the older nurse said. "You spilled a cup of ice chips on yourself in your sleep." She gripped his arm and slowly guided it downward onto the bed. "It's all right."

He peered down at his blue and white printed gown. Wet, but not blood.

"We're going to change your bandage and get you into a dry gown. Are you calm now?"

Nick nodded and leaned back against the pillows. The round-faced young nurse stood back from the bed watching him while the tall black nurse left the room. She returned a few moments later with a short, dark-haired man in a white coat.

"Good morning, I'm Doctor Patel. Let's take a peek at your wound." The doctor leaned and inspected Nick's side as the nurse removed the bandage. "It's healing well." He moved to the head of the bed and made notes on the clipboard while the nurse cleaned and re-bandaged the wound.

"Do you have pain?" the doctor asked.

"Doesn't matter," Nick mumbled.

"Keep him on the pain meds. Get him up in a chair when you're done, Nurse. Later on, try a short walk down the hall. The sooner you're up and moving, the sooner you'll heal." With a curt nod, the doctor left the room.

The two nurses helped Nick into a padded, vinyl chair and changed his gown. The young nurse took the wet gown and hurried out the door.

The tall nurse smiled at him. "The doctor has cleared you to start on soft foods. They'll bring you a tray in a few minutes." She opened the blinds, flooding the room with sunlight. "It's a beautiful spring day outside."

Nick squinted at the window in silence.

"Do you want to watch TV?" She gestured to the mounted set on the wall.

He shook his head.

"How about I get some magazines from the waiting room? You like Sports?"

"No."

"Well, I'm sure your father will be here soon. He'll be relieved to see you awake."

"My father?"

"Yes, he's been here every day since you arrived. Sits in the chair you're in now. He's probably at the funer—. Um, I'm sure he'll be in soon."

Nick waved the nurse away. She checked his IV bags and then left the room.

He rubbed tears from his eyes. Outside the window, the uniformed officer was gone. A younger, huskier man dressed in a dark suit sat with his head turned, staring intently through the glass.

Nick met his curious gaze and then turned away. He looked out the window at the bright blue, cloudless sky. A beautiful day . . . Katie's funeral. The sun shone on the budding leaves of a tree. Droplets of morning dew glistened on the delicate green shoots. The same color as Katie's eyes. Eyes he would never see again.

The man in the suit watched as a nurse and an orderly assisted him on a shaky walk up and down the hall. Afterward, they helped him back into his bed. His father entered as the two were leaving.

"You're awake. Thank, God. How ya feeling, son?" He gripped the side rail of the bed.

Nick shook his head.

"It's good to see you up—"

"You went to K-Katie's funeral?" Nick asked.

His father's gaze dropped to the floor. He cleared his throat. "Who told you that?"

"The nurse."

Dom cursed softly under his breath. He glanced over his shoulder at the man in the suit outside the window. "They told me I can't talk to you about Katie or the funeral."

Nick swallowed hard. The ashen color of his father's face spoke volumes. "You don't have to come here, Pop. I don't expect anyone to come after what I did. I'm surprised the nurses come in here."

His father's eyes watered and he stared out the window as he answered. "You're my son."

"When they release me," Nick pointed to the man in the hallway, "They'll put me in prison, where I belong."

"Concentrate on getting better. Don't think about—"

"It's all I can think about! I k-killed . . . Why am I here? Why didn't the cops fucking shoot me? If I had a gun now, I'd shoot myself. I don't deserve to live. Katie. . .." Nick broke into low, wrenching sobs.

Dom squeezed Nick's shoulder and then paced the room. He finally stopped, lowered himself into the chair and wiped his eyes. "Sal wants to see ya. And Nonna, she's been praying for you every day, Nick. She doesn't like to come to hospitals, ya know that."

"Please, don't let them come. Tell Nonna not to waste her prayers on me." He closed his eyes. Tears streamed down his face.

Chapter 28

Three days later, Nick sat on the edge of the hospital bed and slowly pulled on the tee shirt his father had brought him. Washing and dressing had exhausted him. His father crouched down and tied the laces on his sneakers.

"Pop, I told you not to come today."

Dom stood and rolled his head from side to side to loosen his back after bending over. "The nurse brought your pain pills while you were in the bathroom." He handed Nick a small paper cup with two pills.

Nick grunted and set the cup on the tray table.

His father poured water from a plastic pitcher into a cup and handed it to Nick. "Take the pills, son. It will help the pain."

Taking the cup from his father's shaking hand, he tossed the pills into his mouth and took a long drink of water. "I'll never understand why you're here, but, thank you, Pop."

The husky man in the suit, accompanied by a male orderly pushing a wheelchair, entered the room. Another taller man in a dark suit stood in the doorway watching Nick.

His father gripped him in a bear hug. "I wish . . . I'm so sorry, Nick."

The orderly stood behind the chair as Nick eased himself into it. The husky man held out a pair of handcuffs, slipped them over Nick's wrists and then snapped them closed.

Dom slumped on the edge of the empty bed, his face hidden behind his hands as they wheeled Nick out the door.

The elevator ride downstairs made him light-headed. The orderly pushed him out the front doors of the hospital, down a side ramp and stopped at the curb. Bright sunlight stung his eyes. One of the men waved to a dark brown van parked a few yards away. It pulled closer and parked with the engine running. Nick could barely stand, and the two men had to lift him into the middle row of the van. The tall man slid in beside him and the shorter one got into the front passenger seat. A third man, the driver, shifted into drive and pulled away from the curb. He looked familiar, but Nick couldn't focus his blurry vision on the man's reflection in the rear-view mirror. The sun flickering through the front windshield made him squint and his body fell forward into the back of the driver's seat whenever the van braked at a red light. The man next to him pushed him back with one arm. They rode in silence with only the hypnotic hum of the van's engine and the muffled sounds of traffic filtering through the rolled-up windows. The heaviness in his eyelids spread throughout his body. As the van made a right turn, Nick couldn't stop himself from falling over sideways.

He knew his arms were tied down before he opened his eyes. Small flames clustered around him in the dim room. As his eyes focused, he saw two stands of tall candles on either side of him. He sat in a high-backed chair made of heavy, carved wood, his wrists lashed to its sturdy arms with brown leather straps. Another fastened across his chest and more straps secured his ankles to the thick chair legs. He struggled against the bonds but couldn't budge them or the heavy chair. The small room looked familiar. A green couch to his left and floor to ceiling shelves of books lined the three walls he could see.

"Hey!" he shouted.

The room felt warm, stuffy and smelled of burning candles. A door opened behind him. He turned his head but the tall back of the chair obscured his view. The three men from the van entered and stood in front of him. Instead of dark suits, they wore white albs and purple stoles. One carried a crucifix and another a glass bowl. The third carried a thick leather-bound book. They stepped back as Father Santore entered. He stood in front of Nick, wearing an embroidered purple and gold chasuble over his robe.

"Father? W-what's going on? These men are priests?"

Santore didn't answer. He dipped his fingers into the glass bowl, flicked the water at Nick and made the sign of the cross as he murmured a blessing. The tiny droplets stung Nick's skin, burning like acid. The pain angered him and Santore's monotonous prayers fueled his anger into rage. He spat at Santore and screamed curses to drown out the priest's words.

Father Santore's solemn, brown eyes stayed fixed on Nick. He nodded to the priest holding the book. The young man opened it to a page bookmarked with a long purple ribbon and held it up for Father Santore.

"Let us begin." Santore recited the Litany of Saints. The other three responded in chorus.

"Lord, have mercy on us." The older priest's deep voice filled the room.

The three younger priests answered in unison, "Christ, have mercy on us."

"Lord, have mercy on us." Santore and the priests continued their alternating recitations.

"Christ, hear us."

"Christ, graciously hear us."

"God, the Father of Heaven, have mercy on us."

"God the Son, Redeemer of the World, have mercy on us."

"God the Holy Ghost, have mercy on us."

"Holy Trinity, One God, have mercy on us."

"Holy Mary, pray for us."

"Holy Mother of God, pray for us."

"Holy Virgin of Virgins, pray for us."

Father Santore blessed himself and called out, "Saint Michael, pray for us."

"Saint Gabriel, pray for us."

Nick strained at the straps and shouted for them to stop. Words tumbled from his mouth that sounded foreign to his own ears. His voice deepened into a guttural growl and then rose to a shrill shriek. He glowered at the priests through a red haze that deepened with his fury.

Father Santore continued to call out the seemingly never-ending list of saint's names.

"Saint Cecilia, pray for us.

Saint Catherine, pray for us.

Saint Anastasia, pray for us.

All ye Holy Virgins and Widows, pray for us."

Each syllable the priest uttered stung like a vicious slap across Nick's face. The room temperature soared. He rocked the chair from side to side and fought to kick his legs free.

Santore continued, "From All Evil, O Lord, deliver us.

From all Sin, O Lord, deliver us.

From thy Wrath, O Lord, deliver us.

From a Sudden and Unprovided Death, O Lord, deliver us.

From the Deceits of the Devil, O Lord, deliver us."

A gleeful shriek shot from Nick's mouth as one of the ankle straps broke with a loud snap. The three young priests converged on him.

Two struggled to hold down his flailing leg, while the third used his stole to tie Nick's ankle to the chair leg.

Unruffled, Father Santore recited his monologue, his voice clear and steady. He ignored the obscenities Nick shouted and used a white linen cloth to wipe Nick's saliva from his face.

"Holy Lord, almighty Father, everlasting God and Father of our Lord Jesus Christ, who once and for all consigned that fallen and apostate tyrant to the flames of hell, who sent your only-begotten Son into the world to crush that roaring lion; hasten to our call for help and snatch from ruination and from the clutches of the noonday devil this human being made in your image and likeness. Strike terror, Lord, into the beast now laying waste your vineyard. Fill your servants with courage to fight manfully against that reprobate dragon, lest he despise those who put their trust in you and say with Pharaoh of old: "I know not God, nor will I set Israel free." Let your mighty hand cast him out of your servant, Nick, so he may no longer hold captive this person whom it pleased you to make in your image, and to redeem through your Son; who lives and reigns with you, in the unity of the Holy Spirit, God, forever and ever."

The tall, tapered candles had burned down to tiny nubs in the candelabras. Nick slumped, gasping in the chair, his clothing soaked with sweat and his throat raw from screaming. Still the priest read from the pages of the book, stopping only to bestow blessings and sprinkle holy water over him.

"I command you, unclean spirit, whoever you are, along with all your minions now attacking this servant of God, by the mysteries of the incarnation, passion, resurrection, and ascension of our Lord Jesus Christ, by the descent of the Holy Spirit, by the coming of our Lord for judgment, that you tell me by some sign your name, and the day and hour of your departure. I command you, moreover, to obey me to the letter, I who am a minister of God despite my unworthiness; nor shall you be emboldened to harm in any way this creature of God, or the bystanders, or any of their possessions."

Violent spasms rattled Nick's body and a fiery column surged into his throat. He instinctively opened his mouth to give the vile-tasting acid churning inside his gut an outlet. A dense black mist streamed from his mouth and snaked through his nostrils. The blackness exited his body like a mass of stinging wasps. He writhed in pain and cried out as thousands of burning needles pierced his flesh.

Nick's head lolled forward until his chin touched his chest and his eyelids closed. His bandaged wound throbbed, its rhythm synced with the drumming of his heart. Opening his eyes was an effort.

Father Santore dipped his thumb into the holy water and traced a small cross on Nick's forehead. Cool water drizzled down his nose and cheeks. It soothed the sting of hot needles pricking his skin.

"May the blessing of almighty God, Father, Son, and Holy Spirit, come upon you and remain with you forever."

Nick's head rolled to one side and he looked up at the priest though half-closed lids. "Thank you, Father. Thank you," he whispered.

One of the younger priests unstrapped him. Nick slouched in the chair, too weak to move. He remembered this room. A small library located behind the Sacristy in Saint Michael's church. He and Ray had changed their clothes in here when they were altar boys.

Father Santore held a glass of water to Nick's lips.

He nodded, clutched the glass with trembling hands and gulped the cold water. Santore handed the empty glass to the priest and instructed him to refill it.

The priest returned with the water, wet cloths, folded towels and a clean tee shirt. Nick mopped his sweaty face with a cloth and then let his arms drop limp in his lap.

"Now do I go to jail?" he asked Santore.

"Get dressed." Santore and the three priests filed out of the room and closed the door.

Nick stood on trembling legs and struggled to peel off his sweat-logged shirt. He wiped his torso with a moist cloth and then pulled the dry shirt over his head. Lifting his left arm made the wound in his side throb. He pulled off the shirt and started over, inserting his arms into the sleeves first and then stretching the neck opening over his head. He turned toward the sound of the door opening. He blinked. Katie stood in the doorway.

He yanked the tee shirt over his head and blinked his eyes again. Katie ran toward him. His heart hammered in his chest and his legs shook. She grabbed his arms but couldn't stop him from falling backward onto the couch, pulling her down with him.

Clasping her hands in his, he ran his fingertips over her soft skin. He stared and mumbled, "You're real. You're alive."

She sat next to him and smoothed his damp hair from his face. "I'm so relieved to have you back. They wouldn't let me see you until after the exorcism."

Her words barely registered, but her familiar voice did. He touched her cheek and ran his fingers through her hair. "You're really alive." Tears flooded his eyes.

"Nick, why didn't you tell me what was happening to you sooner?"

"I had to protect you, Katie. That's why I . . . broke up with you." His heart beat quickened. "I thought I'd killed—"

"No." She swiped tears from his cheeks with her fingers.

"I had the bloody knife in my hand. Blood . . . all over me. Blood on your kitchen floor."

"It was Tara's blood."

Nick's eyes widened. "I, I killed Tara? God, I am a murderer."

"Shh, listen to me. You didn't kill anyone." She squeezed his hands. "Sal and I found Tara, murdered. You came after the police and EMTs had arrived. I saw you stagger from your car across the lawn. I called to you, but you were in shock from blood loss. The police wouldn't let me near you."

"They arrested me."

"Yes, but you were injured. They took you to the hospital. Nonna pressured Captain Brannigan. Your knife didn't match the wounds on Tara's body and the only blood on you and the knife was your own." Tears rolled from Katie's eyes. "I knew what you tried to do. Same as your character, Julian, in your story. You tried to kill yourself to save me."

"I failed. Ruby destroyed my gun. He gave Artie more strength. I couldn't stop him."

"You didn't fail. You slowed Artie down. Ruby sent someone else to my apartment."

Nick kissed Katie's lips. "I love you so much. All this time, I believed I'd killed—"

"I'm so sorry. We had to let you believe it until you were strong enough for the exorcism. I showed your letter to Nonna and Father Santore. He thought if you believed you had murdered me, it would calm the demons. Possibly drive them out, if they thought you would end up in prison. Father ordered me to stay away from you." Katie brought his hand to her lips and kissed it. "But I sneaked into the hospital after your surgery. You were still out from the anesthesia, I thought it would be safe. I touched your forehead and your eyes shot open . . . that horrible red. Y-you tried to choke me. A demon possessed you."

Nick fingered the small gold cross dangling from the chain around Katie's neck and recalled the twirling gold star in his dream. "I thought you were an angel. I reached for you, but the demons came, and everything went black."

"It took three orderlies to put restraints on you. I had to stay away after that. Your dad sat with you at the hospital."

"Pop knows?"

"Yes. It about killed him to see you suffering, believing you killed me. He insisted on staying with you, even though he couldn't tell you the truth. Nonna told the hospital psychiatrist the priests were there to take you into counseling program after your attempted suicide."

"I thought they were detectives, there to arrest me."

"I know. It was the best way to bring you here for the exorcism."

"Did they catch Tara's killer? It had to be one of Ruby's thugs."

"Not yet, they have nothing. No forced entry, no witnesses and no weapon." Katie cuddled closer and rested her head on his chest. "Sal walked me home that night. Again. I yelled at him to go away, but he refused to leave me. I feel terrible for treating him so badly now. My door was unlocked. Sal insisted on going in first. He turned on the kitchen light and we saw Tara on the floor. I didn't recognize her at first. We heard a noise and Sal ran to check. Someone was climbing out of Tara's window, but it was too dark to see who." Katie shivered. "It was awful, Nick. The most horrific thing I've ever seen. So much blood."

"The killer was still in your apartment?" Nick wrapped his arms around Katie and pressed his lips to her forehead. "I'm sorry about Tara. She didn't deserve that. But it could have been you. That vicious bastard, Ruby. He'll never leave us alone. All the people he's hurt and killed. Now, Tara. I have to destroy him once and for all."

"You will." Katie stood. "Father Santore and Nonna are waiting for you in the church. You have to light the candle," she said.

"Candle? You mean for my mom?"

"No, for Ruby." She tugged on his hand as she stood. "C'mon. I'll show you."

Nonna and her group of friends gathered in the pews near the alcove of votive candles and the statue of Saint Michael. His fierce eyes, engraved in stone, glared straight ahead over his drawn sword. Nick limped toward the group, his arm around Katie. His side ached, but his relief to be free of the demons and his sheer joy to hold Katie again made the pain bearable.

Nonna rushed up the aisle and hugged and kissed him. Nick continued walking with one arm around Katie and the other around his grandmother. They stopped in front of the alcove.

"Show him." Nonna nodded to Katie and then took her seat in a pew next to Ray's grandmother. The rest of the women sat in the pews behind them, their heads bowed in prayer.

Katie picked up a partially burned white pillar candle from the votive shelf. She turned it over and held it up to show him.

He read the words carved into the wax on the bottom of the candle. "Lamar Evans." He looked at Katie. "The guy who shot Ray? He was hung on the rosary beads."

Katie nodded, took the candle from his hand, replaced it on the rack and took down another. "Frank Jones," she said. "The man who shot your father and tried to burn down the restaurant."

"And was killed in the car chase." Nick reached for the next candle. "Robert Owens," he read. "The name sounds familiar."

"The pedophile who killed little Benjamin Ryan. He was crushed to death in the garbage truck."

Katie put the pillar back and touched two candles in the upper row, "Jimmy Graziano and Big Tony Borrelli. The two men who attacked your mom and threatened you with a knife when you were a baby."

"Pop told me about them." Nick stared at Katie. "They were found in the river with their throats cut."

She pointed to the other candles. "Nonna told me about the others. I forget all the names now, most were from before we were born."

Nick stared at the candles, shaking his head. "Every time something bad happened in the neighborhood, Nonna and her group of ladies would come here to pray . . . and light a candle. All the bad guys died. I had no idea . . ."

Katie slipped her arm around Nick's waist. "You look pale." She led him to a pew. "Sit down." She rolled up his shirt and checked his bandage. "I was worried you might have ripped open your stitches, but I don't see any blood seeping. How do you feel?"

"It's a lot to take in." Nick leaned his head against hers. "Being with you is all that matters."

Footsteps scuffing on the stone floor approached. Father Santore carried a wooden box. He stopped in front of Nick and held out the ornately carved box. "Open it," he said.

Nick lifted the small gold handle. Inside he saw a red pillar candle on a white satin lining.

"Take it out," Santore said.

The top of the candle revealed three, concentric layers of wax. Red on the outside, then a circle of black and finally a pure white center. Nick looked up at the priest.

"It's the one candle I hoped we would never have to light. It was made to destroy the devil himself. The red represents the bloodshed he has caused. The black, the souls he has stolen and corrupted with his evil. The last layer, white is God's pure light. As the flame burns, the outer layers melt away until God's light is all that remains." He sat next to Nick in the pew and asked, "Do you believe in, God, son?"

"Yes."

"Do you love God?"

"I've always believed, Father, especially now after the demons were exorcised, but . . ."

"But?"

"How do you love someone who doesn't care? Who doesn't answer your prayers?"

The priest frowned. "Do you hate God?"

"No." Nick lowered his gaze. "I'm angry at Him for letting Mom die."

Nonna stood and moved behind Nick. She wrapped her arms around his shoulders and spoke softly into his ear, "Nickie, you know how much I loved your grandpapa, Vincente, yes?"

"Of course, Nonna."

"I get angry at him. Sometimes we fight. But I never, never hate him. You angry, yes, but you don't hate God. The devil, he try to take your soul, use your body for his evil. You fought him, because you love Katie, your family, your friends." She patted his chest, over his heart. "You have a pure heart. I know this. The devil could never take that from you. You tried to give your life for your love." She squeezed Katie's shoulder. "There is no greater love."

"Without a pure heart, even this sacred candle will be useless," Father Santore said.

Nick stood and limped to the kneeler in front of the votives. He touched the small candle marked Rose, and then knelt and bowed his head. He closed his eyes and thought about his mom. A bright light filled his vision despite his closed eyes. A figure emerged from the center of the brilliant light. His mother walked toward him. Her eyes sparkled and she looked as he remembered her before her illness. She smiled. "I love you, Nick. You must do this. I know you can." The sweet scent of her tea rose perfume wafted in the air. He drew in a deep breath, squeezed his eyelids tight and held onto the vision as long as he could before it faded away. When he opened his eyes, he saw Katie kneeling next to him. He took her hand and stood.

"I'm ready."

Nonna handed Nick a thin, pen-shaped instrument. The stylus was made of solid gold with a pointed tip and weighed heavy in his hand for its slender size.

"Write the name the devil calls himself," Nonna said. She turned the candle over.

With deep, even strokes, Nick etched Victor Ruby into the smooth wax. Nonna righted the candle and then handed Nick a box of matches.

"Light the candle. Have faith in your heart, Nickie."

He struck a match. A burst of sulfur scent filled his nostrils and a flame flared on the end of the wooden stick. Ruby's black eyes and evil grin flashed in his mind. His sadistic laughter rang in his ears. The flame quivered and shrunk. His hand trembled as he touched the tiny blue ember on the match head to the wick. It caught, flared straight up and then settled into a brilliant, flickering oval atop the candle.

Father Santore placed the candle on the outstretched, flat sword in Saint Michael's hand. He and Nonna knelt in front of the statue. They bowed their heads and made the sign of the cross. Together they recited Saint Michael's prayer. Nick, Katie and the women in the pews repeated the words after them.

"Saint Michael the Archangel, defend us in battle; be our protection against the wickedness and snares of the devil. May God rebuke him, we humbly pray: and do thou, O Prince of the heavenly host, by the power of God, thrust into hell Satan and all the evil spirits who prowl about the world seeking the ruin of souls."

Red wax pooled on top of the candle and dribbled over the rim. Red liquid ribbons ran down the sides exposing stripes of shiny, black wax beneath. The warm red wax dripped and then hung suspended in the cool air like hardened drops of blood from the edges of the sword.

The group continued with a series of prayers. Nick didn't know the words, so he prayed silently in his own words, gazing at the candle and gripping Katie's hand. Gradually the black wax melted, revealing patches of bright white beneath.

Nonna rose from the kneeler and whispered to Nick, "Father Jonathan will drive you two home. You rest, Nickie. Heal." She touched Katie's cheek. "You take care of him, yes?"

Katie hugged Nonna. "Always."

"Is it done? Aren't you coming home with us?" Nick asked.

"Later. Now, we pray." She walked them to the vestibule where Father Jonathan waited. She took Nick's hands in hers, stood on her toes and kissed him on each cheek. "Keep faith, Nickie. And remember, Katie likes sugar in her tea."

Nick nodded. It seemed an odd thing for her to mention, but with his pain, weariness from the prolonged exorcism ritual and the knowledge of the special candles, his thoughts were shrouded in a surreal fog. As they exited the church, he tried not to lean his full weight on Katie's shoulders. Exhaustion overwhelmed him, his side ached, yet an oppressive weight had been lifted from his soul.

Getting out of the church van and climbing the stairs to the apartment sapped the last of his strength. They made it in the front door just as thunder boomed overhead, unleashing a heavy torrent of rain. Nick collapsed into a chair at the kitchen table, still gripping Katie's hand.

His father burst into the kitchen and wrapped his arms around Nick's shoulders. "You're home. The exorcism worked. Thank God."

Nick reached up with his free hand and grasped his dad's beefy arm. "Katie told me everything you did. Thank you, Pop."

His father straightened up. "It was nuthin' compared to what you've been through." He patted Katie's arm. "Both of you. I felt awful when I gave you those drugs to knock you out, Nick. It was the only way to get you to the church without the demons fighting back."

Katie wriggled her hand free of Nick's tight hold. "I have your real pain pills."

His hand felt naked without hers. He watched her walk to the sink, fill a glass with water and take a prescription bottle from her bag. "Here." She handed him a pill and the glass.

"Coffee's brewing. Tea for you." Dom smiled at Katie. He turned up the gas under the kettle. He gripped Nick's shoulder and asked, "Or, would you rather sleep now?"

"I'm beat, but I don't think I can sleep. Coffee sounds great, Pop."

He and Katie sat close together, holding hands, while his father set out cups and spoons.

"Where's Sal?" Nick asked.

"Where else? With Stephanie." Dom laughed. "He sneaks out every night to see her. Thinks we don't know. He got her the job and apartment at Eddie's Gym." Dom sighed. "Sal's a man now, graduated high school and he'll be eighteen next month. Time goes by so fast." He wagged his finger and chuckled. "I remember when you snuck out every night to see Katie."

A dull ripple of pain stabbed Nick's side as he laughed and leaned to kiss Katie's cheek.

His father poured boiling water into Katie's cup and set the coffee pot down on a trivet. He settled into his chair and poured coffee into his and Nick's cups. He passed the cream and then sat back, smiling at Katie and Nick. "Oh, Katie, I forgot the sugar." He started to push himself up from his chair and then stopped. He rubbed his chest where the bullet had hit him.

"Sit, Pop. I'll get it." Nick stood to reach into the cabinet behind him. The pill had removed the stinging edge from his pain. The dull throb in his side paled in comparison to the searing pain of the demons' claws.

Something rattled inside the sugar bowl when he lifted it from the shelf. He removed the small porcelain lid and tilted the bowl under the kitchen light. The diamonds on Katie's engagement ring sparkled inside the empty bowl. Nick laughed out loud.

"What?" Katie and Dom asked simultaneously.

Leaning on the back of Katie's chair, Nick slowly lowered himself down on one knee.

"What's wrong? Are you all right?" Katie asked, rising from her chair.

Nick held up the ring. "Katie, I love you with all my heart. Will you marry me?"

Katie eyes glistened. She smiled. "Again, yes. I will."

He kissed her hand and then slipped the ring onto her finger. With Katie's help, he stood up. Dom rose from his chair and hugged them both. His head bobbed up and down. "Good, good." He grinned as he wiped tears from his eyes.

"You should lie down and rest." Katie slipped her arm around Nick's waist and they walked to his bedroom. "I'm afraid I've taken over your room." She motioned to the boxes lined against the wall. "I was going to stay here until the police allowed me back into the apartment. But after seeing Tara . . . your dad and Sal moved my things here in your Mustang. Must have taken them ten trips. Your family's taken such good care of me this past week." Katie's eyes watered. "I wish Tara and I hadn't fought so much. I wish I had forgiven her before. . . I can't go back to the apartment."

"You won't. You belong here." Nick pulled her close and kissed her.

Katie pressed her face into his chest. "I've missed you so much. The real you." She looked up at him and smiled. "You look exhausted. Lie down in bed. I'll sleep on the couch."

He grasped her hand tighter. "There's plenty of room." He eased himself onto the narrow bed and turned on his right side, pulling Katie next to him. She snuggled her back against him, and he wrapped his arm around her. She clutched his arm with both hands.

"Do you think the candle will work?" he whispered. "If it doesn't, I'll have to find another way to kill Ruby, before he comes after you again."

"Nonna said to have faith," Katie murmured as she brushed her lips over his hand.

They lay in the darkened room holding each other. A cool, moist breeze fluttered the curtains on the open window and let in peeks of yellow light from the streetlamp below. Nick's eyelids drooped as he combed his fingers through Katie's silky hair and breathed in her fragrance as she slept. The steady, drumming of the rain soothed him into a drowsy, twilight state. Still, he fought giving into sleep, afraid he would wake and find tonight had been only a dream. Holding Katie tighter, he closed his eyes and prayed, "Please God, all I want is for Katie, my family and friends to be safe. Nothing else matters."

A thunderous boom shook them both from their sleep. The old sash window rattled inside its wooden casing and the bronze crucifix vibrated on the wall above them. Katie leapt from the bed and ran to the window. "My God! Was that thunder?"

Nick struggled to sit up and rolled his sore body out of bed. He stood behind Katie with his hands on her shoulders and stared out the window. A tower of fire sliced through the purple-gray, predawn sky about a mile away in the downtown business district.

"Sounded and felt more like an explosion," he said.

They watched the flames rise through the early morning fog. A lone siren blared in the distance. Someone knocked on the bedroom door.

Katie opened the door to a wide-eyed Dom standing in the hallway in his robe, running his hand through his disheveled salt and pepper hair. "You heard it?"

"We think something exploded downtown. We can see the fire from here," she said.

Dom shuffled to the window and peered out at the inferno across the city. Billows of black smoke spiraled into the air. More sirens wailed.

"Is it . . . Ruby's building?" Nick asked. "It's the right area and distance from here."

"I'll turn on the news," his father said.

Katie brought coffee into the living room while Nick and his father scanned through news channels. After twenty minutes of fragmented news flashes, a reporter finally confirmed the explosion had occurred at the Ruby International Promotions building.

Firefighters and police officers on the scene gave brief, live interviews. Controlled chaos enveloped the entire block, with fire hoses aimed from all sides at the tall spire of raging flames. One city official speculated a gas main may have blown due to the sheer force of the explosion and the fact it had been felt over a mile away. The gas also accounted for the ferocity of the fire.

A block away, another reporter interviewed a handful of early morning commuters waiting at a bus stop. A young Latina woman stared wide-eyed into the camera and told the reporter she saw a bolt of lightning strike the top floor and then the entire building burst into flames. "A huge bolt of light, so long, so bright! Like nothing I ever see! As if God's finger come down from the sky!" She made a hasty sign of the cross.

The camera turned to the reporter. "Due to the early hour, the buildings here in the business district are hopefully, unoccupied. While it will be some time before firefighters can extinguish this massive blaze and sift through the rubble, city officials are hopeful there will be few, if any, casualties."

Nick stared at Katie. "Ruby lived on the top floor of that building."

Katie pressed closer to him on the couch and squeezed his hand.

They all turned when they heard the kitchen door open. Nonna and Father Santore entered. Both looked exhausted.

Nonna took Nick's hand in hers. "You did it, Nickie. It's over. God's justice came in the fire."

She and Father Santore sank into chairs. Katie poured coffee and brought cups to them.

"Nonna, fire won't kill the devil," Nick said.

Nonna pointed toward the ceiling. "God's cleansing fire, not like the fires of hell. No man can kill the devil. All we can do is chase him away."

Nick leaned forward, wincing from the sting of his wound. "If Ruby's contracts are destroyed, what happens to the people who signed them?" He thought about Chris and Bethany and added, "Both the living and the dead?"

"The fire will destroy the contracts, severing the devil's bond," Father Santore said. "The dead souls will be freed from the eternal despair of Hell. They will be judged according to their deeds on earth. As for the living, they have their God-given free will. They must make their choice; denounce the devil and his demons or join him."

Katie picked up the coffee pot. "I'll make more coffee."

A minute later, she returned and whispered to Nick, "You've got to come see this."

She led him to the kitchen window. The morning had dawned gray and cool. Across the city, shrouded in patchy fog and smoke, stood the blackened silhouette of Ruby's high rise. The only visible flames flared at the roof of the building. From a distance, it looked like a giant candle.

Chapter 29
Six months later

Nick wielded the knife with speed and precision as Katie watched, wide-eyed. The razor-sharp blade made a soft whisking sound as he cut fresh herbs on the wooden chopping block. After mincing cilantro, lemon grass and basil, he used the edge of the knife to scrape the fragrant greens into a saucepan.

Katie smiled and shook her head. "I don't know how you do that. I'd be at Saint Mary's getting my fingers reattached."

Nick's father bustled around the restaurant kitchen and plated the entrees. He waved his hand over the herbed sauce, inhaling the aroma. "Smells fantastic, Nick." He poured the sauce over veal cutlets and then carried the steaming dishes into the dining room.

Nonna entered the kitchen. "Nickie, Mrs. Lepkowski keeps asking me who gave her the check? You want I should tell her?"

"No, Nonna. Tell her it was an anonymous donor."

She reached up and patted Nick's cheek. "She cry when she opened the card. Enough money to send her two children to college and then some."

"Money won't bring back their father." Nick sighed. "I hope it helps his kids."

"Nick, this fund raiser you organized helps all three of the policemen and their families. Plus, you paid for all the food. You've done a lot," Katie said.

Nonna fished a paint chip from her apron pocket and held it out to Katie. "I order the paint at the hardware store this morning."

"Paint for what?" Nick asked.

Nonna squeezed Katie's cheek. "You no tell him?"

"Tell me what?" Nick looked from Katie to Nonna.

Nonna sighed and threw her hands up. "Your bedroom. Paint it blue, Nickie."

"Our spare bedroom?" He frowned at Katie. "I already painted it the green you wanted."

Katie smiled. "Nonna thinks I'm pregnant and the baby's a boy."

Nick wiped his hands on his apron and then grasped Katie's shoulders. "Are you?"

"Of course she is." Nonna folded her arms across her chest, her head nodding.

Katie hesitated. "I don't know. I hope so, but I haven't had time to do a test."

"Eh, tests!" Nonna rolled her eyes. "I see it in your eyes. A grandson. God help me, another boy."

Nick pulled Katie close. "We're gonna have a son? This is incredible."

"Good, now he know." Nonna embraced them both. "I start planning the Christening and the party for after." She left them alone and headed into the dining room.

"I'll pick up a test at the drug store, to be sure." Katie touched his cheek. "I'm so proud of you. You've done everything you said you would. The memorial for Walt at the hospital, helping Tara's mom and the police fund raiser. You deserve to be happy now."

"I am." He kissed her.

The front doorbell jingled, interrupting their embrace. Katie peeked through the porthole window in the door. "They're here." She hurried into the dining room to greet Ray and Alona. Nick followed a few steps behind, carrying a tray.

"Hi Ray, you look great. Not even a limp," Katie said.

"I feel great," Ray said as he hugged Katie. "Wow, this place is jammed."

"Today's the police fund raiser." She smiled at Alona. "And next weekend it'll be your reception dinner. Can you believe it's almost here?"

Alona's shiny, black curls bounced around her radiant face as she nodded her head. "I know. I'm so excited."

"Ray, Alona." Nick waved from the back corner of the dining room. "C'mon back to your private tasting table." He added the tray to the spread of serving dishes on the table.

The three wound their way through the crowded tables. "Oh, my gosh, Nick, this looks and smells wonderful!" Alona's eyes sparkled as she surveyed the colorful foods elegantly displayed on the table.

"I told you, Nick's an incredible chef." Ray pulled out a chair for Alona. The four sat at the table.

"Yes, but I thought cooking was only his hobby. I read your vampire series. I'm impressed—horror novels being on the *Times* best seller list."

"I gave up writing horror stories. I work here as a chef and for the *Daily Record* as a stringer and researcher."

"Huh, I didn't know that," Ray said. "And you run the catering here, too?"

"I like to stay busy."

"Not to mention the beautiful work he's done renovating our brownstone. Only one more room to paint. Re-paint." Katie winked and brushed a lock of hair from Nick's forehead. "Which reminds me, Alona, Ray, your wedding shower on Wednesday night," Katie paused and elbowed Nick, "it isn't an old-fashioned shower, boys are allowed to come, too."

Nick grinned at Ray. "Or we can go out and have an old-fashioned bachelor party."

"You're not a bachelor, you're taken." Katie swatted his arm.

"If our wedding turns out half as beautiful as yours, I'll be ecstatic," Alona said. She pointed to the framed wedding photo of Nick and Katie hanging on the wall next to Sal's graduation picture. She bit into a canape. "Mm, taste this Ray, it's delicious!" She fed the rest of the filled pastry to Ray.

"We still need to decide on desserts, besides the wedding cake, of course," Nick said.

Alona waved her hands excitedly as she chewed and then swallowed. "Can you do one of those cannoli-thingies, like you two had at your reception dinner?"

Nick and Katie looked at each other and then burst out laughing.

"You mean the infamous cannoli tree?" Katie said.

"We called it the great cannoli pyramid. It was as tall as Nonna." Nick laughed, demonstrating the height with his hands.

Ray reached for another pastry. "It's up to you, Alona, I can't choose, I just want to eat it all."

"Alona," Katie said, "Loretta sent over some sample roses for your bouquets, I put them in the cooler in the back. C'mon, I'll show you." The two women walked into the kitchen.

Ray leaned across the table. "I can't let you do all this, Nick." He motioned to the food laid out before them. "Let me pay you something, man."

"Absolutely not. It's my wedding gift," Nick said. "I owe you more than I can ever repay."

"You don't owe me a thing. Seeing you and Katie married and happy is all the payback I need. You two went through a pretty rough time. I'm glad it all worked out."

"Me too. One month of fame damn near ruined my life forever."

"Is that why you quit writing?"

"I still write. I collaborate on reports with Janis Ford, she's an investigative reporter at the *Daily*."

"That's a big switch from vampire books, no?"

Nick shrugged. "I had a contract with the publisher to complete the trilogy, but I don't have any other books planned right now. The royalties have been great, but Janis and I are working on a series of cold case murder articles. Mostly serial killers. The latest is this evil bastard named Artie Mosley. He was put to death for one murder, but from my research, I found he tortured and killed a dozen or more women. Maybe these exposés will give the murdered women's families some closure."

"You said you gave up writing horror. These articles sound pretty grisly."

Nick nodded. "The things people do to each other in real life are more horrific than any fiction I could ever dream up."

Chapter 30

Stephanie sat naked and cross-legged on the narrow bed sipping coffee while she waited for Sal to finish showering. She pushed aside the enormous, stuffed puppy Sal had won for her at a church bazaar and rummaged through a box crammed between the bed and the wall. A pair of peacock-blue, T-straps caught her eye. The two-hundred-and-forty-dollar price tag dangled from a string attached to the leather ankle band. She put her coffee mug down on the windowsill behind the bed and wriggled her left foot into the shoe. Leaning back on the pillows, she lifted her leg and twisted her ankle back and forth admiring the shoe.

"That looks really hot." Sal grinned at her from the foot of the bed. He stood rubbing his dripping body with a towel.

Stephanie's cheeks flushed. She kicked off the shoe. "Coffee's ready. I'm going to take a shower."

Sal dropped his towel and slipped his arms around her waist as she brushed past him on her way to the bathroom.

"Again?" She giggled. "Eddie's going to blame me if you mess up in the ring today."

"I never mess up in the ring. Besides Eddie's wrong. Sex doesn't hurt my endurance." He cupped Stephanie's bare bottom in both his hands and pulled her close. "Sex makes everything better." He walked forward, pushing Stephanie backwards until she fell onto the bed. He climbed on top of her.

"Sal, it's eight forty-five. I have to get ready and be downstairs by nine thir—" She shrieked and then giggled as Sal shook his wet hair and the cold water sprinkled across her breasts. He covered her mouth with his. She wrapped her arms and legs around him.

Sal rolled onto his back until he caught his breath, then he turned over on his side. With his head propped on his elbow, he grinned down at Stephanie. "It gets better each time."

"It does." She combed his damp wavy, hair with her fingers. The giant stuffed dog had fallen over, its face lay next to Sal's elbow on the bed. It stared at her between two long, shaggy brown ears. The puppy's light brown eyes flecked with amber matched Sal's eye color. She smiled, thinking all Sal needed was a long, pink felt tongue lolling from his mouth and he could be the puppy's twin.

"You're such a horn dog. I'm going to be late for work. Again. I bet Eddie knows exactly why I'm late, too."

"I don't care. Old guys tell young guys they can't have sex before a match only 'cause they're jealous that we can." Sal jumped to his feet and danced around the tiny room throwing punches in the air. "See, I have plenty of energy. Not that it matters."

Stephanie sat up in the bed. "You don't sound very excited about this fight."

"It's another of Eddie's stupid local match-ups. A no-name guy from some no-name gym on the west side."

"But, there's prize money, right?"

"Yeah, a couple of hundred bucks, but . . ."

Stephanie waited for Sal to finish his sentence. He stopped hopping from foot to foot and jabbing his fists in the air and started pacing up and down the length of the bed.

"But what?"

"I don't wanna do this anymore."

"But you love boxing."

"I do love boxing. Just not here in these piddly-ass fights. I'm sick of making chump change. I was gonna tell you yesterday, but I was afraid."

"Afraid of what?" Stephanie stood and looked into Sal's eyes.

"Hang on a sec." He ran and retrieved his gym bag and plopped it onto the bed.

Stephanie stood with her arms crossed watching as he dug through its contents. He pulled out a large brown envelope.

"What's that?"

Sal held it out, but then snatched it away before she could take it. "I need to know something first."

She rolled her eyes. "Why are you acting so weird? What do you need to know?"

"If I were to go someplace else, would you come with me?"

"Go where? What are you talking about?"

"Like, if I had a chance to make it big . . ."

Stephanie shrugged in bewilderment when he trailed off without finishing his sentence again. "Sal, what's in the envelope?"

"A contract."

"What kind of contract?"

Sal's eyes lit up and he waved his arms as he talked. "I met this guy the other day. Joe Garnet. A sports promoter from Vegas. This guy's flippin' amazing, Steph. He knows every big shot in the business. And he only promotes the best. All the world class champions. Hagen, Walker, Vargas, O'Hara. The list goes on and on."

"What are you getting at, Sal?"

"Garnet's been traveling the country, scouting for new talent. He's watched three of my matches." Sal grabbed Stephanie's hands. "He told me he was blown away by my talent. Said I have what it takes to be a superstar. He wants to sign me up, Steph. Make me a pro boxer!"

"That sounds major." Stephanie stared at Sal's lopsided grin. He couldn't stand still.

"More than major, it's a flippin' once in a lifetime opportunity. Think about it, Steph. Me and you in Vegas. Garnet said it's a twenty-four-seven party. Night clubs, shows, dancing, casinos, you name it. Here's the best part, he knows some people in the music industry. He promised me he'd help you get your songs recorded. You'll finally be a country singer, like you always dreamed."

"Sal, this all sounds awesome, but—"

"But what?" The sparkle in Sal's eyes dulled. "Don't you want to come with me?"

Stephanie sank down onto the edge of the bed. "I-I don't want to stay here without you. But, what about your family? And Eddie?"

Sal sighed. His shoulders drooped. "I love my family to death. But I can't live my life around what they want. My dad and Nonna are always worried I'll get hurt. 'Play it safe, don't take any chances', that's all they say. Nick's married and has his life with Katie. I love Eddie, too. He's been like a grandfather to me. He's even hinted about leaving me his business since he has no kids of his own."

"Really?"

"Yeah. I mean that's great and all, but I don't want to end up like Eddie. Or my dad. They're both gonna die in the same place they were born. It's depressing. I don't want to hang around this gym all my life. And then there's you."

"Me?"

"I-I love you, Steph. But I saw that fancy apartment you used to live in. All your nice clothes and shoes and stuff are still packed in boxes." He picked up the blue shoe from the floor and turned it over in his hands. "You're so beautiful, but there's no reason for you to get dressed up around here. You can't be happy living in this dump. If I sign with Garnet, we could be flippin' millionaires. We could buy an awesome house. Or a mansion. Hell, a whole bunch of mansions. We could travel around the world. You'd be a famous singer and I'd be a professional boxer. Best of all, we'd be together, if you'll come with me. Whaddaya think?"

"That's the sweetest thing anyone's ever said to me." Stephanie's eyes brimmed with tears. "You really do love me." Her voice faded into a soft whisper. "You think I'm pretty."

Sal brushed his fingers across her cheek. "Beautiful. The most beautiful girl I've ever seen. And sweet. Sexy. Smart. And talented and—hey, what's wrong? Why're you crying?"

Sal knelt in front of her and wrapped his arms around her.

Stephanie's voice trembled. "You never told me you loved me before."

Sal put his cellphone in his pocket and hurried over to where Stephanie sat at the front desk of the gym.

"Garnet's catching a flight back to Vegas at six o'clock."

"Okay, so?"

"So, I thought I had more time. I promised to get the contract to him before he leaves. Would you bring it to him? I have to be in the ring in thirty minutes. If I leave now, Eddie will freak. I didn't want to tell him anything until after the match."

"Yeah, I guess. Where is he?"

"He said he'd be at the Red Owl diner for another hour, then he's heading to the airport. It's on Bay Avenue, about six blocks south of here." Sal lowered his voice. "Garnet always wears a black cowboy hat. Says it's his trademark. Should make him easy to spot."

"Tell Eddie I ran to the drugstore for girl stuff." Stephanie smiled. "He won't ask."

He handed her the envelope and whispered, "We'll be partying in Vegas next weekend."

Sal ran out the back door of Eddie's gym waving his arms and yelling for Stephanie to stop. Her yellow Volkswagen idled in the driveway, poised to pull out into traffic. She backed up and lowered her driver's window. "What's wrong?"

"I forgot to sign!" Sal smacked his open palm against his forehead. "The most important thing and I almost flippin' blew it."

Stephanie frowned as she handed him the envelope.

He patted his boxing shorts and robe. "Um, do you have a pen?"

She dug inside her purse.

Sal reached through the window and grabbed a silver ballpoint from the jumble of items which cascaded into her lap. Ruby International Promotions was engraved on the barrel in red letters.

"No, not that one. Uh, it doesn't work." She held up a pink, plastic pen. "Use this one."

Sal scribbled on the envelope with the silver pen. "This works fine."

He turned to the last page of the thick packet of papers. Laying the contract on the car's hood, he smoothed the page, signed his name and filled in the date.

Eddie yelled from the back door of the gym, "Sal! Stop smooching with that pretty girl of yours. Get your butt in here. We need to tape up your hands and get your gloves on."

Sal shoved the contract through the driver's window, leaned and kissed Stephanie's cheek. "Gotta run."

At three in the afternoon, only a few patrons sat on the red vinyl and chrome stools at the diner's long, Formica counter. Two women sat in the booth closest to the door coaxing a young boy to eat the french fries on his plate. A man wearing a red leather jacket and black cowboy hat sat in the very last booth at the far end of the diner.

Stephanie walked the length of the counter, stools on her right, rows of red vinyl booths and tables on her left. Sunlight shone through the wall of windows and made the tiny gold flecks in the Formica tables glitter. Outside, traffic and pedestrians moved past in a steady flow.

She took a deep breath and stood quietly for a moment by the end booth watching the man read a menu. His head tilted downward, and the hat's wide brim obscured his face in shadow.

"Mr. Garnet?"

He looked up. His dark eyes shone. "Hello, Stephanie. You look well, my dear."

Stephanie slid into the seat across from Garnet. "You're looking well, too, father. The cowboy hat is . . . different."

"My new image." Garnet's lips twisted to reveal gleaming white teeth. "I had a hard time choosing. The white hat or the black."

"Black would seem to be the obvious choice."

"That depends on one's perspective." His unpleasant smile evaporated. "At least I know what side I'm on. Do you?"

She looked down and hugged the brown envelope against her chest.

"You have Sal's contract. Is it signed?"

Stephanie nodded. "Yes, but—"

"With a silver pen?"

"Yes. B-but you can't have it. Something's changed. I'll find you someone else."

Garnet's hand shot across the table. He ripped the envelope from her grasp. "You know my rules."

"No, wait, I agreed to get you Sal before I knew that—"

Garnet threw back his head and laughed. "He loves you? Or, thinks he loves you? Big, stupid jock. Until you, he's only fumbled under girl's skirts in a Catholic school coat closet. Wait until he sees Vegas. Show girls, cocktail waitresses, ring girls—how faithful do you think Sal will be with gorgeous women throwing themselves at him? And where will that leave you? Maybe then you'll appreciate all I've done for you. Such a shame you aren't more like Talon, my perfect daughter."

"Perfect?" Stephanie snorted. "She killed your biggest star."

"Chris had become a whining nuisance. He planned to kill himself anyway. She made a tactical decision and salvaged his soul for me."

"You call shoving him out the window of a fifteen-story building a tactical decision?"

He smiled, showing pointed teeth. "Yes."

"She screwed up again when she stabbed the roommate instead of Katie."

"That wasn't Talon's fault. The information in Janis Ford's report was flawed."

"You always take Talon's side. You made her lead singer in Chris' band. She can't sing. I'm the singer. She's nothing but an evil, cold-blooded . . . slut."

"As I said, my perfect daughter. Instead of your childish sibling jealousy, you'd do well to study your stepsister. You might learn."

A waitress placed a plate with an over-sized hamburger in front of Garnet. "Are you sure the burger's how you want it?" She lowered her voice. "We're not supposed to serve 'em this rare." The limp, blood-red patty flopped over the edges of the bun.

Garnet slipped a folded twenty-dollar bill into the woman's apron pocket. "Just how I like it. Bring dessert now." He tapped his fingernail on a picture on the laminated menu. "Two spoons."

"Yes, sir. Can I get you anything, miss?"

Stephanie shook her head. The woman sauntered off behind the counter.

Garnet picked up the giant burger. Juice from the nearly raw meat saturated the bun into two round, red-soaked sponges. He tore into the sandwich like a ravenous dog. Juice oozed between his fingers and streamed onto the plate. Red droplets spattered the table with each vicious bite. Garnet slurped, grunted and devoured the burger in four bites. He stared at Stephanie as he sucked his fingertips to savor the juice under his nails. Then he picked up the dish and lapped up the crimson puddle with his long, tapered tongue.

Disgusted, Stephanie turned and looked out the window. A bus rolled to a stop outside the diner. The doors opened with a muffled whoosh. A morbidly obese woman approached the bus. She gripped the railings with both hands and hauled her body up the three steps. On the last step, she wavered. Her feet lifted in the air and her body hurled backwards as if shoved by unseen hands. Her floral-print dress billowed up around her waist as she fell. She landed hard, the back of her head impacted the sidewalk, bouncing once. She lay still, her dress bunched up around her waist as a dark, red puddle pooled around her head.

Stephanie spun around and glared at Garnet. "You did that."

His forefinger and thumb were poised in the air as if he had just flicked away a bug. He picked at his teeth with his pinky nail and then shrugged. "I was bored."

The waitress removed Garnet's empty plate with one hand and placed a large ice cream sundae in front of him with the other. The oversized pedestal dish could barely contain the vanilla ice cream slathered in hot fudge. A huge puff of whipped cream wobbled on top with a bright red stain where a cherry had sunk down into the frothy center.

"Two spoons," the waitress said as she laid them on the table. "Oh, my!" She craned her neck to peer out the window. "I'd better call 9-1-1." She hurried away.

Garnet held up the second spoon. "Join me?"

Stephanie wrinkled her nose.

He dug his spoon into a mound of ice cream coated with thick, shiny fudge and shoveled it into his mouth. "Mmm." His tongue scrubbed at the fudge smear on his lips. "Something looks different about you, Stephanie," he said, pointing the spoon at her. "I wonder what it could be?"

"Please, father, I'm begging you, give me back Sal's contract. I swear I'll find you someone else."

"No." He shoved another gob of ice cream into his mouth. Smacking his lips, he waved the spoon near Stephanie's face. "I know what it is. You're not a virgin anymore, are you?" He grinned. Whipped cream encircled his mouth like a foam on a rabid dog.

"That's none of your business."

"*You* are my business. I made you with that pathetic, drug-addicted whore." He plucked the cherry from the sundae and twirled the stem between his fingers. "My little girl has finally lost her virginity." He ripped the fruit from the stem with his teeth and laughed at Stephanie's shocked expression. "No wonder you're protecting Sal."

Outside, a crowd formed. A teen-aged boy aimed his cell phone at the fallen woman and then held it up to show his friend. The two gaped at the phone, laughed and then ambled down the street.

"Is my mother doing better?" Stephanie asked.

"If better means dead, then yes."

Color drained from Stephanie's face, her breath puffed involuntarily through her slackened lips. "Dead? No. You promised—" she swallowed a sob, "you'd help her if I brought you Sal's contract."

"I lied. She overdosed this morning. With a little help." He tapped the silver Rolex on his wrist. "What were you doing at eight forty-five? Your dear mother was choking to death on her own vomit."

Tears welled in Stephanie's eyes. She stared down at the chipped tabletop and willed herself not to cry in front of him. "We had a deal."

"And you betrayed me, twice. First Chris and then Nick. Ultimately, you cost me Ruby International Promotions. All those contracts, all those portals, all those souls, lost. Killing your mother is your punishment. If you weren't my daughter, you'd be dead, too." Garnet sighed. "I'm such a softie when it comes to my little girls."

"You didn't have to kill her!" Stephanie squeezed her eyes shut, hot tears spilled over and rolled down her cheeks.

"Ah, poor Stephanie. Were you still under your weary delusion she would get clean? And then what? She'd frantically search for you. There would be a grand reunion and she'd cradle you against her motherly bosom and proclaim how much she loves you?"

"Shut up! You beat me. Choked me until I blacked out. You said that was my punishment for getting too friendly with Chris and Nick."

"Parents discipline their children. Tough love. I was merely being a good father."

A siren wailed outside as an ambulance pulled up to the curb. EMTs rolled a gurney onto the sidewalk. One knelt and checked the woman's vital signs. They lowered the gurney and then the four men hoisted her onto it. After attaching the straps, raising the stretcher and securing it, they wheeled her into the street toward the open doors of the ambulance.

Garnet scraped his spoon around the bottom of the dish and then sucked it clean with a loud smacking sound. "Your mother threw you away like a used condom. Did you know she tried to trade you for a bag of heroin hours after you were born? But no self-respecting drug dealer wanted to be stuck with you—a pale, sickly, whining baby." He grabbed her wrist. "You should be grateful your father took you in."

Stephanie yanked her hand, but Garnet's sharp fingernails dug into her skin, raising dots of blood.

"Instead of gratitude, you betrayed me. You're just like your mother. Weak. Needy. Always making the wrong choices. Letting your pathetic little girl crushes get in the way. I had to do all the work because you were too stupid to see that Chris and Nick only pitied you. Now you're trying to back out on Sal's contract. This time I'm holding you to your promise."

Outside, a woman screamed. Stephanie jumped when a deafening crash shook the plate glass window. She gasped at the horrific scene outside. A panel truck had plowed into the four EMTs and the gurney, crushing them against the rear of the parked ambulance.

Garnet glanced out the window and grinned. "Tsk, tsk. So sad. And ironic. You would have helped Nick destroy his contract. Yet, he loved

Katie, not you. And now, the brother you betrayed actually does love you. Imagine that, Sal loves scrawny, ugly Stephanie."

"I only made you that promise to get my mom back." She grabbed one end of the brown envelope with her free hand and pulled. "I've made a terrible mistake. Please, give me more time, I'll find someone else. Don't hurt Sal. He loves me . . . I love him."

"How touching." Garnet wrenched the envelope from her desperate grip. "Delivering Sal's signed contract has redeemed you, for now." He gazed at the chaotic scene outside and smiled. Crushed vehicles blocked the road. Bloodied bodies, their limbs bent at unnatural angles, lay in crumpled heaps on the asphalt. The mangled head and torso of the panel truck driver protruded through a jagged hole in the windshield. Flames engulfed the rear of the ambulance, sending thick, black coils of smoke into the air. Horrified pedestrians huddled in doorways and gaped. The shrill shrieks of sirens grew louder.

"If you don't help me destroy Sal, I promise I will destroy you. Think of it as your last chance to become a real daddy's girl. Maybe I'll even let you sit on my lap, like Talon." He leered at her when she winced. "I'll see you and Sal in Vegas. We're going to have a blast."

His image blurred through her tears. He vanished with the envelope. Two airline tickets fluttered on the table.

She dropped her head down onto her folded arms. Her slender shoulders convulsed with her sobs.

"Excuse me, Miss?"

Stephanie gulped back a sob and looked up with tears streaming down her cheeks.

"Oh dear, this is awkward," the waitress said. "Here's the check." She laid the bill on the table and walked away.

End

Now available

Vamped: The Turning

Chapter One

The Black Swan - an event or occurrence that deviates beyond what is normally expected of a situation and is extremely difficult to predict.

A narrow panel in the door, eye-height, slid open. I held up the printed ticket I had purchased online. Unseen eyes studied it and, I assumed, studied me as well. Though I couldn't discern the eyes through the dark narrow slit, I felt their intense scrutiny. A slow chill crept down my back and the slip of paper trembled in my hand. I pushed my eyeglasses up on my nose.

The panel closed. I waited.

A series of clicks, the sound of a heavy bolt sliding, and then the thick steel door opened inward. A broad-shouldered man with a shaven head grunted as he motioned me inside. He snatched the ticket, stamped a small black swan on the back of my left hand and jerked his thumb in the direction of a dim corridor. With the interior as dark as the moonless night outside, my eyes adjusted quickly, and I followed a path of tiny recessed blue lights along the floor.

The hallway opened into a room with burgundy walls. It thrummed with people talking, drinking, smoking and dancing. Smoke hovered overhead like a hazy gray ghost, trapped in the cramped realm between the patrons' heads and low ceiling. Blasts of air-conditioning chilled the space and intermingled odors of perfume, alcohol and cigarettes.

I headed for the oval-shaped bar that dominated the center of the room. To my right, past the dance floor, the band played on an elevated stage, their name scrawled in black script across the base drum head,

Night Train. Lorelei, the undisputed queen of vampire rockers buoyed my hopes. She was the reason I drove over an hour to the secret club. Her long, wild platinum hair matched her pearly complexion and she moved to the music with the stealthy grace of a panther in a black leather halter and skin-tight pants.

Unlike Lorelei, the crowd gyrating to the heavy metal music disappointed me. They wore goth-style clothing and most sported ink-black hair streaked with red, purple or blue. Pale faces and black outlined eyes expressed little interest in me as I walked past. Dressed in a black T-shirt and skinny-legged jeans, my naturally pale completion and thin build—or to use my father's favorite adjective, puny—I blended in with the clientele.

My heart sank a bit more as I climbed onto a blue vinyl bar stool flecked with glitter. A female bartender in a lacy bodice poured a frothy red beverage from a stainless-steel shaker into two tall glasses. She garnished the drinks with cherries and sank black straws into each glass. Laminated tent cards lined the bar top and advertised specialty drinks with ridiculous names—*Bloody Magpies, Draquiris, Fanghattans* and *Sanguintinis.*

I ordered a bottled apple ale. Another barmaid, her eyelids caked with shimmery purple, set the bottle down with a smile as fake as her eyelashes.

"Something wrong?" she asked.

Shaking my head no, I pushed a ten dollar bill across the lacquered bar top. Inwardly, the masquerade sickened me. *The Black Swan* was purported to be a haven where real vampires gathered, or so their website claimed. Yet as I scanned the room surrounded by costumed wannabes, my expectations deflated. This place looked no different than the numerous other vampire clubs I'd visited.

I swiveled around on the stool as I drank my ale, impressed by the size of the club. It's entrance, hidden below street level, belied the square footage inside. The space equaled about half of the huge building above, and as expected on a Saturday night, the industrial park outside appeared deserted, unless of course, you knew where to look.

Steps away from me, patrons danced while *Night Train's* amplifiers rattled the pock-marked acoustic tiles above my head. Bursts of flames shot from the border of the stage in unison with ear-splitting shrieks of electric guitars. The song ended in a barrage of bashing cymbals, then a red velvet curtain dropped over the stage. The band took a break.

The members, four males and Lorelei, exited from a dark stairway to the left of the stage and converged around the bar. She settled on the stool next to mine. Her shocking, silvery-white hair stood out among the mass of mostly raven-haired men and women. It shone blue, red and green as the lights above the bar flickered through their colored repertoire. I tried not to stare at her breasts, perfect pale globes barely reined in by her low-cut top.

The bartender pulled a decanter from underneath the bar and poured a dark crimson liquid into a wine glass. Lorelei clasped the glass with two hands and drank without stopping to take a breath. She tilted the stem upward until the last drop drizzled into her mouth. A red, viscous coating tinted the inside of the glass.

As she swallowed, the movement in her slender, paper-white neck mesmerized me. Her gaze turned to me as she set the empty glass on the bar, her electric blue eyes as startling as the rest of her. Perhaps a trick of the strobe lights, her pupils swelled, covering her irises in a moist black. Thin, spidery veins of black bled into the whites of her eyes. I blinked. The brilliant blue irises and whites returned. She ran her forefinger around the inside of the glass and then stared at me as she sucked the red liquid clinging to her fingertip.

"Why are you here?" Her voice, barely a whisper and her warm breath tickled my ear even though she sat two feet away. A coppery scent wafted beneath my nostrils.

"I want to be transformed."

Her laughter exploded inside my head like particles of glass cascading onto a sheet of tin. She flicked her hand and dismissed me. "You and everyone else."

"No." Urgency welled inside me. I had to convince her. "No. I'm not like them. I'm a true believer. I'm ready to join the Night Flock."

"You are naive." She swept back her pale mane of hair and stood. The male band members gathered around her forming a protective entourage of leather-clad muscle. They walked toward the short flight of stairs leading up to the stage.

I leapt to my feet, raced after her and pushed through a slice of space between two of the male musicians. As my fingers grasped her slim wrist, I was shocked by the chilly firmness of her flesh. Strong hands immediately gripped my shoulders and arms.

Lorelei whirled and faced me, eyes ablaze. Her snarl revealed pointed teeth.

"Please," I said. "You have the power to transform me. I want it. I *need* it."

She waved and the men released me. My bones felt as fragile as a sparrow's in her grasp as she plucked my hand from her wrist. "This is our last set. Stick around." Her full smile showed dazzling white teeth with elongated canines, but whether it held mirth or malevolence, I couldn't quite tell.

An instant later, she stood with the four men on the stage, their ascent up the stairs a blur and her voice still echoing in my ears. As the band warmed up with random keyboard riffs and guitar chords, a mass of black-garbed bodies drifted from the bar and surrounding tables and gathered on the dance floor in front of the stage. Their anticipation jelled into a palpable presence.

I ordered another ale. Taking advantage of the crowd's exodus, I moved to an abandoned table next to the stage. Though I didn't much care for it, heavy metal music embodied the soul of these clubs. Loud, raucous, edgy—it created an audio backdrop of lust, rage, and violence, the same sentiment the patrons attempted to project, though not always achieved, with their sinister make-up and dress.

I sat on the edge of my chair watching Lorelei, my pulse racing from the memory of her touch. More impressive in person than in her online photos, her icy eyes, white face and hair gave off a ghostly aura beneath the bright stage lights. She swung the microphone stand one-handed and belted out lyrics in an impossible range from a deep, throaty growl that made my scalp crawl to stark, piercing screams that pained my ear drums.

Halfway through their set, a tap on my shoulder jolted me from the scene on stage. With the music booming, a young woman mouthed something and motioned to an empty chair at my table.

I nodded automatically. Was she asking to sit with me or just wanted to sit near the stage? She hadn't looked at me the way girls usually did, with a mixture of annoyance and disgust, the same way they might look at ants crawling in their potato salad at a picnic.

Something about her demeanor distracted me. She wasn't a beauty, but *neat and clean.* My mother's words came to mind. She had shoulder-length, sandy brown hair and a tan complexion, both unusual in this setting. Her white tank top and faded blue jeans didn't fit in either. Her eyes sparkled when she looked at me, though I couldn't tell in the dark club if they were blue or green. The fleeting thought she might be interested in me passed as she turned her chair to face the stage. She sat with her back to me. No drink. No purse. Just sat with shoulders squared, back straight and watched the band.

Even as Lorelei fascinated me, a dull ache grew in my temples. The constant, driving drumbeat interspersed with raging electric guitar and keyboard solos wore on my nerves. Jets of freezing air from ceiling vents billowed cigarette smoke into my face. I removed my glasses and rubbed my eyes. My fingers, cold and wet from holding the sweating bottle of ale, soothed the irritation. Disappointment churned with the alcohol in my gut. A light-weight, two drinks were my limit. Besides Lorelei, this club offered nothing I hadn't seen a hundred times before. I should go—to hell with the one hundred and seventy-five dollars I'd paid for admission.

As I stood to leave, the music stopped. The lights went out, submerging the band and the crowded room in a velvety blackness. A drumbeat began, a slow, steady thump-thump that mimicked a heartbeat. The rowdy patrons hushed, save for the barely audible sound of their collective breathing. The dense darkness ebbed and swelled, as if it too, breathed. I sank back into my chair, my heartbeat matching the deep bass beat of the drum. Something was about to happen, but what? Anticipation held me in a state of rapture. Lorelei had said to stick around.

A lone blue spotlight shone down on stage and bathed Lorelei in its spectral glow. Her body undulated like a snake, a boneless creature with pale arms extended and long, spidery fingers that probed the darkness above the crowd.

"Who shall it be tonight?" The microphone amplified her throaty whisper. It reverberated around the silent room.

Gasps and then shouts rose from the crowd. "Me!" "No, me!" The random shouts blended together until they rose into a cacophony of screams.

My heart beat faster as the drummer quickened his pace and the scene at the foot of stage turned riotous. The crowd surged forward, dark silhouettes of bodies jostled against each other, spike-haired heads bobbed, hands stretched upward grasping at air in frantic but futile attempts to touch Lorelei.

"Silence!"

Lorelei's thundering command halted the pandemonium. "I see you all. See who you really are. Posers. Charlatans. Fakes. I will not allow mundane scum to drink my blood."

I jolted upright in my chair. Drink her blood? The website hadn't lied. Lorelei planned to transform someone. Right here, right now.

"There is only one among you tonight who is ready. One who is strong and worthy of my gift."

The pounding in my chest vibrated upward into my throat. *Me.* She was talking about *me.* She told me to stay. My mind reeled. The gravity of how my life was about to change both stunned and thrilled me.

A deathly quiet blanketed the room broken only by the soft shuffle of feet as they backed away from the stage and Lorelei's fierce glare. A spotlight flashed on and scanned the crowd. The white beam sliced through the blackness and swept back and forth across the room, faster and faster. Its strobing effect made me dizzy. I forced myself to look away. The drumbeat sped up, the sound harder, louder, faster—*thump-thump, thump-thump.* My heartbeat synced to it, thundering in my ears.

The roving spotlight stopped. I looked up. Light blinded me.

"You, are the only one here who is worthy." Lorelei pointed to me. "Rise."

I jumped to my feet, light-headed. I squinted through the harsh glare reflecting off my lenses. Lorelei had seen my need. She knew how much I wanted this, deserved this. My impulsive move of grabbing her arm had paid off in a way I could hardly fathom. I sucked in a gasp of smoky air. Fear and desire washed over me. My scalp and fingers tingled, alternating between icy, then fiery waves. Tonight, my life as a vampire would begin and even better, the misery of my human existence would end. My tears magnified the glare of the spotlight.

"What is your name?" Lorelei asked.

Rapid breaths had dried my throat, my tongue stuck to the roof of my mouth. I croaked out, "Tim."

Simultaneously, a vibrant female voice rang out, "Jane." The woman sitting at my table stood and walked toward the stage.

No. *No!* It's *me.* Lorelei pointed at *me.* Spoke to *me.* Words screamed in my head as I watched Lorelei beckon Jane toward the stage. Two of the male musicians reached down, grasped Jane's outstretched arms and lifted her up onto the platform. Jane stood, tall and confident, next to Lorelei. Stood where I should be standing.

My shaking legs could no longer hold me. I collapsed in my chair. The drumbeat slowed, still steady but softer. An ethereal lilt of keyboard notes joined in. My entire body shook as waves of nausea swelled in my gut, then crashed in a sea of bile at the back of my throat. *Get up. Jump on the stage. Take my place next to Lorelei.* Fear of vomiting or passing out paralyzed me. Numb, I sat, my fingers gripping the seat of my chair as I swallowed back the bitter-tasting acid. Shock and anger dueled in my brain.

The two guitarists pushed an ornate, high-backed chair—throne-like—to center stage. Jane settled into it. She gazed out over the murmuring throng standing watch at the foot of the stage.

One of the guitarists brandished a long, thin sword. He swiveled it in the air letting the blue light play off the gleaming metal. Lorelei stood next to the throne and took Jane's hand. They stretched their arms outward, hands clasped, fingers interlaced. In a lightning fast, silvery blur, the blade swiped across their arms. Dark lines immediately formed on their skin. Under the blue light, the liquid welling from the slashes appeared black.

Lorelei leaned forward and licked Jane's arm. Her tongue caressed the skin, a delicate gesture like a cat lapping milk. Then, her mouth widened, glossy red lips enveloped the bleeding wound. My breath caught in my chest. Lorelei's fervor intensified. She clutched the arm with both hands, her head moved up and down in frenzied blood-sucking, a lioness feasting on bloody meat. Jane's eyes squeezed shut, her face twisted with pain or maybe ecstasy. Lorelei pushed the arm away. Tongue lingering on her bloody lips, she pressed her bleeding arm to Jane's mouth.

Jane sucked the dark pool oozing from the wound. The eerie organ music swelled and faded as she drank. Lorelei's body swayed in rhythm to the sensual melody. My breath came fast and shallow and I moved with her as did the pulsating mass of silhouettes in front of the stage. Voyeurs, all of us. Time hung suspended as the lurid scene on stage filled my senses, the faint wet sounds, the metallic scent. Sweat formed under my arms and ran down the center of my back, my shirt stuck to my damp skin. I squirmed in my chair embarrassed by the hardness growing inside the painfully snug crotch of my jeans.

Lorelei shook her head. Her tousled white mane fell across eyes that glittered with lavender light. "Enough!" She pushed Jane's mouth away and withdrew her arm. The dark gash on Lorelei's arm faded to smooth, alabaster skin.

The guitarist stepped from the shadows, this time twirling a strip of filmy white gauze instead of a sword. He knelt on one knee beside the chair and wrapped Jane's wound.

Hypnotized by a spectacle I had only read about until tonight, my anger and nausea dissipated, replaced by awe, lust, and envy. My desire to be transformed renewed. It overwhelmed me.

Jane sat in the chair, eyes closed, and her expression peaceful yet triumphant—smug even—her arms rested on the plush red velvet cushions of the chair's arms. The two guitarists picked up their instruments and the tickle of guitar strings filtered seamlessly into the haunting melody. Lorelei gripped a hand-held mic and sang unidentifiable words in a whisper-soft voice. A demonic lullaby that both soothed and unnerved me. The dark ballad ended in an elongated sigh which Lorelei issued as she slowly bowed from the waist, the ends of her hair grazed the stage floor. The drum beat continued slower, softer, then faded, until it too, stopped.

Jane opened her eyes and stood. The two women embraced as the heavy velvet curtain fell. I stood, craning my neck to peer beneath the curtain. The crowd dwindled. People ambled across the shiny floor, murmuring, whispering as they drifted toward the exit.

The overhead lights in the club flicked on. I turned, squinting in the harsh light as the last of the patrons wandered down the narrow corridor and out the doors. Behind me, bartenders washed glasses, straightened bottles on shelves and wiped down the bar top, their routine no different than closing time in any night club.

I hurried to the bar.

"Last call was an hour ago."

"I don't want a drink. When will she be back?"

"Who?"

"Lorelei—*Night Train*—when are they playing here again?"

"Next Saturday night's their last gig here before they go on tour."

I spun around and raced toward the stage. The bartender yelled, "Hey, you can't go back there."

The curtain obscured the stage. I veered left to the side entrance, took the flight of steps two at a time and burst through the doorway onto the stage.

Lorelei and Jane stood talking. I ran toward them. One of the men stepped into my path and blocked me with his bulk. His hands clamped my shoulders and shoved. I flew backwards, the back of my head slammed against a speaker and my glasses clattered on the wooden floor. The blurry legion of giants standing over me could have been four, or maybe eight.

"Stop." Lorelei's voice.

The hulks separated. She stood over me. "You again. What do you want?"

"T-To be transformed." I rolled up onto my knees and felt on the floor for my glasses. Once I became a vampire, I wouldn't need damned eyeglasses. I stood up, fumbling to fit the thick black frames onto my face. "You told me to stick around, remember? I thought you had chosen me, not her." I nodded in Jane's direction. "I've studied. I'm ready. Strong."

The men broke into laughter. One gripped my jacket collar and yanked me toward the doorway.

With my feet unable to find solid ground in his steely grasp, I twisted my torso around and reached out to Lorelei. "Please! Please Lorelei, I'm begging you."

"Seth, wait," she said. He stopped dragging me and stood, his fingers a tight vice on my upper arm. Lorelei's frigid eyes bore into mine. "I doubt you are ready. Or worthy."

"But—"

"Shush." She turned and opened a battered old trunk behind the speaker. "Complete these six tasks in the next seven days. *If* you succeed, return here and I shall give you what you desire."

She handed me a piece of yellowed parchment paper, the numbers one through six hand-written in black ink down the left side.

"What tasks? The paper's blank."

"Press your finger on the first number and instructions will appear. The next will not appear until you have completed the one prior. The difficulty rises as you progress down the list." Her cold hand encircled my throat, sharp fingernails pressed my skin. "If you fail to complete all six, do not dare return here. Ever." She released my throat and slapped my face with the back of her hand.

Blood smeared my fingertips when I touched my stinging cheek. Lorelei licked the treacherous-looking ring on her right middle finger. Like an inverted spider, a ring of pointy prongs caged a round, ruby-red stone. She nodded to Seth.

Seth shoved me through the doorway to the platform at the top of the stairs. As I started down, his heavy boot struck me square in the ass. Tumbling down the steps, I landed face-down on the shiny floor. The thick velvet curtain muffled their laughter.

"Let me help you."

I straightened my glasses and looked up. Jane crouched beside me, her teal-colored eyes burned with an inner light. Her sandy hair, now a golden mane that surrounded her radiant face. My hopes were confirmed. She was no longer plain. She had been transformed.

"I don't need your help."

She sighed and stood. Her footsteps echoed in the empty club as she strode across the dance floor, turned and then disappeared down the corridor toward the exit.

My butt, knees and arms ached as I climbed to my feet. I tucked the parchment inside my jacket and limped to the exit.

"Ya shouldn'a run backstage." The huge, bald guy's ham-sized fist impacted half of my face. Sucker punched, I barely had time to scoop up my fallen glasses before he heaved me out the door. My outstretched hands saved my face from kissing the concrete stairs outside. Locks clicked behind me. Salty tasting blood oozed from the split in my lower lip and tears blurred my throbbing left eye.

I grasped the railing and climbed up the steps to the parking lot behind the warehouse. Below me, a plain black awning hid the entrance to the Black Swan, only the faint blue light emanating from twin iron sconces gave any indication of what lay beyond the door.

Tonight wasn't the first beating I'd endured, but it would be the last. From elementary school through college, I had drawn bullies like a chunk of bloody chum in the sea drew sharks. But now I knew why. My entire life had prepared me for this—my pending transformation. I smiled in spite of the pain. In fact, I couldn't stop grinning as I staggered to my car in the deserted parking lot.

"In seven days, I'll be a vampire."

Vamped: The Turning

Available now
from

PARANORMALICE PRESS, LLC

While you are waiting, check out *Inky: Nice Neighborhood. Bad Cat* by Chris Holmes on Amazon Kindle.

All books available on Amazon and Kindle.